Peter Straub was born in Milwaukee, Wisconsin in 1943, and was educated at the University of Wisconsin, Columbia University and University College, Dublin. He is the author of *Marriages*, *Under Venus*, *Julia*, *If You Could See Me Now*, *Shadowland*, *Ghost Story*, *Floating Dragon* (winner of the 1983 British Fantasy Award), *The Talisman* (with Stephen King), *Mystery* and *Koko* (winner of the 1989 World Fantasy Award). Peter Straub has spent ten years in Britain and Ireland, and now lives in Connecticut and New York.

By the same author

Novels

Marriages
Under Venus
Julia
If You Could See Me Now
Ghost Story
Shadowland
Floating Dragon
The Talisman (with Stephen King)
Koko
Mystery

Poetry

Open Air
Leeson Park & Belsize Square

Collection

Wild Animals

PETER STRAUB

Houses Without Doors

GraftonBooks

A Division of HarperCollins*Publishers*

For Scott Hamilton and Warren Vaché

GraftonBooks
A Division of HarperCollins*Publishers*
77–85 Fulham Palace Road,
Hammersmith, London W6 8JB

Special overseas edition 1991

First published in Great Britain by
GraftonBooks 1990

Copyright © Seafront Corporation 1990

The Author asserts the moral right to
be identified as the author of this work

ISBN 0-586-21202-7

Printed in Great Britain by
HarperCollinsManufacturing Glasgow

Set in Trump Mediaeval

Contents

Doom is the house without the door –
'Tis entered from the sun –
And then the ladder's thrown away,
Because escape – is done –

Emily Dickinson

She Saw a Young Man

She saw a young man in a loose black sweater and black trousers come towards her down the street. His dark hair was blowing, and his face seemed to be illuminated by a smile. It was always nice to see someone smiling on the street, she thought – a grace note. When he was nearly abreast of her, she saw that he was grimacing, not smiling, and that his eyes were wet. This was on that day in New York when the sky is grey and the air is grey and cold and people are wearing jackets and sweaters for the first time. She turned round and watched him go past her, wondering what had happened to him. Some sort of strange illumination still clung to the young man, and the woman noticed several other people staring at him.

Blue Rose

For Rosemary Clooney

On a stifling summer day the two youngest of the five Beevers children, Harry and Little Eddie, were sitting on cane-backed chairs in the attic of their house on South Sixth Street in Palmyra, New York. Their father called it 'the upstairs junk room', as this large irregular space was reserved for the boxes of tablecloths, stacks of diminishingly sized girls' winter coats, and musty old dresses Maryrose Beevers had mummified as testimony to the superiority of her past to her present.

A tall mirror that could be tilted in its frame, an artefact of their mother's one-time glory, now revealed to Harry the rear of Little Eddie's head. This object, looking more malleable than a head should be, was just peeking above the back of the chair. Even the back of Little Eddie's head looked tense to Harry.

'Listen to me,' Harry said. Little Eddie squirmed in his chair, and the wobbly chair squirmed with him. 'You think I'm kidding you? I had her last year.'

'Well, she didn't kill *you*,' Little Eddie said.

''Course not, she liked me, you little dummy. She only hit me a couple of times. She hit some of those kids every single day.'

'But teachers can't *kill* people,' Little Eddie said.

At nine, Little Eddie was only a year younger than he, but Harry knew that his undersized fretful brother saw him as much a part of the world of big people as their older brothers.

'Most teachers can't,' Harry said. 'But what if they

live right in the same building as the principal? What if they won *teaching awards*, hey, and what if every other teacher in the place is scared stiff of them? Don't you think they can get away with murder? Do you think anybody really misses a snot-faced little brat – a little brat like you? Mrs Franken took this kid, this runty little Tommy Golz, into the cloakroom, and she killed him right there. I heard him scream. At the end, it sounded just like bubbles. He was trying to yell, but there was too much blood in his throat. He never came back, and nobody ever said boo about it. She killed him, and next year she's going to be your teacher. I hope you're afraid, Little Eddie, because you ought to be.' Harry leaned forward. 'Tommy Golz even looked sort of like you, Little Eddie.'

Little Eddie's entire face twitched as if a lightning bolt had crossed it.

In fact, the young Golz boy had suffered an epileptic fit and been removed from school, as Harry knew.

'Mrs Franken especially hates selfish little brats that don't share their toys.'

'I do share my toys,' Little Eddie wailed, tears beginning to run down through the delicate smears of dust on his cheeks. 'Everybody *takes* my toys, that's why.'

'So give me your Ultraglide Roadster,' Harry said. This had been Little Eddie's birthday present, given three days previously by a beaming father and a scowling mother. 'Or I'll tell Mrs Franken as soon as I get inside that school, this fall.'

Under its layer of grime, Little Eddie's face went nearly the same white-grey shade as his hair.

An ominous slamming sound came up the stairs.

'Children? Are you messing around up there in the attic? Get down here!'

'We're just sitting in the chairs, Mom,' Harry called out.

'Don't you bust those chairs! Get down here this minute!'

Little Eddie slid out of his chair and prepared to bolt.

'I want that car,' Harry whispered. 'And if you don't give it to me, I'll tell Mom you were foolin' around with her old clothes.'

'I didn't do nothin'!' Little Eddie wailed, and broke for the stairs.

'Hey, Mom, we didn't break any stuff, honest!' Harry yelled. He bought a few minutes more by adding, 'I'm coming right now,' and stood up and went towards a cardboard box filled with interesting books he had noticed the day before his brother's birthday, and which had been his goal before he had remembered the Roadster and coaxed Little Eddie upstairs.

When, a short time later, Harry came through the door to the attic steps, he was carrying a tattered paperback book. Little Eddie stood quivering with misery and rage just outside the bedroom the two boys shared with their older brother Albert. He held out a small blue metal car, which Harry instantly took and eased into a front pocket of his jeans.

'When do I get it back?' Little Eddie asked.

'Never,' Harry said. 'Only selfish people want to get presents back. Don't you know anything at all?' When Eddie pursed his face up to wail, Harry tapped the book in his hands and said, 'I got something here that's going to help you with Mrs Franken, so don't complain.'

His mother intercepted him as he came down the stairs to the main floor of the little house – here were the kitchen and living room, both floored with faded linoleum, the actual 'junk room' separated by a stiff, brown woollen curtain from the little makeshift room where Edgar Beevers slept, and the larger bedroom reserved for Maryrose. Children were never permitted more than a few steps within this awful chamber, for they might disarrange Maryrose's mysterious 'papers' or interfere with the rows of antique dolls on the windowseat which was the sole, much revered architectural distinction of the Beevers' house.

Maryrose Beevers stood at the bottom of the stairs, glaring suspiciously up at her fourth son. She did not ever look like a woman who played with dolls, and she did not look that way now. Her hair was twisted into a knot at the back of her head. Smoke from her cigarette curled up past the big glasses, shaped like bird's wings, which magnified her eyes.

Harry thrust his hand into his pocket and curled his fingers protectively around the Ultraglide Roadster.

'Those things up there are the possessions of my family,' she said. 'Show me what you took.'

Harry shrugged and held out the paperback as he came down within striking range.

His mother snatched it from him, and tilted her head to see its cover through the cigarette smoke. 'Oh. This is from that little box of books up there? Your father used to pretend to read books.' She squinted at the print on the cover. *'Hypnosis Made Easy.* Some drugstore trash. You want to read this?'

Harry nodded.

'I don't suppose it can hurt you much.' She negligently passed the book back to him. 'People in society read books, you know – I used to read a lot, back before

I got stuck here with a bunch of dummies. *My* father had a lot of books.'

Maryrose nearly touched the top of Harry's head, then snatched back her hand. 'You're my scholar, Harry. You're the one who's going places.'

'I'm gonna do good in school next year,' he said.

'*Well*. You're going to do well. As long as you don't ruin every chance you have by speaking like your father.'

Harry felt that particular pain composed of scorn, shame, and terror that filled him when Maryrose spoke of his father in this way. He mumbled something that sounded like acquiescence, moved a few steps sideways, and skirted her.

2

The porch of the Beevers' house extended six feet on either side of the front door, and was the repository for furniture either too large to be crammed into the junk room or too humble to be enshrined in the attic. A sagging porch swing sat beneath the living room window, to the left of an ancient couch whose imitation green leather had been repaired with black duct tape, on the other side of the front door through which Harry Beevers now emerged stood a useless icebox dating from the earliest days of the Beevers' marriage and two unsteady camp chairs Edgar Beevers had won in a card game. These had never been allowed into the house. Unofficially, this side of the porch was Harry's father's, and thereby had an entirely different atmosphere, defeated, lawless, and shameful, from the side with the swing and couch.

Harry knelt down in neutral territory directly before the front door and fished the Ultraglide Roadster from his pocket. He placed the hypnotism book on the porch and rolled the little metal car across its top. Then he gave the car a hard shove and watched it clunk nose-down onto the wood. He repeated this several times before moving the book aside, flattening himself out on his stomach, and giving the little car a decisive push towards the swing and the couch.

The Roadster rolled a few feet before an irregular board tilted it over on its side and stopped it.

'You dumb car,' Harry said, and retrieved it. He gave it another push deeper into his mother's realm. A stiff, brittle section of paint which had separated from its board cracked in half and rested atop the stalled Roadster like a miniature mattress.

Harry knocked off the chip of paint and sent the car backwards down the porch, where it flipped over again and skidded into the side of the icebox. The boy ran down the porch and this time simply hurled the little car back in the direction of the swing. It bounced off the swing's padding and fell heavily to the wood. Harry knelt before the icebox, panting.

His whole head felt funny, as if wet hot towels had been stuffed inside it. Harry picked himself up and walked across to where the car lay before the swing. He hated the way it looked, small and helpless. He experimentally stepped on the car and felt it pressing into the undersole of his moccasin. Harry raised his other foot and stood on the car, but nothing happened. He jumped on the car, but the moccasin was no better than his bare foot. Harry bent down to pick up the Roadster.

'You dumb little car,' he said. 'You're no good

anyhow, you low-class little jerky thing.' He turned it over in his hands. Then he inserted his thumbs between the frame and one of the little tyres. When he pushed, the tyre moved. His face heated. He mashed his thumbs against the tyre, and the little black dough-nut popped into the tall thick weeds before the porch. Breathing hard, more from emotion than exertion, Harry popped the other front tyre into the weeds. Harry whirled round, and ground the car into the wall beside his father's bedroom window. Long, deep scratches appeared in the paint. When Harry peered at the top of the car, it too was scratched. He found a nail head which protruded a quarter of an inch out from the front of the house, and scraped a long paring of blue paint off the driver's side of the Roadster. Grey metal shone through. Harry slammed the car several times against the edge of the nail head, chipping off small quantities of paint. Panting, he popped off the two small rear tyres and put them in his pocket because he liked the way they looked.

Without tyres, well scratched and dented, the Ultraglide Roadster had lots most of its power. Harry looked it over with a bitter, deep satisfaction and walked across the porch and shoved it far into the nest of weeds. Grey metal and blue paint shone at him from within the stalks and leaves. Harry thrust his hands into their midst and swept his arms back and forth. The car tumbled away and fell into invisibility.

When Maryrose appeared scowling on the porch, Harry was seated serenely on the squeaking swing, looking at the first few pages of the paperback book.

'What are you doing? What was all that banging?'

'I'm just reading. I didn't hear anything,' Harry said.

3

'Well, if it isn't the shitbird,' Albert said, jumping up the porch steps thirty minutes later. His face and T-shirt bore broad black stripes of grease. Short, muscular, thirteen years old, Albert spent every possible minute hanging around the gas station two blocks from their house. Harry knew that Albert despised him. Albert raised a fist and made a jerky, threatening motion towards Harry, who flinched. Albert had often beaten him bloody, as had their two older brothers, Sonny and George, now at army bases in Oklahoma and Germany. Like Albert, his two oldest brothers had seriously disappointed their mother.

Albert laughed, and this time he swung his fist within a couple of inches of Harry's face. On the backswing he knocked the book from Harry's hands.

'Thanks,' Harry said.

Albert smirked and disappeared round the front door. Almost immediately Harry could hear his mother beginning to shout about the grease on Albert's face and clothes. Albert thumped up the stairs.

Harry opened his clenched fingers and spread them wide, closed his hands into fists, then spread them wide again. When he heard the bedroom door slam shut upstairs, he was able to get off the swing and pick up the book. Being around Albert made him feel like a spring coiled up in a box. From the upper rear of the house, Little Eddie emitted a ghostly wail. Maryrose screamed that she was going to start smacking him if he didn't shut up, and that was that. The three unhappy lives within the house fell back into silence.

Harry sat down, found his page, and began reading again.

A man named Dr Roland Mentaine had written *Hypnosis Made Easy* and his vocabulary was much larger than Harry's. Dr Mentaine used words like 'orchestrate' and 'ineffable' and 'enhance', and some of his sentences wound their way through so many subordinate clauses that Harry lost his way. Yet Harry, who had begun the book only half-expecting that he would comprehend anything in it at all, found it a wonderful book. He had made it most of the way through the chapter called 'Mind Power'.

Harry thought it was neat that hypnosis could cure smoking, stuttering, and bedwetting. (He himself had wet the bed almost nightly until months after his ninth birthday. The bedwetting stopped the night a certain lovely dream came to Harry. In the dream he had to urinate terribly, and was hurrying down a stony castle corridor past suits of armour and torches guttering on the walls. At last Harry reached an open door, through which he saw the most splendid bathroom of his life. The floors were of polished marble, the walls white-tiled. As soon as he entered the gleaming bathroom, a uniformed butler waved him towards the rank of urinals. Harry began pulling down his zip, fumbled with himself, and got his penis out of his underpants just in time. As the dream-urine gushed out of him, Harry had blessedly awakened.) Hypnotism could get you right inside someone's mind and let you do things there. You could make a person speak in any foreign language they'd ever heard, even if they'd only heard it once, and you could make them act like a baby. Harry considered how pleasurable it would be to make his brother Albert lie squalling and red-faced on the floor, unable to walk or speak as he pissed all over himself.

Also, and this was a new thought to Harry, you could take a person back to a whole row of lives they had led before they were born as the person they were now. This process of rebirth was called reincarnation. Some of Dr Mentaine's patients had been kings in Egypt and pirates in the Caribbean; some had been murderers, novelists and artists. They remembered the houses they'd lived in, the names of their mothers and servants and children, the locations of shops where they'd bought cake and wine. Neat stuff, Harry thought. He wondered if someone who had been a famous murderer a long time ago could remember pushing in the knife or bringing down the hammer. A lot of the books remaining in the little cardboard box upstairs, Harry had noticed, seemed to be about murderers. It would not be any use to take Albert back to a previous life, however. If Albert had any previous lives, he had spent them as inanimate objects of the order of boulders and anvils.

Maybe in another life Albert was a murder weapon, Harry thought.

'Hey, college boy! Joe College!'

Harry looked towards the sidewalk and saw the baseball cap and T-shirted gut of Mr Petrosian, who lived in a tiny house next to the tavern on the corner of South Sixth and Livermore Street. Mr Petrosian was always shouting genial things at kids, but Maryrose wouldn't let Harry or Little Eddie talk to him. She said Mr Petrosian was common as dirt. He worked as a janitor in the telephone building and drank a case of beer every night while he sat on his porch.

'Me?' Harry said.

'Yeah! Keep reading books, and you could go to college, right?'

Harry smiled noncommittally. Mr Petrosian lifted a wide arm and continued to toil down the street towards his house next to the Idle Hour.

In seconds Maryrose burst through the door, folding an old white dishtowel in her hands. 'Who was that? I heard a man's voice.'

'Him,' Harry said, pointing at the substantial back of Mr Petrosian, now half of the way home.

'What did he say? As if it could possibly be interesting, coming from an Armenian janitor.'

'He called me Joe College.'

Maryrose startled him by smiling.

'Albert says he wants to go back to the station tonight, and I have to go to work soon.' Maryrose worked the night shift as a secretary at St Joseph's Hospital. 'God knows when your father'll show up. Get something to eat for Little Eddie and yourself, will you, Harry? I've just got too many things to take care of, as usual.'

'I'll get something at Big John's.' This was a hamburger stand, a magical place to Harry, erected the summer before in a vacant lot on Livermore Street two blocks down from the Idle Hour.

His mother handed him two carefully folded dollar bills, and he pushed them into his pocket. 'Don't let Little Eddie stay in the house alone,' his mother said before going back inside. 'Take him with you. You know how scared he gets.'

'Sure,' Harry said, and went back to his book. He finished the chapter on 'Mind Power' while first Maryrose left to wait at the bus stop on the corner, and then while Albert noisily departed. Little Eddie sat frozen before his soap operas in the living room. Harry turned a page and started reading 'Techniques of Hypnosis'.

4

At eight-thirty that night the two boys sat alone in the kitchen, on opposite sides of the table covered in yellow bamboo-patterned formica. From the living room came the sound of Sid Caesar babbling in fake German to Imogene Coca on 'Your Show of Shows'. Little Eddie claimed to be scared of Sid Caesar, but when Harry had returned from the hamburger stand with a Big Johnburger (with 'the works') for himself and a Mama Marydog for Eddie, double fries, and two chocolate shakes, he had been sitting in front of the television, his face moist with tears of moral outrage. Eddie usually liked Mama Marydogs, but he had taken only a couple of meagre bites from the one before him now, and was disconsolately pushing a french fry through a blob of ketchup. Every now and then he wiped at his eyes, leaving nearly symmetrical smears of ketchup to dry on his cheeks.

'Mom *said* not to leave me alone in the house,' said Little Eddie. 'I heard. It was during *The Edge of Night* and you were on the porch. I think I'm gonna tell on you.' He peeped across at Harry, then quickly looked back at the french fry and drew it out of the puddle of ketchup. 'I'm ascared to be alone in the house.' Sometimes Eddie's voice was like a queer speeded-up mechanical version of Maryrose's.

'Don't be so dumb,' Harry said, almost kindly. 'How

can you be scared in your own house? You live here, don't you?'

'I'm ascared of the attic,' Eddie said. He held the dripping french fry before his mouth and pushed it in. 'The attic makes noise.' A little squirm of red appeared at the corner of his mouth. 'You were supposed to take me with you.'

'Oh Jeez, Eddie, you slow everything down. I wanted to just get the food and come back. I got you your dinner, didn't I? Didn't I get you what you like?'

In truth, Harry liked hanging around Big John's by himself because then he could talk to Big John and listen to his theories. Big John called himself a 'renegade Papist' and considered Hitler the greatest man of the twentieth century, followed closely by Paul XI, Padre Pio who bled from the palms of his hands, and Elvis Presley.

All these events occurred in what is usually but wrongly called a simpler time, before Kennedy and feminism and ecology, before the Nixon presidency and Watergate, and before American soldiers, among them a 21-year-old Harry Beevers, journeyed to Vietnam.

'I'm still going to tell,' said Little Eddie. He pushed another french fry into the puddle of ketchup. 'And that car was my birthday present.' He began to snuffle. 'Albert hit me, and you stole my car, and you left me alone, and I was scared. And I don't wanta have Mrs Franken next year, cuz I think she's gonna hurt me.'

Harry had nearly forgotten telling his brother about Mrs Franken and Tommy Golz, and this reminder brought back very sharply the memory of destroying Eddie's birthday present.

Eddie twisted his head sideways and dared another

quick look at his brother. 'Can I have my Ultraglide Roadster back, Harry? You're going to give it back to me, aren't cha? I won't tell Mom you left me alone if you give it back.'

'Your car is okay,' Harry said. 'It's in a sort of a secret place I know.'

'You hurt my car!' Eddie squalled. 'You did!'

'Shut up!' Harry shouted, and Little Eddie flinched. 'You're driving me crazy!' Harry yelled. He realized that he was leaning over the table, and that Little Eddie was getting ready to cry again. He sat down. 'Just don't scream at me like that, Eddie.'

'You did something to my car,' Eddie said with a stunned certainty. 'I knew it.'

'Look, I'll prove your car is okay,' Harry said, and took the two rear tyres from his pocket and displayed them on his palm.

Little Eddie stared. He blinked, then reached out tentatively for the tyres.

Harry closed his fist around them. 'Do they look like I did anything to them?'

'You took them *off*!'

'But don't they look okay, don't they look fine?' Harry opened his fist, closed it again, and returned the tyres to his pocket. 'I didn't want to show you the whole car, Eddie, because you'd get all worked up, and you gave it to me. Remember? I wanted to show you the tyres so you'd see everything was all right. Okay? Got it?'

Eddie miserably shook his head.

'Anyway, I'm going to help you, just like I said.'

'With Mrs Franken?' A fraction of his misery left Little Eddie's smeary face.

'Sure. You ever hear of something called hypnotism?'

'I heard a hypmotism.' Little Eddie was sulking. 'Everybody in the whole world heard a that.'

'Hypnotism, stupid, not hypmotism.'

'Sure, hypmotism. I saw it on the TV. They did it on *As The World Turns*. A man made a lady go to sleep and think she was going to have a baby.'

Harry smiled. 'That's just TV, Little Eddie. Real hypnotism is a lot better than that. I read all about it in one of the books from the attic.'

Little Eddie was still sulky because of the car. 'So what makes it better?'

'Because it lets you do amazing things,' Harry said. He called on Dr Mentaine. 'Hypnosis unlocks your mind and lets you use all the power you really have. If you start now, you'll really knock those books when school starts up again. You'll pass every test Mrs Franken gives you, just like the way I did.' He reached across the table and grasped Little Eddie's wrist, stalling a fat brown french fry on its way to the puddle. 'But it won't just make you good in school. If you let me try it on you, I'm pretty sure I can show you that you're a lot stronger than you think you are.'

Eddie blinked.

'And I bet I can make you so you're not scared of anything any more. Hypnotism is real good for that. I read in this book, there was this guy who was afraid of bridges. Whenever he even *thought* about crossing a bridge he got all dizzy and sweaty. Terrible stuff happened to him, like he lost his job, and once he just had to ride in a car across a bridge and he dumped a load in his pants. He went to see Dr Mentaine, and Dr

Mentaine hypnotized him and said he would never be afraid of bridges again, and he wasn't.'

Harry pulled the paperback from his hip pocket. He opened it flat on the table and bent over the pages. 'Here. Listen to this. "Benefits of the course of treatment were found in all areas of the patient's life, and results were obtained for which he would have paid any price."' Harry read these words haltingly, but with complete understanding.

'Hypmotism can make me strong?' Little Eddie asked, evidently having saved this point in his head.

'Strong as a bull.'

'Strong as Albert?'

'A lot stronger than Albert. A lot stronger than me, too.'

'And I can beat up on big guys that hurt me?'

'You just have to learn how.'

Eddie sprang up from the chair, yelling nonsense. He flexed his stringlike biceps and for some time twisted his body into a series of muscleman poses.

'You want to do it?' Harry finally asked.

Little Eddie popped into his chair and stared at Harry. His T-shirt's neckband sagged all the way to his breastbone without ever actually touching his chest. 'I wanna start.'

'Okay, Eddie, good man.' Harry stood up and put his hand on the book. 'Up to the attic.'

'Only, I don't wanna go in the attic,' Eddie said. He was still staring at Harry, but his head was tilted over like a weird little echo of Maryrose, and his eyes had filled with suspicion.

'I'm not gonna *take* anything from you, Little Eddie,' Harry said. 'It's just, we should be out of everybody's way. The attic's real quiet.'

Little Eddie stuck his hand inside his T-shirt and let his arm dangle from the wrist.

'You turned your shirt into an armrest,' Harry said.

Eddie jerked his hand out of its sling.

'Albert might come waltzing in and wreck everything if we do it in the bedroom.'

'If you go up first and turn on the lights,' Eddie said.

5

Harry held the book open on his lap, and glanced from it to Little Eddie's tense, smeary face. He had read these pages over many times while he sat on the porch. Hypnotism boiled down to a few simple steps, each of which led to the next. The first thing he had to do was to get his brother started right, 'relaxed and receptive', according to Dr Mentaine.

Little Eddie stirred in his cane-backed chair and kneaded his hands together. His shadow, cast by the bulb dangling overhead, imitated him like a black little chair-bound monkey. 'I wanna get started, I wanna get to be strong,' he said.

'Right here in this book it says you have to be relaxed,' Harry said. 'Just put your hands on top of your legs, nice and easy, with your fingers pointing forward. Then close your eyes and breathe in and out a couple of times. Think about being nice and tired and ready to go to sleep.'

'I don't wanna go to sleep!'

'It's not really sleep, Little Eddie, it's just sort of like it. You'll still really be awake, but nice and relaxed. Or else it won't work. You have to do everything I tell you. Otherwise everybody'll still be able to beat up on

you, like they do now. I want you to pay attention to
everything I say.'

'Okay.' Little Eddie made a visible effort to relax. He
placed his hands on his thighs and twice inhaled and
exhaled.

'Now close your eyes.'

Eddie closed his eyes.

Harry suddenly knew that it was going to work – if
he did everything the book said, he would really be
able to hypnotize his brother.

'Little Eddie, I want you just to listen to the sound
of my voice,' he said, forcing himself to be calm. 'You
are already getting nice and relaxed, as easy and peaceful as if you were lying in bed, and the more you listen
to my voice the more relaxed and tired you are going
to get. Nothing can bother you. Everything bad is far
away, and you're just sitting here, breathing in and
out, getting nice and sleepy.'

He checked his page to make sure he was doing it
right, and then went on.

'It's like lying in bed, Eddie, and the more you hear
my voice the more tired and sleepy you're getting, a
little more sleepy the more you hear me. Everything
else is sort of fading away, and all you can hear is my
voice. You feel tired but good, just like the way you do
right before you fall asleep. Everything is fine, and
you're drifting a little bit, drifting and drifting, and
you're getting ready to raise your right hand.'

He leaned over and very lightly stroked the back of
Little Eddie's grimy right hand. Eddie sat slumped in
the chair with his eyes closed, breathing shallowly.
Harry spoke very slowly.

'I'm going to count backwards from ten and, every
time I get to another number, your hand is going to get

lighter and lighter. When I count, your right hand is going to get so light it floats up and finally touches your nose when you hear me say "one". And then you'll be in a deep sleep. Now I'm starting. Ten. Your hand is already feeling light. Nine. It wants to float up. Eight. Your hand really feels light now. It's going to start to go up now. Seven.'

Little Eddie's hand obediently floated an inch up from his thigh.

'Six.' The grimy little hand rose another few inches. 'It's getting lighter and lighter now, and every time I say another number it gets closer and closer to your nose, and you get sleepier and sleepier. Five.'

The hand ascended several inches nearer Eddie's face.

'Four.'

The hand now dangled like a sleeping bird half of the way between Eddie's knee and his nose.

'Three.'

It rose nearly to Eddie's chin.

'Two.'

Eddie's hand hung a few inches from his mouth.

'One. You are going to fall asleep now.'

The gentle curved, ketchup-streaked forefinger delicately brushed the tip of Little Eddie's nose, and stayed there while Eddie sagged against the back of the chair.

Harry's heart beat so loudly that he feared the sound would bring Eddie out of his trance. Eddie remained motionless. Harry breathed quietly by himself for a moment. 'Now you can lower your hand to your lap, Eddie. You are going deeper and deeper into sleep. Deeper and deeper and deeper.'

Eddie's hand sank gracefully downwards.

The attic seemed hot as the inside of a furnace to

Harry. His fingers left blotches on the open pages of
the book. He wiped his face on his sleeve and looked
at his little brother. Little Eddie had slumped so far
down in the chair that his head was no longer visible
in the tilting mirror. Perfectly still and quiet, the attic
stretched out on all sides of them, waiting – or so it
seemed to Harry – for what would happen next. Maryrose's trunks sat in rows under the eaves far behind
the mirror; her old dresses hung silently within the
dusty wardrobe.

Harry rubbed his hands on his jeans to dry them, and
flicked a page over with the neatness of an old scholar
who had spent half his life in libraries.

'You're going to sit up straight in your chair,' he
said.

Eddie pulled himself upright.

'Now I want to show you that you're really hypnotized, Little Eddie. It's like a test. I want you to hold
your right arm straight out before you. Make it as rigid
as you can. This is going to show you how strong you
can be.'

Eddie's pale arm rose and straightened to the wrist,
leaving his fingers dangling.

Harry stood up and said, 'That's pretty good.' He
walked the two steps to Eddie's side and grasped his
brother's arm and ran his fingers down the length of it,
gently straightening Eddie's hand. 'Now I want you to
imagine that your arm is getting harder and harder. It's
getting as hard and rigid as an iron bar. Your whole
arm is an iron bar, and nobody on earth could bend it.
Eddie, it's stronger than Superman's arm.' He removed
his hands and stepped back.

'Now. This arm is so strong and rigid that you can't
bend it no matter how hard you try. It's an iron bar,

and nobody on earth could bend it. Try. Try to bend it.'

Eddie's face tightened up, and his arm rose perhaps two degrees. He grunted with invisible effort, unable to bend his arm.

'Okay, Eddie, you did real good. Now your arm is loosening up and, when I count backwards from ten, it's going to get looser and looser. When I get to *one*, your arm'll be normal again.' He began counting, and Eddie's fingers loosened and drooped, and finally the arm came to rest again on his leg.

Harry went back to his chair, sat down, and looked at Eddie with great satisfaction. Now he was certain that he would be able to do the next demonstration, which Dr Mentaine called 'The Chair Exercise'.

'Now you know that this stuff really works, Eddie, so we're going to do something a little harder. I want you to stand up in front of your chair.'

Eddie obeyed. Harry stood up too, and moved his chair forward and to the side so that its cane seat faced Eddie, about four feet away.

'I want you to stretch out between these chairs, with your head on your chair and your feet on mine. And I want you to keep your hands at your sides.'

Eddie hunkered down uncomplainingly and settled his head back on the seat of his chair. Supporting himself with his arms, he raised one leg and placed his foot on Harry's chair. Then he lifted the other foot. Difficulty immediately appeared in his face. He raised his arms and clamped them in so that he looked trussed.

'Now your whole body is slowly becoming as hard as iron, Eddie. Your entire body is one of the strongest things on earth. Nothing can make it bend. You could hold yourself there for ever and never feel the slightest pain or discomfort. It's like you're lying on a mattress, you're so strong.'

The expression of strain left Eddie's face. Slowly his arms extended and relaxed. He lay propped string-straight between the two chairs, so at ease that he did not even appear to be breathing.

'While I talk to you, you're getting stronger and stronger. You could hold up anything. You could hold up an elephant. I'm going to sit down on your stomach to prove it.'

Cautiously, Harry seated himself down on his brother's midriff. He raised his legs. Nothing happened. After he had counted slowly to fifteen, Harry lowered his legs and stood. 'I'm going to take my shoes off now, Eddie, and stand on you.'

He hurried over to a piano stool embroidered with fulsome roses and carried it back; then he slipped off his moccasins and stepped on top of the stool. As Harry stepped on top of Eddie's exposed thin belly, the chair supporting his brother's head wobbled. Harry stood stock-still for a moment, but the chair held. He lifted the other foot from the stool. No movement from the chair. He set the other foot on his brother. Little Eddie effortlessly held him up.

Harry lifted himself experimentally up on his toes and came back down on his heels. Eddie seemed entirely unaffected. Then Harry jumped perhaps half an inch into the air, and, since Eddie did not even grunt when he landed, he kept jumping, five, six, seven, eight times, until he was breathing hard. 'You're amazing, Little Eddie,' he said, and stepped off onto the stool. 'Now you can begin to relax. You can put your feet on the floor. Then I want you to sit back up in your chair. Your body doesn't feel stiff any more.'

Little Eddie had been rather tentatively lowering one foot, but as soon as Harry finished speaking he buckled in the middle and thumped his bottom on the floor. Harry's chair (Maryrose's chair) tipped over sickeningly, but landed soundlessly on a neat woollen stack of layered winter coats.

Moving like a robot, Little Eddie slowly sat upright on the floor. His eyes were open but unfocused.

'You can stand up now and get back in your chair,' Harry said. He did not remember leaving the stool, but he had left it. Sweat ran into his eyes. He pressed his face into his shirtsleeve. For a second, panic had brightly beckoned. Little Eddie was sleepwalking back to his chair. When he sat down, Harry said, 'Close your eyes. You're going deeper and deeper into sleep. Deeper and deeper, Little Eddie.'

Eddie settled into the chair as if nothing had happened, and Harry reverently set his own chair upright again. Then he picked up the book and opened it. The print swam before his eyes. Harry shook his head and looked again, but still the lines of print snaked across the page. He pressed the palms of his hands against his eyes, and red patterns exploded across his vision.

He removed his hands from his eyes, blinked, and found that, although the lines of print were now behaving themselves, he no longer wanted to go on. The attic was too hot, he was too tired, and the toppling of the chair had been too close a brush with actual disaster. But for a time he leafed purposefully through the book while Eddie tranced on, and then he found the sub-heading 'Post-Hypnotic Suggestion'.

'Little Eddie, we're just going to do one more thing.

If we ever do this again, it'll help us go faster.' Harry shut the book. He knew exactly how this went; he would even use the same phrase Dr Mentaine used with his patients. *Blue rose*. Harry did not quite know why, but he liked the sound of that.

'I'm going to tell you a phrase, Eddie, and from now on, whenever you hear me say this phrase, you will instantly go back to sleep and be hypnotized again. The phrase is "blue rose". Blue Rose. When you hear me say "blue rose", you will go right to sleep, just the way you are now, and we can make you stronger again. "Blue rose" is our secret, Eddie, because nobody else knows it. What is it?'

'Blue rose,' Eddie said in a muffled voice.

'Okay. I'm going to count backwards from ten, and when I get to "one" you will be wide awake again. You will not remember anything we did, but you will feel happy and strong. Ten.'

As Harry counted backwards, Little Eddie twitched and stirred, let his arms fall to his sides, thumped one foot carelessly on the floor, and at 'one' opened his eyes.

'Did it work? What'd I do? Am I strong?'

'You're a bull,' Harry said. 'It's getting late, Eddie – time to go downstairs.'

Harry's timing was accurate enough to be uncomfortable. As soon as the two boys closed the attic door behind them they heard the front door slide open in a cacophony of harsh coughs and subdued mutterings followed by the sound of unsteady footsteps proceeding to the bathroom. Edgar Beevers was home.

6

Late that night the three housebound Beevers sons lay in their separate beds in the good-sized second-floor room next to the attic stairs. Directly above Maryrose's bedroom, its dimensions were nearly identical to it except that the boy's room, the 'dorm', had no window-seat and the attic stairs shaved a couple of feet from Harry's end. When the other two boys had lived at home, Harry and Little Eddie had slept together, Albert had slept in a bed with Sonny, and only George, who at the time of his induction into the army had been six feet tall and weighed two hundred and one pounds, had slept alone. In those days, Sonny had often managed to make Albert cry out in the middle of the night. The very idea of George could still make Harry's stomach freeze.

Though it was now very late, enough light from the street came in through the thin white net curtains to give complex shadows to the bunched muscles of Albert's upper arms as he lay stretched out atop his sheets. The voices of Maryrose and Edgar Beevers, one approximately sober and the other unmistakably drunk, came clearly up the stairs and through the open door.

'*Who* says I waste my time? I don't say that. I don't waste my time.'

'I suppose you think you've done a good day's work when you spell a bartender for a couple of hours – and then drink up your wages! That's the story of your life, Edgar Beevers, and it's a sad, sad story of W-A-S-T-E. If

my father could have seen what would become of
you . . .'

'I ain't so damn bad.'

'You ain't so damn good, either.'

'Albert,' Eddie said softly from his bed between his
two brothers.

As if galvanized by Little Eddie's voice, Albert suddenly sat up in bed, leaned forward, and reached out to
try to smack Eddie with his fist.

'I didn't do nothin'!' Harry said, and moved to the
edge of his mattress. The blow had been for him, he
knew, not Eddie, except that Albert was too lazy to get
up.

'I hate your lousy guts,' Albert said. 'If I wasn't too
tired to get out of this here bed, I'd pound your face
in.'

'Harry stole my birthday car, Albert,' Eddie said.
'Makum gimme it back.'

'One day,' Maryrose said from downstairs, 'at the
end of the summer when I was seventeen, late in the
afternoon, my father said to my mother, "Honey, I
believe I'm going to take out our pretty little Maryrose
and get her something special," and he called up to me
from the drawing-room to make myself pretty and get
set to go, and because my father was a gentleman and
a Man of His Word I got ready in two shakes. My father
was wearing a very handsome brown suit and a red
bow-tie and his boater. I remember just like I can see
it now. He stood at the bottom of the staircase, waiting
for me, and when I came down he took my arm and
we just went out that front door like a courting couple.
Down the stone walk, which my father put in all by
himself even though he was a white-collar worker,
down Majeski Street, arm in arm down to South

Palmyra Avenue. In those days all the best people, all
the people who counted, did their shopping on South
Palmyra Avenue.'

'I'd like to knock your teeth down your throat,'
Albert said to Harry.

'Albert, he took my birthday car, he really did, and I
want it back. I'm ascared he busted it. I want it back
so much I'm gonna die.'

Albert propped himself up on an elbow and for the
first time really looked at Little Eddie. Eddie whim-
pered. 'You're such a twerp,' Albert said. 'I wish you
would die, Eddie. I wish you'd just drop dead so we
would stick you in the ground and forget about you. I
wouldn't even cry at your funeral. Prob'ly I wouldn't
even be able to remember your name. I'd just say, "Oh
yeah, he was that little creepy kid used to hang around
cryin' all the time. Glad he's dead, whatever his name
was."'

Eddie had turned his back on Albert and was weeping softly, his unwashed face distorted by the shadows
into an uncanny image of the mask of tragedy.

'You know, I really wouldn't mind if you dropped
dead,' Albert mused. 'You neither, shitbird.'

'. . . realized he was taking me to Allouette's. I'm
sure you used to look in their windows when you were
a little boy. You remember Allouette's, don't you?
There's never been anything so beautiful as that store.
When I was a little girl and lived in the big house, all
the best people used to go there. My father marched
me right inside, with his arm around me, and took me
up in the elevator, and we went straight to the lady
who managed the dress department. "Give my little
girl the best," he said. Price was no object. Quality was

all he cared about. "Give my little girl the best." *Are you listening to me, Edgar?'*

Albert snored face-down into his pillow; Little Eddie twitched and snuffled. Harry lay awake for so long he thought he would never get to sleep. Before him he kept seeing Little Eddie's face all slack and dopey under hypnosis . . . Little Eddie's face made him feel hot and uncomfortable. Now that Harry was lying down in bed, it seemed to him that everything he had done since returning from Big John's seemed really to have been done by someone else, or to have been done in a dream. Then he realized that he had to use the bathroom.

Harry slid out of bed, quietly crossed the room, went out onto the dark landing, and felt his way downstairs to the bathroom.

When he emerged, the bathroom light showed him the squat black shape of the telephone atop the Palmyra directory. Harry moved to the low telephone table beside the stairs. He lifted the phone from the directory and opened the book, the width of a Big 5 tablet, with his other hand. As he had done on many other nights when his bladder forced him downstairs, Harry leaned over the page and selected a number. He kept the number in his head as he closed the directory and replaced the phone. He dialled. The number rang so often Harry lost count. At last a hoarse voice answered. Harry said 'I'm watching you, and you're a dead man.' He softly replaced the receiver in the cradle.

7

Harry caught up with his father the next afternoon just as Edgar Beevers had begun to move up South Sixth Street towards the corner of Livermore. His father wore his usual costume of baggy grey trousers cinched far above his waist by a belt with a double buckle, a red-and-white plaid shirt, and a brown felt hat stationed low over his eyes. His long fleshy nose swam before him, cut in half by the shadow of the hat brim.

'Dad!'

His father glanced incuriously at him, then put his hands back in his pockets. He turned sideways and kept walking down the street, though perhaps a shade more slowly. 'What's up, kid? No school?'

'It's summer, there isn't any school. I just thought I'd come with you for a little.'

'Well, I ain't doing much. Your Ma asked me to pick up some hamburg on Livermore, and I thought I'd slip into the Idle Hour for a quick belt. You won't turn me in, will you?'

'No.'

'You ain't a bad kid, Harry. Your Ma's just got a lot of worries. I worry about Little Eddie too, sometimes.'

'Sure.'

'What's with the books? You read when you walk?'

'I was just sort of looking at them,' Harry said.

His father insinuated his hand beneath Harry's left elbow and extracted two luridly jacketed paperback books. They were titled *Murder, Incorporated* and *Hitler's Death Camps*. Harry already loved both of these books. His father grunted and handed *Murder,*

Incorporated back to him. He raised the other book nearly to the tip of his nose and peered at the cover, which depicted a naked woman pressing herself against a wall of barbed wire while a uniformed Nazi aimed a rifle at her back.

Looking up at his father, Harry saw that beneath the harsh line of shadow cast by the hat brim his father's whiskers grew in different colours and patterns. Black and brown, red and orange, the glistening spikes swirled across his father's cheek.

'I bought this book, but it didn't look nothing like that,' his father said, and returned the book.

'What didn't?'

'That place. Dachau. That death camp.'

'How do you know?'

'I was there, wasn't I? You wasn't even born then. It didn't look anything like that picture on that book. It just looked like a piece a shit to me, like most of the places I saw when I was in the army.'

This was the first time Harry had heard that his father had been in the service.

'You mean, you were in World War Two?'

'Yeah, I was in the Big One. They made me a corporal over there. Had me a nickname, too. "Beans". "Beans" Beevers. And I got a Purple Heart from the time I got an infection.'

'You saw Dachau with your own eyes?'

'Damn straight, I did.' He bent down suddenly. 'Hey – don't let your Ma catch you readin' that book.'

Secretly pleased, Harry shook his head. Now the book and the death camp were a bond between himself and his father.

'Did you ever kill anybody?'

His father wiped his mouth and both cheeks with

one long hand. Harry saw a considering eye far back in the shadow of the brim.

'I killed a guy once.' A long pause. 'I shot him in the back.'

His father wiped his mouth again, and then motioned forward with his head. He had to get to the bar, the butcher, and back again in a very carefully defined period of time. 'You really want to hear this?'

Harry nodded. He swallowed.

'I guess you do, at that. Okay. We was sent into this camp, Dachau, at the end of the war to process the prisoners and arrest the guards and the commandant. Everything was all arranged. A bunch of brass hats from Division were going to come on an inspection, so we had to wait there a couple of days. We had these guards lined up, see, and these skinny old wrecks would come up and give 'em hell. We wasn't supposed to let 'em get too near.'

They were passing Mr Petrosian's little tar-paper house, and Harry felt a spasm of relief that Mr Petrosian was not out on his tiny porch, working on his case of beer. The Idle Hour was only a few paces ahead.

'Anyhow, one of these guards, one of the worst ones, suddenly decided he's going to run for it. He takes off, runnin' like crazy towards the woods. What do I do? I ask. Nobody knows what the hell to do. Shoot him, somebody says. So I shot him in the back. That was all she wrote.'

Now they had reached the screen door which led into the Idle Hour, and the smells of malt and hops filled the air. 'See you back at the house,' his father said, and disappeared through the screen door like a magician.

8

After Harry had read a hundred pages of *Murder, Incorporated*, his favourite murderers were Louis 'Lepke' Buchalter and Abe 'Kid Twist' Reles. They were dependable professionals. A kind of black light surrounded them and made them glitter. Lepke Buchalter and Abe Reles looked out at the world from the shadows of their hat brims. They lived in shadowy rooms and peered out through the curtains. They appeared on a dark corner before their terrified victim, did their work, and walked away, turning up their coat collars.

Suppose you had some kind of job that took you round the country, like a salesman's job, Harry thought as he read away the afternoon in the porch swing; suppose you had a job that took you from one town to another. Suppose you killed someone in each one of those towns, carefully and quietly, and hid the bodies so it would take people a long time to find them. Your work would never be done.

9

'Blue rose,' Harry said.

Little Eddie sagged open-mouthed against the cane of his chair, his hands loose in his lap.

It had worked. Harry looked around as if he expected applause, and did feel that all the things in the attic looked back at him with warm approval. It was nine-thirty at night; he and Eddie, alone in the house, occupied the attic in perfect safety. Harry wanted to see if he could put other people under and make them do things, but for now, for tonight, he was content to experiment with Eddie.

'You're going deeper and deeper asleep, Eddie, deeper and deeper, and you're listening to every word I say. You're just sinking down and down, hearing my voice come to you, going deeper and deeper with every word, and now you are real deep asleep and ready to begin.'

Little Eddie sat sprawled over Maryrose's cane-backed chair, his chin touching his chest and his little pink-mouth drooping open. He looked like a slightly undersized seven-year-old, like a second-grader instead of the fourth-grader he would be when he joined Mrs Franken's class in the fall. Suddenly he reminded Harry of the Ultraglide Roadster, scratched and dented and stripped of its tyres.

'Tonight you're going to see how strong you really are. Sit up, Eddie.'

Eddie pulled himself upright and closed his mouth, almost comically obedient.

Harry thought it would be fun to make Little Eddie believe he was a dog and trot around the attic on all fours, barking and lifting his leg. Then he saw Little Eddie staggering across the attic, his tongue bulging out of his mouth, his own hands squeezing and squeezing his throat. Maybe he would try that too, after he had done several other exercises he had discovered in Dr Mentaine's book. He checked the underside of his collar for maybe the fifth time that evening, and felt the long thin shaft of the pearl-headed hatpin which he had stopped reading *Murder, Incorporated* long enough to smuggle out of Maryrose's bedroom after she had left for work.

'Eddie,' he said, 'now you are very deeply asleep, and you will be able to do everything I say. I want you to hold your right arm straight out in front of you.'

Eddie stuck his arm out like a poker.

'That's good, Eddie. Now I want you to notice that all the feeling is leaving that arm. It's getting number and number. It doesn't even feel like flesh and blood any more. It feels like it's made out of steel or something. It's so numb that you can't feel anything there any more. You can't even feel pain in it.'

Harry stood up, went towards Eddie, and brushed his fingers along his arm. 'You didn't feel anything, did you?'

'No,' Eddie said in a slow, gravel-filled voice.

'Do you feel anything now?' Harry pinched the underside of Eddie's forearm.

'No.'

'Now?' Harry used his nails to pinch the side of Eddie's bicep, hard, and left purple dents in the skin.

'No,' Eddie repeated.

'How about this?' He slapped his hand against Eddie's forearm as hard as he could. There was a sharp loud smacking sound, and his fingers tingled. If Little Eddie had not been hypnotized, he would have tried to screech down the walls.

'No,' Eddie said.

Harry pulled the hatpin out of his collar and inspected his brother's arm. 'You're doing great, Little Eddie. You're stronger than anybody in your whole class – you're probably stronger than the whole rest of the school.' He turned Eddie's arm so that the palm was up and the white forearm, lightly traced by small blue veins, faced him.

Harry delicately ran the point of the hatpin down

Eddie's pale, veined forearm. The pinpoint left a narrow chalk-white scratch in its wake. For a moment Harry felt the floor of the attic sway beneath his feet; then he closed his eyes and jabbed the hatpin into Little Eddie's skin as hard as he could.

He opened his eyes. The floor was still swaying beneath him. From Little Eddie's lower arm protruded six inches of the eight-inch hatpin, the mother-of-pearl head glistening softly in the light from the overhead bulb. A drop of blood the size of a watermelon seed stood on Eddie's skin. Harry moved back to his chair and sat down heavily. 'Do you feel anything?'

'No,' Eddie said again in that surprisingly deep voice.

Harry stared at the hatpin embedded in Eddie's arm. The oval drop of blood lengthened itself out against the white skin and began slowly to ooze towards Eddie's wrist. Hafry watched it advance across the pale underside of Eddie's forearm. Finally he stood up and returned to Eddie's side. The elongated drop of blood had ceased moving. Harry bent over and twanged the hatpin. Eddie could feel nothing. Harry put his thumb and forefinger on the glistening head of the pin. His face was so hot he might have been standing before an open fire. He pushed the pin a further half-inch into Eddie's arm, and another small quantity of blood welled up from the base. The pin seemed to be moving in Harry's grasp, pulsing back and forth as if it were breathing.

'Okay,' Harry said. 'Okay.'

He tightened his hold on the pin and pulled. It slipped easily from the wound. Harry held the hatpin before his face just as a doctor holds up a thermometer to read a temperature. He had imagined that the entire bottom section of the shaft would be painted with red, but saw that only a single winding glutinous streak of blood adhered to the pin. For a dizzy second he thought of slipping the end of the pin in his mouth and sucking it clean.

He thought: maybe in another life I was Lepke Buchalter.

He pulled his handkerchief, a filthy square of red paisley, from his front pocket and wiped the streak of blood from the shaft of the pin. Then he leaned over and gently wiped the red smear from Little Eddie's underarm. Harry refolded the handkerchief so the blood would not show, wiped sweat from his face, and shoved the grubby cloth back into his pocket.

'That was good, Eddie. Now we're going to do something a little bit different.'

He knelt down beside his brother and lifted Eddie's nearly weightless, delicately veined arm. 'You still can't feel a thing in this arm, Eddie, it's completely numb. It's sound asleep and it won't wake up until I tell it to.' Harry repositioned himself in order to hold himself steady while he knelt, and put the point of the hatpin nearly flat against Eddie's arm. He pushed it forward far enough to raise a wrinkle of flesh. The point of the hatpin dug into Eddie's skin but did not break it. Harry pushed harder, and the hatpin raised the little bulge of skin by a small but appreciable amount.

Skin was a lot tougher to break through than anyone imagined.

The pin was beginning to hurt his fingers, so Harry opened his hand and positioned the head against the base of his middle finger. Grimacing, he pushed his hand against the pin. The point of the pin popped through the raised wrinkle.

'Eddie, you're made out of beer cans,' Harry said, and tugged the head of the pin backwards. The wrinkle flattened out. Now Harry could shove the pin forwards again, sliding the shaft deeper and deeper under the surface of Little Eddie's skin. He could see the raised line of the hatpin marching down his brother's arm, looking as prominent as the damage done to a cartoon lawn by a cartoon rabbit. When the mother-of-pearl head was perhaps three inches from the entry hole, Harry pushed it down into Little Eddie's flesh, thus raising the point of the pin. He gave the head a sharp jab, and the point appeared at the end of the ridge in Eddie's skin, poking through a tiny smear of blood. Harry shoved the pin in further. Now it showed about an inch and a half of grey metal at either end.

'Feel anything?'

'Nothing.'

Harry jiggled the head of the pin, and a bubble of blood walked out of the entry wound and began to slide down Eddie's arm. Harry sat down on the attic floor beside Eddie and regarded his work. His mind seemed pleasantly empty of thought, filled only with a variety of sensations. He *felt* but could not hear a buzzing in his head, and a blurry film seemed to cover his eyes. He breathed through his mouth. The long pin stuck through Little Eddie's arm looked monstrous seen one way; seen another, it was sheerly beautiful. Skin, blood, and metal. Harry had never seen anything like it before. He reached out and twisted the pin, causing another little blood-snail to crawl from the exit wound. Harry saw all this as if through smudgy glasses, but he did not mind. He knew the blurriness was only mental. He touched the head of the pin again and moved it from side to side. A little more blood leaked from both punctures. Then Harry shoved the pin in, partially withdrew it so that the point nearly disappeared back into Eddie's arm, moved it forward again; and went on like this, back and forth, back and forth, as if he were sewing his brother up, for some time.

Finally he withdrew the pin from Eddie's arm. Two long streaks of blood had nearly reached his brother's wrist. Harry ground the heels of his hands into his eyes, blinked, and discovered that his vision had cleared.

He wondered how long he and Eddie had been in the attic. It could have been hours. He could not quite remember what had happened before he had slid the hatpin into Eddie's skin. Now his blurriness really was mental, not visual. A loud, uncomfortable pulse beat in his temples. Again he wiped the blood from Eddie's arm. Then he stood on wobbling knees and returned to his chair.

'How's your arm feel, Eddie?'

'Numb,' Eddie said in his gravelly sleepy voice.

'The numbness is going away now. Very, very slowly. You are beginning to feel your arm again, and it feels very good. There is no pain. It feels like the sun was shining on it all afternoon. It's strong and healthy. Feeling is coming back into your arm, and you can move your fingers and everything.'

When he had finished speaking Harry leaned back against the chair and closed his eyes. He rubbed his forehead with his hand and wiped the moisture off on his shirt.

'How does your arm feel?' he said without opening his eyes.

'Good.'

'That's great, Little Eddie.' Harry flattened his palms against his flushed face, wiped his cheeks, and opened his eyes.

I can do this every night, he thought. I can bring Little Eddie up here every single night, at least until school starts.

'Eddie, you're getting stronger and stronger every day. This is really helping you. And the more we do it the stronger you'll get. Do you understand me?'

'I understand you,' Eddie said.

'We're almost done for tonight. There's just one more thing I want to try. But you have to be really deep asleep for this to work. So I want you to go deeper and deeper, as deep as you can go. Relax . . . and now you are really deep asleep, deep, deep, and relaxed and ready and feeling good.'

Little Eddie sat sprawled in his chair with his head tilted back and his eyes closed. Two tiny dark spots of blood stood out like mosquito bites on his lower right forearm.

'When I talk to you, Eddie, you're slowly getting younger and younger. You're going backwards in time, so now you're not nine years old any more, you're eight – it's last year and you're in the third grade. And now you're seven . . . and now you're six years old . . . and now you're five, Eddie, and it's the day of your fifth birthday. You're five years old today, Little Eddie. How old are you?'

'I'm five.' To Harry's surprised pleasure, Little Eddie's voice actually seemed younger, as did his hunched posture in the chair.

'How do you feel?'

'Not good. I hate my present. It's terrible. Dad got it, and Mom says it should never be allowed in the house because it's just junk. I wish I wouldn't ever have to have birthdays, they're so terrible. I'm gonna cry.'

His face contracted. Harry tried to remember what Eddie had got for his fifth birthday, but could not – he caught only a dim memory of shame and disappointment. 'What's your present, Eddie?'

In a teary voice, Eddie said, 'A radio. But it's busted and Mom says it looks like it came from the junkyard. I don't want it any more. I don't even wanna *see* it.'

Yes, Harry thought: yes, yes, yes. He could remember. On Little Eddie's fifth birthday, Edgar Beevers had produced a yellow plastic radio which even Harry had seen was astoundingly ugly. The dial was cracked, and it was marked here and there with brown circular scab-like marks where someone had mashed out cigarettes on it.

The radio had long since been buried in the junk room, where it now lay beneath several geological layers of trash.

'Okay, Eddie, you can forget the radio now, because you're going backwards again . . . you're getting younger . . . you're going backwards through being four years old, and now you're three.'

He looked with interest at Little Eddie, whose entire demeanour had changed. From being tearfully unhappy, Eddie now demonstrated a self-sufficient good cheer Harry could not remember ever seeing in him. His arms were folded over his chest. He was smiling, and his eyes were bright and clear and childish.

'What do you see?' Harry asked.

'Mommy-ommy-om.'

'What's she doing?'

'Mommy's at her desk. She's smoking and looking

through her papers.' Eddie giggled. 'Mommy looks funny. It looks like smoke is coming out of the top of her head.' Eddie ducked his chin and hid his smile behind a hand. 'Mommy doesn't see me. I can see her, but she doesn't see me. Oh! Mommy works hard! She works hard at her desk!'

Eddie's smile abruptly left his face. His face froze for a second in a comic rubbery absence of expression; then his eyes widened in terror and his mouth went loose and wobbly.

'What happened?' Harry's mouth had gone dry.

'No, Mommy!' Eddie wailed. 'Don't, Mommy! I wasn't spying. I wasn't, I promise – ' His words broke off into a screech. *'No, Mommy! Don't! Don't, Mommy!'* Eddie jumped upwards, sending his chair flying back, and ran blindly towards the rear of the attic. Harry's head rang with Eddie's screeches. He heard a sharp *crack!* of wood breaking, but only as a small part of all the noise Eddie was making as he charged round the attic. Eddie had run into a tangle of hanging dresses, spun round, enmeshing himself deeper in the dresses, and was now tearing himself away from the web of dresses, pulling some of them off the rack. A long-sleeved purple dress with an enormous lace collar had draped itself around Eddie like a ghostly dance partner, and another dress, this of dull red velvet, snaked around his right leg. Eddie screamed again and yanked himself away from the tangle. The entire rack of clothes wobbled and then went over in a mad jangle of sound.

'No!' he screeched. *'Help!'* Eddie ran straight into a big wooden beam marking off one of the eaves, bounced off, and came windmilling towards Harry. Harry knew his brother could not see him.

'Eddie, stop,' he said, but Eddie was past hearing him. Harry tried to make Eddie stop by wrapping his arms around him, but Eddie slammed right into him, hitting Harry's chest with a shoulder and knocking his head painfully against Harry's chin; Harry's arms closed on nothing and his eyes lost focus, and Eddie went crashing into the tilting mirror. The mirror yawned over sideways. Harry saw it tilt with dream-like slowness towards the floor, then in a eyeblink drop and crash. Broken glass sprayed across the attic floor.

'*Stop!*' Harry yelled. '*Stand still, Eddie!*'

Eddie came to rest. A ripped and dirty dress of dull red velvet still clung to his right leg. Blood oozed down his temple from an ugly cut above his eye. He was breathing hard, releasing air in little, whimpering exhalations.

'Holy shit,' Harry said, looking round at the attic. In only a few seconds Eddie had managed to create what looked at first like absolute devastation. Maryrose's ancient dresses lay tangled in a heap of dusty fabrics from which wire hangers skeletally protruded; grey Eddie-sized footprints lay like a pattern over the muted explosion of colours the dresses now created. When the rack had gone over, it had knocked a section the size of a dinner plate out of a round wooden coffee table Maryrose had particularly prized for its being made from a single section of teak – 'a single piece of *teak*, the rarest wood in all the world, all the way from Ceylon!' The much-prized mirror lay in hundreds of glittering pieces across the attic floor. With growing horror, Harry saw that the wooden frame had cracked like a bone, showing a bone-pale, shockingly white fracture in the expanse of dark stain.

Harry's blood tipped within his body, nearly tipping him with it, like the mirror. 'Oh God, oh God, oh God.'

He turned slowly round. Eddie stood blinking two feet to his side, wiping ineffectually at the blood running from his forehead and now covering most of his left cheek. He looked like an Indian in warpaint — a defeated, lost Indian, for his eyes were dim and his head turned aimlessly from side to side.

A few feet from Eddie lay the chair in which he had been sitting. One of its thin, curved wooden arms lay beside it, crudely severed. It looked like an insect's leg, Harry thought, like a toy gun.

For a moment Harry thought that his face too was red with blood. He wiped his hand over his forehead and looked at his glistening palm. It was only sweat. His heart beat like a bell. Beside him Eddie said, 'Aaah . . . what . . . ?' The injury to his head had brought him out of the trance.

The dresses were ruined, stepped on, tangled, torn. The mirror was broken. The table had been mutilated. Maryrose's chair lay on its side like a murder victim, its severed arm ending in a bristle of snapped ligaments.

'My head *hurts*,' Eddie said in a weak, trembling voice. 'What happened? Aaah! I'm all blood! I'm all blood, Harry!'

'You're all blood, you're all blood?' Harry shouted at him. 'Everything's *all blood*, you dummy! Look around!' He did not recognize his own voice, which sounded high and tinny and seemed to be coming from somewhere else. Little Eddie took an aimless step away from him, and Harry wanted to fly at him, to pound his bloody head into a pancake, to destroy him, smash him . . .

Eddie held up his bloodstained palm and stared at it. He wiped it vaguely across the front of his T-shirt and took another wandering step. 'I'm ascared, Harry,' his tiny voice said.

'Look what you did!' Harry screamed. 'You wrecked everything! Damn it! What do you think is going to happen to us?'

'What's Mom going to do?' Eddie asked in a voice only slightly above a whisper.

'You don't know?' Harry yelled. 'You're dead!'

Eddie started to weep.

Harry bunched his hands into fists and clamped his eyes shut. They were both dead, that was the real truth. Harry opened his eyes, which felt hot and oddly heavy, and stared at his sobbing, red-smeared, useless little brother. 'Blue rose,' he said.

10

Little Eddie's hands fell to his sides. His chin dropped, and his mouth fell open. Blood ran in a smooth wide band down the left side of his face, dipped under the line of his jaw, and continued on down his neck and into his T-shirt. Pooled blood in his left eyebrow dripped steadily onto the floor, as if from a tap.

'You are going deep *asleep*,' Harry said. Where was the hatpin? He looked back to the single standing chair and saw the mother-of-pearl head glistening on the floor near it. 'Your whole body is *numb*.' He moved over to the pin, bent down, and picked it up. The metal shaft felt warm in his fingers. 'You can feel no *pain*.'

He went back to Little Eddie. 'Nothing can *hurt* you.' Harry's breath seemed to be breathing itself, forcing itself into his throat, in hot, harsh, shallow pants, then expelling itself out.

'Did you *hear* me, Little Eddie?'

In his gravelly, slow-moving hypnotized voice, Little Eddie said, 'I heard you.'

'And you can feel no *pain*?'

'I can feel no pain.'

Harry drew his arm back, the point of the hatpin extending forward from his fist, and then jerked his hand forward as hard as he could and stuck the pin into Eddie's abdomen right through the blood-soaked T-shirt. He exhaled sharply, and tasted a sour misery on his breath.

'You don't feel a thing.'

'I don't feel a thing.'

Harry opened his right hand and drove his palm against the head of the pin, hammering it in another few inches. Little Eddie looked like a voodoo doll. A kind of sparkling light surrounded him. Harry gripped the head of the pin with his thumb and forefinger and yanked it out. He held it up and inspected it. Glittering light surrounded the pin too. The long shaft was painted with blood. Harry slipped the point into his mouth and closed his lips around the warm metal.

He saw himself, a man in another life, standing in a row with men like himself in a bleak grey landscape defined by barbed wire. Emaciated people in rags shuffled up towards them and spat on their clothes. The smells of dead flesh and of burning flesh hung in the air. Then the vision was gone, and Little Eddie stood before him again, surrounded by layers of glittering light.

Harry grimaced or grinned, he could not have told the difference, and drove his long spike deep into Eddie's stomach.

Eddie uttered a small *oof*.

'You don't feel anything, Eddie,' Harry whispered. 'You feel good all over. You never felt better in your life.'

'Never felt better in my life.'

Harry slowly pulled out the pin and cleaned it with his fingers.

He was able to remember every single thing anyone had ever told him about Tommy Golz.

'Now you're going to play a funny, funny game,' he said. 'This is called the Tommy Golz game because it's going to keep you safe from Mrs Franken. Are you ready?' Harry carefully slid the pin into the fabric of his shirt collar, all the while watching Eddie's slack, blood-streaked person. Vibrating bands of light beat rhythmically and steadily about Eddie's face.

'Ready,' Eddie said.

'I'm going to give you your instructions now, Little Eddie. Pay attention to everything I say and it's all going to be okay. Everything's going to be okay – as long as you play the game exactly the way I tell you. You understand, don't you?'

'I understand.'

'Tell me what I just said.'

'Everything's gonna be okay as long as I play the game exactly the way you tell me.' A dollop of blood slid off Eddie's eyebrow and splashed onto his already soaked T-shirt.

'Good, Eddie. Now the first thing you do is fall down – not now, when I tell you. I'm going to give you all the instructions, and then I'm going to count backwards from ten, and when I get to *one*, you'll start playing the game. Okay?'

'Okay.'

'So first you fall down, Little Eddie. You fall down real hard. Then comes the fun part of the game. You bang your head on the floor. You start to go crazy. You twitch, and you bang your hands and feet on the floor. You do that for a long time. I guess you do that until you count to about a hundred. You foam at the mouth, you twist all over the place. You get real stiff, and then you get real loose, and then you get real stiff, and then real loose again, and all this time you're banging your head and your hands and feet on the floor, and you're twisting all over the place. Then when you finish counting to a hundred in your head, you do the last thing. You swallow your tongue. And that's the game. When you swallow your tongue, you're the winner. And then nothing bad can happen to you, and Mrs Franken won't be able to hurt you ever, ever, ever.'

Harry stopped talking. His hands were shaking. After a second he realized that his insides were shaking too. He raised his trembling fingers to his shirt collar and felt the hatpin.

'Tell me how you win the game, Little Eddie. What's the last thing you do?'

'I swallow my tongue.'

'Right. And then Mrs Franken and Mom will never be able to hurt you, because you won the game.'

'Good,' said Little Eddie. The glittering light shimmered about him.

'Okay, we'll start playing right now,' Harry said. 'Ten.' He went towards the attic steps. 'Nine.' He reached the steps. 'Eight.'

He went down one step. 'Seven.' Harry descended another two steps. 'Six.' When he went down another two steps, he called up in a slightly louder voice, 'Five.'

Now his head was beneath the level of the attic floor, and he could not see Little Eddie any more. All he could hear was the soft, occasional plop of liquid hitting the floor.

'Four.'

'Three.'

'Two.' He was now at the door to the attic steps. Harry opened the door, stepped through it, breathed hard, and shouted 'One!' up the stairs.

He heard a thud, and then quickly closed the door behind him.

Harry went across the hall and into the 'dormitory' bedroom. There seemed to be a strange absence of light in the hallway. For a second he saw – was sure he saw – a line of dark trees across a wall of barbed wire. Harry closed this door behind him too, and went to his narrow bed and sat down. He could feel blood beating in his face; his eyes seemed oddly warm, as if they were heated by filaments. Harry slowly, almost reverently, extracted the hatpin from his collar and set it on his pillow. 'A hundred,' he said. 'Ninety-nine, ninety-eight, ninety-seven, ninety-six, ninety-five, ninety-four . . .'

When he had counted down to *'one'*, he stood up and left the bedroom. He went quickly downstairs without looking at the door behind which lay the attic steps. On the ground floor he slipped into Maryrose's bedroom, crossed over to her desk, and slid open the bottom right-hand drawer. From the drawer he took a velvet-covered box. This he opened, and jabbed the hatpin in the ball of material, studded with pins of all sizes and descriptions, from which he had taken it. He replaced the box in the drawer, pushed the drawer into the desk, and quickly left the room and went upstairs.

Back in his own bedroom, Harry took off his clothes and climbed into his bed. His face still burned.

He must have fallen asleep very quickly, because the next thing he knew Albert was slamming his way into the bedroom and tossing his clothes and boots all over the place. 'You asleep?' Albert asked. 'You left the attic light on, you fuckin' dummies, but if you think I'm gonna save your fuckin' asses and go up and turn it off, you're even stupider than you look.'

Harry was careful not to move a finger, not to move even a hair.

He held his breath while Albert threw himself onto his bed, and when Albert's breathing relaxed and slowed Harry followed his big brother into sleep. He did not awaken again until he heard his father half-screeching, half-sobbing up in the attic, and that was very late at night.

I I

Sonny came from Fort Sill, George all the way from Germany. Between them, they held up a sodden Edgar Beevers at the graveside while a minister Harry had never seen before read from a Bible as cracked and rubbed as an old brown shoe. Between his two older sons, Harry's father looked bent and ancient, a skinny old man only steps from the grave himself. Sonny and George despised their father, Harry saw – they held him up on sufferance, in part because they had chipped in thirty dollars apiece to buy him a suit and did not want to see it collapse with its owner inside onto the lumpy clay of the graveyard. His whiskers glistened in the sun, and moisture shone beneath his eyes and at the corners of his mouth. He had been shaking too severely for either Sonny or George to shave him, and had been capable of moving in a straight line only after George let him take a couple of long swallows from a leather-covered flask he took out of his duffel bag.

The minister uttered a few sage words on the subject of epilepsy.

Sonny and George looked as solid as brick walls in their uniforms, like prison guards or actual prisons themselves. Next to them, Albert looked shrunken and unfinished. Albert wore the green plaid sports jacket in which he had graduated from the eighth grade, and his wrists hung prominent and red four inches below the bottom of the sleeves. His motor-cycle boots were visible beneath his light grey trousers, but they, like the green jacket, had lost their flash. Like Albert, too: ever since the discovery of Eddie's body, Albert had gone round the house looking as if he'd just bitten off the end of his tongue and was trying to decide whether or not to spit it out. He never looked anybody in the eye, and he rarely spoke. Albert acted as though a gigantic padlock had been fixed to the middle of his chest and *he* was damned if he'd ever take it off. He had not asked Sonny or George a single question about the army. Every now and then he would utter a remark about the gas station so toneless that it suffocated any reply.

Harry looked at Albert standing beside their mother, kneading his hands together and keeping his eyes fixed as if by decree on the square foot of ground before him.

Albert glanced over at Harry, knew he was being
looked at, and did what to Harry was an extraordinary
thing. Albert *froze*. All expression drained out of his
face, and his hands locked immovably together. He
looked as little able to see or hear as a statue. *He's that
way because he told Little Eddie that he wished he
would die*, Harry thought for the tenth or eleventh
time since he had realized this, and with undiminished
awe. Then was he lying? Harry wondered. And if he
really did wish that Little Eddie would drop dead, why
isn't he happy now? Didn't he get what he wanted?
Albert would never spit out that piece of his tongue,
Harry thought, watching his brother blink slowly and
sightlessly towards the ground.

Harry shifted his gaze uneasily to his father, still
propped up between George and Sonny, heard that the
minister was finally reaching the end of his speech,
and took a fast look at his mother. Maryrose was
standing very straight in a black dress and black
sunglasses, holding the straps of her bag in front of her
with both hands. Except for the colour of her clothes,
she could have been a spectator at a tennis match.
Harry knew by the way she was holding her face that
she was wishing she could smoke. Dying for a cigarette, he thought, ha ha, the Monster Mash, it's a
graveyard smash.

The minister finished speaking, and made a rhetori-
cal gesture with his hands. The coffin sank on ropes
into the rough earth. Harry's father began to weep
loudly. First George, then Sonny, picked up large,
damp, shovel-marked pieces of clay and dropped them
on the coffin. Edgar Beevers nearly fell in after his own
tiny clod, but George contemptuously swung him
back. Maryrose marched forward, bent and picked up a

random piece of clay with thumb and forefinger as if using tweezers, dropped it and turned away before it struck. Albert fixed his eyes on Harry – his own clod had split apart in his hand and crumbled away beneath his fingers. Harry shook his head *no*. He did not want to drop dirt on Eddie's coffin and make that noise. He did not want to look at Eddie's coffin again. There was enough dirt around to do the job without him hitting that metal box like he was trying to ring Eddie's doorbell. He stepped back.

'Mom says we have to get back to the house,' Albert said.

Maryrose lit up as soon as they got into the single black car they had rented through the funeral parlour, and breathed out acrid smoke over everybody crowded into the back seat. The car backed into a narrow graveyard lane, and turned down the main road towards the front gates.

In the front seat, next to the driver, Edgar Beevers drooped sideways and leaned his head against the window, leaving a blurred streak on the glass.

'How in the name of hell could Little Eddie have epilepsy without anybody knowing about it?' George asked.

Albert stiffened and stared out the window.

'Well, that's epilepsy,' Maryrose said. 'Eddie could have gone on for years without having an attack.' That she worked in a hospital always gave her remarks of this sort a unique gravity, almost as if she were a doctor.

'Must have been some fit,' Sonny said, squeezed into place between Harry and Albert.

'*Grand mal*,' Maryrose said, and took another hungry drag on her cigarette.

'Poor little bastard,' George said. 'Sorry, Mom.'

'I know you're in the armed forces, and armed forces people speak very freely, but I wish you would not use that kind of language.'

Harry, jammed into Sonny's rock-hard side, felt his brother's body twitch with a hidden laugh, though Sonny's face did not alter.

'I said I was sorry, Mom,' George said.

'Yes. Driver! Driver!' Maryrose was leaning forward, reaching out one claw to tap the chauffeur's shoulder. 'Livermore is the next right. Do you know South Sixth Street?'

'I'll get you there,' the driver said.

This is not my family, Harry thought. I came from somewhere else and my rules are different from theirs.

His father mumbled something inaudible as soon as they got in the door and disappeared into his curtained-off cubicle. Maryrose put her sunglasses in her purse and marched into the kitchen to warm the coffee cake and the macaroni casserole, both made that morning, in the oven. Sonny and George wandered into the living room and sat down on opposite ends of the couch. They did not look at each other. George picked up a *Reader's Digest* from the table and began leafing through it backwards, and Sonny folded his hands in his lap and stared at his thumbs. Albert's footsteps plodded up the stairs, crossed the landing, and went into the dormitory bedroom.

'What's she in the kitchen for?' Sonny asked, speaking to his hands. 'Nobody's going to come. Nobody ever comes here, because she never wanted them to.'

'Albert's taking this kind of hard, Harry,' George said. He propped the magazine against the stiff folds of his uniform and looked across the room at his little brother. Harry had seated himself beside the door, as out of the way as possible. George's attentions rather frightened him, though George had behaved with consistent kindness ever since his arrival two days after Eddie's death. His crewcut still bristled and he could still break rocks with his chin, but some violent demon seemed to have left him. 'You think he'll be okay?'

'Him? Sure.' Harry tilted his head, grimaced.

'He didn't see Little Eddie first, did he?'

'No, Dad did,' Harry said. 'He saw the light on in the attic when he came home, I guess. Albert went up there, though. I guess there was so much blood Dad thought somebody broke in and killed Eddie. But he just bumped his head, and that's where the blood came from.'

'Head wounds bleed like bastards,' Sonny said. 'A guy hit me with a bottle once in Tokyo. I thought I was gonna bleed to death right there.'

'And Mom's stuff got all messed up?' George asked quietly.

This time Sonny looked up.

'Pretty much, I guess. The dress rack got knocked down. Dad cleaned up what he could the next day. One of the cane-back chairs got broke, and a hunk got knocked out of the teak table. And the mirror got broken into a million pieces.'

Sonny shook his head, and made a soft whistling sound through his pursed lips.

'She's a tough old gal,' George said. 'I hear her coming, though, so we have to stop, Harry. But we can talk tonight.'

Harry nodded.

12

After dinner that night, when Maryrose had gone to bed – the hospital had given her two nights off – Harry sat across the kitchen table from a George who clearly had something to say. Sonny had polished off a sixpack by himself in front of the television and gone up to the dormitory bedroom by himself. Albert had disappeared shortly after dinner, and their father had never emerged from his cubicle beside the junk room.

'I'm glad Pete Petrosian came over,' George said. 'He's a good old boy. Ate two helpings, too.'

Harry was startled by George's use of their neighbour's first name – he was not even sure that he had ever heard it before.

Mr Petrosian had been their only caller that afternoon. Harry had seen that his mother was grateful that someone had come, and despite her preparations wanted no more company after Mr Petrosian had left.

'Think I'll get a beer, that is if Sonny didn't drink it all,' George said, and stood up and opened the fridge. His uniform looked as if it had been painted on his body, and his muscles bulged and moved like a horse's. 'Two left,' he said. 'Good thing you're underage.' George popped the caps off both bottles and came back to the table. He winked at Harry, then tilted the first bottle to his lips and took a good swallow. 'So what the devil was Little Eddie doing up there, anyhow? Trying on dresses?'

'I don't know,' Harry said. 'I was asleep.'

'Hell, I know I kind of lost touch with Little Eddie, but I got the impression he was scared of his own shadow. I'm surprised he had the nerve to go up there and mess around with Mom's precious stuff.'

'Yeah,' Harry said. 'Me too.'

'You didn't happen to go with him, did you?' George tilted the bottle to his mouth and winked at Harry again.

Harry just looked back. He could feel his face getting hot.

'I just was thinking maybe you saw it happen to Little Eddie, and got too scared to tell anybody. Nobody would be mad at you, Harry. Nobody would blame you for anything. You couldn't know how to help someone who's having an epileptic fit. Little Eddie swallowed his tongue. Even if you'd been standing next to him when he did it and had the presence of mind to call an ambulance, he would have died before it got here. Unless you knew what was wrong and how to correct it. Which nobody would expect you to know, not in a million years. Nobody'd blame you for anything, Harry, not even Mom.'

'I was asleep,' Harry said.

'Okay, okay. I just wanted you to know.'

They sat in silence for a time, then both spoke at once.

'Did you know – ?'

'We had this – '

'Sorry,' George said. 'Go on.'

'Did you know that Dad used to be in the army? In World War Two?'

'Yeah, I knew that. Of course I knew that.'

'Did you know that he committed the perfect murder once?'

'*What?*'

'Dad committed the perfect murder. When he was at Dachau, that death camp.'

'Oh Christ, is that what you're talking about? You got a funny way of seeing things, Harry. He shot an enemy who was trying to escape. That's not murder, it's war. There's one hell of a big difference.'

'I'd like to see war someday,' Harry said. 'I'd like to be in the army, like you and Dad.'

'Hold your horses, hold your horses,' George said, smiling now. 'That's sort of one of the things I wanted to talk to you about.' He set down his beer bottle, cradled his hands around it, and tilted his head to look at Harry. This was obviously going to be serious. 'You know, I used to be crazy and stupid, that's the only way to put it. I used to look for fights. I had a chip on my shoulder the size of a house, and pounding some dipshit into a coma was my idea of a great time. The army did me a lot of good. It made me grow up. But I don't think you need that, Harry. You're too smart for that – if you have to go, you go, but out of all of us you're the one who could really amount to something in this world. You could be a doctor. Or a lawyer. You ought to get the best education you can, Harry. What you have to do is stay out of trouble and get to college.'

'Oh, college,' Harry said.

'Listen to me, Harry. I make pretty good money, and I got nothing to spend it on. I'm not going to get married and have kids, that's for sure. So I want to make you a proposition. If you keep your nose clean and make it through high school, I'll help you out with college. Maybe you can get a scholarship – I think you're smart enough, Harry, and a scholarship would be great. But either way, I'll see you make it through.' George emptied the first bottle, set it down, and gave

Harry a quizzical look. 'Let's get one person in this family off on the right track. What do you say?'

'I guess I better keep reading,' Harry said.

'I hope you'll read your ass off, little buddy,' George said, and picked up the second bottle of beer.

13

The day after Sonny left, George put all of Eddie's toys and clothes into a box and squeezed the box into the junk room; two days later, George took a bus to New York so he could get his flight to Munich from Idle-wild. An hour before he caught his bus, George walked Harry up to Big John's and stuffed him full of hamburg-ers and French fries and said, 'You'll probably miss Eddie a lot, won't you?' 'I guess,' Harry said, but the truth was that Eddie was now only a vacancy, a blank space. Sometimes a door would close and Harry would know that Little Eddie had just come in; but when he turned to look, he saw only emptiness. George's ques-tion, asked a week ago, was the last time Harry had heard anyone pronounce his brother's name.

In the seven days since the charmed afternoon at Big John's and the departure on a southbound bus of George Beevers, everything seemed to have gone back to the way it was before, but Harry knew that really everything had changed. They had been a loose, divided family of five, two parents and three sons. Now they seemed to be a family of three, and Harry thought that the actual truth was that the family had shrunk down to two, himself and his mother.

Edgar Beevers had left home – he too was an absence. After two visits from policemen who parked their cars right outside the house, after listening to his mother's muttered expressions of disgust, after the spectacle of his pale, bleary, but sober and cleanshaven father trying over and over to knot a necktie in front of the bathroom mirror, Harry finally accepted that his father had been caught shoplifting. His father had to go to court, and he was scared. His hands shook so uncontrollably that he could not shave himself, and in the end Maryrose had to knot his tie – doing it in one, two, three quick movements as brutal as the descent of a knife, never removing the cigarette from her mouth.

GRIEF-STRICKEN AREA MAN FORGIVEN OF SHOPLIFTING CHARGE read the headline over the little story in the evening newspaper which at last explained his father's crime. Edgar Beevers had been stopped on the sidewalk outside the Livermore Avenue National Tea, T-bone steaks hidden inside his shirt and a bottle of Rhinegold beer in each of his front pockets. He had stolen two steaks! He had put beer bottles in his pockets! This made Harry feel like he was sweating inside. The judge had sent him home, but home was not where he went. For a short time, Harry thought, his father had hung out on Oldtown Road, Palmyra's Skid Row, and slept in vacant lots with winos and bums. (Then a woman was supposed to have taken him in.)

Albert was another mystery. It was as though a creature from outer space had taken him over and was using his body, like *Invasion of the Body-Snatchers*. Albert looked like he thought somebody was always standing behind him, watching every move he made. He was still carrying around that piece of tongue, and pretty soon, Harry thought, he'd get so used to it that he would forget he had it.

Three days after George left Palmyra, Albert actually tagged along after Harry on the way to Big John's. Harry turned around on the sidewalk and saw Albert in his black jeans and grease-blackened T-shirt halfway down the block, shoving his hands in his pockets and looking hard at the ground. That was Albert's way of pretending to be invisible. The next time he turned around, Albert growled, 'Keep walking.'

Harry went to work on the pinball machine as soon as he got inside Big John's. Albert slunk in a few minutes later and went straight to the counter. He took one of the stained paper menus from a stack squeezed in beside a napkin dispenser and inspected it as if he had never seen it before.

'Hey, let me introduce you guys,' said Big John, leaning against the far side of the counter. Like Albert, he wore black jeans and motorcycle boots but his dark hair, daringly for the 1950s, fell over his ears. Beneath his stained white apron he wore a long-sleeved black shirt with a pattern of tiny azure palm trees. 'You two are the Beevers boys, Harry and Bucky. Say hello to each other, fellows.'

Bucky Beaver was a toothy rodent in an Ipana television commercial. Albert blushed, still grimly staring at his menu sheet.

'Call me "Beans",' Harry said, and felt Albert's gaze shift wonderingly to him.

'Beans and Bucky, the Beevers boys,' Big John said. 'Well, Buck, what'll you have?'

'Hamburger, fries, shake,' Albert said.

Big John half-turned and yelled the order through the hatch to Mama Mary's kitchen. For a time the three of them stood in uneasy silence. Then Big John said, 'Heard your old man found a new place to hang his hat. His new girlfriend is a real pistol, I heard. Spent some time in County Hospital. On account of she picked up little messages from outer space on the good old Philco. You hear that?'

'He's gonna come home real soon,' Harry said. 'He doesn't have any new girlfriend. He's staying with an old friend. She's a rich lady and she wants to help him out because she knows he had a lot of trouble and she's going to get him a real good job, and then he'll come home, and we'll be able to move to a better house and everything.'

He never even saw Albert move, but Albert had materialized beside him. Fury, rage, and misery distorted his face. Harry had time to cry out only once, and then Albert slammed a fist into his chest and knocked him backwards into the pinball machine.

'I bet that felt real good,' Harry said, unable to keep down his own rage. 'I bet you'd like to kill me, huh? Huh, Albert? How about that?'

Albert moved backwards two paces and lowered his hands, already looking impassive, locked into himself.

For a second in which his breath failed and dazzling light filled his eyes, Harry saw Little Eddie's slack, trusting face before him. Then Big John came up from nowhere with a big hamburger and a mound of French fries on a plate and said, 'Down, boys. Time for Rocky here to tackle his dinner.'

That night Albert said nothing at all to Harry as they lay in their beds. Neither did he fall asleep. Harry knew that for most of the night Albert just closed his eyes and faked it, like a possum in trouble. Harry tried to stay awake long enough to see when Albert's fake sleep melted into the real thing, but he sank into dreams long before that.

* * *

He was rushing down the stony corridor of a castle past suits of armour and torches guttering in sconces. His bladder was bursting, he had to let go, he could not hold it more than another few seconds . . . At last he came to the open bathroom door and ran into that splendid gleaming place. He began to tug at his zip, and looked round for the butler and the row of marble urinals. Then he froze. Little Eddie was standing before him, not the uniformed butler. Blood ran in a gaudy streak from a gash high on his forehead over his cheek and right down his neck, neat as paint. Little Eddie was waving frantically at Harry, his eyes bright and hysterical, his mouth working soundlessly because he had swallowed his tongue.

Harry sat up straight in bed, about to scream, then realized that the bedroom was all around him and Little Eddie was gone. He hurried downstairs to the bathroom.

14

At two o'clock the next afternoon Harry Beevers had to pee again, and just as badly, but this time he was a long way from the bathroom across from the junk room and his father's old cubicle. Harry was standing in the humid sunlight across the street from 45 Oldtown Way. This short street connected the bums, transient hotels, bars, and seedy movie theatres of Oldtown Road with the more respectable hotels, department stores, and restaurants of Palmyra Avenue – the real downtown. Forty-five Oldtown Way was a four-storey brick tenement with an exoskeleton of fire escapes. Black iron bars covered the ground-floor windows. On one side of 45 Oldtown Way were the large soap-smeared windows of a bankrupted shoe store, on the other a vacant lot where loose bricks and broken bottles nestled amongst dandelions and tall Queen Anne's Lace. Harry's father lived in that building now. Everybody else knew it and, since Big John had told him, now Harry knew it too.

He jigged from leg to leg, waiting for a woman to come out through the front door. It was as chipped and peeling as his own, and a broken fanlight sat drunkenly atop it. Harry had checked the row of dented mailboxes on the brick wall just outside the door for his father's name, but none bore any names at all. Big John hadn't known the name of the woman who had taken Harry's father, but he said that she was large, black-haired and crazy, and that she had two children in foster care. About half an hour ago a dark-haired woman had come through the door, but Harry had not followed her because she had not looked especially large to him. Now he was beginning to have doubts. What did Big John mean by 'large', anyhow? As big as he was? And how could you tell if someone was crazy? Did it show? Maybe he should have followed that woman. This thought made him even more anxious, and he squeezed his legs together.

His father was in that building now, he thought. Harry thought of his father lying on an unmade bed, his brown winter coat around him, his hat pulled low on his forehead like Lepke Buchalter's, drawing on a cigarette, looking moodily out of the window.

Then he had to pee so urgently that he could not have held it in for more than a few seconds, and trotted across the street and into the vacant lot. Near the back

fence the tall weeds gave him some shelter from the
street. He frantically unzipped and let the braided
yellow stream splash into a nest of broken bricks.
Harry looked up at the side of the building beside him.
It looked very tall, and seemed to be tilting slightly
towards him. The four blank windows on each floor
looked back down at him. Just as he was tugging at his
zip, he heard the front door of the building slam shut.

His heart slammed too. Harry hunkered down
behind the tall white weeds. Anxiety that she might
walk the other way, towards downtown, made him
twine his fingers together and bend them back. If he
waited about five seconds, he figured, he'd know she
was going towards Palmyra Avenue and he would be
able to get across the lot in time to see which way she
turned. His knuckles cracked. He felt like a soldier
hiding in a forest, like a murder weapon.

He raised himself up on his toes and got ready to
dash back across the street, because an empty grocery
cart closely followed by a moving belly with a tiny
head and basketball shoes, a cigar tilted in its mouth
like a flag, appeared past the front of the building. He
could go back and wait across the street. Harry settled
down and watched the stomach go down the sidewalk
past him. Then a shadow separated itself from the
street side of the fat man, and the shadow became a
black-haired woman in a long loose dress now striding
past the grocery cart. She shook back her head, and
Harry saw that she was tall as a queen and that her
skin was darker than olive. Deep lines cut through her
cheeks. It had to be the woman who had taken his
father. Her long rapid strides had taken her well past
the fat man's grocery cart. Harry ran across the rubble
of the lot and began to follow her up the sidewalk.

His father's woman walked in a hard, determined way. She stepped down into the street to get round groups too slow for her. At the Oldtown Road corner she wove her way through a group of saggy-bottomed men passing around a bottle in a paper bag and cut in front of two black children dribbling a basketball up the street. She was on the move, and Harry had to hurry along to keep her in sight.

'I bet you don't believe me,' he said to himself, practising, and skirted the group of winos on the corner. He picked up his speed until he was nearly trotting. The two black kids with the basketball ignored him as he kept pace with them, then went on ahead. Far up the block, the tall woman with bouncing black hair marched right past a flashing neon sign in a bar window. Her bottom moved back and forth in the loose dress, surprisingly big whenever it bulged out the fabric of the dress; her back seemed as long as a lion's. 'What would you say if I told you . . . ?' Harry said to himself.

A block and a half ahead, the woman turned on her heel and went through the door of the A&P store. Harry sprinted the rest of the way, pushed the yellow wooden door marked ENTER, and walked into the dense, humid air of the grocery store. Other A&P stores may have been air-conditioned, but not the little shop on Oldtown Road.

What was foster care, anyway? Did you get money if you gave away your children?

A good person's children would never be in foster care, Harry thought. He saw the woman turning into the third aisle past the cash register. He realized, with a small shock, that she was taller than his father. If I told you, you might not believe me . . . He went slowly around the corner of the aisle. She was standing on the pale wooden floor about fifteen feet in front of him, carrying a wire basket in one hand. He stepped forward. What I have to say might seem ... For good luck, he touched the hatpin inserted into the bottom of his collar. She was staring at a row of brightly coloured bags of potato crisps. Harry cleared his throat. The woman reached down and picked up a big bag and put it in the basket.

'Excuse me,' Harry said.

She turned her head to look at him. Her face was as wide as it was long, and in the mellow light from the store's low-wattage bulbs her skin seemed a very light shade of brown. Harry knew he was meeting an equal. She looked like she could do magic, as if she could shoot fire and sparks out of her fierce black eyes.

'I bet you don't believe me,' he said, 'but a kid can hypnotize people just as good as an adult.'

'What's that?'

His rehearsed words now sounded crazy to him, but he stuck to his script.

'A kid can hypnotize people. I can hypnotize people. Do you believe that?'

'I don't think I even care,' she said, and wheeled away towards the rear of the aisle.

'I bet you don't think I could hypnotize you,' Harry said.

'Kid, get lost.'

Harry suddenly knew that if he kept talking about hypnotism the woman would turn down the next aisle and ignore him no matter what he said, or else begin to speak in a very loud voice about seeing the manager. 'My name is Harry Beevers,' he said to her back. 'Edgar Beevers is my dad.'

She stopped and turned around and looked expressionlessly into his face.

Harry dizzyingly saw a wall of barbed wire before him, a dark green wall of trees at the other end of a barren field.

'I wonder if you . . . maybe you call him Beans,' Harry said.

'Oh, great,' she said. 'That's just great. So you're one of his boys. Terrific. *Beans* wants potato crisps; what do you want?'

'I want you to fall down and bang your head and swallow your tongue and *die* and get buried and have people drop dirt on you,' Harry said. The woman's mouth fell open. 'Then I want you to puff up with *gas*. I want you to *rot*. I want you to turn green and *black*. I want your *skin* to slide off your bones.'

'You're crazy!' the woman shouted at him. 'Your whole family's crazy! Do you think your mother wants him any more?'

'My father shot us in the back,' Harry said, and turned and bolted down the aisle for the door.

Outside, he began to trot down seedy Oldtown Road. At Oldtown Way he turned left. When he ran past number 45, he looked at every blank window. His face, his hands, his whole body felt hot and wet. Soon he had a stitch in his side. Harry blinked, and saw a dark line of trees, a wall of barbed wire before him. At the top of Oldtown Way he turned into Palmyra Avenue. From there he could continue running past Allouette's boarded-up windows, past all the stores old and new to the corner of Livermore, and from there, he only now realized, to the little house that belonged to Mr Petrosian.

15

On a sweltering mid-afternoon eleven years later at a camp in the central highlands of Vietnam, Lieutenant Harry Beevers closed the flap of his tent against the mosquitoes and sat on the edge of his temporary bunk to write a long-delayed letter back to Pat Caldwell, the young woman he wanted to marry – and to whom he would be married for a time, after his return from the war to New York State.

This is what he wrote, after frequent crossings-out and hesitations. Harry later destroyed this letter.

Dear Pat:
   First of all I want you to know how much I miss you, my darling, and that if I ever get out of this beautiful and terrible country, which I am going to do, that I am going to chase you mercilessly and unrelentingly until you say that you'll marry me. Maybe in the euphoria of relief (YES!!!), I have the future all worked out, Pat, and you're a big part of it. I have eighty-six days until DEROS, when they pat me on the head and put me on that big bird out of here. Now that my record is clear again, I have no doubts that Columbia Law School will take me in. As you know, my law board scores were pretty respectable (modest me!) when I took them at Adelphi. I'm pretty sure I could even get into Harvard Law, but I settled on Columbia because then we could both be in New York.
   My brother George has already told me that he will help me out with whatever money I – you and I – will need. George put me through Adelphi. I don't think you knew this. In fact, nobody knew this. When I look back, in college I was such a jerk. I wanted everybody to think my family was well-to-do, or at least middle-class. The truth is, we were damn poor, which I think makes my accomplishments all the more noteworthy, all the more loveworthy!

You see, this experience, even with all the ugly and self-doubting and humiliating moments, has done me a lot of good. I was right to come here, even though I had no idea what it was really like. I think I needed the experience of war to complete me, and I tell you this even though I know that you will detest any such idea. In fact, I have to tell you that a big part of me loves being here, and that in some way, even with all this trouble, this year will always be one of the high points of my life. Pat, as you see I'm determined to be honest — to be an honest man. If I'm going to be a lawyer, I ought to be honest, don't you think? (Or maybe the reverse is the reality!) One thing that has meant a lot to me here has been what I can only call the close comradeship of my friends and my men — I actually like the grunts more than the usual officer types, which of course means that I get more loyalty and better performance from my men than the usual Lieutenant. Some day I'd like you to meet Mike Poole and Tim Underhill and Pumo the Puma and the most amazing of all, M. O. Dengler, who of course was involved with me in the Ia Thuc cave incident. These guys stuck by me. I even have a nickname, 'Beans'. They call me 'Beans' Beevers, and I like it.

There was no way my court martial could have really put me in any trouble, because all the facts, and my own men, were on my side. Besides, could you see me actually killing children? This is Vietnam and you kill people, that's what we're doing here — we kill Charlies. But we don't kill babies and children. Not even in the heat of wartime — and Ia Thuc was pretty hot!

Well, this is my way of letting you know that at the court martial of course I received a complete and utter vindication. Dengler did too. There were even unofficial mutterings about giving us medals for all the BS we put up with for the past six weeks — including that amazing story in Time magazine. Before people start yelling about atrocities, they ought to have all the facts straight. Fortunately, last week's magazines go out with the rest of the trash.

Besides, I already knew too much about what death does to people.

I never told you that I once had a little brother named

Edward. When I was ten, my little brother wandered up into the top floor of our house one night and suffered a fatal epileptic fit. This event virtually destroyed my family. It led directly to my father's leaving home. (He had been a hero in WWII, something else I never told you.) It deeply changed, I would say even damaged, my older brother Albert. Albert tried to enlist in 1964, but they wouldn't take him because they said he was psychologically unfit. My Mom too almost came apart for a while. She used to go up in the attic and cry and wouldn't come down. So you could say that my family was pretty well destroyed, or ruined, or whatever you want to call it, by a sudden death. I took it, and my Dad's desertion, pretty hard myself. You don't get over these things easily.

The court martial lasted exactly four hours. Big deal, hey! as we used to say back in Palmyra. We used to have a neighbour named Pete Petrosian who said things like that and, against what must have been million-to-one odds, who died exactly the same way my brother did, about two weeks after – lightning really did strike twice. I guess it's dumb to think about him now, but maybe one thing war does is to make you conversant with death. How it happens, what it does to people, what it means, how all the dead in your life are somehow united, joined, part of your eternal family. This is a profound feeling, Pat, and no damn whipped-up failed court martial can touch it. If there were any innocent children in that cave, then they are in my family forever, like little Edward and Pete Petrosian, and the rest of my life is a poem to them. But the army says there weren't, and so do I.

I love you and love you and love you. You can stop worrying now and start thinking about being married to a Columbia Law student with one hell of a good future. I won't tell you any more war stories than you want to hear. And that's a promise, whether the stories are about Nam or Palmyra.

 Always yours,
 Harry
 (a.k.a. 'Beans'!)

INTERLUDE:

In the Realm of Dreams

For a long time after the war, he dreamed about his childhood. He heard screams from the bedroom or the bathroom of the little duplex where they had lived when he was a small boy, and when he turned in panic to look out of the window he knew that the street with its rising lawns and tall elms was only a picture over the face of a terrible fire. In the dreams, he knew that none of this had anything at all to do with the war. It had all happened before. Screams floated inside the brown and yellow house, and smoke and fire billowed beneath the streets.

The screams would stop as soon as he touched the bathroom door knob. When he opened the door, he would see the shower curtain pulled across the tub. It was splashed with blood, and curls and loops of blood lay scattered on the floor and the white toilet seat. The hard part was pushing back the shower curtain, but there was never anybody in the tub – only a big bloodstain moving towards the drain like a living thing. That was exactly what had happened, in and before the war.

The Juniper Tree

It is a school yard in my Midwest of empty lots, waving green and brilliant with tiger lilies, of ugly new 'ranch' houses set down in rows in glistening clay, of treeless avenues cooking in the sun. Our school yard is asphalt – on June days, patches of the asphalt loosen and stick like gum to the soles of our high-top basket-ball shoes.

Most of the playground is black empty space from which heat radiates up like the wavery images on the screen of a faulty television set. Tall wire mesh surrounds it. A new boy named Paul is standing beside me.

Though it is now nearly the final month of the semester, Paul came to us, carroty-haired, pale-eyed, too shy to ask even the whereabouts of the lavatory, only six weeks ago. The lessons baffle him, and his Southern accent is a fatal error of style. The popular students broadcast in hushed, giggling whispers the terrible news that Paul 'talks like a nigger'. Their voices are *almost* awed – they are conscious of the enormity of what they are saying, of the enormity of its consequences.

Paul is wearing a brilliant red shirt too heavy, too enveloping, for the weather. He and I stand in the shade at the rear of the school, before the cream-coloured brick wall in which is placed at eyelevel a newly broken window of pebbly green glass reinforced with strands of copper wire. At our feet is a little scatter of green, edible-looking pebbles. The pebbles dig into the soles of our shoes, too hard to shatter against the softer asphalt. Paul is singing to me in his slow, lilting voice that he will never have friends in this school. I put my foot down on one of the green candy pebbles and feel it push up, hard as a bullet, against my foot. 'Children are so cruel,' Paul casually sings. I think of sliding the pebble of broken glass across my throat, slicing myself wide open to let death in.

Paul did not return to school in the fall. His father, who had beaten a man to death down in Mississippi, had been arrested while leaving a movie theatre near my house named the Orpheum-Oriental. Paul's father had taken his family to see an Esther Williams movie costarring Fernando Lamas, and when they came out, their mouths raw from salty popcorn, the baby's hands sticky with spilled Coca-Cola, the police were waiting for them. They were Mississippi people, and I think of Paul now, seated at a desk on a floor of an office building in Jackson filled with men like him at desks: his tie perfectly knotted, a good shine on his cordovan shoes, a necessary but unconscious restraint in the set of his mouth.

In those days I used to spend whole days in the Orpheum-Oriental.

I was seven. I held within me the idea of a disappearance like Paul's, of never having to be seen again. Of being an absence, a shadow, a place where something no longer visible used to be.

*   *   *

Before I met that young-old man whose name was
'Frank' or 'Stan' or 'Jimmy', when I sat in the rapture of
education before the movies at the Orpheum-Oriental, I
watched Alan Ladd and Richard Widmark and Glenn
Ford and Dane Clark. *Chicago Deadline.* Martin and
Lewis, tangled up in the same parachute in *At War with
the Army.* William Boyd and Roy Rogers. Open-
mouthed, I drank down movies about spies and crimi-
nals, wanting the passionate and shadowy ones to fulfil
themselves, to gorge themselves on what they needed.

The feverish gaze of Richard Widmark, the anger of
Alan Ladd, Berry Kroeger's sneaky eyes, girlish and
watchful – vivid, total elegance.

When I was seven, my father walked into the bathroom
and saw me looking at my face in the mirror. He
slapped me, not with his whole strength, but hard,
raging instantly. 'What do you think you're looking
at?' His hand was cocked and ready. 'What do you
think you see?'

'Nothing,' I said.

'Nothing is right.'

A carpenter, he worked furiously, already defeated,
and never had enough money – as if, permanently
beyond reach, some quantity of money existed that
would have satisfied him. In the mornings he went to
the job site hardened like cement into anger he barely
knew he had. Sometimes he brought men from the
taverns home with him at night. They carried transparent bottles of Miller High Life in paper bags and set
them down on the table with a bang that said: Men are
here! My mother, who had returned from her secretary's job a few hours earlier, fed my brothers and

me, washed the dishes, and put the three of us to bed
while the men shouted and laughed in the kitchen.

He was considered an excellent carpenter. He
worked slowly, patiently; and I see now that he spent
whatever love he had in the rented garage that was his
workshop. In his spare time he listened to baseball
games on the radio. He had professional, but not
personal, vanity, and he thought that a face like mine
should not be examined.

Because I saw 'Jimmy' in the mirror, I thought my
father, too, had seen him.

One Saturday my mother took the twins and me on
the ferry across Lake Michigan to Saginaw. The point
of the journey was the journey, and at Saginaw the
boat docked for twenty minutes before wallowing back
out into the lake and returning. With us were women
like my mother, her friends, freed by the weekend
from their jobs, some of them accompanied by men
like my father, with their felt hats and baggy weekend
trousers flaring over their weekend shoes. The women
wore blood-bright lipstick that printed itself onto their
cigarettes and smeared across their front teeth. They
laughed a great deal and repeated the words that had
made them laugh. 'Hot dog', 'slippin' 'n' slidin', 'opera
singer'. Thirty minutes after departure, the men disappeared into the enclosed deck bar; the women, my
mother among them, arranged deck chairs into a long
oval tied together by laughter, attention, gossip. They
waved their cigarettes in the air. My brothers raced
around the deck, their shirts flapping, their hair glued
to their skulls with sweat. When they squabbled, my
mother ordered them into empty deck chairs. I sat on
the deck, leaning against the railings, quiet. If someone

had asked me: What do you want to do this afternoon, what do you want to do for the rest of your life? I would have said, I want to stay right here, I want to stay here forever.

After a while I stood up and left the women. I went across the deck and stepped through a hatch into the bar. Dark, deeply grained imitation wood covered the walls. The odours of beer and cigarettes and the sound of men's voices filled the enclosed space. About twenty men stood at the bar, talking and gesturing with half-filled glasses. Then one man broke away from the others with a flash of dirty blond hair. I saw his shoulders move, and my scalp tingled and my stomach froze and I thought: Jimmy. 'Jimmy'. But he turned all the way round, dipping his shoulders in some ecstasy of beer and male company, and I saw that he was a stranger, not 'Jimmy' after all.

*   *   *

I was thinking: Someday when I am free, when I am out of this body and in some city whose name I do not even know now, I will remember this from beginning to end and then I will be free of it.

The women floated over the empty lake, laughing out clouds of cigarette smoke, the men, too, as boisterous as the children on the sticky asphalt playground with its small green spray of glass like candy.

*   *   *

In those days I knew I was set apart from the rest of my family, an island between my parents and the twins. Those pairs that bracketed me slept in double beds in adjacent rooms at the back of the ground floor of the duplex owned by the blind man who lived above us. My bed, a cot coveted by the twins, stood in their room. An invisible line of great authority divided my territory and possessions from theirs.

This is what happened in the mornings in our half of the duplex. My mother got up first – we heard her showering, heard drawers closing, the sounds of bowls and milk being set out on the table. The smell of bacon frying for my father, who banged on the door and called out my brothers' names. 'Don't you make me come in there, now!' The noisy, puppylike turmoil of my brothers getting out of bed. All three of us scramble into the bathroom as soon as my father leaves it. The bathroom was steamy, heavy with the odour of shit and the more piercing, almost palpable smell of shaving – lather and amputated whiskers. We all pee into the toilet at the same time. My mother frets and frets, pulling the twins into their clothes so that she can take them down the street to Mrs Candee, who is given a five-dollar bill every week for taking care of them. I am supposed to be running back and forth on the playground in Summer Play School, supervised by two teenage girls who live a block away from us. (I went to Play School only twice.) After I dress myself in clean underwear and socks and put on my everyday shirt and trousers, I come into the kitchen while my father finishes his breakfast. He is eating strips of bacon and golden-brown pieces of toast shiny with butter. A cigarette smoulders in the ashtray before him. Everybody else has already left the house. My father and I can hear the blind man banging on the piano in his living room. I sit down before a bowl of cereal. My father looks at me, looks away. Angry at the blind man for banging at the piano this early in the

morning, he is sweating already. His cheeks and forehead shine like the golden toast. My father glances at
me, knowing he can postpone this no longer, and
reaches wearily into his pocket and drops two quarters
on the table. The high-school girls charge twenty-five
cents a day, and the other quarter is for my lunch.
'Don't lose that money,' he says as I take the coins.
My father dumps coffee into his mouth, puts the cup
and his plate into the crowded sink, looks at me again,
pats his pockets for his keys, and says, 'Close the door
behind you.' I tell him that I will close the door. He
picks up his grey toolbox and his black lunch pail,
claps his hat on his head, and goes out, banging his
toolbox against the door frame. It leaves a broad grey
mark like a smear left by the passing of some angry
creature's hide.

Then I am alone in the house. I go back to the bedroom,
close the door and push a chair beneath the knob, and
read *Blackhawk* and *Henry* and *Captain Marvel* comic
books until at last it is time to go to the theatre.

While I read, everything in the house seems alive
and dangerous. I can hear the telephone in the hall
rattling on its hook, the radio clicking as it tries to
turn itself on and talk to me. The dishes stir and rattle
in the sink. At these times all objects, even the heavy
chairs and sofa, become their true selves, violent as
the fire that fills the sky I cannot see and races through
the secret ways and passages beneath the streets. At
these times other people vanish like smoke.

When I pull the chair away from the door, the house
immediately goes quiet, like a wild animal feigning
sleep. Everything inside and out slips cunningly back
into place, the fires bank, men and women reappear on

the sidewalks. I must open the door and I do. I walk
swiftly through the kitchen and the living room to the
front door, knowing that if I look too carefully at any
one thing I will wake it up again. My mouth is so dry
my tongue feels fat. 'I'm leaving,' I say to no one.
Everything in the house hears me.

* * *

The quarter goes through the slot at the bottom of the
window, the ticket leaps from its slot. For a long time,
before 'Jimmy', I thought that unless you kept your
stub unfolded and safe in a shirt pocket the usher could
rush down the aisle in the middle of the movie, seize
you, and throw you out. So into the pocket it goes, and
I slip through the big doors into the cool, cross the
lobby and pass through a swinging door with a porthole
window.

Most of the regular daytime patrons of the Orpheum-
Oriental sit in the same seats every day – I am one of
those who comes here every day. A small, talkative
gathering of bums sit at the right of the theatre, in the
rows beneath the sconces fastened like bronze torches
to the walls. The bums choose these seats so that they
can examine their bits of paper, their 'documents', and
show them to each other during the movies. Always
on their minds is the possibility that they might have
lost one of these documents, and they frequently
consult the tattered envelopes in which they are kept.

I take the end seat on the left side of the central
block of seats, just before the broad horizontal middle
aisle. There I can stretch out. At other times I sit in
the middle of the last row, or the first; sometimes
when the balcony is open I go up and sit in its first
row. From the first row of the balcony, seeing a movie

is like being a bird and flying down into the movie
from above. To be alone in the theatre is delicious.
The curtains hang heavy, red, anticipatory; the mock
torches glow on the walls. Swirls of gilt wind through
the red paint. On days when I sit near a wall, I reach
out towards the red, which seems warm and soft, and
find my fingers resting on a chill dampness. The carpet
of the Orpheum-Oriental must once have been a bot-
tomlessly rich brown; now it is a dark non-colour,
mottled with the pink and grey smears, like melted
Band Aids, of chewing gum. From about a third of the
seats dirty grey wool foams from slashes in the worn
plush.

On an ideal day I sit through a cartoon, a travelogue,
a sequence of previews, a movie, another cartoon, and
another movie before anyone else enters the theatre.
This whole cycle is as satisfying as a meal. On other
mornings old women in odd hats and young women
wearing scarves over their rollers, a few teenage couples, are scattered throughout the theatre when I come
in. None of these people ever pays attention to anything but the screen and, in the case of the teenagers,
each other.

Once, a man in his early twenties, hair like a haystack,
sat up in the wide middle aisle when I took my seat.
He groaned. Rusty-looking dried blood was spattered
over his chin and his dirty white shirt. He groaned
again and then got to his hands and knees. The carpet
beneath him was spotted with what looked like a
thousand red dots. The young man stumbled to his
feet and began reeling up the aisle. A bright, depthless
pane of sunlight surrounded him before he vanished
into it.

* * *

At the beginning of July, I told my mother that the high-school girls had increased the hours of the Play School because I wanted to be sure of seeing both features twice before I had to go home. After that I could learn the rhythms of the theatre itself, which did not impress themselves upon me all at once but revealed themselves gradually, so that by the middle of the first week I knew when the bums would begin to move towards the seats beneath the sconces. They usually arrived on Tuesdays and Fridays shortly after eleven o'clock, when the liquor store down the block opened up to provide them with the pints and half-pints that nourished them. By the end of the second week, I knew when the ushers left the interior of the theatre to sit on padded benches in the lobby and light up their Luckies and Chesterfields, when the old men and women would begin to appear. By the end of the third week, I felt like the merest part of a great, orderly machine. Before the beginning of the second showing of *Beautiful Hawaii* or *Curiosities Down Under*, I went out to the counter and with my second quarter purchased a box of popcorn or a packet of Good 'n' Plenty candy.

In a movie theatre nothing is random except the customers and hitches in the machine. Filmstrips break and lights fail; the projectionist gets drunk or falls asleep; and the screen presents a blank yellow face to the stamping, whistling audience. These inconsistencies are summer squalls, forgotten as soon as they have ended.

The occasion for the lights, the projectionist, the boxes of popcorn and packets of candy, the movies, enlarged when seen over and over. The truth gradually came to me that this deepening and widening out, this enlarging, was why movies were shown over and over all day long. The machine revealed itself most surely in the exact, limpid repetitions of the actors' words and gestures as they moved through the story. When Alan Ladd asked 'Blackie Frachot', the dying gangster, 'Who did it, Blackie?' his voice widened like a river, grew *sandier* with an almost unconcealed tenderness I had to learn to hear – the voice within the speaking voice.

* * *

Chicago Deadline was the exploration by a newspaper reporter named 'Ed Adams' (Alan Ladd) of the tragedy of a mysterious young woman, 'Rosita Jandreau', who had died alone of tuberculosis in a shabby hotel room. The reporter soon learns that she had many names, many identities. She had been in love with an architect, a gangster, a crippled professor, a boxer, a millionaire, and had given a different facet of her being to each of them. Far too predictably, the adult me complains, the obsessed 'Ed' falls in love with 'Rosita'. When I was seven, little was predictable – I had not yet seen *Laura* – and I saw a man driven by the need to understand, which became identical to the need to protect. 'Rosita Jandreau' was the embodiment of memory, which was mystery.

Through the sequence of her identities, the various selves shown to brother, boxer, millionaire, gangster, all the others, her memory kept her whole. I saw, twice a day for two weeks, before and during 'Jimmy', the machine deep within the machine. Love and memory were the same. Both love and memory accommodated us to death. (I did not understand this, but I saw it.)

The reporter, Alan Ladd, with his dirty blond hair, his perfect jawline, and brilliant, wounded smile, gave her life by making her memory his own.

'I think you're the only one who ever understood her,' Arthur Kennedy – 'Rosita's' brother – tells Alan Ladd.

Most of the world demands the kick of sensation, most of the world must gather and spend money, hunt for easier and more temporary forms of love, must feed itself, sell newspapers, destroy the enemy's plots with plots of its own . . .

'I don't know what you want,' 'Ed Adams' says to the editor of *The Journal*. 'You got two murders . . .'

*   *   *

'. . . and a mystery woman,' I say along with him. His voice is tough and detached, the voice of a wounded man acting. The man beside me laughs. Unlike his normal voice, his laughter is breathless and high-pitched. It is the second showing today of *Chicago Deadline*, early afternoon. After the next showing of *At War with the Army* I will have to walk up the aisle and out of the theatre. It will be twenty minutes to five, and the sun will still burn high over the cream-coloured buildings across wide, empty Sherman Boulevard.

I met the man, or he met me, at the candy counter. He was at first only a tall presence, blond, dressed in dark clothing. I cared nothing for him, he did not matter. He was vague even when he spoke. 'Good popcorn.' I looked up at him – narrow blue eyes, bad teeth smiling at me. Stubble on his face. I looked away and the uniformed man behind the counter handed me popcorn. 'Good for you, I mean. Good stuff in popcorn – comes right out of the ground. Grows on big plants tall as I am, just like other corn. You know that?'

When I said nothing, he laughed and spoke to the man behind the counter.

'*He* didn't know that – the kid thought popcorn grew inside poppers.' The counterman turned away. 'You come here a lot?' the man asked me.

I put a few kernels of popcorn in my mouth and turned towards him. He was showing me his bad teeth.

'You do,' he said. 'You come here a lot.'

I nodded.

'Every day?'

I nodded again.

'And we tell little fibs at home about what we've been doing all day, don't we?' he asked, and pursed his lips and raised his eyes like a comic butler in a movie. Then his mood shifted and everything about him became serious. He was looking at me, but he did not see me. 'You got a favourite actor? I got a favourite actor. Alan Ladd.'

And I saw – both saw and understood – that he thought he looked like Alan Ladd. He did, too, at least a little bit. When I saw the resemblance, he seemed like a different person, more glamorous. Glamour surrounded him, as though he were acting, impersonating a shabby young man with stained, irregular teeth.

'The name's Frank,' he said, and stuck out his hand. 'Shake?'

I took his hand.

'Real good popcorn,' he said, and stuck his hand into the box. 'Want to hear a secret?'

A secret.

'I was born twice. The first time, I died. It was on an

army base. Everybody *told* me I should have joined the navy, and everybody was right. So I just had myself get born somewhere else. Hey – the army's not for everybody, you know?' He grinned down at me. 'Now I told you my secret. Let's go in – I'll sit with you. Everybody needs company, and I like you. You look like a good kid.'

He followed me back to my seat and sat down beside me. When I quoted the lines along with the actors, he laughed.

Then he said –

Then he leaned towards me and said –

He leaned towards me, breathing sour wine over me, and took –

No.

'I was just kidding out there,' he said. 'Frank ain't my real name. Well, it was my name. Before. See? Frank *used* to be my name for a while. But now my good friends call me Stan. I like that. Stanley the Steamer. Big Stan. Stan the Man. See? It works real good.'

*   *   *

'You'll never be a carpenter,' he told me. 'You'll never be anything like that – because you got that look. *I* used to have that look, okay? So I know. I know about you just by looking at you.'

He said he had been a clerk at Sears; after that he had worked as the custodian for a couple of apartment buildings owned by a guy who used to be a friend of his but was no longer. Then he had been the janitor at the high school where my grade school sent its graduates. 'Good old booze got me fired. Story of my life,' he said. 'Tight-ass bitches caught me drinking down in the basement, in a room I used there, and threw me out without a fare-thee-well. Hey, that was my *room*. My *place*. The best things in the world can do the worst things to you; you'll find that out someday. And when you go to that school, I hope you'll remember what they done to me there.'

These days he was resting. He hung around; he went to the movies.

He said: 'You got something special in you. Guys like me, we're funny, we can tell.'

We sat together through the second feature, Dean Martin and Jerry Lewis, comfortable and laughing. 'Those guys are bigger bums than we are,' he said. I thought of Paul backed up against the school in his enveloping red shirt, imprisoned within his inability to be like anyone around him.

'You coming back tomorrow? If I get here, I'll check around for you.'

'Hey. Trust me. I know who you are.'

'You know that little thing you pee with?' Leaning sideways he whispered into my ear. 'That's the best thing a man's got. Trust me.'

*   *   *

The big providential park near our house, two streets past the Orpheum-Oriental, is separated into three different areas. Nearest the wide iron gates on Sherman Boulevard through which we enter was a wading pool divided by a low green hedge, so rubbery it seemed artificial, from a playground with a climbing frame, swings, and a row of seesaws. When I was a child of two and three, I splashed in the warm pool and clung to the chains of the swings, making myself go higher and higher, terror and joy and grim duty so woven together that no one could pull them apart.

Beyond the children's pool and playground was the zoo. My mother walked my brothers and me to the playground and wading pool and sat smoking on a bench while we played; both of my parents took us into the zoo. An elephant extended his trunk to my father's palm and delicately lipped peanuts towards his maw. The giraffe stretched towards the constantly diminishing supply of leaves, ever fewer and higher, above his cage. The lions drowsed on amputated branches or paced behind the bars, staring out not at what was there but at the long grassy plains imprinted on their memories. I knew the lions had the power not to see us, to look straight through us to Africa. But when they saw you instead of Africa, they looked right into your bones, they saw the blood travelling through your body. The lions were golden brown, patient, green-eyed. They recognized me and could read thoughts. The lions neither liked nor disliked me; they did not miss me during their long weekdays, but they took me into the circle of known beings.

('You shouldn't have looked at me like that,' June Havoc – 'Leona' – tells 'Ed Adams'. She does not mean it, not at all.)

Past the zoo and across a narrow park road, down which khaki-clothed park attendants pushed barrows heavy with flowers stood a wide, unexpected lawn bordered with flower beds and tall elms – open space hidden like a secret between the caged animals and the

elm trees. Only my father brought me to this section
of the park. Here he tried to make a baseball player of
me.

'Get the bat off your shoulders,' he says. 'For God's
sake, will you try to hit the ball, anyhow?'

When I fail once again to swing at his slow, perfect
pitch, he spins around, raises his arm, and theatrically
asks everyone in sight. 'Whose kid is this, anyway?
Can you answer me that?'

He has never asked me about the Play School I am
supposed to be attending, and I have never told him
about the Orpheum-Oriental. I will never come any
closer to talking to him than now, for 'Stan', 'Stanley
the Steamer', has told me things that cannot be true,
that must be inventions and fables, part of the world
of children wandering lost in the forest, of talking cats
and silver boots filled with blood. In this world, dismembered children buried beneath juniper trees can
rise and speak, made whole once again. Fables boil
with underground explosions and hidden fires and, for
this reason, memory rejects them, thrusts them out of
its sight, and they must be repeated over and over. I
cannot remember 'Stan's' face – cannot even be sure I
remember what he said. Dean Martin and Jerry Lewis
are bums like us. I am certain of only one thing:
tomorrow I am again going to see my newest, scariest,
most interesting friend.

'When I was your age,' my father says, 'I had my
heart set on playing pro ball when I grew up. And
you're too damned scared or lazy to even take the bat
off your shoulder. Kee-rist! I can't stand looking at you
anymore.'

He turns round and begins to move quickly towards

the narrow park road and the zoo, going home, and I run after him. I retrieve the softball when he tosses it into the bushes.

'What the hell do you think you're going to do when you grow up?' my father asks, his eyes still fixed ahead of him. 'I wonder what you think life is all *about*. I wouldn't give you a job, I wouldn't trust you round carpenter tools, I wouldn't trust you to blow your nose right – to tell you the truth, I wonder if the hospital mixed up the goddamn babies.'

I follow him, dragging the bat with one hand, in the other cradling the softball in the pouch of my mitt.

At dinner my mother asks if Summer Play School is fun, and I say yes. I have already taken from my father's dresser drawer what 'Stan' asked me to get for him, and it burns in my pocket as if it were alight. I want to ask: is it actually true and not a story? Does the worst thing always have to be the true thing? Of course, I cannot ask this. My father does not know about worst things – he sees what he wants to see, or he tries so hard he thinks he does see it.

'I guess he'll hit a long ball someday. The boy just needs more work on his swing.' He tries to smile at me, a boy who will someday learn to hit a long ball. The knife is upended in his fist – he is about to smear a pat of butter on his steak. He does not see me at all. My father is not a lion, he cannot make the switch to seeing what is really there in front of him.

Late at night Alan Ladd knelt beside my bed. He was wearing a neat grey suit, and his breath smelled like cloves. 'You okay, son?' I nodded. 'I just wanted to tell you that I like seeing you out there every day. That means a lot to me.'

* * *

'Do you remember what I was telling you about?'

And I knew: it was true. He had said those things, and he would repeat them like a fairy tale, and the world was going to change because it would be seen through changed eyes. I felt sick – trapped in the theatre as if in a cage.

'You think about what I told you?'

'Sure,' I said.

'That's good. Hey, you know what? I feel like changing seats. You want to change seats too?'

'Where to?'

He tilted his head back, and I knew he wanted to move to the last row. 'Come on. I want to show you something.'

We changed seats.

For a long time we sat watching the movie from the last row, nearly alone in the theatre. Just after eleven, three of the bums filed in and proceeded to their customary seats on the other side of the theatre – a rumpled greybeard I had seen many times before; a fat man with a stubby, squashed face, also familiar; and one of the shaggy, wild-looking young men who hung around the bums until they became indistinguishable from them. They began passing a flat brown bottle back and forth. After a second I remembered the young man – I had surprised him awake one morning, passed out and spattered with blood, in the middle aisle.

Then I wondered if 'Stan' was not the young man I

had surprised that morning; they looked as alike as twins, though I knew they were not.

'Want a sip?' 'Stan' said, showing me his own pint bottle. 'Do you good.'

Bravely, feeling privileged and adult, I took the bottle of Thunderbird and raised it to my mouth. I wanted to like it, to share the pleasure of it with 'Stan', but it tasted horrible, like garbage, and the little bit I swallowed burned all the way down my throat.

I made a face, and he said, 'This stuff's really not so bad. Only one thing in the world can make you feel better than this stuff.'

He placed his hand on my thigh and squeezed. 'I'm giving you a head start, you know. Just because I liked you the first time I saw you.' He leaned over and stared at me. 'You believe me? You believe the things I tell you?'

I said I guessed so.

'I got proof. I'll show you it's true. Want to see my proof?'

When I said nothing, 'Stan' leaned closer to me, inundating me with the stench of Thunderbird. 'You know that little thing you pee with? Remember how I told you how it gets really big when you're about thirteen? Remember I told you about how incredible that feels? Well, you have to trust Stan now, because Stan's going to trust you.' He put his face right beside my ear. 'Then I'll tell you another secret.'

He lifted his hand from my thigh and closed it round mine and pulled my hand down onto his crotch. 'Feel anything?'

I nodded, but I could not have described what I felt any more than the blind men could describe the elephant.

'Stan' smiled tightly and tugged at his zip in a way even I could tell was nervous. He reached inside his pants, fumbled, and pulled out a thick, pale club that looked like nothing human. I was so frightened I thought I would throw up, and I looked back up at the screen. Invisible chains held me to my seat.

'See? Now you understand me.'

Then he noticed that I was not looking at him. 'Kid. Look. I said, look. It's not going to hurt you.'

I could not look down at him. I saw nothing.

'Come on. Touch it, see what it feels like.'

I shook my head.

'Let me tell you something. I like you a lot. I think the two of us are friends. This thing we're doing, it's unusual to you because this is the first time, but people do this all the time. Your mommy and daddy do it all the time, but they just don't tell you about it. We're pals, aren't we?'

I nodded dumbly. On the screen, Berry Kroeger was telling Alan Ladd, 'Drop it, forget it, she's poison.'

'Well, this is what friends do when they really like each other, like your mommy and daddy. Look at this thing, will you? Come on.'

Did my mommy and daddy like each other? He squeezed my shoulder, and I looked.

Now the thing had folded up into itself and was drooping sideways against the fabric of his trousers. Almost as soon as I looked, it twitched and began to push itself out like the slide of a trombone.

'There,' he said. 'He likes you, you got him going. Tell me you like him too.'

Terror would not let me speak. My brains had turned to powder.

'I know what – let's call him Jimmy. We'll say his

name is Jimmy. Now that you've been introduced, say hi to Jimmy.'

'Hi, Jimmy,' I said, and, despite my terror, could not keep myself from giggling.

'Now go on, touch him.'

I slowly extended my hand and put the tips of my fingers on 'Jimmy'.

'Pet him. Jimmy wants you to pet him.'

I tapped my fingertips against 'Jimmy' two or three times, and he twitched up another few degrees, as rigid as a surfboard.

'Slide your fingers up and down on him.'

If I run, I thought, he'll catch me and kill me. If I don't do what he says, he'll kill me.

I rubbed my fingertips back and forth, moving the thin skin over the veins.

'Can't you imagine Jimmy going in a woman? Now you can see what you'll be like when you're a man. Keep on, but hold him with your whole hand. And give me what I asked you for.'

I immediately took my hand from 'Jimmy' and pulled my father's clean white handkerchief from my back pocket.

He took the handkerchief with his left hand and with his right guided mine back to 'Jimmy'. 'You're doing really great,' he whispered.

In my hand 'Jimmy' felt warm and slightly gummy. I could not join my fingers around its width. My head was buzzing. 'Is Jimmy your secret?' I was able to say.

'My secret comes later.'

'Can I stop now?'

'I'll cut you into little pieces if you do,' he said, and when I froze he stroked my hair and whispered, 'Hey, can't you tell when a guy's kidding around? I'm really happy with you right now. You're the best kid in the world. You'd want this, too, if you knew how good it felt.'

After what seemed an endless time, while Alan Ladd was climbing out of a taxicab, 'Stan' abruptly arched his back, grimaced, and whispered, 'Look!' His entire body jerked and, too startled to let go, I held 'Jimmy' and watched thick, ivory-coloured milk spurt and drool almost unendingly onto the handkerchief. An odour utterly foreign but as familiar as the toilet or the lakeshore rose from the thick milk. 'Stan' sighed, folded the handkerchief, and pushed the softening 'Jimmy' back into his trousers. He leaned over and kissed the top of my head. I think I nearly fainted. I felt lightly, pointlessly dead. I could still feel him pulsing in my palm and fingers.

When it was time for me to go home, he told me his secret — his own real name was Jimmy, not Stan. He had been saving his real name until he knew he could trust me.

'Tomorrow,' he said, touching my cheek with his fingers. 'We'll see each other again tomorrow. But you don't have anything to worry about. I trust you enough to give you my real name. You trusted me not to hurt you, and I didn't. We have to trust each other not to say anything about this, or both you and I'll be in a lot of trouble.'

'I won't say anything,' I said.

I love you.

I love you, yes, I do.

* * *

Now *we're* a secret, he said, folding the handkerchief into quarters and putting it back in my pocket. A lot of love has to be a secret. Especially when a boy and a man are getting to know each other and learning how to make each other happy and be good, loving friends – not many people can understand that, so the friendship has to be protected. When you walk out of here, he said, you have to forget that this happened. Otherwise people will try to hurt us both.

Afterwards I remembered only the confusion of *Chicago Deadline*, how the story had abruptly surged forward, skipping over whole characters and entire scenes, how for long stretches the actors had moved their lips without speaking. I could see Alan Ladd stepping out of the taxicab, looking straight through the screen into my eyes, knowing me.

My mother said that I looked pale, and my father said that I didn't get enough exercise. The twins looked up from their plates, then went back to spooning macaroni and cheese into their mouths. 'Were you ever in Chicago?' I asked my father, who asked what it was to me. 'Did you ever meet a movie actor?' I asked, and he said, 'This kid must have a fever.' The twins giggled.

Alan Ladd and Donna Reed came into my bedroom together late that night, moving with brisk, cool theatricality, and kneeled down beside my bed. They smiled at me. Their voices were very soothing.

'I saw you missed a few things today,' Alan said. 'Nothing to worry about. I'll take care of you.'

'I know,' I said, 'I'm your number one fan.'

Then the door cracked open, and my mother put her head inside the room. Alan and Donna smiled and stood up to let her pass between them and the cot. I missed them the second they stepped back. 'Still awake?' I nodded. 'Are you feeling all right, honey?' I nodded again, afraid that Alan and Donna would leave if she stayed too long. 'I have a surprise for you,' she said. 'The Saturday after this, I'm taking you and the twins all the way across Lake Michigan on the ferry. There's a whole bunch of us. It'll be a lot of fun.' Good, that's nice, I'll like that.

*   *   *

'I thought about you all last night and all this morning.'

When I came into the lobby, he was leaning forward on one of the padded benches where the ushers sat and smoked, his elbows on his knees and his chin in his hand, watching the door. The metal tip of a flat bottle protruded from his side pocket. Beside him was a package rolled up in brown paper. He winked at me, jerked his head towards the door into the theatre, stood up, and went inside in an elaborate charade of not being with me. I knew he would be just inside the door, sitting in the middle of the last row, waiting for me. I gave my ticket to the bored usher, who tore it in half and handed over the stub. I knew exactly what had happened yesterday, just as if I had never forgotten any of it, and my insides began shaking. All the colours of the lobby, the red and the shabby gilt, seemed much brighter than I remembered them. I could smell the popcorn in the case and the oily butter heating in the machine. My legs moved me over a mile of sizzling brown carpet and past the sweets counter.

Jimmy's hair gleamed in the empty, darkening theatre. When I took the seat next to him, he ruffled my hair and grinned down and said he had been thinking about me all night and all morning. The package in brown paper was a sandwich for my lunch: a kid had to eat more than popcorn.

The lights went all the way down as the series of curtains opened over the screen. Loud music, beginning in the middle of a note, suddenly jumped from the speakers, and the Tom and Jerry cartoon *Bull Dozing* began. When I leaned back, Jimmy put his arm around me. I felt sweaty and cold at the same time, and my insides were still shaking. I suddenly realized that part of me was glad to be in this place, and I shocked myself with the knowledge that all morning I had been looking forward to this moment as much as I had been dreading it.

'You want your sandwich now? It's liver sausage, because that's my personal favourite.' I said no thanks, I'd wait until the first movie was over. 'Okay,' he said, 'just as long as you eat it.' Then he said, 'Look at me.' His face was right above mine, and he looked like Alan Ladd's twin brother. 'You have to know something,' he said. 'You're the best kid I ever met. Ever.' The man squeezed me up against his chest and into a dizzying funk of sweat and dirt and wine, along with a trace (imagined?) of that other, more animal odour that had come from him yesterday. Then he released me.

'You want me to play with your little "Jimmy" today?'
    'No.'
'Too small, anyhow,' he said with a laugh. He was in perfect good humour. 'Bet you wish it was the same size as mine.'
    That wish terrified me, and I shook my head.

'Today we're just going to watch the movies together,' he said. 'I'm not greedy.'

Except for when one of the ushers came up the aisle, we sat like that all day, his arm around my shoulders, the back of my neck resting in the hollow of his elbow. When the credits for *At War with the Army* rolled up the screen, I felt as though I had fallen asleep and missed everything. I couldn't believe that it was time to go home.

Jimmy tightened his arm around me and in a voice full of amusement said *Touch me.* I looked up into his face. Go on, he said, I want you to do that little thing for me. I prodded his fly with my index finger. 'Jimmy' wobbled under the pressure of my fingers, seeming as long as my arm, and for a second of absolute wretchedness I saw the other children running up and down the school playground behind the girls from the next block.

'Go on,' he said.

* * *

'*Trust me,*' he said, investing 'Jimmy' with an identity more concentrated, more focused, than his own. 'Jimmy' wanted 'to talk', 'to speak his piece', 'was hungry', 'was dying for a kiss'. All these words meant the same thing. *Trust me*: I trust you, so you must trust me. Have I ever hurt you?

No.

Didn't I give you a sandwich?

Yes.

Don't I love you? You know I won't tell your parents what you do – as long as you keep coming here, I won't tell your parents anything because I won't *have* to,

see? And you love me, too, don't you? There. You see
how much I love you?

I dreamed that I lived underground in a wooden room.
I dreamed that my parents roamed the upper world,
calling out my name and weeping because the animals
had captured and eaten me. I dreamed that I was buried
beneath a juniper tree, and the cut-off pieces of my
body called out to each other and wept because they
were separate. I dreamed that I ran down a dark forest
path towards my parents and, when I finally reached
the small clearing where they sat before a bright fire,
my mother was Donna and Alan was my father. I
dreamed that I could remember everything that was
happening to me, every second of it, and that when the
teacher called on me in class, when my mother came
into my room at night, when the policeman went past
me as I walked down Sherman Boulevard, I had to spill
it out. But when I tried to speak, I could not remember
what it was that I remembered, *only that there was
something to remember*, and so I walked again and
again towards my beautiful parents in the clearing,
repeating myself like a fable, like the jokes of the
women on the ferry.

Don't I love you? Don't I show you, can't you tell
that I love you?

Yes.

Don't you, can't you, love me too?

He stares at me as I stare at the movie. He could see
me, the way I could see him, with his eyes closed. He
has me memorized. He has stroked my hair, my face,
my body into his memory, stroke after stroke, stealing
me from myself. Eventually he took me in his mouth

and his mouth memorized me too, and I knew he wanted me to place my hands on that dirty-blond head resting so hugely in my lap, but I could not touch his head.

I thought: I have already forgotten this. I want to die. I am dead already. Only death can make this not have happened.

When you grow up, I bet you'll be in the movies and I'll be your number one fan.

* * *

By the weekend, those days at the Orpheum-Oriental seemed to have been spent under water; or underground. The spiny anteater, the lyrebird, the kangaroo, the Tasmanian devil, the nun bat, and the frilled lizard were creatures found only in Australia. Australia was the world's smallest continent, the world's largest island. It was cut off from the Earth's great landmasses. Beautiful girls with blonde hair strutted across Australian beaches, and Australian Christmases were hot and sunbaked – everybody went outside and waved at the camera, exchanging presents from lawn chairs. The middle of Australia, its heart and gut, was a desert. Australian boys excelled at sports. Tom Cat loved Jerry Mouse, though he plotted again and again to murder him, and Jerry Mouse loved Tom Cat, though to save his life he had to run so fast he burned a track through the carpet. Jimmy loved me and he would be gone someday, and then I would miss him a lot. Wouldn't I?
Say you'll miss me.
I'll –
I'll miss –

* * *

I think I'd go crazy without you.

When you're all grown up, will you remember me?

Each time I walked out past the usher tearing in half
the tickets of the people just entering, handing them
the stubs, every time I pushed open the door and
walked out onto the heat-filled sidewalk of Sherman
Boulevard and saw the sun on the buildings across the
street, I lost my hold on what had happened inside the
darkness of the theatre. I didn't know what I wanted. I
had two murders and a ... My right hand felt as
though I had been holding a smaller's child's sticky
hand very tightly between my palm and fingers. If I
lived in Australia, I would have blond hair like Alan
Ladd and run for ever across tan beaches on Christmas
Day.

*   *   *

I walked through high school in my sleep, reading
novels, daydreaming in classes I did not like but
earning spuriously good grades; in the middle of my
senior year Brown University gave me a full scholarship. Two years later I amazed and disappointed all my
old teachers and my parents and my parents' friends
by dropping out of school shortly before I would have
failed all my courses but English and history, in which
I was getting As. I was certain that no one could teach
anyone else how to write. I knew exactly what I was
going to do, and all I would miss of college was the
social life.

For five years I lived inexpensively in Providence,
supporting myself by stacking books in the school
library and by petty thievery. I wrote when I was not

working or listening to the local bands; then I destroyed what I had written and wrote it again. In this way I saw myself to the end of a novel, like walking through a park one way and then walking backwards and forwards through the same park, over and over, until every nick on every swing, every tawny hair on every lion's hide had been witnessed and made to gleam or allowed to sink back into the importunate field of details from which it had been lifted. When this novel was rejected by the publisher to whom I sent it, I moved to New York City and began another novel while I rewrote the first all over again at night. During this period an almost impersonal happiness, like the happiness of a stranger, lay beneath everything I did. I wrapped parcels of books at the Strand Bookstore. For a short time, no more than a few months, I lived on Shredded Wheat and peanut butter. When my first book was accepted, I moved from a single room on the Lower East Side into another, larger single room, a 'studio apartment', on Ninth Avenue in Chelsea, where I continue to live. My apartment is just large enough for my wooden desk, a convertible couch, two large crowded bookshelves, a shelf of stereo equipment, and dozens of cardboard boxes of records. In this apartment everything has its place and is in it.

My parents have never been to this enclosed, tidy space, though I speak to my father on the phone every two or three months. In the past ten years I have returned to the city where I grew up only once, to visit my mother in the hospital after her stroke. During the four days I stayed in my father's house I slept in my old room, my father upstairs. After the blind man's death my father bought the duplex and on my first night home he told me that we were both successes.

Now, when we speak on the telephone, he tells me of the fortunes of the local baseball and basketball teams and respectfully inquires about my progress on 'the new book'. I think: This is not my father, he is not the same man.

My old cot disappeared long ago, and late at night I lay on the twins' double bed. Like the house as a whole, like everything in my old neighbourhood, the bedroom was larger than I remembered it. I brushed the wallpaper with my fingers, then looked up to the ceiling. The image of two men tangled up in the ropes of the same parachute, comically berating each other as they fell, came to me, and I wondered if the image had a place in the novel I was writing, or if it was a gift from the as yet unseen novel that would follow it. I could hear the floor creak as my father paced upstairs in the blind man's former territory. My inner weather changed, and I began brooding about Mei-Mei Levitt, whom fifteen years earlier at Brown I had known as Mei-Mei Chung.

Divorced, an editor at a paperback firm, she had called to congratulate me after my second novel was favourably reviewed in the *Times*, and on this slim but well-intentioned foundation we began to construct a long and troubled love affair. Back in the surroundings of my childhood, I felt profoundly uneasy, having spent the day beside my mother's hospital bed without knowing if she understood or even recognized me, and I thought of Mei-Mei with sudden longing. I wanted her in my arms, and I yearned for my purposeful, orderly, dreaming adult life in New York. I wanted to call Mei-Mei, but it was past midnight in the Midwest, an hour later in New York, and Mei-Mei, no owl, would have gone to bed hours earlier. Then I remembered my mother lying stricken in the narrow hospital bed, and suffered a spasm of guilt for thinking about my lover. For a deluded moment I imagined that it was my duty to move back into the house and see if I could bring my mother back to life while I did what I could for my retired father. At that moment I remembered, as I often did, an orange-haired boy enveloped in a red wool shirt. Sweat poured from my forehead, my chest.

Then a terrifying thing happened to me. I tried to get out of bed to go to the bathroom and found that I could not move. My arms and legs were cast in cement; they were lifeless and *would not move.* I thought that I was having a stroke, like my mother. I could not even cry out — my throat, too, was paralysed. I strained to push myself up off the narrow bed and smelled that someone very near, someone just out of sight or around a corner, was making popcorn and heating butter. Another wave of sweat gouted out of my inert body, turning the sheet and the pillowcase slick and cold.

I saw — as if I were writing it — my seven-year-old self hesitating before the entrance of a theatre a few blocks from this house. Hot, flat, yellow sunlight fell over everything, cooking the life from the wide boulevard. I saw myself turn away, felt my stomach churn with the smoke of underground fires, saw myself begin to run. Vomit backed up in my throat. My arms and legs convulsed, and I fell out of bed and managed to crawl out of the room and down the hall to throw up in the toilet behind the closed door of the bathroom.

* * *

My age, as I write these words, is forty-three. I have written five novels over a period of nearly twenty years

– 'only' five, each of them more difficult, harder to write than the one before. To maintain this hobbled pace of a novel every four years, I must sit at my desk at least six hours every day; I must consume hundreds of boxes of typing paper, scores of yellow legal pads, forests of pencils, miles of black ribbon. It is a fierce, voracious activity. Every sentence must be tested three or four ways, made to clear fences like a horse. The purpose of every sentence is to be an arrow into the secret centre of the book. To find my way into the secret centre I must hold the entire book, every detail and rhythm, in my memory. This comprehensive act of memory is the most crucial task of my life.

My books get flattering reviews, which usually seem to describe other, more linear novels, and they win occasional awards – I am one of those writers whose advances are funded by the torrents of money spun off by best-sellers. Lately I have had the impression that the general perception of me, to the extent that such a thing exists, is that of a hermetic painter inscribing hundreds of tiny, grotesque, fantastical details over every inch of a large canvas. (My books are unfashionably long.) I teach writing at various colleges, give occasional lectures, am modestly enriched by grants. This is enough, more than enough. Now and then I am both dismayed and amused to discover that a young writer I have met at a PEN reception or a workshop regards my life with envy. Envy misses the point completely.

'If you were going to give me one piece of advice,' a young woman at a conference asked me, 'I mean, *real* advice, not just the obvious stuff about keeping on writing, what would it be? What would you tell me to do?'

'I won't tell you, but I'll write it out,' I said, and picked up one of the conference flyers and printed a few words on its back. 'Don't read this until you are out of the room,' I said, and watched while she folded the flyer into her bag.

What I had printed on the back of the flyer was: GO TO A LOT OF MOVIES.

On the Sunday after the ferry trip I could not hit a single ball in the park. My eyes kept closing and, as soon as my eyelids came down, visions started up like movies – quick, automatic dreams. My arms seemed too heavy to lift. After I had trudged home behind my dispirited father, I collapsed on the sofa and slept straight through to dinner. In a dream a spacious box confined me, and I drew coloured pictures of elm trees, the sun, wide fields, mountains, and rivers on its walls. At dinner loud noises, never scarce around the twins, made me jump. 'That kid's not right, I swear to you,' my father said. When my mother asked if I wanted to go to Play School on Monday, my stomach closed up like a fist. 'I have to,' I said, 'I'm really fine, I have to go.' Sentences rolled from my mouth, meaning nothing, or meaning the wrong thing. For a moment of confusion I thought that I really was going to the playground, and saw black asphalt, deep as a field, where a few children, diminished by perspective, clustered at the far end. I went to bed right after dinner. My mother pulled down the shades, turned off the light, and finally left me alone. From above came the sound, like a beast's approximation of music, of random notes struck on a piano. I knew only that I was scared, not why. The next day I had to go to a certain place, but I could not think where until my fingers recalled the velvety plush of the end seat on the middle aisle. Then black-and-white images, full of intentional menace, came to me from the previews I had seen for two weeks – *The Hitchhiker*, staring Edmund O'Brien. The spiny anteater and nun bat were animals found only in Australia.

I longed for Alan Ladd, 'Ed Adams', to walk into the room with his reporter's notebook and pencil, and knew that I had *something to remember* without knowing what it was.

After a long time the twins cascaded into the bedroom, undressed, put on pyjamas, brushed their teeth. The front door slammed – my father had gone out to the taverns. In the kitchen, my mother ironed shirts and talked to herself in a familiar, rancorous voice. The twins went to sleep. I heard my mother put away the ironing board and walk down the hall to the living room.

I saw 'Ed Adams' calmly walking up and down on the sidewalk outside our house, as handsome as a god in his neat grey suit. 'Ed' went all the way to the end of the block, put a cigarette in his mouth, and leaned into a sudden, round flare of brightness before exhaling smoke and walking away. I knew I had fallen asleep only when the front door slammed for the second time that night and woke me up.

In the morning my father struck his fist against the bedroom door and the twins jumped out of bed and began yelling round the bedroom, instantly filled with energy. As in a cartoon, into the bedroom drifted tendrils of the odour of frying bacon. My brothers jostled towards the bathroom. Water rushed into the basin and the toilet bowl, and my mother hurried in, her face tightened down over her cigarette, and began yanking the twins into their clothes. 'You made your decision,' she said to me; 'now I hope you're going to make it to the playground on time.' Doors opened, doors slammed shut. My father shouted from the kitchen, and I got out of bed. Eventually I sat down before the bowl of cereal. My father smoked and did not meet my eyes. The cereal tasted of dead leaves. 'You look the way that asshole upstairs plays piano,' my father said. He dropped quarters on the table and told me not to lose that money.

After he left, I locked myself in the bedroom. The piano dully resounded overhead like a sound track. I heard the cups and dishes rattle in the sink, the furniture moving by itself, looking for something to hunt down and kill. *Love me, love me*, the radio called from beside a family of brown-and-white porcelain spaniels. I heard some light, whispery thing, a lamp or a magazine, begin to slide around the living room. *I am imagining all this*, I said to myself, and tried to concentrate on a *Blackhawk* comic book. The pictures jigged and melted in their panels. *Love me*, Blackhawk cried out from the cockpit of his fighter as he swooped down to exterminate a nest of yellow, slant-eyed villains. Outside, fire raged beneath the streets, trying to pull the world apart. When I dropped the comic book and closed my eyes, the noises ceased and I could hear the hovering stillness of perfect attention. Even Blackhawk, belted into his aeroplane within the comic book, was listening to what I was doing.

* * *

In thick, hazy sunlight I went down Sherman Boulevard towards the Orpheum-Oriental. Around me the

world was motionless, frozen like a frame in a comic
strip. After a time I noticed that the cars on the
boulevard and the few people on the sidewalk had not
actually frozen into place but instead were moving
with great slowness. I could see men's legs advancing
within their trousers, the knee coming forward to
strike the crease, the cuff slowly lifting off the shoe,
the shoe drifting up like Tom Cat's paw when he crept
towards Jerry Mouse. The warm, patched skin of Sherman Boulevard . . . I thought of walking along Sherman
Boulevard for ever, moving past the nearly immobile
cars and people, past the theatre, past the liquor store,
through the gates, and past the wading pool and
swings, past the elephants and lions reaching out to be
fed, past the secret park where my father flailed in a
rage of disappointment, past the elms and out the
opposite gate, past the big houses on the opposite side
of the park, past picture windows and past lawns with
bikes and plastic pools, past slanting driveways and
basketball hoops, past men getting out of cars, past
playgrounds where children raced back and forth on a
surface shining black. Then past fields and crowded
markets, past high yellow tractors with mud dried like
old wool inside the enormous hubs, past wagons piled
high with hay, past deep woods where lost children
followed trails of breadcrumbs to a gingerbread door,
past other cities where nobody would see me because
nobody knew my name – past everything, past
everybody.

At the Orpheum-Oriental, I stopped still. My mouth
was dry and my eyes would not focus. Everything
around me, so quiet and still a moment earlier, jumped
into life as soon as I stopped walking. Horns blared,

cars roared down the boulevard. Beneath these sounds I heard the pounding of great machines, and the fires gobbling up oxygen beneath the street. As if I had gulped them from the air, fire and smoke poured into my stomach. Flame slipped up my throat and sealed the back of my mouth. In my mind I saw myself taking the first quarter from my pocket, exchanging it for a ticket, pushing through the door, and moving into the cool air. I saw myself holding out the ticket to be torn in half, going over an endless brown carpet towards the inner door. From the last row of seats on the other side of the inner door, inside the shadowy but not yet dark theatre, a shapeless monster whose wet black mouth said *Love me, love me*, stretched yearning arms towards me. Shock froze my shoes to the sidewalk, then shoved me firmly in the small of the back, and I was running down the block, unable to scream because I had to clamp my lips against the smoke and fire trying to explode from my mouth.

The rest of that afternoon remains vague. I wandered through the streets, not in the clean, hollow way I had imagined but almost blindly, hot and uncertain. I remember the taste of fire in my mouth and the loudness of my heart. After a time I found myself before the elephant enclosure in the zoo. A newspaper reporter in a neat grey suit passed through the space before me, and I followed him, knowing that he carried a notebook in his pocket, that he had been beaten by gangsters, that he could locate the speaking secret that hid beneath the disconnected and dismembered pieces of the world. He would fire his pistol on an empty chamber and trick evil 'Solly Wellman', Berry Kroeger, with his girlish, watchful eyes. And when 'Solly Well-man' came gloating out of the shadows, the reporter would shoot him dead.

Dead.

Donna Reed smiled down from an upstairs window: has there ever been a smile like that? Ever? I was in Chicago, and behind a closed door 'Blackie Franchot' bled onto a brown carpet. 'Solly Wellman', something like 'Solly Wellman', called and called to me from the decorated grave where he lay like a secret. The man in the grey suit finally carried his notebook and his gun through a front door, and I saw that I was only a few blocks from home.

Paul leans against the wire fence surrounding the playground, looking out, looking backwards. Alan Ladd brushes off 'Leona', for she had no history that matters and exists only in the world of work and pleasure, of cigarettes and cocktail bars. Beneath this world is another, and 'Leona's' life is a blind, strenuous denial of that other world.

My mother held her hand to my forehead and declared that I not only had a fever but had been building up to it all week. I was not to go to the playground the next day, I had to spend the day lying down on Mrs Candee's couch. When she lifted the telephone to call one of the high-school girls, I said not to bother, other kids were gone all the time, and she put down the receiver.

*   *   *

I lay on Mrs Candee's couch staring up at the ceiling of her darkened living room. The twins squabbled outside, and maternal, slow-witted Mrs Candee brought me orange juice. The twins ran towards the sandbox, and Mrs Candee groaned as she let herself fall into a wobbly lawn chair. The morning newspaper folded beneath the lawn chair said that *The Hitchhiker* and *Double Cross* had begun playing at the Orpheum-Oriental. *Chicago Deadline* had done its work and travelled on. It had broken the world in half and sealed the monster deep within. Nobody but me knew this. Up and down the block, sprinklers whirred, whipping loops of water onto the dry lawns. Men driving slowly up and down the street hung their elbows out of their windows. For a moment, free of regret and nearly without emotion of any kind, I understood that I belonged utterly to myself. Like everything else, I had been torn asunder and glued back together with shock, vomit, and orange juice. The knowledge sifted into me that I was all alone. 'Stan', 'Jimmy', whatever his name was, would never come back to the theatre. He would be afraid that I had told my parents and the police about him. I knew that I had killed him by forgetting him, and then I forgot him again.

The next day I went back to the theatre and went through the inner door and saw row after row of empty seats falling towards the curtained screen. I was all alone. The size and grandeur of the theatre surprised me. I went down the long, descending aisle and took the last seat, left side, on the broad middle aisle. The next row seemed nearly a playground's distance away. The lights dimmed and the curtains rippled slowly away from the screen. Anticipatory music filled the air, and the first letters appeared on the screen.

* * *

What I am, what I do, why I do it. I am simultaneously a man in his early forties, that treacherous time, and a boy of seven before whose bravery I shall forever fall short. I live underground in a wooden room and patiently, in joyful concentration, decorate the walls. Before me, half unseen, hangs a large and appallingly complicated vision I must explore and memorize, must witness again and again in order to locate its hidden centre. Around me, everything is in its proper place. My typewriter sits on the sturdy table. Beside the typewriter a cigarette smoulders, raising a grey stream of smoke. A record revolves on the turntable, and my small apartment is dense with music. ('Bird of Prey Blues', with Coleman Hawkins, Buck Clayton, and Hank Jones.) Beyond my walls and windows is a world towards which I reach with outstretched arms and an ambitious and divided heart. As if 'Bird of Prey Blues' has evoked them, the voices of sentences to be written this afternoon, tomorrow, or next month stir and whisper, beginning to speak, and I lean over the typewriter towards him, getting as close as I can.

INTERLUDE:

Going Home

They had come back to their home town to help her father move into a high-rise nursing home that looked like a luxury hotel. The rooms had a bland impersonality that made even the residents' old furniture look like it belonged in a hotel suite, and everybody liked the home a good deal. Most of the new residents experienced a period of euphoria after moving in. In the mornings, a girl at a desk pushed a button that set off a buzzer in every room, and if you did not answer your buzzer they sent a man up to see what had happened to you. The food was substantial and tasteless, and the large dining room was always crowded. There were prayer meetings and discussion groups. Everyone watched a lot of television. She and her husband sat in her father's new living room, on furniture she had known all her life, and listened to her father talk over the noise from the television.

One afternoon, they drove across town to her husband's old neighbourhood – the neighbourhood where he had been a small child, before his family had moved even farther away, to the suburbs. They got out of the car and walked up, then down the block, then crossed into the alley and walked up and down behind his old house. It looked as he remembered it – a two-storey brown and yellow duplex with a small, patchy backyard. The house had been cared for. Yet the neighbourhood was not what he remembered. All the elm trees had died, and the neighbourhood was mysteriously larger – everything was bigger than he remembered, everything was cleaner and brighter. It was he who was smaller now. They walked a little bit away, into another of the little side streets that ran alongside a broad avenue, and here too everything was charged with a blazing, glowing familiarity. He felt a sudden emotion move into his chest like an alien force: a large, virtually featureless block of feeling that constricted his breathing and pushed tears into his eyes. He could not tell if this feeling were grief or joy or some unbearable mixture of the two. He had been a child right here, in this place, and the unbearable feeling came from the centre of his childhood.

They returned to the car. She drove them back across town, and he cried the whole way, too deep inside the feeling to understand it or even identify it. When they left the city, he felt for the first time in his life that he was leaving his home town, leaving home.

A Short Guide to the City

The viaduct killer, named for the location where his victims' bodies have been discovered, is still at large. There have been six victims to date, found by children, people exercising their dogs, lovers, or – in one instance – by policemen. The bodies lay sprawled, their throats slashed, partially sheltered by one or another of the massive concrete supports at the top of the slope beneath the great bridge. We assume that the viaduct killer is a resident of the city, a voter, a renter or property owner, a product of the city's excellent public school system, perhaps even a parent of children who even now attend one of its seven elementary schools, three public high schools, two parochial schools or single nondenomenational private school. He may own a boat or belong to the Book of the Month Club; he may frequent one or another of its many bars and taverns; he may have subscription tickets to the concert series put on by the city symphony orchestra. He may be a factory worker with a library ticket. He owns a car, perhaps two. He may swim in one of the city's public pools or the vast lake, punctuated with sailboats, during the hot, moist August of the city.

For this is a Midwestern city, northern, with violent changes of season. The extremes of climate, from ten or twenty below zero to up around one hundred in the summer, cultivate an attitude of acceptance in its citizens, of insularity – it looks inwards, not out, and few of its children leave for the more temperate, uncertain, and experimental cities of the eastern or western coasts. The city is proud of its modesty: it cherishes the ordinary, or what it sees as the ordinary, which is not. (It has had the same mayor for twenty-four years, a man of limited-to-average intelligence who has aged gracefully and has never had any other occupation of any sort.)

Ambition, the yearning for fame, position, and achievement, is discouraged here. One of its citizens became the head of a small foreign state, another a famous bandleader, yet another a Hollywood staple who for decades played the part of the star's best friend and confidant; this, it is felt, is enough – and besides, all of these people are now dead. The city has no literary tradition. Its only mirror is provided by its two newspapers, which have thick sports sections and are comfortable enough to be read in bed.

The city's characteristic mode is *denial*. For this reason, an odd fabulousness permeates every quarter of the city, a receptiveness to fable, to the unrecorded. A river runs through the centre of the business district, as the Liffey runs through Dublin, the Seine through Paris, the Thames through London and the Danube through Budapest, though our river is smaller and less consequential than any of these.

Our lives are ordinary and exemplary, the citizens would say. We take part in the life of the nation, history courses through us for all our immunity to the national illnesses: it is even possible that in our ordinary lives . . . We too have had our pulse taken by the great national seers and opinion-makers, for in us you may find . . .

Forty years ago, in winter, the body of a woman was found on the banks of the river. She had been raped and murdered, cast out of the human community – a prostitute, never identified – and the noises of struggle that must have accompanied her death went unnoticed by the patrons of The Green Woman Taproom, located directly above that point on the river where her body was discovered. It was an abnormally cold winter that year, a winter of shared misery, and within The Green Woman the music was loud, feverish, festive.

In that community, which is Irish and lives above its riverfront shops and bars, neighbourhood children were supposed to have found a winged man huddling in a packing case, an aged man, half-starved, speaking a strange language none of the children knew. His wings were ragged and dirty, many of the feathers as cracked and threadbare as those of an old pigeon's, and his feet dirty and swollen. '*Ull! Li! Gack!*' the children screamed at him, mocking the sounds that came from his mouth. They pelted him with rocks and snowballs, imagining that he had crawled up from that same river which sent chill damp – a damp as cold as cancer – into their bones and bedrooms, which gave them earaches and chilblains, which in summer bred rats and mosquitoes.

One of the city's newspapers is Democratic, the other Republican. Both papers ritually endorse the mayor who, though consumately political, has no recognizable politics. Both of the city's newspapers also support the Chief of Police, crediting him with keeping the city free of any kind of violence that has undermined so many other American cities. None of our citizens goes armed, and our church attendance is still far above the national average.

We are ambivalent about violence.

We have very few public statues, mostly of Civil

War generals. On the lakefront, separated from the rest
of the town by a six-lane expressway, stands the cube-
like structure of the Arts Center, otherwise called the
War Memorial. Its rooms are hung with mediocre
paintings, before which schoolchildren are led on tours
by their teachers, most of whom were educated in our
local school system.

Our teachers are satisfied, decent people, and the
statistics about alcohol and drug abuse among both
students and teachers are very encouraging.

There is no need to linger at the War Memorial.

Proceeding directly north, you soon find yourself
among the orderly, impressive precincts of the
wealthy. It was in this sector of the town, known
generally as the East Side, that the brewers and tanners
who made our city's first great fortunes set up their
mansions. Their houses have a northern, Germanic,
even Baltic, look which is entirely appropriate to our
climate. Of grey stone or red brick, the size of factories
or prisons, these stately buildings seem to conceal that
vein of fantasy that is actually our most crucial inher-
itance. But it may be that the style of life – the
invisible, hidden life – of these inbred merchants is
itself fantastic: the multitude of servants, the maids
and coachmen, the cooks and laundresses, the private
zoos, the elaborate dynastic marriages and fleets of
cars, the rooms lined with silk wallpaper, the twenty-
course meals, the underground wine cellars and bomb
shelters . . . Of course, we do not know if all of these
things are true, or even if *some* of them are true. Our
society folk keep to themselves, and what we know of
them we learn chiefly from the newspapers, where
they are pictured at their balls, standing with their
beautiful daughters before fountains of champagne.

The private zoos have been broken up long ago. As citizens, we are free to walk down the avenues, past the magnificent houses, and to peer in through the gates at their coach-houses and lawns. A uniformed man polishes a car, four tall young people in white play tennis on a private court.

The viaduct killer's victims have all been adult women.

While you continue moving north you will find that, as the houses diminish in size, the distance between them grows greater. Through the houses, now without gates and coach-houses, you can glimpse a sheet of flat greyish-blue – the lake. The air is free, you breathe it in. That is freedom, breathing this air from the lake. Free people may invent themselves in any image, and you may imagine yourself a prince of the earth, walking with an easy stride. Your table is set with linen, china, crystal, and silver, and as you dine, as the servants pass among you with the serving trays, the talk is educated, enlightened, without prejudice of any sort. The table-talk is mainly about ideas, it is true, ideas of a conservative cast. You deplore violence, you do not recognize it.

Further north lie suburbs, which are uninteresting.

If from the War Memorial you proceed south, you cross the viaduct. Beneath you is a valley – the valley is perhaps best seen in the dead of winter. All of our city welcomes winter, for our public buildings are grey stone fortresses which, on days when the temperature dips below zero and the old grey snow of previous storms swirls in the avenues, seem to blend with the leaden air and become dreamlike and cloudy. This is how they were meant to be seen. The valley is called . . . it is called the Valley. Red flames tilt and waver at the tops of columns, and smoke pours from factory chimneys. The trees seem to be black. In the winter, the smoke from the factories becomes solid, like dark grey glaciers, and hangs in the dark air in defiance of gravity, like wings that are a light, feathery grey at their tips and darken imperceptibly towards black, towards pitchy black at the point where these great frozen glaciers, these dirigibles, would join the body at the shoulder. The bodies of the great birds to which these wings are attached must be imagined.

In the old days of the city, the time of the private zoos, wolves were bred in the Valley. Wolves were in great demand in those days. Now the wolf-ranches have been entirely replaced by factories, by rough taverns owned by retired shop foremen, by spurs of the local railroad line, and by narrow streets lined with rickety frame houses and shoe-repair shops. Most of the old wolf-breeders were Polish and, though their kennels, grassy yards, and barbed-wire exercise runs have disappeared, at least one memory of their existence endures: the Valley's street signs are in the Polish language. Tourists are advised to skirt the Valley, and it is always recommended that photographs be confined to the interesting views obtained by looking down from the viaduct. The more courageous visitors, those in search of pungent experience, are cautiously directed to the taverns of the ex-foremen, in particular the oldest of these – The Rusty Nail and The Brace 'n' Bit – where the wooden floors have so softened and furred with lavings and scrubbings that the boards have come to resemble the pelts of long, narrow, short-haired animals. For the intrepid, these words of caution: do not dress conspicuously, and carry only small amounts of cash. Some working knowledge of Polish is also advised.

Continuing further south, we come to the Polish district proper, which also houses pockets of Estonians and Lithuanians. More than the city's sadly declining downtown area, this district has traditionally been regarded as the city's heart, and has remained unchanged for more than a hundred years. Here the visitor may wander freely among the markets and street fairs, delighting in the sight of well-bundled children rolling hoops, patriarchs in tall fur hats and long beards, and women gathering around the numerous communal water pumps. The sausages and stuffed cabbage sold at the foodstalls may be eaten with impunity, and the local beer is said to be of an unrivalled purity. Violence in this district is invariably domestic, and the visitor may feel free to enter the frequent political discussions, which in any case partake of a nostalgic character. In later January or early February the 'South Side' is at its best, with the younger people dressed in multi-layered heavy woollen garments decorated with the 'reindeer' or 'snowflake' motif, and the older women of the community seemingly vying to see which of them can outdo the others in the thickness, blackness, and heaviness of her outer garments and in the severity of the traditional headscarf known as the *babushka*. In late winter the neatness and orderliness of these colourful folk may be seen at its best, for the wandering visitor will often see the bearded paterfamilias sweeping and shovelling not only his immaculate bit of sidewalk (for these houses are as close together as those of the wealthy along the lakefront, so near to one another that until very recently telephone service was regarded as an irrelevance), but his tiny front lawn as well, with its Marian shrines, *crèches*, ornamental objects such as elves, trolls, postboys, etc. It is not unknown for residents here to proffer the stranger an invitation to inspect their houses, in order to display the immaculate condition of the kitchen with its well-blackened woodstove and polished ornamental tiles, and perhaps even extend a thimble-glass of their own peach or plum brandy to the thirsty visitor.

Alcohol, with its associations of warmth and comfort, is ubiquitous here, and it is the rare family that does not devote some portion of the summer to the preparation of that winter's plenty.

For these people, violence is an internal matter, to be resolved within or exercised upon one's own body and soul or those of one's immediate family. The inhabitants of these neat, scrubbed little houses with their statues of Mary and cathedral tiles, the descendants of the hard-drinking wolf-breeders of another time, have long since abandoned the practice of crippling their children to ensure their continuing exposure to parental values, but self-mutilation has proved more difficult to eradicate. Few blind themselves now, but many a grandfather conceals a three-fingered hand within his embroidered mitten. Toes are another frequent target of self-punishment, and the prevalence of cheerful, even boisterous, shops, always crowded with old men telling stories, which sell the hand-carved wooden legs known as 'pegs' or 'dollies', speaks of yet another.

No one has ever suggested that the viaduct killer is a South Side resident.

The South Siders live in a profound relationship to

violence, and its effects are invariably implosive rather than explosive. Once a decade, perhaps twice a decade, one member of a family will realize, out of what depths of cultural necessity the outsider can only hope to imagine, that the whole family must die – *be sacrificed*, to speak with greater accuracy. Axes, knives, bludgeons, bottles, *babushkas*, ancient derringers: virtually every imaginable implement has been used to carry out this aim. The houses in which this act of sacrifice has taken place are immediately if not instantly cleaned by the entire neighbourhood, acting in concert. The bodies receive a Catholic burial in consecrated ground, and a mass is said in honour of both the victims and their murderer. A picture of the departed family is installed in the church which abuts Market Square, and for a year the house is kept clean and dust-free by the grandmothers of the neighbourhood. Men young and old will quietly enter the house, sip the brandy of the 'removed', as they are called, meditate, now and then switch on the wireless or the television set, and reflect on the darkness of earthly life. The departed are frequently said to appear to friends and neighbours, and often accurately predict the coming of storms and assist in the location of lost household objects – a treasured button or Mother's sewing-needle. After the year has elapsed, the house is sold, most often to a young couple, a young blacksmith or market-vendor and his bride, who find the furniture and even the clothing of the 'removed' welcome additions to their small household.

Further south are suburbs and impoverished hamlets, which do not compel a visit.

Immediately west of the War Memorial is the city's

downtown. Before its decline, this was the city's business district and administrative centre, and the monuments of its affluence remain. Marching directly west on the wide avenue which begins at the expressway are the Federal Building, the Post Office, and the great edifice of City Hall. Each is an entire block long and constructed of granite blocks quarried far north in the state. Flights of marble stairs lead up to the massive doors of these structures, and crystal chandeliers can be seen through many of the windows. The facades are classical and severe, uniting in an architectural landscape of granite revetments and colonnades of pillars. (Within, these grand and inhuman buildings have long ago been carved and partitioned into warrens illuminated by bare light bulbs or flickering fluorescent tubing, each tiny office with its worn counter for petitioners and a stamped sign proclaiming its function: Tax & Excise, Dog Licences, Passports, Graphs & Charts, Registry of Notary Publics, and the like. The larger rooms with chandeliers which face the avenue, reserved for civic receptions and banquets, are seldom used.)

In the next sequence of buildings are the Hall of Records, the Police Headquarters, and the Criminal Courts building. Again, wide, empty marble steps lead up to massive bronze doors, rows of columns, glittering windows which on wintry days reflect back the grey, empty sky. Local craftsmen, many of them descendants of the city's original French settlers, forged and installed the decorative iron bars and grilles on the facade of the Criminal Courts building.

After we pass the massive, nearly windowless brick facades of the Gas and Electric buildings, we reach the arching metal drawbridge over the river. Looking downriver, we can see its muddy banks and the lights of the terrace of The Green Woman Taproom, now a popular gathering for the city's civil servants. (A few feet further east is the spot from which a disgruntled lunatic attempted and failed to assassinate President Dwight D. Eisenhower.) Further on stand the high cement walls of several breweries. The drawbridge has not been raised since 1956, when a corporate yacht passed through.

Beyond the drawbridge lies the old mercantile centre of the city, with its adult bookstores, pornographic theatres, coffee shops, and its rank of old department stores. These now house discount outlets selling roofing tiles, silencers and other car parts, plumbing equipment, and cut-rate clothing, and most of their display windows have been boarded or bricked in since the civic disturbances of 1968. Various civic plans have failed to revive this area, though the cobblestones and gas streetlamps installed in the optimistic mid-seventies can for the most part still be seen. Connoisseurs of the poignant will wish to take a moment to appreciate them, though they should seek to avoid the bands of ragged children that frequent this area at nightfall, for though these children are harmless they can become pressing in their pleas for small change.

Many of these children inhabit dwellings they have constructed themselves in the vacant lots between the adult bookstores and fast-food outlets of the old mercantile district, and the 'treehouses' atop mounds of tyres, most of them several storeys high and utilizing fire escapes and flights of stairs scavenged from the old department stores, are of some architectural interest. The stranger should not attempt to penetrate these 'children's cities', and on no account should offer them any more than the pocket change they request, or display a camera, jewellery, or an expensive wrist-watch. The truly intrepid tourist seeking excitement may hire one of these children to guide him to the diversions of his choice. Two dollars is the usual gratuity for this service.

It is not advisable to purchase any of the goods the children themselves may offer for sale, although they have been affected by the same self-consciousness evident in the impressive buildings on the other side of the river and do sell picture postcards of their largest and most eccentric constructions. It may be that the naïve architecture of these treehouses represents the city's most authentic artistic expression, and the post-cards, amateurish as most of them are, provide interesting, perhaps even valuable, documentation of this expression of what may be called folk art.

These industrious children of the mercantile area have ritualized their violence into highly formalized tattooing and 'spontaneous' forays and raids into the treehouses of opposing tribes, during which only super-ficial injuries are sustained, and it is not supposed that the viaduct killer comes from their number.

Further west are the remains of the city's museum and library, devastated during the civic disturbances, and beyond these picturesque, still-smoking hulls lies the ghetto. It is not advisable to enter the ghetto on foot, though the tourist who has arranged to rent an automobile may safely drive through it after he has negotiated his toll at the gatehouse. The ghetto's residents are completely self-sustaining, and the atten-tive tourist who visits this district will observe the multitude of tents housing hospitals, wholesale food and drug warehouses, and the like. Within the ghetto

are believed to be many fine poets, painters, and
musicians, as well as the historians known as 'memor-
ists', who are the district's living encyclopaedias and
archivists. The memorist's tasks include the memor-
ization of the works of the area's poets, painters, etc.
for the district contains no printing presses or art-
supply shops, and these inventive and self-reliant
people have devised this method of preserving their
works. It is not believed that a people capable of
inventing the genre of 'oral painting' could have
spawned the viaduct killer, and in any case no ghetto
resident is permitted access to any other area of the
city.

The ghetto's relationship to violence is unknown.

Further west the annual snowfall increases greatly,
for seven months of the year dropping an average of
two point three feet of snow each month upon the
shopping malls and paper mills which have concentrated here. Dust storms are common during the sum-
mers, and certain infectious viruses, to which the
inhabitants have become immune, are carried in the
water.

Still further west lies the Sports Complex. The
tourist who has ventured thus far is well advised to
turn back at this point and return to our beginning, the
War Memorial. Your car may be left in the ample and
clearly posted parking lot on the Memorial's eastern
side. From the Memorial's wide empty terraces, you
are invited to look south-east, where a great unfinished
bridge crosses half the span to the hamlets of Wyatt
and Arnoldville. Construction was abandoned on this
noble civic project, subsequently imitated by many
cities in our western states and in Australia and
Finland, immediately after the disturbances of 1968,

when its lack of utility became apparent. When it was noticed that many families chose to eat their bag lunches on the Memorial's lakeside terraces in order to gaze silently at its great interrupted arc, the bridge was adopted as the symbol of the city, and its image decorates the city's many flags and medals.

The 'Broken Span', as it is called, which hangs in the air like the great frozen wings above the Valley, serves no function but the symbolic. In itself, and entirely by accident, this great non-span memorializes violence, not only by serving as reference to the workmen who lost their lives during its construction (its non-construction). It is not rounded or finished in any way, for labour on the bridge ended abruptly, even brutally, and from its truncated floating end dangle lengths of rusting iron webbing, thick wire cables weighted by chunks of cement, and bits of old planking material. In the days before access to the un-bridge was walled off by an electrified fence, two or three citizens each year elected to commit their suicide by leaping from the end of the span; and one must resort to a certain lexical violence when referring to it. Ghetto residents are said to have named it 'Whitey', and the treehouse children call it 'Ursula', after one of their own killed in the disturbances. South-Siders refer to it as 'The Ghost', civil servants 'The Beast', and East-Siders simply as 'that thing'. The 'Broken Span' has the violence of all unfinished things, of everything interrupted or left undone. In violence there is often the quality of *yearning* – the yearning for completion. For closure. For that which is absent and would if present bring to fulfilment. For the body without which the wing is a useless frozen ornament. It ought not to go unmentioned that most of the city's residents have never seen the bridge except in its representations, and for this majority the bridge is little more or less than a myth, being without any actual referent. It is pure idea.

Violence, it is felt though unspoken, is the physical form of sensitivity. The city believes this. Incompletion, the lack of referent which strands you in the realm of pure idea, demands release from itself. We are above all an American city, and what we believe most deeply we . . .

The victims of the viaduct killer — that citizen who excites our attention, who makes us breathless with outrage and causes our police force to ransack the humble dwellings along the riverbank — have all been adult women. These women in their middle years are taken from their lives and set like statues beside the pillar. Each morning there is more pedestrian traffic on the viaduct; in the frozen mornings men (mainly men) come with their lunches in paper bags, walking slowly along the cement walkway, not looking at one another, barely knowing what they are doing, looking down over the edge of the viaduct, looking away, dawdling, finally leaning like fishermen against the railing, waiting until they can no longer delay going to their jobs.

The visitor who has done so much and gone so far in this city may turn his back on the 'Broken Span', the focus of civic pride, and look in a south-westerly direction past the six lanes of the expressway, perhaps on tiptoe (children may have to mount one of the convenient retaining walls). The dull flanks of the viaduct should just now be visible, with the heads and shoulders of the waiting men picked out in the grey air like brush strokes. The quality of their yearning, its expectancy, is visible even from here.

INTERLUDE:

The Poetry Reading

The department chairman pronounced his name, and the famous poet got to his feet and began to move uncertainly towards the podium. The young woman who had written to him several days before (and had not received an answer) held her breath ... For a second, it seemed that the poet might walk off the stage, or collapse. He seemed much older and weaker than she had imagined – she would have walked straight past him on the street. He looked like the sort of old man who would have dirty fingernails, who would no longer be able to shave himself well. He gained the podium, leaned on it, opened his folio, frowned, wiped his forehead. He was perspiring. He began to read, and his voice was a glorious surprise. It sounded as if another man, much younger and stronger, were reading from inside him. This young man spoke with the voice of an orchestra, in the voices of trombones and trumpets. The old poet never looked up from his papers, but she thought that his eyes looked glazed, as if he were drunk, or nearly asleep.

The next day she could remember the sound of his voice, but the poems were only a golden blur. She was glad he had not answered her letter. She couldn't think of a single place where she could go with a man like that. Where could you take a guy who looked like a bum?

The Buffalo Hunter

For Rona Pondick

At the peasant's words ... undefined but significant ideas seemed to burst out as though they had been locked up and, all striving towards one goal, they thronged whirling through his head, blinding him with their light.

Anna Karenina, Leo Tolstoy

ONE

Bob Bunting's parents surprised him with a telephone call on the Sunday that was his thirty-fifth birthday. It was his first conversation with his parents in three years, though he had received a monthly letter from them during this period, along with cards on his birthdays. These usually reflected his father's abrasive comic style. Bunting had written back with the same frequency, and it seemed to him that he had achieved a perfect relationship with his parents. Separation was health; independence was health.

During his twenties, when he was sometimes between jobs and was usually short of money, he had flown from New York to spend Thanksgivings and Christmases with his parents in Michigan – Battle Creek, Michigan. Thanksgiving disappeared first, when Bunting finally got a job he liked, and in his thirtieth year Bunting had realized how he could avoid making the dreary Christmas journey into the dark and frigid Midwest. It was to this inspiration that his father referred after wishing him what sounded to Bunting like a perfunctory and insincere 'Happy Birthday' and alluding to the rarity of their telephone conversations.

'I suppose Veronica keeps you pretty busy, huh? You guys go out a lot?'

'Oh, you know,' Bunting said. 'About the usual.'

Veronica was entirely fictional. Bunting had not had a date with a member of the opposite sex since certain disastrous experiments in high school. Over the course of a great many letters, Veronica had evolved from a vaguely defined 'friend' into a tall, black-haired, Swiss-born executive of DataComCorp, Bunting's employer. Still somewhat vague, she looked a little like Sigourney Weaver and a little like a woman in horn-rimmed glasses he had twice seen on the M104 bus.

'Well, something's keeping you pretty busy, because you never answer your phone.'

'Oh, Robert,' said Bunting's mother, addressing her husband's implication more than his actual words. Bunting, who had also been named Robert, was supposed to be scattering some previously unsuspected wild oats.

'Sometimes I think you just lie there and listen to the phone ring,' his father said, mollifying and critical at once.

'He's *busy*,' his mother breathed. 'You know how they are in New York.'

'Do I?' his father asked. 'So you went to see *Cats*, hey, Bobby? You liked it?'

Bunting sighed. 'We left at the intermission.' This was what he had intended to write when the next letter came due. 'I liked it okay, but Veronica thought it was terrible. Anyhow, some Swiss friends of hers were in town, and we had to go downtown to meet them.'

His father asked, 'Girls or boys?'

'A couple, a very good-looking young couple,' Bunting said. 'We went to a nice new restaurant called The Blue Goose.'

'Is that a Swiss restaurant, Bobby?' his mother asked,

and he glanced across the room to the mantel above the unusable fireplace of his single room, where the old glass baby bottle he had used in his childhood stood beside a thrift-shop mirror. He was used to inventing details about imaginary restaurants on paper, and improvisation made him uneasy.

'No, just an American sort of a place,' he said.

'While we're on the subject of Veronica, is there any chance you could bring her back here this Christmas? We'd sure like to meet the gal.'

'No – no – no, Christmas is no good, you know that. She has to get back to Switzerland to see her family. It's a really big deal for her: they all troop down to the church in the snow – '

'Well, it's kind of a big deal for us, too,' his father said.

Bunting's scalp grew sweaty. He unbuttoned his shirt collar and pulled down his tie, wondering why he had answered the telephone. 'I know, but . . .'

None of them spoke for a moment.

'We're just grateful you write so often,' his mother finally said.

'I'll get back home one of these days, you know I will. I'm just waiting for the right time.'

'Well, I suggest you make it snappy,' his father said. 'We're both getting older.'

'But, thank God, you're both healthy.'

'Your mother fainted in the Red Owl parking lot last week. Passed right out and banged her head. Racked up her knee, too.'

'Fainted? Why did you faint?' Bunting said. He pictured his mother swaddled in bandages.

'Oh, I don't want to talk about it,' she said. 'It's not

really serious. I can still get around, what with my cane.'

'What do you mean, "not really serious"?'

'I get a headache when I think of all those eggs I broke,' she said. 'You're not to worry about me, Bobby.'

'You didn't even go to a doctor, did you?'

'Oh hell, we don't need any *doctors*,' said his father. 'Charge you an arm and a leg for nothing. Neither one of us has been to a doctor in twenty years.'

There was a silence during which Bunting could hear his father computing the cost of the call. 'Well, let's wrap this up, all right?' his father said at last.

This conversation, with its unspoken insinuations, suspicions, and judgements, left Bunting feeling jittery and exhausted. He set down the telephone, rubbed his hands over his face, and stood up to pick his way through his crowded, untidy room to the mantel of the useless fireplace. He bent to look at himself in the mirror. His thinning hair stood up in little tufts where he had tortured it while talking to his parents. He pulled a comb from his jacket pocket and flattened the tufts over his scalp. His pink, inquisitive face looked reassuringly back at him from above the collar of his crisp white shirt. In honour of his birthday he had put on a new tie and one of his best suits, a grey nail-head worsted that instantly made its wearer look like the CEO of a Fortune 500 company. He posed for a moment before the mirror, bending his knees to consult the image of his torso, neck, and boyish, balding head. Then he straightened up and looked at his watch. It was four-thirty: not too early for a birthday drink.

Bunting took his old baby bottle from the mantel and stepped over a pile of magazines to enter his tiny kitchen area and open the freezer compartment of his refrigerator. He set the baby bottle down on the meagre counter beside the sink and removed a quart bottle of Popov vodka from the freezer, which he placed beside the baby bottle. Bunting unscrewed the nipple from the bottle, inspected the pink, chewed-looking nipple and the interior of the bottle for dust and foreign substances, blew into each, and then set down bottle and nipple. He removed the cap from the vodka and tilted it over the baby bottle. A stream of liquid like silvery treacle poured from one container into the other. Bunting half-filled the baby bottle with frigid vodka, and then, because it was his birthday, added another celebratory gurgle that made it nearly three-quarters full. He capped the vodka bottle and put it back in the otherwise empty freezer. From the refrigerator he removed a plastic bottle of Schweppes Tonic Water, opened it, and added tonic until the baby bottle was full. He screwed the nipple back onto the neck of the bottle and gave it two hard shakes. A little of the mixture squirted through the opening of the nipple, which Bunting had enlarged with the tip of a silver pocket-knife. The glass bottle grew cold in his hand.

Bunting skirted the wing-chair that marked the boundary of his kitchen, stepped back over the mound of old newspapers, dropped the bottle on his hastily made bed, and shrugged off his suit jacket. He hung the jacket over the back of a wooden chair and sat down on the bed. There was a Luke Short novel on the rush seat of the wooden chair, and he picked it up and swung his legs onto the bed. When he leaned back into the pillows, the bottle tilted and expressed a transparent drop of vodka and tonic onto the rumpled blue coverlet. Bunting snatched up the bottle, awkwardly opened the book, and grunted with satisfaction as the words lifted, full of consolation and excitement, from the page. He brought the bottle to his mouth and began to suck cold vodka through the hole in the spongy pink nipple.

On one of his Christmas visits home, Bunting had unearthed the bottle while rummaging through boxes in the attic of his parents' house. He had not even seen it at first – a long glass shape at the bottom of a paper bag containing an empty wartime ration book, two small, worn pairs of moccasins, and a stuffed monkey, partially dismembered. He had gone upstairs to escape his father's questions and his mother's looks of worry – Bunting at the time being employed in the mail room of a magazine devoted to masturbatory fantasies – and had become absorbed in the record of his family's past life which the attic contained. Here were piles of old winter coats, boxed photograph albums containing tiny pictures of strangers and empty streets and long-dead dogs, stacks of yellowed newspapers with giant wartime headlines (ROMMEL SMASHED! and VICTORY IN EUROPE!), paperback novels in rows against a slanting wall, bags of things swept from the backs of closets.

The monkey came firmly into this category, as did the shoes, though Bunting was not certain about the ration book. Wedged beneath the moccasins, the tubular glass bottle glinted up from the bottom of the bag. Bunting discarded the monkey, a barely-remembered toy, and fished out the thick, surprisingly weighty baby bottle. An ivory-coloured ring of plastic with a wide opening for a rubber nipple had been screwed down over the bottle's top. Bunting examined the bottle, realizing that once, in true helplessness, he had clutched this object to his infant chest. Once his own tiny fingers had spread over the thick glass while he had nursed. This proxy, this imitation and simulated breast had kept him alive: it was a period piece, it was something like an object of everyday folk art, and it had survived when his childhood – visible now only as a small series of static moments that seemed plucked from a vast darkness – had not. Above all, perhaps, it made him smile. He held on to it as he walked around the little attic – he did not want to let go of it – and, when he came back downstairs, hid it in his suitcase. And then forgot it was there.

When he got home, the baby bottle's presence in his suitcase, wrapped in a coil of dirty shirts, startled him: it was as if the glass tube had followed him from Battle Creek to Manhattan by itself. Then he remembered wrapping it in the shirts on the night before his departure, a night when his father got drunk during dinner and said three times in succession, each time louder than the last, 'I don't think you're ever going to amount to anything in this world, Bobby,' and his mother started crying, and his father got disgusted with them both and stomped outside to lurch around in the snow. His mother had gone upstairs to the bedroom, and Bunting had switched on the television and sat without feelings before depictions of other people's Christmases. Eventually his father had come back inside and joined him in front of the television without speaking to him or even looking at him. At the airport the next morning, his father had scratched his face in a whiskery embrace and said that it had been good to see him again, and his mother looked brave and stricken. They were two old people, and working-class Michigan seemed unbearably ugly, with an ugliness he remembered.

He put the bottle away in a cupboard on a high shelf and forgot about it again.

Over the following years, Bunting saw the bottle on only the few occasions he had to reach for something on its shelf. He either ate most of his meals in inexpensive neighbourhood restaurants or ordered them from Empire Szechuan, so he had little use for the pots and pans that stood there. During these years he found the job in the mail room of DataComCorp, invented Veronica for his parents' pleasure and his own, reduced and then finally terminated his visits to Michigan, moved into his early thirties, and settled into what he imagined were the habits of his adult life.

He saved his money, having little to spend it on apart from his rent. Every autumn and every spring, he went to a good men's clothing store and brought two suits, several new shirts, and three or four new neckties: these excursions were great adventures, and he prepared for them carefully, examining advertisements and comparing the merits of the goods displayed at Barney's, Paul Stuart, Polo, Armani, and two or three other shops he considered to be in their class. He read the same westerns and mystery novels his father had once read. He ate his two meals a day in the fashion described. His hair was cut once every two weeks by a Japanese barber round the corner who remarked on the smoothness of his collar as he tucked the protective sheet next to his neck. He washed his dishes only when they were all used up, and once a month or so he swept the floor and put things into piles. He set out roach killer and mouse traps and closed his eyes when he disposed of corpses. No one but himself ever entered his apartment, but at work he sometimes talked with Frank Herko, the man at the next word processor.

Frank envied Bunting's wardrobe, and swapped tales of his own sex life, conducted in bars and discos, for Bunting's more sedate accounts of evenings with Veronica.

Bunting liked to read lying down, and liked to drink while he read. His little apartment was cold in the winter, and the only place to lie down in it was the bed, so for four months of every year Bunting spent much of every weekend and most of his evenings wrapped up fully clothed in his blankets, a glass of cold vodka (without tonic, for this was after Labor Day) in one hand, a paperback book in the other. The only difficulty with this system, otherwise perfectly adapted to Bunting's desires and needs, had been the occasional spillage. There had been technical problems concerning the uprightness of the glass during the turning of the pages. One solution was to prop the glass against the side of his body as he turned the page, but this method met with frequent failure, as did the technique of balancing the glass on his chest. Had he cleared all the books, wads of Kleenex used and unused, pill bottles, cotton balls, ear cleaners, jar of vaseline, and the hand mirror from the chair beside his bed, he could have placed the glass on the seat between sips; but he did not want to have to reach for his drink. Bunting wanted his satisfactions prompt and ready to hand.

Depending on the time of the day, the drink Bunting might choose to go with *New Gun in Town* or *Saddles and Sagebrush* could be herbal tea, orange juice, warm milk, Tab or Pepsi-Cola, mineral water: should he not be enabled to take in such pleasurable and harmless liquids without removing his eye from the page? Every

other area of life was filled with difficulty and compro-
mise; this – bed and a book – should be pristine.

The solution came to him one November after a
mysterious and terrifying experience that occurred as
he was writing his monthly letter home.

Dear Mom and Dad,
* Everything is still going so well I sometimes think I must*
be dreaming. Veronica says she has never seen any employee
anywhere come so far so fast. We went dancing at the
Rainbow Room last night following dinner at Quaglino's, a
new restaurant all the critics are raving about. As I walked
her back to Park Avenue through the well-dressed crowds
on Fifth Avenue, she told me that she felt she would once
again really need me by her side in Switzerland this
Christmas. It's hard for her to defend herself against her
brother's charges that she has sold out her native country,
and the local aristocracy is all against her too . . .

The mention of Christmas caused him to see, as if
printed on a postcard, the image of the dingy white
house in Battle Creek, with his parents standing before
the front steps, his father scowling beneath the peak of
plaid cap and his mother blinking with apprehension.
They faced forward, like the couple in 'American
Gothic'. He stopped writing and his mind spun past
them up the steps, through the door, up the stairs into
a terrifying void. For a moment he thought he was
going to faint, or that he *had* fainted. Distant white
lights wheeled above him, and he was falling through
space. Some massive knowledge moved within him,
thrusting powerfully upwards from the darkness where
it had been jailed, and he understood that his life
depended on keeping this knowledge locked inside
him, in a golden casket within a silver casket within a
leaden casket. It was a wild beast with claws and teeth,

a tiger, and this tiger had threatened to surge into his
conscious mind and destroy him. Bunting was panting
from both the force and the threat of the tiger locked
within him, and he was looking at the white paper
where his pen had made a little scratchy scrawl after
the word *too*, aware that he had not fainted – but it
was, just then and only for a second, as if his body had
been hurled through some dark barrier.

Drained, he lay back against the headboard and tried
to remember what had just happened. It was already
blurred by distance. He had seen his parents and flown
. . . ? He remembered the expression on his mother's
face, the blinking, almost simian eyes and the deep
parallel lines in her forehead, and felt his heart beating
with the relief that he had escaped whatever it was
that had surged up from within him. So thoroughly
had he escaped it that he now wondered about the
reality of his experience. A thick shield had slammed
back into place, where it emphatically belonged.

And then came Bunting's revelation.

He thought of the old baby bottle on its shelf and
saw how he could use it. He set aside the letter and
went across his room to take down the bottle from its
high shelf. It came away from the shelf with a faint
kissing sound.

The bottle was covered with fluffy grey dust, and a
sticky brown substance from the shelf circled its base.
Bunting squeezed dishwashing liquid into the bottle
and held it under a stream of hot water. He scrubbed
the bottom clean, unscrewed the plastic cap, and
washed the grooves on the cap and the neck of the
bottle. As he dried the warm bottle with his clean tea-
towel, he saw his mother bent over the sink in her

dark little kitchen, her arms sunk in soapy water and steam rising past her head.

Bunting thrust this image away and regarded the bottle. It seemed surprisingly beautiful for so functional an object. The bottle was a perfect cylinder of clear glass, which sparkled as it dried. Oddly, its smooth, caressing weight felt as comfortable in his adult palm as it must have in his childish hand. The plastic cap twirled gracefully down over the moulded O of the bottle's mouth. One tiny air bubble had been caught ascending from the thick rim at the bottom. The manufacturers's name, Prentiss, was spelled out in thick transparent letters circling the bottle's shoulders.

He placed it on the cleanest section of the counter and squatted to admire his work. The bottle was an obelisk made of a miraculous transparent skin. The wall behind it turned to a swarmy, elastic blur. For a moment Bunting wished that his two windows, which looked out onto a row of decrepit brownstones on the west side of Manhattan, were of the same thick, distorting glass.

He went out onto Eighth Avenue to search for nipples, and found them in a drugstore, hanging slightly above eye level, wrapped in packages of three like condoms, and surrounded by a display of bottles. He snatched the first pack of nipples off the hook and carried it to the register. He practised what he would say if the sullen Puerto Rican girl asked him why he was buying baby-bottle nipples – *darn kid goes through these things in a hurry* – but she charged him ninety-six cents, pushed the package into a bag, took his dollar and gave him change without a comment or even a curious glance.

He carried the bag back to his building rejoicing, as if he had narrowly escaped some great danger. The ice had not broken beneath his feet: he was in command of his life.

At home, he drew the package of nipples from the bag and noticed first that they were stacked vertically, like the levels of a pagoda, secondly that they were Evenflo nipples, 'designed especially for juice'. That was all right: he was going to use them to get juiced.

Dear Parent, read the back of the package. *All babies are unique*. Bunting cheered the wise patriarchs of the Evenflo Products Company. The Evenflo system let you adjust the flow rate to ensure that Baby always got a smooth, even flow. *Baby swallows less air, too*. Sure-Seal nipples had twin air valves. They were called The Pacers, as if they were members of a swift, confident family.

Bunting was warned not to put the nipples into a microwave oven, and cautioned that every nipple wore out. There was an 800 number to call, if you had questions.

He took his quart of Popov from the freezer and carefully decanted vodka into the sparkling bottle. The clear liquid sprang to the top and formed a trembling meniscus above the glass mouth. Bunting used his pocket knife to cut the nipples from the pack, taking care to preserve the instructions for their use, and removed the topmost level of the pagoda. The nipple felt surprisingly firm and resilient between his fingers. Impatiently, he fitted the nipple into the cap ring and screwed the ring down onto the bottle. Then he tilted it to his mouth and sucked.

The nipple met his teeth and tongue, which instantly accepted it, for what suits a mouth better than a nice new nipple? But a frustratingly thin stream of vodka came through the cross-cut opening. Bunting sucked harder, working the nipple between his teeth like gum, but the vodka continued to stream through the opening at the same even, deliberate rate.

Now Bunting took his little silver knife, actually Frank Herko's, from his pocket. Bunting had seen it lying on Herko's desk for several days before borrowing it. He intended to give it back someday, but no one could dispute that the elegant knife suited someone like Bunting far more than Frank Herko – in fact, Herko had probably found it on a sidewalk, or beneath a table in a restaurant (for Frank Herko really did go to restaurants, the names of which Bunting appropriated for his tales of Veronica), and therefore it was as much Bunting's as his. Very cautiously, Bunting inserted the delicate blade into one of the smooth cross-cut incisions. He lengthened the cut in the rubber by perhaps an eighth of an inch, then did the same to the other half of the cross-cut. He replaced the nipple in the cap ring, tightened the ring onto the bottle, and tested his improvement. A mouthful of vodka slipped through the enlarged opening and chilled his teeth.

Bunting had taken his wonderful new invention directly to bed, shedding his tie and his jacket as he went. He picked up his Luke Short novel and sucked vodka through the nipple. When he turned the page, he clamped the nipple between his teeth and let the bottle dangle, jutting downwards past his lower lip like a monstrous cigar. A feeling of discontinuity, unfinished business, troubled him. He was riding down onto a grassy plateau atop a dun horse named Shorty. He gazed out across a herd of grazing buffalo. The bottle dangled again as the bottom half of the letter to his parents slipped down his legs into the herd of buffalo. 'Oh,' he said. 'Oh, yes.'

The baby bottle, inspired by the event which had befallen him as he wrote the letter, had *replaced* it. All Bunting wanted to do was luxuriate in his bed, rolling atop old Shorty, clutching his trusty bottle in pursuit of buffalo hides, but more than a sense of duty compelled him to fold down the corner of the page and close the book on Shorty and the browsing herd. Bunting's heart had lightened. He picked up the pad on which he had been writing to far-away Battle Creek, found his pen in the folds of the blanket, and resumed writing.

So I'll have to go with her again, he wrote, then turned over the page to begin a paragraph dictated from the centre of his new satisfaction.

Have I ever really told you about Veronica, Mom and Dad? I mean, really told you about her? Do you know how beautiful she is, and how intelligent, and how successful? I bet not a day goes by that some photographer doesn't ask her to pose for her, or an editor doesn't stop her on the street to say that she has to be on the cover of his magazine.

She has dark hair and high, wide cheekbones, and sometimes I think she looks like a great cat getting ready to spring. She has an MBA, and she reads a novel in one day. She does all the crossword puzzles in ink. And fashion sense! It's no wonder she looks like a model! You look at those top models in the newspaper ads, the ones with long dark hair and full lips, and you'll see her, you'll see how graceful Veronica is. The way she bends, the way she moves, the way she holds her glasses in one hand, and how cute she looks when she looks out through them, just like a beautiful kitten. And she loves this country, Dad, you should hear her talk about the benefits America gives its people – honestly, there's never been a girl like this before, and I thank my stars I found her and won her love.

With this letter Bunting had come into his own. Despite all the lies he had told about her, lies which had become woven into his life so deeply that a beautiful shadow had seemed to accompany him on the bus back and forth to work, Veronica had never been so present to him, so visible. She had come out of the shadows.

He continued:

In fact, my relationship with Veronica is getting better and better. She gives me what I need, that comfort and stability you need when you come home from the business world, close your door behind you, and want to be free from the troubles and pressures of the day. Did I tell you about the way she'll pout at me in the middle of some big meeting with a DataComCorp client, just a little tiny movement that no one but me would possibly notice! It gives me the shivers, Mom and Dad. And she has shown me so much of the life and excitement of this town, the ins and outs of having fun in the Big Apple – I really think this is going to last, and one fine day I'll probably pop the question! She'd say yes in a minute, I know, because she really does love me as much as I love her . . .

TWO

Bunting woke up with a hangover on the Monday after his birthday and immediately decided that it would not be necessary to go to work.

His room offered evidence of a disorderly night. The Popov bottle, nearly empty, stood on the counter beside the refrigerator, and one of his lamps had been on all night, shedding a yellow circle of light upon a mass of folds and wrinkles that resolved into his grey worsted suit from Paul Stuart. Evidently he had tossed aside the jacket, undone his belt, and stepped out of his trousers as he moved towards the bed. His shoes lay widely separated, as if he had torn them off his feet and tossed them away. Closer to the bed were his tie, yesterday's white shirt, and his underwear, all of which formed points on a line leading towards his poisoned body. Beside him lay the empty Prentiss baby bottle and a paperback copy of *The Buffalo Hunter*, splayed open on the sheet. Evidently he had tried to read after finally getting out of his clothes and making it to bed: his body had followed its habits although his mind had stopped working.

He moved his legs off the bed, and sudden nausea made him fear that he was going to vomit before he could get to the toilet. The clarity he had experienced on first waking vanished into headache and other physical miseries. Some other, more decayed body had replaced the one he knew. The nausea ebbed away, and Bunting pushed himself off the bed. He looked down at long, white, skinny legs. These were certainly not his. The legs took him to the bathroom, where he sat on the toilet. He heard himself moaning. Eventually he was able to get into the shower, where the hot water sizzled down on the stranger's body. The stranger's wrinkled hands pushed soap across his white skin and rubbed shampoo into his lifeless hair.

Slowly, he dressed himself in a dark suit, a clean white shirt, and a navy blue necktie with white stripes, the clothes he would have worn to a funeral. His head seemed to float farther from the ground than he remembered, and his arms and legs were spindly and breakable. Bunting experienced a phantasmal happiness, a ghastly good cheer released by the disappearance of so much of his everyday self.

The mirror showed him a white, aged Bunting with sparkling eyes. He was still a little drunk, he realized, but did not remember why he had taken so much of the vodka. He wondered if there had been a reason and decided that he had simply celebrated his birthday too vigorously. 'Thirty-five,' he said to the white spectre in the mirror. 'Thirty-five and one day.' Bunting was not accustomed to giving much attention to any birthdays or anniversaries, even his own, and only the call from Battle Creek had reminded him that anyone else knew that the day was anything but ordinary. He had not even given himself a present.

That was how he would spend this peculiar morning. He would buy himself a thirty-fifth birthday present. Then, if he felt more like himself, he would go in to work.

Bunting located his sunglasses on his dining table, pushed them into his breast pocket, and let himself out of his room. The corridor looked even shabbier than usual. Sections of wallpaper curled down from the seams and corners, and whole sections of the wall had been spray-painted with puffy, cartoonish nonsense words. *Bango Skank. Jeepy.* Bunting's feeling of breakability increased. He worked his way through the murk of the hallway to the elevator and pushed the button several times. A few minutes later, he stepped out of the elevator and permitted himself to breathe. After the elevator, the lobby smelled like a freshly-mown hayfield. Two ripped couches of imitation leather faced each other across a dirty stone floor. A boxy wooden desk stood empty against a grey wall miraculously keep clean of graffiti. A six-foot fern was turning a crisp, pale brown in a pot beside the desk. Bunting pushed his way through the smudgy glass

doors, then the heavy wooden doors past the row of
buzzers, and came out into bright sunlight that
instantly bounced into his eyes from the tops of a
dozen cars, from clean shop windows, from the steel
wristbands of watches and glittering earrings, from a
hundred bright things large and small. Bunting yanked
his sunglasses from his pocket and put them on.

When he passed the drugstore, he remembered that
he needed a new pack of nipples, and turned in. Inside,
a slanted mirror gave him a foreshortened version of
himself, all bulging forehead and sinister glasses. He
looked like an alien being in disguise. Bunting walked
through the glaring aisles to the back of the store and
the displays of goods for infants.

Here were the wonderful siblings of the Pacer family,
but as he reached for them he saw what he had missed
the first time. The drugstore carried not only the
orange nipples with the special cross-cut opening, but
in rows on both sides of the juice nipples, flesh-
coloured nipples for drinking formula, white nipples
for drinking milk, and blue nipples for drinking water.

He took down packets of each kind of nipple, and
then realized that perfect birthday presents were dangling all over the wall before him. On his first visit, he
had not even noticed all the baby bottles displayed
alongside the nipples; he had not been interested in
baby bottles then, apart from his own. He had not
imagined that he would ever be interested in other
baby bottles. And in other ways also he had been
mistaken. He had assumed that baby bottles remained
the same over time, like white dress shirts and black
business shoes and hardcover books, that the form had
been perfected sometime early in the twentieth century and seventy or eighty years later was simply

reproduced in larger numbers. This had been an error. Baby bottles were objects like automobiles and breakfast cereals, capable of astonishing variation.

Smiling with this astonished pleasure, Bunting walked up and down past the display, carrying his packets of white, orange, blue, and flesh-coloured nipples. The first transformation in bottles had been in shape, the second in material, the third in colour. There had also been an unexplained change of manufacturers. None of these bottles before him were Prentiss baby bottles. Every single one was made either by Evenflo or Playtex. What had happened to Prentiss? The manufacturers of his long-lasting, extremely serviceable bottle had gone out of business – skunked, flushed, busted.

Bunting felt a searing flash of shame for his parents: they had backed a loser.

Most baby bottles were not even round any more. They were six-sided, except for those (Easy Hold) that looked like elongated doughnuts, with a long narrow oval in the middle through which a baby's fingers could presumably slide. And the round ones, the Playtex bottles, were nothing more than shells around collapsible plastic bags. These hybrid objects, redolent of menopausal old age, made Bunting shudder. Of the six-sided bottles – nursers, as they were now called – some were yellow, others orange, and some had a row of little smiling faces marching up the ounce markings on the side. Some of these new types of bottles were glass, but most were made of a thin transparent plastic.

Bunting instantly understood that, except for the ones that contained the collapsing breast, he had to have *all* of these bottles. Even his headache seemed to loosen its grip. He had found the perfect birthday present for himself. Now that he had seen them, it was not possible not to buy one each of most of these varieties of 'nursers'. Another brilliant notion penetrated him, as if sent by arrow from a heavenly realm.

He saw lined up on the shelf beside his stove a bottle for coffee and one for tea, a bottle for cold vodka, another for nice warm milk, bottles for soft drinks and different kinds of beer and one for mineral water: a library of bottles. There could be morning bottles and evening bottles and late-night bottles. He'd need a lot more nipples, he realized, and began taking things down from their hooks.

Back in his apartment, Bunting washed his birthday presents and set them out on his counter. The row did not look as imposing as he had envisioned it would – there were only seven bottles in all, his old Prentiss and six new ones. Seven seemed too few. He remembered all the bottles left on the wall. He should have bought more of them. A double row of bottles – 'nursers' – would be twice as impressive. It was his birthday, wasn't it?

Still, he had a collection – a small collection. He ran his fingers over the row of bottles and selected one made of clear plastic, to sample the difference between it and the old round glass Prentiss. Because he felt a bit dehydrated, he filled it with tap water and pushed a blue Water Nipple through the cap ring. The new nipple was deliciously slippery on his tongue. Bunting yawned, and half-consciously took the new blue-tipped bottle to his bed. He promised himself he would lie down for just a few minutes, and collapsed onto the unmade bed. He opened his book, began to suck water through the new nipple, and fell asleep so immediately

and thoroughly he might have been struck in the back
of the head with a mallet.

When Bunting awoke two hours later, he could not
remember exactly where, or even exactly who, he was.
Nothing around him looked familiar. The light – more
precisely, the relative quality of the darkness – was all
wrong. He did not understand why he was wearing a
suit, a shirt, a tie, and shoes, and he felt some deep,
mysterious sense of shame. He had betrayed himself,
he had been *found out*, and now he was in disgrace.
His mouth tasted terrible. Gradually, his room took
shape around him, but it was the wrong time for this
room. Why wasn't he at work? His heart began to beat
faster. Bunting sat up, groaning, and saw the rank of
sparkling new baby bottles, each with its new nipple,
beside his sink. The sense of shame and disgrace
retreated. He remembered that he had taken the morning off, and for a moment thought that he really should
write a letter to his parents as soon as his head cleared.

But he had just talked to his parents. He had escaped
another Christmas, though this was balanced by some
alarming news his father had given to him. The exact
nature of this news would not yield itself: it felt like a
large, tender bruise, and his mind recoiled from the
memory of injury.

He looked at his watch, and was surprised that it
was only eleven-thirty.

Bunting got out of bed, thinking that he might as
well go to work. In the bathroom, he splashed water
on his face and brushed his teeth, taking care not to
get water or toothpaste on his jacket or tie. While he
gargled mouthwash, he remembered: his mother had
fallen down in some supermarket parking lot. Had his
father insinuated that he ought to come back to Battle

Creek? No, there had been no such insinuation. He was sure of that. And what could he do to help his mother, even if he went back? She was all right – what she had really minded was breaking a lot of eggs.

THREE

An oddly energetic exhilaration, as if he had narrowly escaped some great danger, came to Bunting when he walked back out into the sunlight, and when his bus did not arrive immediately, he found himself walking to DataComCorp's offices. His body felt in some way still not his, but capable of moving at a good rate down the sidewalks towards Columbus Circle and then mid-town. The mid-autumn air felt fresh and cool, and the memory of the six new baby bottles back in his apartment was a bubbling inner spring, surfacing in his thoughts, then disappearing underground before coming to the surface again.

Did ever a young mother go into a drugstore in search of a baby bottle for her new infant, and not find one?

Bunting arrived at the door of the Data Entry room just at the time that one of his fellow workers was leaving with orders for sandwiches and drinks. Few of Bunting's fellow workers chose to spend their salaries on restaurant lunches, and nearly all of them ate delicatessen sandwiches in a group by the coffee machine or alone at their desks. Bunting generally ate in his cubicle or in Frank Herko's, for Frank disdained most of their fellow clerks, as did Bunting. Though some of the other clerks had attended trade or technical schools, only Bunting and Frank Herko had been in college. Bunting had two years at Lansing College, Herko two at Yale. Frank Herko looked nothing like Bunting's idea of a Yale student. He was stocky and barrel-chested, with a black beard and long, curly black hair. He generally dressed in baggy trousers and shabby sweaters, some with actual holes in the wool. Neither did Herko behave like his office friend's idea of a Yalie, being aggressive, loud, and frank to the point of crudity. Bunting had been disturbed and annoyed by Herko during his first months in Data Entry, an attitude undermined and finally changed by the other man's persistent, oddly delicate deference, friendliness and curiosity. Herko had seemed to decide that the older man was a sort of treasure, a real *rara avis*, deserving of special treatment.

Bunting asked the messenger to bring him a Swiss cheese and Black Forest ham sandwich on whole wheat, mustard and mayonnaise, lettuce and tomato. 'Oh, and coffee,' he said. 'Black coffee.'

Herko was winding his way towards the door, beaming at him. 'Uh huh, black coffee,' he said. 'You *look* like black coffee today. Nice of you to make it in, Bunting, my man. I take it you had an unusually late night.'

'You could say that.'

'Oh yes, oh yes. And we show up for work right after getting out of bed, don't we? With our beautiful suit all over wrinkles from the night before.'

'Well,' Bunting said, looking down. Long, pronounced wrinkles ran down the length of the suit jacket, intersecting longitudinal wrinkles that matched other wrinkles in his tie. He had been too disoriented to notice them when he had awakened from his nap. 'I did just get out of bed.' He began trying to smooth out the wrinkles in his jacket.

Frank took a step nearer and sniffed the air. 'A stench of alcohol is still oozing from the old pores. Had a little party, didn't we?' He bent towards Bunting and peered into his face. 'My God. You really look like shit, you know that? Why'd you come to work anyhow, you dumb fuck? You couldn't take a day off?'

'I wanted to come to work,' Bunting said. 'I took the morning off, didn't I?'

'Rolling around in bed with the beautiful Veronica,' Herko said. 'Hurry up and get into your cubicle before one of the old cunts gets a whiff of you and keels over.'

He propelled Bunting towards his row and cubicle. Bunting pushed open his door and fell into the chair facing his terminal. A stack of paper several inches high had been placed beside his keyboard.

Herko pulled a tube of Binaca from his trousers pocket. 'For God's sake, give yourself a shot of this, will you?'

'I brushed my teeth,' Bunting protested. 'Twice.'

'Use it anyhow. Keep it. You're going to need it.'

Bunting dutifully squirted cinnamon flavoured vapour onto his tongue and put the tube in his jacket pocket.

'Bunting cuts loose,' Herko said. 'Bunting gets down and dirty. Bunting the party animal.' He was grinning. 'Did Veronica do a number on you, or did you do a number on her, man?'

Bunting rubbed his eyes.

'Hey man, you can't just show up in last night's clothes, still wasted from the night before – on top of everything else three hours late! – and not expect me to be curious.' He leaned forward and stretched out his arms, enlarging the baggy blue sweater. 'Talk to me! What the hell happened? Did you and Veronica have an anniversary or a fight?'

'Neither one,' said Bunting.

Herko put his hands on his hips and shook his head, silently pleading for more of the story.

'Well, I was somewhere else,' Bunting said.

'Obviously. You sure as hell didn't go *home* last night.'

'And I was with someone else,' Bunting said.

Herko crowed and balled his fist and pumped his arm, elbow bent. 'Attaboy! Attaway! Bunting's on a roll.'

Again Bunting saw his parents posed before their peeling house like the couple in 'American Gothic', his father on the verge of uttering some banal heart-lessness and his mother virtually twitching with anxi-ety. They were small, Bunting realized, the size of dolls.

'I've been seeing a couple of new people. Now and then. Off and on.'

'A couple of new people,' Herko said.

'Two or three. Three, actually.'

'What does Veronica have to say about that? Does she even know?'

'Veronica and I are cooling off a little bit. We're creating some space between us. She's probably seeing other people too, but she says she isn't.' These inven-tions came easily to Bunting, and he propped his chin in the palm of his hand and looked into Frank Herko's luminous eyes. 'I guess I was getting a little bored or something. I wanted some variety. You don't want the same thing all the time, do you?'

'You don't want to be stultified,' Herko said quickly.

'You get stultified, going with the same person all the time.'

'It was always hard for Veronica to relax. People like that don't ever really slow down and take things easy. They're always thinking about getting ahead, about how to make more money, get a little more status.'

'I didn't know Veronica was like that,' Herko said. He had been given a very different picture of Bunting's girlfriend.

'Believe me, it even took me a long time to see it. You don't want to admit a kind of thing like that.' He shrugged. 'But once she starts looking around, she'll find somebody more suitable. I mean, we still love each other, but . . .'

'It wasn't working out, that's obvious,' Herko supplied. 'She wasn't right for you, she didn't have the same values, it could never turn out happily. You're doing the right thing. Besides, you're going out and having fun, aren't you? What more do you want?'

'I want my headache to go away,' Bunting said. The sensation of a slight, suspended drunkenness had passed, and with it the feeling of inhabiting an unfamiliar body.

'Oh, for God's sake, why didn't you say so?' asked Herko, and disappeared into his own cubicle. Bunting could see the top of his head floating back and forth like a wig over the top of the partition. Desk drawers moved in and out. In a moment Herko was back with two aspirin, which he set atop Bunting's desk before going out to the water cooler. Bunting sat motionless as royalty. Herko returned with a conical paper cup brimming with water just as the woman came in with a cardboard box filled with the department's orders from the deli.

'Hand over our wonderful four-star lunches and leave us alone,' Herko said.

They unwrapped their sandwiches and began to eat, Herko casting eager and importunate looks towards the older man. Bunting ate with fussy deliberation, and Herko chomped. There was a long silence.

'This sandwich tastes good,' Bunting said at last.

'Yeah, yeah,' Herko said. 'Right now *Alpo* would taste good to you. What about the girl? Tell me about the girl.'

'Oh, Carol?'

'What's this "Oh, Carol?" shit, Bunting? You think I know the girl, or something? Tell me about her – where did you meet her, how old is she, what does she do for a living, does she have good legs and big tits, you know – *tell* me!'

Bunting chewed on slowly, deliberately, regarding Herko. The younger man looked like a large, shaggy puppy. 'I met her in an art gallery.'

'You devil.'

'I was just walking past the place, and when I looked in the window I saw her sitting behind the desk. The next day when I walked past, she was there again, so I went in and walked around, pretending to look at the pictures. I started talking with her, and then I started coming back to the gallery, and after a while I asked her out.'

'Those girls in art galleries are incredible,' Herko said. 'That's why they're working in art galleries. You can't have a dog selling beautiful pictures, right?' He shook his head. His sandwich oozed a whitish liquid onto the thick white paper, and a trace of the liquid clung to the side of his mouth. 'You know what you are, Bunting? You're a secret weapon.' A bit more white liquid squirted from the corner of his mouth. 'You're a god-damned *missile silo*.'

'Carol is more like my kind of person, that's all,' Bunting said. Secretly, this description thrilled him. 'She's more like an artistic kind of person, not so into her career and everything. She's willing to focus more on me.'

'Which means she's a hundred per cent better in bed, am I right?'

'Well,' Bunting said, thinking vaguely that Veronica had after all been very good in bed.

'It's obvious, it goes without saying,' Herko said. 'You don't even have to tell me.'

Bunting shrugged.

'What's her last name?'

'Even,' Bunting said. 'Carol Even. It's an English name.'

'At least English is her first language. She's a product of your own culture – of course she's more your type than some Swiss money machine. Tell me about the other two.'

'Oh, you know,' Bunting said. He sipped from the styrofoam container of coffee. 'It's the usual kind of thing.'

'Do they all work in art galleries? Do you boff 'em all at once, or do you just take them one by one? Where do you go? Do you make the club scene? Concerts? Or do you just invite them back to your place for a nice soulful *talk*?' He was chewing frantically as he talked, waving his free hand. A pink paste filled his mouth, a pulp of compressed roast beef, mayonnaise, and whole-grain bread. 'You're a madman, Bunting, you're a stone wacko. I always knew it – I knew you were gonzo from the moment you first walked into this place. You can fool all these old ladies with your fancy clothes, but I can see your fangs, my friend, and they are long, long fangs.' Herko swallowed the mess in his mouth and twinkled at Bunting.

'You could see that, huh?'

'First thing. Long fangs, my friend. Now tell me about these other women.' He suppressed a burp. 'Go on, we only got a couple of minutes.'

Lunch ended twenty minutes later, and the day slid forward. Though Bunting felt tired, his odd exhilar-ation had returned – an exhilaration that seemed like a freedom from some heavy, painful responsibility – and, as his fingers moved across the keyboard of his computer, he thought about the women he had described to Frank Herko. Images of the wonderful new baby bottles back in his room flowed in and out of his fantasies.

He found he was making a surprising number of typing mistakes.

Late in the afternoon, Herko's head appeared over the top of the partition separating their two cubicles.

'How's it going?'

'Slowly,' Bunting said.

'Forget about it, you're still convalescing. Listen, I had a great idea. You're not really going out with Veronica any more, right?'

'I didn't say that,' Bunting said.

'You know what I mean. You're basically a free man, aren't you? My friend Lindy has this girlfriend, Marty, who wants to go out with someone new. Marty's a great kid. You'd like her. That's a promise, man. If I could, I'd take her out myself, but Lindy would kill me if I did. No kidding – I wouldn't put you on about this, I think you'd like her a lot and you could have a good time with her, and if everything works out, which I don't see why it should not, all four of us could go out somewhere together.'

'Marty?' Bunting asked. 'You want me to go out with someone named Marty?'

Frank snickered. 'Hey, she's really cute, don't act that way with me. This is actually Lindy's idea. I guess I talked about you with her, and she thought you sounded okay, you know, so when her friend Marty started saying this and that, she was breaking up with a guy, she asked me about you. And I said: no way, this guy is all wrapped up. But since you're going wild, you really ought to check Marty out. I'm not kidding.'

He was not. His head looked even bigger than usual, his beard seemed to jump out of his skin, his hair foamed from his scalp, his eyes bulged. Bunting had a brief, unsettling image of what it would be like to be a girl, fending off all this insistent male energy.

'I'll think about it,' he said.

'Great. Do I have your phone number? I do, don't I?'

Bunting could not remember having given Herko his telephone number – he very rarely gave it out – but he recited it to the eager head looking down at him, and the head disappeared below the partition as Herko went to his desk to write down the number. A moment later, the head reappeared. 'You're not going to be sorry about this. I promise!' Herko disappeared behind the partition.

Bunting's entire body went cold. 'Now, wait just a second. What are you going to do?' He could feel his heart racing.

'What do you think I'm going to do?' Herko called over the partition.

'You can't give anybody my number!' Bunting heard his own voice come up in a squeaky wail, and realized that everybody else in the Data Entry Room had also heard him.

Herko's upper body appeared, leaning around the door to Bunting's cubicle. He was frowning. 'Hey, man. Did I say I was going to give anybody your number?'

'Well, don't,' Bunting said. He felt as though he had been struck by a bolt of lightning a second ago. He looked down at his hands and saw that they, and presumably the rest of his body, had turned a curious lobster-red flecked with white spots.

'You're going to piss me off, man, because you ought to know you can trust me. I'm not just some jerk, Bunting. I'm trying to do something nice for you.'

Bunting stared furiously down at his keyboard.

'You're starting to piss me off,' Herko said in a low, quiet voice.

'Okay, I trust you,' Bunting said, and continued staring at his keyboard until Herko retreated into his own cubicle.

At the end of the day Bunting left the office quickly and took the staircase to avoid having to wait for the elevator. When he reached the ground floor, he sensed two elevators opening simultaneously off to his right, and hurried towards the door, dreading that someone would call out his name. Bunting spun through the door and walked as quickly as he could to the corner, where he turned off on a deeply shadowed cross-town street. He pulled his sunglasses from his pocket and put them on. Strangers moved past him, and even the Oriental rug outlets and Indian restaurants that lined the street seemed interchangeable and anonymous. His pace slowed. It came to him that, without consciously planning to do so, he was walking away from his bus stop. Bunting experienced every sensation of running away from something, but had no clear idea of what he was running from. It was all an illusion: there was nothing to run from. Herko? The idea was absurd. He certainly did not have to run from fuzzy, noisy Frank Herko.

Bunting ambled along, too tired to walk all the way back to his building but aware of some new dimension, an anticipatory expectancy, in his life that made it pleasant to walk along the cross-town street.

He crossed Broadway and kept walking, thinking that he might even try to figure out which subway could take him uptown. Bunting had taken the subway only once, shortly after his arrival in New York, and on the hot, crowded train he had felt in mortal danger. Every inch of the walls had been filled with lunatic scribbling; every other male on the subway had looked like a mugger. But Frank Herko took the subway in from Brooklyn every day. According to the newspapers, all the subway graffiti had been removed. Bunting had lived in New York for a decade without getting mugged; he walked all alone down dark streets; the subway could not possibly seem so threatening to him now. And it was much faster than the bus.

Bunting passed the entrance to a subway station just as he had these thoughts, and he paused to look at it. Stairs led down to a smoky blackness filled with noise: up the filthy steps floated a stench of zoo, of other people's private parts.

Bunting twitched away like a cat and kept walking west, committed now to walking to Eighth Avenue.

He suddenly felt nearly bad enough to hail a cab and spend five dollars on the trip home. It had come to him that Frank Herko and his friend Lindy were going to set about making him go out on a date with a girl named Marty, and that this must have been the vague pleasure that had lightened his mood only minutes ago.

Nothing was right about this; the whole idea was nightmarishly grotesque.

But why did the idea of a date have to be grotesque? He was a well-dressed man with a steady job. His looks were okay – definitely on the okay side. Worse people had millions of dates. Above all, Veronica had given him a kind of history, a level of experience no other data clerk could claim. He had spent hundreds of hours talking to Veronica in restaurants, another hundred in aeroplanes. He had travelled to Switzerland and stayed in luxury hotel suites.

Bunting realized that if something happened in your mind, it had happened – you had a memory of it, you could talk about it. It changed you in the same way as an event in the world. In the long run, there was very little difference between events in the world and events in the mind, because one reality inhabited them both. He had been the lover of a sophisticated Swiss woman named Veronica, and he could certainly handle a date with a scruffy acquaintance of Frank Herko's. Named Marty.

In fact, he could see her. He could summon her up. Her name and her friendship with Frank evoked a short, dark-haired, undemanding girl who liked to have a good time. She would be passably pretty, wear short skirts and fuzzy sweaters, and go to a lot of movies. A passive, good-hearted quality would balance her occasional crudeness. He would appear patrician, aloof, ironic to her – a sophisticated older man.

He could take her out once, in some indeterminate future time. The differences between them would speak for themselves, and he and Marty would part with a mixture of regret and relief. It was this infinitely postponable scenario that had hovered about him with such delightful vagueness.

Bunting turned up Eighth Avenue smiling to himself. When he saw that he was walking past a drugstore he turned in and moved through the aisles until he came to a large display of baby bottles. Here beside the three kinds of Evenflo and the Playtex hung bottles he had never heard of – no sturdy Prentisses, but squat little blue bottles and bottles with patterns and flags and teddy bears: a whole new range of baby bottles made by a company named Ama. Bunting saw instantly that Ama was a wonderful company. They were located in Florida, and they had a sunny, inventive, Floridian sensibility. Bunting began scooping up the bottles, and ended by carrying an awkward armful to the counter.

'How many babies you *got*?' the young woman behind the register asked him.

'These are for a project,' Bunting said.

'Like a collection?' she asked. Her head tilted prettily in the dusty light through the big plate-glass window on Eighth Avenue.

'Yes, like a collection,' Bunting said. 'Exactly.' He smiled at her bushy hair and puzzled eyes.

Outside the drugstore, he moved to the curb and raised his hand for a cab. With the same heightened sense of self that came when he bought his splendid suits, he rode back to his building in the ripped back seat of a jouncing, smelly taxi, splurging another fifteen cents every time the meter changed.

FOUR

That night he ate a microwaved Lean Cuisine dinner and divided his attention between the evening news on his television set and the array of freshly washed bottles on both sides of it. The news seemed outmoded and repetitious, the bottles various and pristine. The news had happened before, the same murders and explosions and declarations and demonstrations had occurred yesterday and the day before and the week and month before that, but the bottles existed in present time, unprecedented and extraordinary. The news was routine, the bottles possessed wonder. It was difficult for him to take his eyes from them.

How many bottles, he wondered, would it take to fill up his table? Or his bed?

For an instant, he saw his entire room festooned, engorged with cylindrical glass and plastic bottles – blue bottles covering one wall, yellow ones another, a curving path between bottles on the floor, a smooth cushion of nippled bottles on his bed. Bunting blinked and smiled as he chewed on turkey. He sipped Spanish burgundy from one of the new glass Evenflos.

When he had dumped the Lean Cuisine tray in the garbage and dropped his silverware in the sink, Bunting scrubbed out the bottle, rinsed the nipple, and set them on his draining board. He put a kettle of hot water on the stove, two teaspoons of instant coffee in one of his new bottles, and added boiling water and cold milk before screwing on the nipple. He poured a generous slug of cognac into another new bottle, a squat, pink, friendly-looking little Ama, and took both bottles to his bed along with a pen and a pad of paper.

Bunting pulled coffee, then cognac, into his mouth, and let the little pink Ama dangle from his mouth while he wrote.

Dear Mom and Dad,
There have been some changes that I ought to tell you about. For some time there have been difficulties between Veronica and me which I haven't told you about because I didn't want you to worry about me. I guess what it all boils down to is that I've been feeling you could say stultified by our relationship. This has been difficult for both of us, after all the time we've been together, but things are finally resolved, and Veronica and I are only distant friends now. Of course there has been some pain, but I felt that my freedom was worth that price.

Lately I have been seeing a girl named Carol, who is really great. I met her in an art gallery where she works, and we hit it off right away. Carol makes me feel loved and cared for, and I love her already, but I'm not going to make the mistake of tying myself down so soon after breaking up with Veronica, and I'm going out with two other great girls too. I'll tell you all about them in the weeks to come.

Unfortunately, I still will not be able to come for Christmas, since New York is getting so expensive, and my rent just went up to an astronomical sum . . .

If nobody hears the tree falling down in the forest, does it make any sound?

Does the air hear?

When his letter was done, Bunting folded it into an envelope and set it aside to be mailed in the morning. It was two hours to bedtime. He removed his jacket, loosened his tie, and slipped off his shoes. He thought of Veronica, sitting on the edge of a bed on the east side of town. A Merlin phone on a long cord sat beside her. Veronica's eyes were dark and hard, and a deep vertical line between her harsh thick eyebrows cut into her forehead. Bunting noticed for the first time that her calves were skinny, and that the loose skin beneath her eyes was a shade darker than the rest of her face. Without his noticing it, Veronica had been getting old. She had been hardening and drying like something left out in the sun. It came to him that he had always been unsuitable for her, and that was why she had chosen him. In her personal life, she set up situations destined from the first to fail. He had spent years 'with' Veronica, but he had never understood this before.

He had been an actor in a psychic drama, and he had done no more than to play his role.

It came to him that Veronica had deliberately introduced him to a way of life he could not afford by himself in order to deprive him of it later. If he had not broken off with her, she would have dropped him. Veronica was a poignant case. Those winks and flashes of leg in office meetings had simply been aspects of a larger plan unconsciously designed to leave him gasping with pain. Without Bunting, she would find someone else – an impoverished young poet, say – and do the whole thing all over again, dinner at the Blue Goose and first-class trips to Switzerland (Bunting had not told his parents about travelling first class), orchestra seats at Broadway plays, until what was twisted in her made her discard him.

Bunting felt sort of . . . awed. He knew someone like that.

He washed the Evenflo, refilled the pink little bottle with cognac, picked up his novel and went back to bed to read. For a moment he squirmed around on top of his sheets, getting into the right position. He sucked cognac into his mouth, swallowed, and opened the book.

The lines of print swam up to meet him, and instantly he was on top of a quick little grey horse named Shorty, looking down the brown sweep of a hill towards a herd of grazing buffalo. An enormous, nearly cloudless sky hung above him; far ahead, so distant they were colourless and vague, a bumpy line of mountains rose up from the yellow plain. Shorty began to pick his way down the hill, and Bunting saw that he was wearing stained leather chaps over his trousers, a dark blue shirt, a sheepskin vest, and muddy brown boots with tarnished spurs. Two baby bottles had been inserted, nipple-down, into the holsters on his hips, and a rifle hung in a long sheath from the pommel of his saddle. Shorty's muscles moved beneath his legs, and a strong smell of horse came momentarily to Bunting, then was gone in a general wave of fresh, living odours from the whole scene before him. A powerful smell of grass dominated, stronger than the faint, tangy smell of the buffalo. From a long way off, Bunting smelled fresh water. Off to the east, someone was burning dried sod in a fireplace. The strength and clarity of these odours nearly knocked Bunting off his horse, and Shorty stopped moving and looked around at him with a large, liquid brown eye. Bunting smiled and prodded Shorty with his heels, the horse continued walking quietly down the hill, and the astonishing freshness of the air sifted around and through him. It was the normal air of this world, the air he knew.

Shorty reached the bottom of the hill and began moving slowly alongside the great herd of buffalo. He

wanted to break into a gallop, to cut towards the
buffalo and divide them, and Bunting pulled back on
the reins. Shorty's hide quivered, and the short coarse
hairs scratched against Bunting's chaps. It was important to proceed slowly and get into firing range before
scattering the buffalo. A few of the massive bearded
heads swung towards Bunting and Shorty as they
plodded west towards the front of the herd. One of the
females snorted and pushed her way towards the centre
of the herd, and the others grunted and moved aside to
let her pass. Bunting slipped his rifle from its case,
checked to make sure it was fully loaded, and held it
across his lap. He stuffed six extra shells in each pocket
of the sheepskin vest.

Shorty was ambling away past the front of the herd
now, something like fifty yards away from the nearest
animals. A few more of the buffalo watched him. Their
furry mouths drizzled onto the grass. When he passed
out of their immediate field of vision, they did not
turn their heads but went back to nuzzling the thick
grass. Bunting kept moving until he was far past the
front of the herd, and then cut Shorty back around in a
wide circle behind them.

The herd moved very slightly apart: now the males
had noticed him, and were watching to see what he
would do. Bunting knew that if he got off the horse
and stood in the sun for a few minutes the males
would walk up to him and stand beside him and find
on him the smell of every place he had ever been in
his life. Then the ones who liked those smells would
stay around him and the rest would wander off a little
way. That was what buffalo did, and it was fine if you
could stand their own smell.

Bunting cocked his rifle, and one big male raised his head and shook it, as if trying to get rid of a bad dream.

Bunting kept Shorty moving on a diagonal line towards the middle of the herd, and the buffalo began moving apart very slowly.

The big male who had been watching seemed to come all the way out of his dream, and started ambling towards him. Bunting was something like ten yards from the big male, and twenty yards from most of the rest of the herd. It wasn't too bad: it could have been better, but it would do.

Bunting raised his rifle and aimed it at the centre of the big male's forehead. The buffalo instantly stopped moving and uttered a deep sound of alarm that made the entire herd ripple. A single electrical impulse seemed to pass through all the animals ranged out before Bunting. Bunting squeezed the trigger, and the rifle made a flat, cracking sound that instantly spread to all parts of the long grassy plain, and the big male went down on his front knees and then collapsed onto his side.

The rest of the herd exploded. Buffalo ran towards the hill and scattered across the plain. Bunting kicked Shorty into action and rode into their midst, shooting as he went. Two others fell instantly, then a third around whose body Shorty wheeled. Two of the fastest buffaloes had reached the hill, and Bunting aimed and fired and brought them down. He reloaded as a line of panicked buffalo swung away from the hill and bolted deeper into the meadow. The leader fell and rolled, and Shorty carried Bunting up alongside the second in line. Bunting shot the second buffalo in the eye, and it shuddered and fell. He swivelled in the saddle and brought down two more that were pounding towards the opposite end of the endless meadow.

By now the grass was spattered with blood, and the air had become thick with the screams of dying animals and the buzzing of flies. Bunting's own hands were spotted with blood, and long smears of blood covered his chaps. He fired until the rifle was empty, and then he reloaded and fired again as Shorty charged and separated the stampeding buffalo, and in the end he thought that only a few of the fastest animals had escaped. Dead and dying buffalo like huge sacks of dark brown wool lay all over the meadow, males and females. A few infant buffaloes who had been trampled in the panic lay here and there in the tall grass.

Bunting swung himself off Shorty and went moving among the prone buffaloes, slitting open the bellies of the dead. A great rush of purple and silver entrails fell out of the dead buffaloes' body cavities, and Bunting's arms grew caked with drying blood. At last he came to a young female that was struggling to get onto its feet. He took one of the baby bottles from its holster, put the barrel behind the animal's ear, and pulled the trigger. The female jerked forward and slammed its dripping muzzle into the grass. Bunting sliced open its belly.

He skinned the female, then moved to another. He managed to skin four of the buffalo, a third of all he had killed, before it grew too dark to work. His arms and shoulders ached from tearing the thick flesh away from the animals' fatty hides. The entire meadow reeked of blood and death. Bunting built a small fire and unrolled his pack beside it and lay down to doze until morning.

Then the meadow and the night and the piles of dead

animals slid away into nothingness, into white space; and Bunting's head jerked up. He was lying in his bed, and there was no fire, and for a moment he did not understand why he could not see the sky. A close, stuffy odour, the odour of himself and his room, surrounded him. Bunting looked back at the book and saw that he had reached the end of a chapter. He shook his head, rubbed his face, and took in that he was wearing a shirt, a tie, the trousers to a good suit.

More than three hours had passed since he had picked up *The Buffalo Hunter*. He had been reading, and what he had read was a single chapter of a novel by Luke Short. The chapter had seemed incomparably more real than his own life. Now Bunting regarded the book as though it were a bomb, a secret weapon – it had stolen him out of the world. While he had been in the book, he had been more purely alive than at any other time during the day.

Bunting could not keep himself from testing the book again. His mouth was dry, and his heart was thumping hard enough nearly to shake the bed. He picked up the book and sucked cognac, for courage, from the little pink bottle. The book opened in his hand to the words *Chapter Three*. He looked down to the first line of print, saw the words 'The sun awakened him . . .' and in an instant he was lying on a bed of thick grass beside a low, smoky fire. His horse whickered softly. The sun, already warm, slanted into his eyes and dazzled him, and he threw off his blanket and got to his feet. His hips ached. A thick mat of flies covered the heaps of entrails, dark blood glistened on the grass, and Bunting closed his eyes and *wrenched* himself out of the page and back into his own body.

He was breathing hard. The world of the book still seemed to be present, just out of sight, calling to him.

Hurriedly he put the book on the seat of his chair and stood up. The room swayed twice, right to left, left to right, and Bunting put out his hand to steady himself. He had been lost inside the book for only a few hours, but now it felt like he had spent an entire night asleep in a bloody meadow, keeping uneasy watch over a slaughtered herd. He turned the book over so that its cover was face down on the chair and carried the bottle to the counter. He refilled it with cognac and took two large swallows before screwing the nipple back on.

What had happened to him was both deeply disturbing and powerfully, seductively pleasurable. It was as if he had travelled backwards in time, gone into a different body and a different life, and there lived at a pitch of responsiveness and openness not available to him in his real, daily life. In fact, it had felt far more real than his 'real' life. Bunting began to tremble again, remembering the clarity and freshness of the air, the touch of Shorty's coarse hair against his legs, the way the big male buffalo had come slowly towards him as the others began to stir apart – in that world, everything had possessed consequence. No detail was wasted because every detail overflowed with meaning.

He sucked the cognac into his mouth, troubled by something else that had just occurred to him.

Bunting had read *The Buffalo Hunter* three or four times before – he had a small shelf of western and mystery novels, and he read them over and over. What troubled him was that there was no slaughter of buffaloes in *The Buffalo Hunter*. Bunting could remember – vaguely, without any particularity – a few scenes in which the hunter rode down buffalo and killed them, but none in which he massacred great numbers and waded through their bloody entrails.

Bunting let the bottle hang from the nipple in his teeth and looked around his cramped, disorderly little room. For a moment – less than that, for an almost imperceptible fraction of a second – his familiar squalor seemed almost to tremble with promise, like the lips of one on the verge of telling a story. Bunting had the sense of some unimaginable anticipation, and then it was gone, so quickly it barely had time to leave behind the trace of an astonished curiosity.

He wondered if he dared go back to *The Buffalo Hunter*, and then knew he could not resist it. He would give himself a few more hours reading, then pull himself out of the book and make sure he got enough sleep.

Bunting took off the rest of his clothes and hung up the excellent suit. He brushed his teeth and ran hot water over the dishes in the sink to discourage the roaches. Then he turned off the overhead light and the other lamp and got into bed. His heart was beating fast again: it was he who trembled with an almost sexual anticipation: and he licked his lips and took the book off the crowded seat of the chair. He nestled into the sheets and folded his pillow. Then at last Bunting opened the book once again.

FIVE

When the white spaces came he held himself in suspension as he turned the page and in this way went without a break from waking in the morning and

skinning the buffaloes and rigging a sledge to drag
them behind Shorty to selling them to a hide broker
and being ambushed and nearly killed for his money.
Bunting was thrown in jail and escaped, found Shorty
tethered in a feed lot, and spent two nights sleeping in
the open. He got a job as a ranch hand and overheard
enough to learn that the hide broker ran the town;
after that Bunting shot a man in a gunfight, escaped
arrest again, stole his hides back from a locked warehouse, killed two more men in a gunfight, faced down
the crooked broker, and was offered and refused the
position of town sheriff. He rode out of the town back
towards the freedom he needed, and two days later he
was looking again across a wide plain towards grazing
buffalo. Shorty began trotting towards them, moving
at an angle that would take him past the top of the
herd. Bunting patted the extra shells in the pockets of
his sheepskin vest and slowly drew the rifle from its
sheath. A muscle twitched in Shorty's flank. A shaggy
female buffalo cocked her head and regarded Bunting
without alarm. Something was coming to an end,
Bunting knew, some way of life, some ordained, flawless narrative of what it meant to be alive at this
moment. A cold breeze carried the strong aroma of
buffalo towards him, and the sheer beauty and rightness – a formal rightness, inescapable and exact – of
who and where he was went through Bunting like
music, and as he sailed off into the final, the most
charged and pregnant, white space he could no longer
keep himself from weeping.

   Bunting let the book fall from his hands, back in a
shrunken and diminished world. He experienced a long
moment of pure loss from which only tremendous

hunger and certain physical urgencies imperfectly distracted him. He needed, with overpowering urgency, to get into the bathroom; his legs had fallen asleep, his neck ached, and his knees creaked with pain. When he finally sat down on the toilet he actually cried out – it was as if he had gone days without moving. He realized that he was incredibly thirsty and, as he sat, he forced his arms to move to the sink, take up the glass, fill it with water. He swallowed, and the water forced its way down his throat and into his chest, breaking passage for itself. The world of Shorty, the meadow of endless green, and the grazing buffalo was already swimming backwards, like a long night's dream. He was left behind in this littler, less eloquent world.

He turned on his shower and stepped inside to soak away his pains.

When he dried himself off, he realized that he had no proper idea of the time. Nor was he really certain what day it was. He remembered seeing grey darkness outside his windows, so presumably it would soon be time to go to work – Bunting always awakened at the same time every day, seven-thirty, and had no need of an alarm – but suppose that he had read very late into the night, and had managed to get drunk, as on the night of his birthday . . . Had he really just finished reading the book? *Living in* the book, as it actually seemed? That would mean that he had not slept at all, though it seemed to Bunting that he'd had the *experience* of sleeping, in gullies and in a little jailhouse, in a bunkhouse and a tavern's back room and beside a fire in a wide meadow with millions of pinpoint stars overhead.

He dressed in a fresh shirt, a glen plaid suit, and a pair of cracked, well-polished brown shoes. When he strapped on his watch, he saw that it was six-thirty. He had read all night long, or most of it: he supposed he must have slept now and then, and dreamed certain passages of the book. Hunger forced him out of his room as soon as he was dressed, although he was an hour early: Bunting supposed he could walk to work again and get there early enough to clean up everything from Monday. Now that he was no longer so stiff, his body and his mind both felt, beneath a lingering layer of tiredness like that after a session of strenuous exercise, refreshed and energetic.

The light in the corridor seemed darker than it should have been, and in the lobby two teenage boys who had stayed up all night sucking on crack pipes and plotting crimes shared a thin hand-rolled cigarette beside the dying fern. Bunting hurried past them to the street. It was surprisingly crowded. He had gone half-way to the diner before the fact of the crowd, the darkness, and the whole feeling of the city combined into the recognition that it was evening, not morning. An entire day had disappeared.

Outside the diner he bought a paper, looked at the date, and found that it was even worse than that. It was Thursday, not Tuesday: he had not left his apartment – not even his bed – for two and a half days. For something like sixty hours he had lived inside a book.

Bunting went into the bright diner, and the man behind the cash register, who had seen him at least four mornings a week for the past ten years, gave him an odd, apprehensive look. For a second or two the counterman also seemed wary of him. Then the man recognized him, and his face relaxed. Bunting tried to smile, and realized that he was still showing the shock he had felt at the loss of those sixty hours. His smile felt like a mask.

Bunting ordered a feta cheese omelette and a cup of coffee, and the counterman turned away towards the coffee machine. Headlines and rows of black print at Bunting's elbow seemed to lift up from the surface of the folded newspaper and blare out at him; the whole dazzle of the restaurant surged and chimed, as if saying *wait for it, wait for it*: but the counterman turned carrying a white cup brimming with black coffee, the ink sifted down into the paper, and the sense of promise and anticipation faded back into the general bright surface of things.

Bunting lifted the thick china cup. Its rim was chalky and abraded with use. He was at a counter where he had eaten a thousand meals; the people around him offered the combination of anonymity and familiarity that most represents safety in urban life; but Bunting wanted overwhelmingly to be in his crowded little room, flat on his unmade bed, with the nipple of a baby bottle clamped between his teeth and a book open in his hands. If there was a promised land – a Promised Land – he had lived in it from Monday night to Thursday evening.

He was still in shock, and still frightened by the intensity of what had happened to him, but he knew more than anything else that he wanted to go back there.

When his omelette came it was overcooked and too salty, but Bunting bolted it down so quickly he scarcely tasted it. 'You were hungry,' the counterman said, and gave him his check without coming any nearer than he had to.

Bunting came out of the restaurant into what at first

looked like an utter darkness punctuated here and there by street lamps and the headlights of the cars streaming down upper Broadway. Red lights flashed off and on. A massive policeman motioned Bunting aside, away from some commotion in the middle of the sidewalk. Bunting glanced past him and saw a body curled on the pavement, another man lying almost serenely prone with his hands stapled into handcuffs. A sheet of smooth black liquid lay across half the sidewalk. The policeman moved towards him, and Bunting hurried away.

More shocks, more disturbance – savage, pale faces came out of the dark, and cars sizzled past, honking. The red of the traffic lights burned into his eyes. All about him were creatures of another species, more animal, more instinctual, more brutal than he. They walked past him, unnoticing, flaring their lips and showing their teeth. He heard steps behind him and imagined his own body limp on the pockmarked concrete, his empty wallet tossed into the pool of his blood. The footsteps accelerated, and a white frozen panic filled Bunting's body. He stepped sideways, and a hand fell on his shoulder.

Bunting jumped, and a deep voice said, 'Just hold it, will you?'

Bunting looked over his shoulder at a wide, brutal face filled with black dots – little holes full of darkness – and a black moustache. He nearly fainted.

'I just wanted to ask some questions, sir.'

Bunting took in the uniform at the same time as he saw the amusement on the policeman's face.

'You came out of that diner, didn't you, sir?'

Bunting nodded.

'Did you see what happened?'

'What?'

'The shooting, sir. Did you see a shooting?'

Bunting was trembling. 'I saw – ' He stopped talking, having become aware that he had intended to say *I saw myself shoot a man out west in a gunfight*. He looked wildly back towards the diner. A dozen policemen stood around a roped-off area of the sidewalk, and red lights flashed and spun. 'I really didn't see anything at all. I barely saw . . .' He gestured towards the confusion.

The man nodded wearily and folded his notebook with a contemptuous, disbelieving snap. 'Yeah,' he said. 'You have a good night, sir.'

'I didn't see – I didn't – '

The policeman had already turned away.

On Bunting's side of the avenue, the lobby of his bank offered access to their rows of cash machines; across it, the drugstore's windows blared out light through a display of stuffed cartoon characters. A cardboard cutout of a girl in a bathing suit held a camera. Bunting watched the policeman go back to his colleagues. Before they could begin talking about him, he ducked into the bank and removed a hundred dollars from his checking account.

When he came out again, he went to the corner, crossed the street without looking at the police cars lined up in front of the diner, and went into the drugstore. There he bought five tubes of epoxy glue and ninety dollars' worth of baby bottles and nipples, enough to fill a large box. He carried this awkwardly back to his building, peering over the top to see where he was going.

Bunting had to set down the box to push his button in the elevator, and again to let himself into his apartment. When he was finally safe inside his room, with the police bolt pushed back in front of the door, his lights on, and a colourful little Ama filled with vodka in his hand, he felt his true self returning to him, ragged and shredded from his nightmare on the streets. Except for the curious tingle of anticipation that had come to him in the diner, everything since being driven from his room by hunger had been like being attacked and beaten. Bunting could not even remember buying all the bottles and nipples, which had taken place in a tense, driven flurry.

Bunting began unpacking the baby bottles from the giant box, now and then stopping to suck cold Popov from the Ama. When he got to sixty-five, he saw that he was only one layer from the bottom, and was immediately sorry that he had not taken another hundred from the cash machine. He was going to need at least twice as many bottles as he had to fulfil his plan, unless he spaced them out. He did not want to space them out, he wanted a nice, tight look. A nice, tight look was essential: a kind of *blanketing* effect.

Bunting thought he would try to do as much this night as he could with what he had, then get more money from the bank tomorrow evening and see how far another seventy or eighty bottles got him. When he was done tonight, he would read some more – not *The Buffalo Hunter* again, but some other novel, to see if the same incredible state of grace, like the ultimate movie, would come to him.

Bunting did not understand how, but what he wanted to do with all the new baby bottles was tied to what had happened to him when he read the Luke Short novel. It had to do with . . . with *inwardness*. That was as close as he could come to defining the connection. They led him *inward*, and inward was where everything important lay. He felt that though his entire way of life could be seen as a demonstration of this principle, he had never really understood it before – never seen it clearly. And he thought that this insight must have been what he felt coming towards him at the coffee shop: what mattered about his life took place entirely in this room.

When all the bottles were out of the box, Bunting began slicing open the packages of nipples and attaching the nipples to the bottles. When this was done, he opened a tube of epoxy and put a few dots on the base of one of the bottles. Then he pressed the bottle to the corner of a blank wall and held it there until it stuck. At last he lowered his arm and stepped away. The pink-tipped bottle adhered to the wall and jutted out into the room like an illusion. It took Bunting's breath away. The bottle appeared to be on the point of shooting or dripping milk, juice, water, vodka, any sort of fluid onto anyone in front of it.

He dotted epoxy onto the base of another bottle and held it to the wall snugly alongside the first.

An hour and a half later, when he ran out of new bottles, more than a third of the wall was covered: perfectly aligned horizontal bottles and jutting nipples marched along its surface from the entrance to the kitchen alcove to the door frame. Bunting's arms ached from holding the bottles to the wall, but he wished that he could finish the wall and go on to another. Beautiful now, the wall would be even more beautiful when he finished.

Bunting stretched and yawned and went to the sink to wash his hands. A number of roaches ambled into their hiding places, and Bunting decided to wash the stacked dishes and glasses before the roaches started crowding each other out of the sink. He had his hands deep in soapy water when a thought disquieted him: he had not thought about the loss of all Tuesday, all Wednesday, and most of Thursday since buying the box of nipples and bottles, but what if his radical redecoration of his apartment was no more than a reaction to that loss?

But that was the viewpoint of another kind of mind. The world in which he went to work and came home was the world of public life. In that world, according to people like his father and Frank Herko, one 'counted', 'amounted to something', or did not. For a dizzy second, Bunting imagined himself entirely renouncing this worthless, superficial world to become a Magellan of the interior.

At that moment the telephone rang. Bunting dried his hands on the greasy dishtowel, picked up the phone, and heard his father pronounce his name as if he were grinding it to powder. Bunting's heart stopped. The world had heard him. This unnerving impression was strong enough to keep him from taking in the meaning of his father's first few sentences.

'She fell down again?' he finally said.

'Yeah, something wrong with your ears? I just *said* that.'

'Did she hurt herself?'

'About the same as before,' his father said. 'Like I say, I just thought you ought to know about stuff like this, when it happens.'

'Well, is she bruised? Is her knee injured?'

'No, she mainly fell on her face this time, but her knee's just the same. She wears that big bandage on it, you know, probably kept her from busting the knee all up.'

'What's making her fall down?' Bunting asked. 'What does the doctor say?'

'I don't know, he don't say much at all. We're taking her in for some tests Friday; probably find out something then.'

'Can I talk to her?'

'Nah, she's down in the basement, washing clothes. That's why I could call – she didn't even want me to tell you about what happened. She's on this washing thing now: she does the wash two, three times a day. Once I caught her going downstairs with a dishtowel. She was going to put it in the machine.'

Bunting glanced at his own filthy dishtowel. 'Why does she – what is she trying to – ?'

'She forgets,' his father said. 'That's it, pure and simple. She forgets.'

'Should I come out there? Is there anything I could do?'

'You made it pretty clear you *couldn't* come here, Bobby. We got your letter, you know, about Veronica and Carol and the rent and everything else. You tell us you got a busy social life, you tell us you got a steady job but you don't have much extra money. That's your life. And what could you do anyhow?'

Bunting said, 'Not much, I guess,' feeling stung and dismissed by this summary.

'Nothing,' his father said. 'I can do everything that has to be done. If she does the wash twice a day, what's the big deal? That's okay with me. We got the doctor appointment Friday, that's all set. And what's he going to say? Take it easy, that's what. It'll cost us thirty-five bucks to hear this guy telling your mother to take it easy. So as far as we know yet, everything's basically okay. I just wanted to keep you up to date. Glad I caught you in.'

'Oh, sure. Me, too.'

''Cause you must be out a lot these days, huh? You must get out even more than you used to, right?'

'I'm not sure,' Bunting said.

'I never could get a straight answer out of you, Bobby,' his father said. 'Sometimes I wonder if you know how to give one. I been calling you for two days, and all you say is *I'm not sure.* Anyhow, keep in touch.'

Bunting promised to keep in touch, and his father cleared his throat and hung up without actually saying goodbye.

Bunting sat staring at the telephone receiver for a long time, barely conscious of what he was doing, not thinking and not aware of not thinking. He could not remember what he had been doing before the telephone rang: he had been puffed up with self-importance, it seemed to him now, as inflated as a bullfrog. He pictured his mother trotting down the basement stairs towards the washing machine with a single dishtowel in her hands. Her bruised face was knotted with worry, and a thick white pad had been clamped to her knee with a tightly rolled Ace bandage. She looked as driven as if she held a dying baby. He saw her drop the cloth into the washing machine, pour in a cup of Oxydol, close the lid and punch the starting button. Then what did she do? Nod and walk away, satisfied that one tiny scrap of the universe had been nailed into place? Go upstairs and wander around in search of another dishcloth, a single sock, a handkerchief?

Did she fall down inside the house?

He set the receiver back in its cradle and stood up. Before he knew he intended to go there, he was across the room and in front of the rows of bottles. He spread his arms and leaned forward. Rubber nipples pressed against his forehead, his closed eyes, cheeks, shoulders, and chest. He turned his face sideways, spread his arms, and moved in tighter. It was something like lying on a fakir's bed of nails, he thought. It was pretty good. It wasn't bad at all. He liked it. The nipples were harder than he had expected, but not painfully hard. Not a single bottle moved – the epoxy clamped them to the wall. Nothing would get those bottles off the wall, short of a blowtorch or a cold chisel. Bunting was slightly in awe of what he had done. He sighed. *She forgets. That's it, pure and simple.* Tough little nipples pressed lightly against the palms of his hands. He began to feel better. His father's voice and the image of his mother darting downstairs to drop a single cloth into the washing machine receded to a safe distance. He straightened up and passed his palms over the rows of nipples, which flattened against his skin and then bounced back into position. Tomorrow he would have to go to the bank and withdraw more money. Another hundred to a hundred and fifty would finish the wall.

He couldn't go to Battle Creek, anyhow: it would be a waste of time. His mother already had an appointment with a doctor.

He backed away from the wall. The image of the fakir's bed resurfaced in his mind: nails, blood leaking from punctured skin. He shook it off by taking a long drink from the Ama. The vodka burned all the way down his throat. Bunting realized that he was slightly drunk.

He could do no more tonight; his arms and shoulders still ached from gluing the bottles onto the wall; he would tip just a little more vodka into the Ama – another inch, for an hour's reading – and get into bed. He had to go to work tomorrow.

As he folded and hung up the day's clothes, Bunting looked over his row of books, wondering if the *Buffalo Hunter* experience would ever be given to him again, afraid that reading might just be reading again.

On the other hand, he was also afraid that it might not be. Did he want to jump down the rabbit hole every time he opened a book?

Bunting had been groping towards the clothes rail with the suit hanger in his hand while looking down at his row of books, and finally he leaned into his closet and put the hook on the rail so that he could really inspect the books. There were thirty or forty, all of them paperbacks and all at least five or six years old. Some of them dated to his first days in New York. All the paperbacks had curling covers, cracked spines, and pulpy pages that looked as if they had been dunked in a bathtub. Slightly more than half of these were westerns, many of these taken from Battle Creek. Most of the others were mysteries. He finally selected one of these, *The Lady in the Lake*, by Raymond Chandler.

It would be a relatively safe book to see from the inside – it wasn't one of the books where Philip Marlowe got beaten up, shot full of drugs, or locked away in a mental hospital. As importantly, he had read it last year and remembered it fairly well. He would be able to see if any important details changed once he got inside the book.

Bunting carefully brushed his teeth and washed his face. He peered through his blinds and looked out at the dingy brownstones, wondering if any of the people who lived behind those lighted windows had ever felt anything like his fearful and impatient expectancy.

Bunting checked the level in his bottle and turned off his other lamp. Then he switched it on again and ducked into his closet to find an alarm clock he had brought with him from Michigan but never needed. Bunting extracted the clock from a bag behind his shoes, set it to the proper time, shoved various things off the bedside chair to make room for it, and wound it up. After he had set the alarm for seven-thirty, he switched off the light near the sink. Now the only light burning in his room was the reading lamp at the head of the bed. Bunting turned down his covers with an almost formal sense of ceremony and got into bed. He folded his pillow in half and wedged it behind his head. He licked his lips and opened *The Lady in the Lake* to the first chapter. Blood pounded in his temples, his fingertips, and at the back of his head. The first sentence swam up at him, and he was gone.

SIX

Nearly everything was different – the cloudy air, the loud ringing sounds, the sense of a wide heartbreak, his taller, more detached self – and one of the greatest differences was that this time he had a vast historical memory, comprehensive and investigatory: he knew that the city around him was changing, that its air was far more poisoned than the beautiful clean air of the meadow where the buffalo grazed but much cleaner than the air of New York City forty-five years hence. Some aspect of himself was familiar with a future in which violence, ignorance, and greed had finally won the battle. He was walking through downtown Los Angeles, and men were tearing up a rubber sidewalk at Sixth and Olive. The world beat in on him, its sharp particulars urged him towards knowledge, and as he entered a building and was instantly in a seventh-floor office his eye both acknowledged and deflected that knowledge by assessing the constant stream of details – double plate-glass doors bound in platinum, Chinese rugs, a glass display case with tiers of creams and soaps and perfumes in fancy boxes. A man named Kingsley wanted him to find his mother. Kingsley was a troubled man of sixty-two, elegant in a chalk-striped, grey flannel suit, and he moved round his office a lot as he talked. His mother and his stepfather had been in their cabin up in the mountains at Puma Point for most of the summer, and then had suddenly stopped communicating.

'Do you think they left the cabin?' Bunting asked.

Kingsley nodded.

'What have you done about it?'

'Nothing. Not a thing. I haven't even been up there.' Kingsley waited for Bunting to ask why, and Bunting could smell the man's anger and impatience. He was like a cocked and loaded gun.

'Why?' he asked.

Kingsley opened a desk drawer and took out a telegraph form. He passed it over, and Bunting unfolded it under Kingsley's smouldering gaze. The wire had been sent to Derace Kingsley at a Beverly Hills address and said: I AM DIVORCING CHRIS STOP MUST GET AWAY FROM HIM AND THIS AWFUL LIFE STOP   PROBABLY   FOR   GOOD   STOP   GOOD LUCK   MOTHER.

When Bunting looked up, Kingsley was handing him an eight-by-ten glossy photograph of a couple in bathing suits sitting on a beach beneath a sun umbrella. The woman was a slim blonde in her sixties, smiling and still attractive. She looked like a good-looking widow on a cruise. The man was a handsome, brainless animal with a dark tan, sleek black hair, and strong shoulders and legs.

'My mother,' Kingsley said. 'Crystal. And Chris Lavery. Former playmate. He's my stepfather.'

'Playmate?' Bunting asked.

'To a lot of rich women. My mother was just the one who married him. He's a no-good son of a bitch, and there's never been any love lost between us.'

Bunting asked if Lavery was at the cabin.

'He wouldn't stay a minute if my mother went away. There isn't even a telephone. He and my mother have a house in Bay City. Let me give you the address.' He scribbled *Derace Kingsley, Gillerlain Company* on a stiff sheet of stationery from the top of his desk, folded the card in half, and handed it to Bunting like a state secret.

'Were you surprised that your mother wanted out of the marriage?'

Kingsley considered the question while he took a panatella out of a copper and mahogany box and beheaded it with a silver guillotine. He took his time about lighting it. 'I was surprised when she wanted *in*, but I wasn't surprised when she wanted to dump him. My mother has her own money, a lot of it, from her family's oil leases, and she always did as she pleased. I never thought her marriage to Chris Lavery would last. But I got that wire three weeks ago, and I thought I'd hear from her long before now. Two days ago a hotel in San Bernardino called me to say that my mother's Packard Clipper was unclaimed in their garage. It's been there for better than two weeks. I figured she was out of the state, and sent them a cheque to hold the car. Yesterday I ran into Chris Lavery in front of the Athletic Club and he acted as if nothing had happened. When I confronted him with what I knew, he denied everything and said that, as far as he knew, she was enjoying herself up at the cabin.'

'So that's where she is,' Bunting said.

'That bastard would lie just for the fun of it. But there's another angle here. My mother has had trouble with the police occasionally.'

He looked genuinely uncomfortable now, and Bunting helped him out. 'The police?'

'She helps herself to things from stores. Especially when she's had too many martinis at lunch. We've had some pretty nasty scenes in managers' offices. So far nobody's filed charges, but if something happened in a strange city where nobody knew her . . .' He lifted his hands and let them fall back onto the desk.

'Wouldn't she call you, if she got into trouble?'

'She might call Chris first,' Kingsley admitted. 'Or she might be too embarrassed to call anybody.'

'Well, I think we can almost throw the shoplifting angle out of this,' Bunting said. 'If she'd left her husband and gotten into trouble, the police would be likely to get in touch with you.'

Kingsley poured himself a drink to help himself with his worrying. 'You're making me feel better.'

'But a lot of other things could have happened. Maybe she ran away with some other man. Maybe she had a sudden loss of memory – maybe she fell down and hurt herself somewhere, and she can't remember her name or where she lives. Maybe she got into some jam we haven't thought of. Maybe she met foul play.'

'Good God, don't say that,' Kingsley said.

'You've got to consider it,' Bunting told him. 'All of it. You never know what's going to happen to a woman your mother's age. Plenty of them go off the rails, believe me — I've seen it again and again. They start washing dishcloths in the middle of the night. They fall down in parking lots and mess up their faces. They forget their own names.'

Kingsley stared at him, horrified. He took another slug of his drink.

'I get a hundred dollars a day, and a hundred right now,' Bunting said.

Bunting drove to an address in Bay City that Kingsley's secretary gave him. The house where Kingsley's mother had lived with Chris Lavery lay on the edge of the V forming the inner end of a deep canyon. It was built downward, and the front door was slightly below street level. Patio furniture stood on the roof. The bedrooms were in the basement, and lowest of all, like the corner pocket on a pool table, was the garage. Korean moss edged the flat stones of the front walk. An iron knocker hung on the narrow door below a metal grille.

Bunting pounded the knocker against the door. When nothing happened, he pushed the bell. Then he hammered on the knocker again. No one came to the door. He walked around the side of the house and lifted the garage door to eyelevel. A car with white sidewalls was inside the garage. He went back to the front door.

Bunting pushed the bell and banged on the door, thinking that Chris Lavery might have been sleeping off a hangover. When there was still no response, Bunting twisted back and forth in front of the door, uncertain of his next step. He would have to drive up to the lake, that was certain, but now he felt that he would drive all day and get nowhere – at Puma Point there would be another empty building, and he would stand at another door, knocking and ringing, and nobody would ever let him in. He would stand outside in the dark, banging on a locked door.

How had he become a detective? What had made him do it? *That* was the mystery, it seemed to him, not the whereabouts of some rich idiot who had married a playboy. He touched the little pink Ama bottle in his shoulder holster, for comfort.

Bunting stepped off the porch and walked back around the side of the house to the garage. He swung up the door, went inside, and pulled the door down behind him. The car with whitewalls was a big roadster convertible that would gulp down gasoline like it was vodka and looked as if it could hit a hundred and twenty on the highway. Bunting realized that if he had the key he could turn on the ignition, lean back in the seat, stick his good old bottle in his mouth, and take the long, long ride. He could make the long goodbye, the one you never came back from.

But he did not have the key to the roadster and, even if he did, he had a business card with a tommy-gun in the corner; he had to detect. At the back of the garage was a plywood door leading into the house. The door was locked with something the builder had bought at a five and dime, and Bunting kicked at the door until it broke open. Wooden splinters and tinny pieces of metal sprayed into the hallway.

Bunting stepped inside. His heart was beating fast,

and he thought with sudden clarity: *this is why I'm a detective*. It was not just the excitement, it was the sense of imminent discovery. The whole house lay above him like a beating heart, and he was in a passage *inside* that heart.

The hushed warm smell of late morning in a closed house came to him, along with the odour of Vat 69. Bunting began moving down the hall. He glanced into a guest bedroom with drawn blinds. At the end of the hall he stepped into an elaborately furnished bedroom where a crystal greyhound stood on a smeary mirror-top table. Two pillows lay side by side on the unmade bed, and a pink towel with lipstick smears hung over the side of the wastebasket. Red lipstick smears lay like slashes across one of the pillows. Some foul, emphatic perfume hung in the air.

Bunting turned to the bathroom door and put his hand on the knob.

No, he did not want to look in the bathroom. He suddenly realized that he wanted to be anywhere at all – a Sumatran jungle, a polar icecap – rather than where he was. The lipstick stain on the towel dripped steadily onto the carpet, turning it into a squashy red mush. He looked at the bed, and saw that the second pillow glistened with red that had leaked onto the sheet.

No, he said inside himself, please no, not again. One of them is in there, or both of them are in there, and it'll look like a butcher shop . . . You don't want, you can't, it's too much . . .

He turned the knob and opened the door. His eyes were nearly closed. Drools and sprays of blood covered the floor. A fine spattering of blood misted the shower curtain.

It's only Bunting finding another body. Body-a-day Bunting, they call him.

He walked through the blood and pushed back the shower curtain.

The tub was empty – only a thick layer of blood lay on the bottom of the tub, slowly oozing down the drain.

The hideous clanging of a bell came to him through the bathroom windows. A white space in the air filled with the sound of the bell. Bunting clapped his hands to his ears. His neck hurt, and his back ached. He turned to flee the bathroom, but the bathroom had disappeared into empty white space. His legs could not move. Pain encased his body like St Elmo's fire, and he groaned aloud and closed his eyes and opened them to the unbearable enclosure of his room and the shrieking clock.

For a moment he knew that the walls of this room were splashed with someone's blood, and he dropped the book and scuttled off the bed, gasping with pain and terror. His legs folded away, and he fell full-length on the floor. His legs cried out, his entire body cried out. He could not move. He began writhing towards the door, moaning, and stopped only when he realized that he was back in his room. He lay on his carpet, panting, until the blood had returned to his legs enough for him to stand and go into the bathroom. He had a difficult moment when he had to pull back the shower curtain, but none of the numerous stains on the porcelain and the wall tiles were red, and hot water soon brought him back into his daily life.

SEVEN

The next significant event in Bunting's life followed the strange experience just described as if it had been rooted in or inspired by it, and began shortly after he left his building to go to work. He had a slight headache, and his hands trembled: it had seemed to him while tying his necktie that his face had subtly altered in a way that the discoloured bags under his eyes did not entirely account for. His cheeks looked sunken, and his skin was an almost unnatural white. He supposed that he had not slept at all. He looked as if he were still staring at the bloody bathtub.

A layer of skin had been peeled away from him. All the colours and noises on the street seemed brighter and louder; everything seemed several notches more alive – the cars streaming down the avenue, the men and women rushing along the sidewalk, the ragged bums holding their paper bags. Even the little pieces of grit and paper whirled by the wind seemed like messages. Although he was never truly conscious of this, Bunting usually tried to take in as little as possible on his way to work. He thought of himself as in a transparent bubble which protected him from unnecessary pain and distraction. That was how you lived in New York City – you moved around inside an envelope of tough, resistant varnish. A crew of men in orange hard hats and jackets were taking up the concrete sidewalk down the block from his building, and the sound of a jackhammer pounded in Bunting's ears. For a second the world wobbled around him, and he was back in the Los Angeles of forty years before, on his way to see a man named Derace Kingsley. He shuddered, then remembered: in the first paragraph of *The Lady in the Lake* he had seen workmen taking up a rubber sidewalk.

For a second the clouds parted, and bright sunlight fell upon Bunting and everything before him. The air went dark.

The sound of the jackhammers abruptly ceased, and the workmen behind Bunting began shouting indistinct, urgent words. They had found something under the sidewalk and, because Bunting had to get away from what they had found, he took one quick step towards his bus stop. Then a wall of water smashed against his head – without any warning a thick, drenching rainfall had soaked his clothes, his hair, and everything and everybody about him. The air turned black in an instant, and a loud roll of thunder, followed immediately by a crack of lightning that illuminated the frozen street, obliterated the shouts of the workmen. The lightning turned the world white for a brief electric moment; Bunting could not move. His suit was a wet rag, and his hair streamed down the sides of his face. The sudden rainfall and the lightning that illuminated the water bouncing crazily off the roof of the bus shelter threw Bunting right out of his frame. What had been promised for days had finally arrived. His eyes had been washed clean of habit, and he *saw*.

People thrust past him to get into doorways and beneath the roof of the bus shelter, but he neither could, nor wanted to, move. It was as if all of life had gloriously opened itself before him. If he could have moved, he would have fallen to his knees with thanks. For long, long seconds after the lightning faded, everything blazed and burned with life. Being streamed from every particle of the world – wood, metal, glass or flesh. Cars, fire hydrants, the concrete and crushed stones of the road, each individual raindrop: all contained the same living substance that Bunting himself contained – and this was what was significant about himself and them. If Bunting had been religious, he would have felt that he had been given a direct, unmediated vision of God; since he was not, his experience was of the sacredness of the world itself.

All of this took place in a few seconds, but those seconds were out of time altogether. When the experience began to fade, and Bunting began to slip out of eternity back into time, he wiped the mixture of rain and tears from his face and started to move towards the bus shelter. It seemed that he too had overflowed. He moved beneath the roof of the bus shelter. Several people were looking at him oddly. He wondered what his face looked like – it seemed to him that he might be glowing. The bus appeared in the rainy darkness up the avenue, lurching and rolling through the potholes like an ocean liner. What had happened to him – what he was already beginning to think of as his 'experience' – was similar, he realized, to what he felt when he tumbled into *The Buffalo Hunter*.

He sighed loudly and wiped his eyes. The people nearest him moved away.

EIGHT

He arrived at DataComCorp soaked and irritable, not knowing why. He wanted to push people who got in his way, to yell at anyone who slowed him down. He blamed this feeling on having to arrive at the office in wet clothes. The truth was that discomfort caused only the smallest part of his anger. Bunting felt as if he had been forced into an enclosure too small for him: he had left a mansion and returned to a hovel. The glimpse of the mansion made the hovel unendurable.

He came stamping out of the elevator and scowled at the receptionist. As soon as he was inside his cubicle, he ripped off his suit jacket and threw it at a chair. He yanked down his tie and rubbed his neck and forehead with his damp handkerchief. In a dull, ignorant fury he banged his fist against his computer's 'on' switch and began punching in data. If Bunting had been in a better mood, his natural caution would have protected him from the mistake he made after Frank Herko appeared in his cubicle. As it was, he didn't have a chance – foolhardy anger spoke for him.

'The Great Lover returns at last,' Herko said.

'Leave me alone,' said Bunting.

'Bunting the Infallible shows up still drunk after partying with his lovely bimbo, misses work for two days, doesn't answer his phone, shows up half-drowned – '

'Get out, Frank,' Bunting said.

' – and madder than a stuck bull, probably suffering from flu if not your actual pneumonia – '

Bunting sneezed.

' – and expects the only person who really understands him to shut up and leave him alone. God, you're *soaked*. Don't you have any sense? Hold on, I'll be right back.'

Bunting growled. Herko slipped out of the cubicle, and a minute later returned with both hands full of wadded, brown paper napkins from the dispenser in the men's room. 'Dry yourself off, will you?'

Bunting snarled and swabbed his face with some of the napkins. He scrubbed napkins in his hair, unbuttoned his shirt and rubbed napkins over his damp chest.

'So what were you doing?' Herko asked. 'Coming down with double pneumonia?'

Herko was a hysterical fool. Also, he thought he owned Bunting. Bunting did not feel ownable. 'Thanks for the napkins,' he said. 'Now get out of here.'

Herko threw up his hands. 'I just wanted to tell you that I set up your date with Marty for tomorrow night. I suppose that's still all right, or do you want to kill me for that, too?'

Around Bunting the world went white. His blood stopped moving in his veins. 'You set up my date?'

'Well, Marty was eager to meet you. Eight o'clock, at the bar at One Fifth Avenue. Then you're in the Village, you can go to eat at a million places right around there.' Herko leaned forward to peer at Bunting's face. 'What's the matter? You sick again? Maybe you should go home.'

Bunting whirled to face his computer. 'I'm okay. Will you get the hell out of here?'

'Jesus,' Herko said. 'How about some thanks?'

'Don't do me any more favours, okay?' Bunting did not take his eyes from his screen, and Herko retreated.

Late in the afternoon, Bunting put his head around the door of his friend's cubicle. Herko glanced up, frowning. 'I'm sorry,' Bunting said. 'I was in a bad mood this morning. I know I was rude, and I want to apologize.'

'Okay,' Herko said. 'That's all right.' He was still a little stiff and wounded. 'It's okay about the date, right? Tomorrow night?'

'Well,' Bunting said, and saw Herko's face tighten. 'No, it's fine. Sure. That's great. Thanks.'

'You'll love the bar,' Herko said. 'And then you're right down there in the Village. Million restaurants, all around you.'

Bunting had never been in Greenwich Village, and knew only of the restaurants, many of them invented, to which he had taken Veronica. Then something else occurred to him.

'You like Raymond Chandler, don't you?' he asked, having remembered an earlier conversation.

'Ray is my man, my *main* man.'

'Do you remember that part in *The Lady in the Lake* where Marlowe first goes to Chris Lavery's house?'

Herko nodded, instantly in a better mood.

'What does he find?'

'He finds Chris Lavery.'

'Alive?'

'Well, how else could he talk to him?'

'He doesn't find a lot of blood splashed all over the bathroom, does he?'

'What's happened to you?' Herko asked. 'You starting to put the great literature of our time through a mental shredder, or what?'

'Or what,' Bunting said, though it seemed that he had certainly shuffled, if not actually shredded, the pages he had read. He backed out of the cubicle and disappeared into his own.

Herko sat quiet with surprise for a moment, then yelled, 'Long fangs! Long, long fangs! Bunting's gone a-hunting!' He howled like a wolf.

Some of the ladies giggled, and one of them said that he shouldn't tease. Herko started laughing big, chesty barrelhouse laughs.

Bunting sat behind his computer, trying to force himself to concentrate on his work. Herko gasped for breath, then went on rolling out laughter. The bubble of noise about him suddenly evoked the image of the workmen who had exclaimed, an instant before the sudden storm, over the hole they had made in the sidewalk: they had found a dead man in that hole.

Bunting knew this with a sudden and absolute certainty. The men working on the sidewalk had looked down into that hole and seen a rotting corpse, or a heap of bones and a skull in a dusty suit, or a body in some stage between these two. Bunting saw the open mouth, the matted hair, the staring eyes and the writhing maggots. He tried to wrench himself back into the present, where his own living body sat in a damp shirt before a computer terminal filled with what for the moment looked alarmingly like gibberish. DATATRAX 30 CARTONS MONMOUTH NJ BLUE CODE RED CODE.

Jesus stepped past the rock at the mouth of the tomb, spread his arms wide, and sailed off in his dusty white robe into a flawless blue sky.

That's my body, he thought. *My* body.

Something the size of a walnut rattled in his stomach, grew to the size of an apple, then developed a point that lengthened into a needle. Bunting held his hands to his stomach and rushed out of the Data Room into the corridor. He banged through the men's room door and entered a toilet stall not much smaller than his cubicle. He pressed his necktie to his chest to avoid splattering it, bent over, and vomited.

In the middle of the afternoon, Bunting looked up from his screen and saw the flash of a green dress moving past the door of his cubicle. The colour was a dark, flat green that both stood out from the office's pale walls and harmonized with them, and for an instant it seemed to float towards Bunting, who had been daydreaming about nothing in particular. The flat green jumped into sharp focus; then it was gone. The air the woman had filled hummed with her absence, and suddenly all the world Bunting could see promised to overflow with sacred and eternal being, as it had that morning. Bunting braced himself and fought the rising sense of expectancy – he did not know why, but he had to resist. The world instantly lost the feeling of trembling anticipation which had filled it a moment before: every detail fell back into itself. Jesus went back into his cave and rolled the rock back across the entrance. The workmen standing in the rain looked down into an empty hole. Bunting was still alive, or still dead. He had been saved. The tree had fallen in the deep forest and no one had heard it, so it still stood.

That night Bunting again set his alarm and went back into *The Lady in the Lake*. He was driving into the mountains, and once he got to a place called Bubbling Springs the air grew cool. Canoes and rowing boats went back and forth on the Puma Lake, and speedboats filled with squealing girls zipped past, leaving wide, foamy wakes. Bunting drove through meadows dotted with white irises and purple lupins. He turned off at a sign for Little Fawn Lake and crawled past granite rocks. He drove past a waterfall and through a maze of black oak trees. Now everything about him sang with meaning, and he was alive within this meaning, as alive as he was supposed to be, equal to the significance of every detail within the landscape. A woodpecker peered around a tree trunk, an oval lake curled at the bottom of a valley, a small bark-covered cabin stood against a stand of oaks. This information came towards and into him in a steady stream, every glowing feather and shining outcrop of rock and inch of wood overflowing with its portion of being, and Bunting, the eye around which this speaking world cohered, moved through this stream of information undeflected and undisturbed.

He got out of his car and pounded on the cabin door, and a man named Bill Chess came limping into view. Bunting gave Bill Chess a drink from a pint of rye in his pocket and they sat on a flat rock and talked. Bill Chess's wife had left him and his mother had died. He was lonely in the mountains. He didn't know anything about Derace Kingsley's mother. Eventually, they went up the heavy wooden steps to Kingsley's cabin and Chess unlocked the door and they went inside to the hushed warmth. Bunting's heart was breaking. Everything he saw looked like a postcard from a world without grief. The floors were plain and the beds were neat. Bill Chess sat down on one of the cream-coloured bedspreads while Bunting opened the door to the bathroom. The air was hot, and the stink of blood stopped him as soon as he stepped inside. Bunting moved to the shower curtain, knowing that what was left of Crystal Kingsley's body lay inside the tub. He held his breath and grasped the curtain. When he pushed it aside, Bill Chess cried out behind him. 'Muriel! Sweet Christ, it's Muriel!' But there was no body in the tub, only a bloodstain hardening as it oozed towards the drain.

NINE

At seven thirty on Friday night, Bunting sat at a table facing the entrance of One Fifth Avenue, alternately checking his watch and looking at the door. He had arrived fifteen minutes before, dressed in one of his best suits, showered, freshly shaved, black wingtips and teeth brushed, his mouth tingling with Bianca. To get to the bar, which was already crowded, you had to walk past the tables, and Bunting planned to get a good look at this woman before she saw him. After that he would know what to do. The waitress came round, and he ordered another vodka martini. Bunting thought he felt comfortable. His heart was beating fast, and his hands were sweaty, but that was okay, Bunting thought – after all, this was his first date, his first *real* date, since he had broken up with Veronica. In another sense, one he did not wish to consider, this was his first date in twenty years. Every couple of minutes, he went to the men's room and splashed water on his face. He fluffed up his hair and buffed his shoes with paper towels. Then he went back to his table and sipped his drink and watched the door.

He wished that he had thought of secreting an Ama in one of his pockets. Even a loose nipple would work: he could tuck it into his mouth whenever he felt anxious. Or just keep it in his pocket.

Bunting shot his cuffs, ran a hand over his hair, looked at his watch. He leaned on his elbows and stared at the people in the bar. Most of them were younger than himself, and all of them were talking and laughing. He checked the door again. A young woman with black hair and round glasses had just entered, but it was still only twenty minutes to eight – far too early for Marty. He pulled out his handkerchief and wiped his forehead, wondering if he ought to go back into the bathroom and splash more water on his face. He felt a little bit hot. Still okay, but just a tad hot. He advised himself to think about all those times he'd gone to fancy places with Veronica, and shoved his hands in his pockets and tried to remember the exact feelings of walking into Quaglino's beside his tall, executive girlfriend . . .

'Bob? Bob Bunting?' someone said in his ear, and he jumped forward as if he had been jabbed with a fork. His chest struck the table, and his glass wobbled. He stabbed out a hand to grasp the drink and knocked it over. Clear liquid spilled out and stained the tablecloth dark. Two large olives rolled across the table, and one of them fell to the floor. Bunting uttered a short, mortifying shriek. The woman who had spoken to him was laughing. She placed a hand on his arm. He whirled around on his chair, bumping his elbow on the table's edge, and found the black-haired woman who had just entered the restaurant staring down at him with quizzical alarm.

'After all that, I hope you *are* Bob Bunting,' she said.

Bunting nodded. 'I hope I am, too,' he said. 'I don't seem to be too sure, do I? But who are you? Do we know each other?'

'I'm Marty,' she said. 'Weren't you waiting for me?'

'Oh,' he said, understanding everything at last. She was a short, round-faced young woman with a restless, energetic quality that made Bunting instantly feel tired. Her eyes were very blue and her lipstick was very red. At the moment she seemed to be inwardly laughing at him. 'Excuse me, my goodness,' he said, 'yes, of course, how nice to meet you.' He got to his feet and held out his hand.

She took it, not bothering to conceal her amusement. 'You been here long?' She had a strong New York accent.

'A little while,' he confessed.

'You wanted to check me out, didn't you?'

'Well, no. Not really.' He thought with longing of his room, his bed, his wall of bottles, and *The Lady in the Lake*. 'How did you know who I was?'

'Frank described you, how else? He said you'd be dressed like a lawyer and that you looked a little shy. Do you want to have another drink here, now that I made you spill that one? I'll have one, too.'

He took her coat to the cloakroom, and when he returned he found a fresh martini at his place, a glass of white wine in front of Marty, and a clean tablecloth on the table. She was smiling at him. He could not decide if she was unusually pretty or just disconcerting.

'You did get here early to check me out, didn't you?' she asked. 'If you didn't like the way I looked, you could duck out when I went to the bar.'

'I'd never do that.'

'Why not? I would. Why do you think I got here so early? I wanted to check you out. Blind dates make me feel funny. Anyhow, I knew who you were right away, and you didn't look so bad. I was afraid you might be real stuffy, from what Frank said about you, but I knew that anybody as nervous as you couldn't really be stuffy.'

'I'm not nervous,' Bunting said.

'Then why did you go off like a bomb when I said your name?'

'You startled me.'

'Well, I couldn't have startled you if you weren't nervous. It's okay. You never saw me before, either. So tell me the truth – if you saw me walk in the door, and if I didn't notice you, would you have cut out? Or would you have gone through with it?'

She raised her glass and sipped. Her eyes were so blue that the colour had leaked into the whites, spreading a faint blue nimbus around the irises. He saw for the first time that she was wearing a black dress that fit her tightly, and that her eyebrows were firm black lines. She seemed exotic, almost mysterious, despite her forthright manner. She was, he realized, startlingly good-looking. Then he suddenly saw her naked, a vision of smooth white skin and large soft breasts.

'Oh,' he said, 'I would have gone through with it, of course.'

'Why are you blushing? Your whole face just turned red.'

He shrugged in an agony of embarrassment. He was certain that she knew what he had been thinking. He gulped at his drink.

'You're not exactly what I expected, Bob,' she said in a very dry voice.

'Well, you're not quite what I expected, either,' was all he could think to say. Unable to look at her, he was sitting straight upright on his chair and facing the happy crowd in the bar. How were those men able to be so casual? How did they think of things to say?

'How well do you know Frank and Lindy?' she asked.

'I work with Frank.' He glanced over at her, then

looked back at the happy, untroubled people in the bar. 'We're in the same office.'

'That's all? You don't see him after work?'

He shook his head.

'You made a big impression on Frank,' she said. 'He seems to think . . . Bob, would you mind looking at me, Bob? When I'm talking to you?'

Bunting cleared his throat and turned to face her. 'Sorry.'

'Is anything wrong? Anything I should know about? Do I look just like the person you hated most in the fourth grade?'

'No, I like the way you look,' Bunting said.

'Frank acted like you were this real swinger. This wild man. "Long fangs, Marty," he says to me, "this guy has got long, long fangs." You know how Frank talks. This means he likes you. So I figured if Frank Herko liked you so much, how bad could you be? Because Frank Herko acts like a real asshole, but underneath he's a real sweetheart.' She sipped her wine and continued looking at him coolly. 'So I got all dolled up and took the train into Manhattan, figuring at least I might get some fun out of the evening, go to some clubs, maybe a good restaurant, meet this wild man. If I have to fight him off when it's all over, well, I can do that. But it's not like that, is it? You don't know any clubs – you don't really go out much, do you, Bobby?'

Bunting stood up and took a twenty out of his wallet. He was blushing so hard his ears felt twice their normal size. He put the money down on the table and said, 'I'm sorry, I didn't mean to waste your time.'

Marty grinned. 'Hold on, will you?' She reached across the table and grabbed his wrist. 'Don't act that way. I'm just saying you're different from what I expected. Sit down. Please. Don't be so . . .'

Bunting sat down, and she let go of his wrist. He could still feel her fingers around him. The sensation made him feel slightly dizzy. He was looking at her pale, clever, pretty face.

'So *scared*,' she said. 'There's no reason for that. Let's just sit here and talk. In a while, we can go out and eat somewhere. Or we could even eat here. Okay?'

'Sure,' he said, recovering. 'We can just sit here and talk.'

'So say something,' Marty said. She frowned. 'Do you always sweat this much? Or is it just me?'

He wiped his forehead. 'I, uh, had a kind of funny week. Things have been affecting me in an odd way. I broke up with somebody a little while ago.'

'Frank told me. Me, too. That's why he thought we ought to meet each other. But I think you ought to think of another topic.'

'I don't have any topics,' Bunting said.

'Guys all talk about sports. I like sports. Honest, I really do. I'm a Yankee fan from way back. And I like Islanders' games. But basketball is my favourite sport. Who do you like? Larry Bird, I bet – you look like a Larry Bird type. Guys who like Larry Bird never like Michael Jordan, I don't know why.'

'Michael who?' Bunting said.

'Okay, football. Phil Simms. The Jets. The good old Giants. Lawrence Tayler.'

'I hate football.'

'Okay, what about music? What kind of music do you like? You ever hear house music?'

Bunting imagined a house like a child's drawing, two windows at either side of a simple door, dancing to notes spilling from the chimney attached to its pointed roof.

Marty tilted her head and smiled at him. 'On second thoughts, I bet you like classical music. You sit around in your place and listen to symphonies and stuff like that. You make yourself a little martini and then you put on a little Beethoven, right? And then you're right in the groove. I like classical music sometimes too, I think it's good.'

'People are too interested in sports and music,' Bunting said. 'All they talk about is some game they saw on television, or some series, or some record. It's like there isn't anything else.'

'You forgot one,' she said. 'You forgot money.'

'That's right – they pay too much attention to money.'

'So what should they pay attention to?'

'Well . . .' He looked up, for the moment wholly distracted from his embarrassment and discomfort. It seemed to him that there existed an exact answer to this question, and that he knew it. 'Well, more important things.' He raised his hands, as if he could catch the answer while it flew past him.

'More important than sports, television, and music. Not to mention money.'

'Yes. None of that is important at all – it's worthless, when you come right down to it.'

'So what is important?' She looked at him with her eyes narrowed behind her big glasses. 'I'm dying to hear about it.'

'Um, what's inside us.'

'What's *inside* us? What does that mean?'

Bunting made another large, vague gesture with his hands. 'I sort of think God is inside us.' This sentence came out of his mouth by itself, and it startled him as much as it did Marty. 'Something like God is inside us. Outside of us, too.' Then he found a way to say it. 'God is what lets us see.'

'So you're religious.'

'No, the funny thing is, I'm not. I haven't gone to church in twenty-five years.' He flattened his hands against his eyes for a moment, then took them away. His whole face had a naked look, as if he had just taken off a pair of glasses. 'Lct's say you're just walking down the street. Let's say you're not thinking about anything in particular. You're trying to get to work, and you're even a little worried about something – the rent, or the way your boss was acting, or something. You're absolutely, completely, inside the normal world. And then something happens – a car backfires, or a woman with a gorgeous voice starts to sing behind you – and suddenly you see what's really there: that everything, absolutely everything is alive. The whole world is one living thing, and that living thing is just *beating* with life. Every rock, every blade of grass, every speck of dust, every raindrop, even the windshield wipers and the headlights . . . It's like you're floating in space, or no, it's like you're gone, disappeared, like you don't really exist any more in the old way at all because you're the same as everything else, no more alive, no more conscious, *just* as alive, *just* as conscious, everything is overflowing, light streams and pours out of every little detail . . .' Bunting fought down the desire to cry.

'I'll give you one thing, it makes a double play against Los Angeles sound pretty small.'

'The double play would be part of it, too,' he said, understanding that now as well. 'Us sitting here is part of it. We're talking, and that's a big part of it. If churches were about what they're supposed to be about, they'd open their windows and concentrate on us sitting here. Look at that, they'd say, Look at all that beauty and feeling, look at that radiance, that incredible radiance, that's what's holy. But do you know what they say instead?' He hitched his chair closer to her, and took another big gulp of his drink. 'Maybe they really know all this – I think some of them must know it, it must be their secret – but instead, what they say is just the *opposite*. The world is evil and ugly, they say: turn your back on it. You need blood, they say: you need sacrifice. We're back to savages jumping around in front of a fire. Kill that child, kill that goat; the body is sinful and the world is bad. Ignore it long enough and you'll get a reward in heaven. People get old believing in this, they get sick and forgetful; they begin to fade out of the world without ever having seen it.'

Marty was looking at him intently, and her mouth was open. She blinked when he stopped talking. 'I can see why Frank is impressed with you. He can go on like this for hours. You must have a great time at work.'

'We never talk about this at work. I never talked about it with anybody until now.' It came to Bunting that he was sitting at a table with a pretty woman. He was in the world and enjoying himself. He was on a date, talking. It was not a problem. He was like the men in the bar behind him, talking to their dates. He wondered if he could tell Marty about the baby bottles.

'Didn't you talk like this with your old girlfriend?'

Bunting shook his head. 'She was only interested in her career. She would have thought I was crazy.'

'Well, I think you're crazy, too,' Marty said. 'But that's okay. Frank is crazy in another way, and among other, less harmful things, my old boyfriend was crazy about doo-wop music. Johnny Maestro? He worshipped Johnny Maestro. He thought it summed it all up.'

'I suppose it did,' Bunting said. 'But no more than anything else.'

'Did you get a lot of this stuff out of books? Do you read a lot?'

Another flare went off in Bunting's brain, and he took another gulp of his drink, waving his free hand in the air, semaphoring that she hadn't quite understood matters, but that he had plenty to say about her question. 'Books!' he said after he had swallowed. 'You wouldn't believe what I've . . .' He shook his head. She was smiling at him. 'Think about what reading a book is really *like*. A novel, I mean – you're reading a novel. What's happening? You're in another world, right? Somebody made it, somebody selected everything in it, and so suddenly you're not in your apartment any more, you're walking along this mountain road, or you're sitting on top of a horse. You look out and you see things. What you see is partly what the guy put there for you to see, and partly what you make up on the basis of that. Everything means something, because it was all chosen. Everything you see, touch, feel, smell, everything you notice and everything you think, is organized to take you somewhere. Do you see? Everything *glows*! In paintings too, don't you suppose? There's some force pushing away at all the details, making them *bulge*, making them *sing*. Because the act of painting or writing about a leaf or a house or whatever, if the guy does it right, amounts to saying: I saw the amazing overflowing life in this thing, and now you can see it too. So wake up!' He gestured with both arms, like a conductor calling for a great swell of sound.

'Have you ever thought about becoming a teacher?' Marty asked. 'You get all fired up, Bobby, you'd be great in a classroom.'

'I just want to say something.' Bunting held his hands over his heart. 'This is the greatest night of my life. I never really felt like this before. At least, not since I was really small, three or four, or something. I feel wonderful!'

'Well, you're certainly not nervous any more,' Marty said. 'But I still say you're religious.'

'I never heard of any religion that preaches about this, did you? If you hear of one, let me know and I'll sign up. It has to be a church that says: Don't come in here, stay outside in the weather. Wake up and open your eyes. What we do in here, with the crosses and stuff, that's just to remind you of what's *really* sacred.'

'You're something else,' she said, laughing. 'You and Frank Herko are quite the pair. The two of you must get that office all stirred up.'

'Maybe we should.' For a giddy instant, Bunting saw himself and shaggy, overbearing Frank Herko conducting loud debates over the partition. He would speak as he was speaking now, and Frank would respond with delight and abandon, and the two of them would carry on their talks after work, in apartments and restaurants and bars. It was a vision of a normal and joyous life – he would call up Frank Herko at his apartment, and Frank would say: Why don't you come on over? Bring Marty, we'll go out for dinner, have a little fun.

Bunting and Marty were smiling at each other.

'You're sort of like Frank, you know. You like saying outrageous things. You're not at all the way I thought you were when I came in. I mean, I liked you, and I thought you were interesting, but I thought it might be kind of a long evening. You don't mind my saying that now? I really don't want to hurt your feelings, and I shouldn't be, because you seem so different now. I mean, I never heard anybody talk that way before, not even Frank. It might be crazy, but it's fascinating.'

Nobody had ever told Bunting he was fascinating before this, especially not a young woman staring at him with wonderful blue eyes past a fall of pure black hair. He realized, and this was one of the most triumphant moments of his life, that he could very likely bring this amazing young woman back to his apartment.

Then he remembered what his apartment – his room – actually looked like, and what he had done to it.

'Don't start blushing again,' Marty said. 'It's just a compliment. You're an interesting man, and you hardly know it.' She reached across the table and rested her fingers lightly on the back of his hand. 'Why don't we finish these drinks and order some food? It's Friday. We don't have to go anywhere else. This is fine. I'm enjoying myself.'

Marty's light cool fingers felt as heavy as anvils on his skin. A wave of pure guilt made him pull his hand away. She was still smiling at him, but a shadow passed behind her wonderful eyes. 'I have to do something,' he said. 'I shouldn't have let myself forget,' he said. 'There must be a telephone in this place somewhere.' He began looking wildly around the restaurant.

'You have to call someone?'

'It's urgent, I'm sorry, I can't believe I've been acting

like . . .' Bunting wiped his face and pushed himself away from the table and stood up. He moved clumsily towards the people standing at the bar.

'Like *what*?' she asked, but he was already pushing clumsily through the crowd.

Bunting found a pay telephone outside the men's room. He scooped change out of his pockets and stacked it up. Then he dialled the area code for Battle Creek and his parents' number. He dropped in most of the money. The phone rang and rang, and Bunting fidgeted and cupped his ear against the roar of voices from the bar.

Finally his mother answered.

'Mom! How are you? How'd it go?'

'Yes, who is this?'

'Bobby. It's Bobby.'

'Bobby isn't here,' she said.

'No, *I*'m Bobby, Mom. How are you feeling?'

'Fine. Why wouldn't I feel fine?'

'Did you see the doctor today?'

'Why would I see him?' She sounded sharp, almost angry. 'That was stupid. I don't have to see *him*, listen to your father gripe about the money for the rest of his life.'

'Didn't you have an appointment?'

'Did I?'

'I think so,' he said, feeling his grip on reality loosen.

'Well, what if I did? This isn't Russia. Your father wanted to bully me about the money, that's all it is. I pretended – just sat in my car, that's all I did. He wants to humiliate me, that's what it is; thirty-seven years of humiliation.'

'He didn't go with you?'

'He *couldn't*, there wasn't any *appointment*. And

when I came home, I drove and drove. I kept seeing Kellogg's and the sanatorium, but I never knew where I was and so I had to keep driving – and then, like a miracle, I saw I was turning into our street, and I was so mad at him I swore I'd never ever go to that doctor again.'

'You got lost driving home?' His body felt hot all over.

'Now, you stop talking about that. You sound like *him*. I want to know about that beautiful girlfriend of yours. Tell me about Veronica. Someday you have to bring that girl home, Bobby. We want to meet her.'

'I'm not going out with her any more,' Bunting said. 'I wrote you.'

'You're just like that horrible old crosspatch. Brutal is the word for him. Brutal all his life, brutal, brutal, brutal. Says things just to *confuse* me, and then he gets upset when I want to do a little wash, acts as if I haven't been his punching bag for the past thirty years – '

Bunting heard only heavy breathing for a moment. 'Mom?'

'I don't know who you are, and I wish you'd stop calling,' she said. Bunting heard his father's voice, loud and indistinct, and his mother said, 'Oh, you can leave me alone, too.' Then he heard a startled outcry.

'Hello, what's going on?' Bunting said. All the sounds from Battle Creek had dwindled into a muffled silence overwhelmed by the din from the bar. His father had put his hand over the mouthpiece. This almost certainly meant that he was yelling. 'Someone talk to me!' Bunting shouted, and the yelling in the bar abruptly ceased. Bunting hunched his shoulders and tried to burrow into the hood over the telephone.

'All right, who is this?' his father asked.

'Bob, it's Bobby,' he said.

'You've got some nerve, calling up out of the blue, but you never did care much about what anybody else might be going through, did you? Look, I know you're sensitive and all that, but this isn't the best time to give us bullshit about your little girlfriends. You got your mother all upset, and she was upset enough already, believe me.' He hung up.

Bunting replaced the receiver. He was not at all clear about what was going on in Battle Creek. It had seemed that his mother had forgotten who he was during the course of their worrying conversation. He pushed his way through the men and women at the bar and came out into the restaurant where a young woman with a round face framed in black hair was looking at him curiously from one of the rear tables. It took him a moment to remember her name. He tried to smile at her, but his face would not work right.

'What happened to you?' she asked.

'This isn't . . . um, I can't, ah . . . I'm afraid that I have to go home.'

Her face hardened with a recognition: in an instant, all the sympathy dropped away. 'We were having a nice time, and you go make a phone call, and now everything's off?'

Bunting shrugged and looked at his feet. 'It's a personal thing – I can't really explain it – but, uh – '

'*But, uh,* that's it? What happened to "This is the greatest night of my life"?' She squinted at him. 'Oh, boy. I guess I get it. You ran out, didn't you? You thought you could get through an evening, and then you realized you can't, so you called your guy. And everything you said wasn't really you, it was just – just that crap you take. You're pathetic.'

'I don't know what you're talking about,' Bunting said. His misery seemed to be compounding itself second by second.

'I know guys like you,' she said, her eyes blazing at him. 'One in particular.' She stood up and held out her hand for the cloakroom ticket. 'I know a few inadequate children who can't handle relationships, one in particular, but I thought I was all done hanging around a guy who spent half the night making phone calls and the other half in the bathroom – and I guess I really am done! Because I'm going!' She retrieved her coat and shoved her arms into its sleeves. People at the other tables were staring at them.

'You must have the wrong idea about something,' Bunting said.

'Oh, that's good,' she said. She buttoned her coat. Her small face seemed cold, a cold white stone with a red smear near the bottom. 'Sleep on it, if you do sleep; see if you can come up with something a little snappier.' Marty walked quickly through the tables, passed the lounging headwaiter, and went outside. Frigid air swept into the room as the door closed on the empty darkness.

Bunting paid for the drinks and noticed that the waitress would not look directly at him. An artificial quiet had settled on the bar. Bunting put on his coat and wandered outside, feeling lost and aimless. He had no appetite. He buttoned his coat and watched cars scream towards him down the wide avenue. A short distance to his left, the avenue ended at a massive arch which stood at the entrance to a park. He had no idea where he was. That didn't matter: all places were the same place. Traffic continued to come towards him out of the dark, and he realized that he was in Battle Creek, Michigan – he was back in Battle Creek, downtown in the business district, a long way from home.

TEN

When Jesus flew to heaven he had wounds in his hands and feet. They had torn his flesh and killed him on a cross, there was blood on the ground, and when he rolled the rock away in his dusty robe he left bloody palm prints on the rock.

Jesus said, so you have some fucking doubts, Bobby? Take a look at this. And he opened his clothes and showed Bunting the great open wound in his side. Go on, he said, stick your god-damned hand on it, stick your mitt in there; how about them god-damn apples, Bobby? You get it, you get it now, good buddy? This shit is for real.

And Jesus walked on his bleeding feet through Battle Creek, leaving his bloodstains on the sidewalks unseen by those assholes who had never been wounded by anything more serious than a third martini, and who had never wounded anyone else with a weapon deadlier than an insult. There was a savage grin on his face. He slammed the palm of his hand against the side of one of those little houses, and blood squirted onto the peeling paint. Holy, holy, holy. The palm print was holy, the flecks of paint were holy, the cries of pain and sorrow too.

* * *

Go home, you little asshole, said Jesus. You're never gonna get it, never. But neither do most people, so that part's okay. Go home and read a book. That'll do – it's a piss-poor way to get there, but I guess it's about the best you can do.

Suffer the little children, said Jesus, suffer everybody else too. You think this shit is easy?

Still muttering to himself, Jesus turned off on a side street, his bloody footprints following after him, his thin robe whipping around him in the wind, and Bunting saw the frame houses of working-class Battle Creek all around him. Some were covered with hideous brickface, some with grainy tar-paper that peeled away from the seams around the window frames. Most of these houses had porches where skeletal furniture turned brittle in the cold, and birdbaths and shrines to Mary stood in a few tiny front yards. Before one of these unhappy two-storey houses his parents had posed for the only photograph ever taken of the two of them together, a testament to ignorance, incompatibility, resentment, violence, and disorder. His father scowls out from under the brim of his hat, his mother twitches. Holy, holy, holy. From this chaos, from this riot, the overpowering sacred bounty. He was standing on his old street, Bunting realized, the ultimate example in this dwindled and partial world of blazing real life. Jesus's bloody palm print shone from the ugly wall, even uglier now in winter when the dirty, chipping paint looked like a skin disease. Here was his childhood, which he had not been intended to escape – its smallness and meanness had been supposed to accompany him always.

Bunting stared at the shabby building in which his

childhood had happened, and heard the old screams, the grunts and shrieks of pain and passion, sail through the thin walls. This was the bedrock. His childhood reached forth and touched him with a cold, cold finger. He could not survive it now, he could not even bear to witness a tenth of it. But neither could he live without it.

He turned round and found that he had left Battle Creek and walked all the way from Washington Square to the Upper West Side. Across the street, on the other side of several hundred jostling, honking cars, stood his apartment building. Home again.

ELEVEN

Bunting's weekend was glacial. He had trouble getting out of bed, and remembered to eat only when he realized that the sun had gone down. He felt so tired it was difficult to walk to the bathroom, and fell asleep in front of the television, watching programmes that seemed without point or plot. It was all one great formless story, a story with no internal connections, and its incoherence made it watchable.

On Sunday afternoon Bunting scratched his face and remembered that he had not bathed or shaved since Friday evening. He took off the clothes he had worn since Saturday morning, showered, shaved, dressed in grey slacks and a sports jacket, put on his coat, and went around the corner through brittle wintry air to the diner. The man at the register and the counterman treated him normally. He ordered something from the enormous menu, ate what he ordered without tasting it, and forgot it as soon as he was done. When he walked back out into the cold he realized that he could buy more baby bottles. He had to finish the wall he had begun, and there was another wall he could cover with bottles, if he chose – he was under no real compulsion to do this, he knew, but it would be like finishing an old project. Bunting had always liked to complete his projects. There were several other things he could do with baby bottles, too, once he got started.

He walked to the cash machine and took out three hundred dollars, leaving only five hundred and change in his account. At the drugstore he bought a gross of mixed bottles and another gross of mixed nipples, and asked for them to be delivered. Then he walked again out into the cold and turned towards his building. His entire attitude towards the bottles, even the redecoration project, had changed – he could remember his first, passionate purchases, the haste and embarrassment, the sheer weight of the need. Bunting supposed that this calm, passive state was a dull version of what most people felt all the time. It was probably what they called sanity. Sanity was what took over when you got too tired for anything else.

He stopped off at the liquor store and bought two litres of vodka and a bottle of cognac.

This time when he walked out into the cold, it came to him that Veronica had never existed. Of course he had always known at some level that his executive, Swiss-born mistress was a fantasy, but it seemed to him that he had never quite admitted this to himself. He had lived with his stories for so long he had forgotten that they had begun as an excuse for not going back to Battle Creek.

Battle Creek had come to him instead, two nights ago. *Suffer the little children, suffer everybody, suffer,*

suffer. The furious, complaining Jesus had shown what was real. This dry, reduced world was what was left when he stormed back into his cave to lie down dead again.

Bunting walked past the leavings of *Bango Skank* and *Jeepy* and let himself back into his room. He switched on the television and poured cold vodka into an Ama. Words and phrases of unbelievable ugliness, language murdered by carelessness and indifference, dead bleeding language, came from the television. People all over the nation listened to stuff like this every day and heard nothing wrong in it. Bunting watched the action on the screen for a moment, trying to make at least some kind of primitive sense out of it. A blond man ran down a flight of stairs and punched another man in the face. The second man, taller and stronger than the first, collapsed and fell all the way down the stairs. A car sped down a highway, and lights flashed. Bunting sighed and snapped off the television.

Bunting wandered through the stacks of magazines and newspapers and picked up *The Lady in the Lake*. He wondered if the buzzing of the delivery boy would pull him out of the book and then remembered with a deepening sense of gloom – with something very close to despair – that he probably would not have to be pulled out of the book. He was sane now. Or, if that was an error of terminology, he was in the same relationship to the world that he had been in before everything had changed.

Bunting held his breath and opened the book. He let his eyes drop to the lines of print, which resolutely stayed on the page. He sighed again and sat down on the bed to read until the new baby bottles arrived.

It was another book – the details were the same but

all the essentials had changed. Chris Lavery was apparently still alive, and Muriel Chess had been found in Little Fawn Lake, not in the bathroom of a mountain cabin. Crystal Kingsley was Derace Kingsley's wife, not his mother. All the particulars of weather, appearances, and speech, the entire atmosphere of the book, came to Bunting in a flawed and ordinary way, sentence by sentence. For Bunting, this way of reading was like having lost the ability, briefly and mysteriously gained, of being able to fly. He stumbled along after the sentences, remembering what had been. When the buzzer rang he put the book down with relief, and spent the rest of the night gluing bottles to his walls.

On Monday morning, Frank Herko came into his cubicle even before going into his own. His eyes looked twice their normal size, and his forehead was still red from the cold. Static electricity had given his hair a lively, unbridled, but stiff look, as if it had been starched or deep-fried. 'What the hell went on?' he yelled as soon as he came in. Bunting could feel the attention of everyone else in the data room focusing on his cubicle.

'I don't know what you mean,' he said.

Herko actually bared his teeth at him. His eyes grew even larger. He unzipped his down jacket, ripped it off his body, and startled Bunting by throwing it to the floor. 'Then I'll try to tell you,' he said, speaking so softly he was nearly whispering. 'My girlfriend Lindy has a girlfriend. A person named Marty. This is a person she likes. Particularly likes. You could even go so far as to say that Marty is a person very dear to my friend Lindy, and that what affects Marty affects my girlfriend Lindy. So the little ups and downs of this person Marty's life, who by the way is also kind of dear to me, though not of course to the extent that she is dear to my friend, these ups and downs affect my friend Lindy and therefore, in a roundabout sort of way, also affect me.' Frank leaned forward from the waist and extended his arms. 'So! When Marty has a bad experience with a guy she calls a sleazeball and blames this experience on her friend Lindy Berman and Lindy Berman's friend Frank Herko, then Frank Herko winds up eating *shit*! Is it starting to fall into place, Bobby? Are you starting to get why I asked you what the *hell* happened?' He planted his fists on his hips and glowered, then shook his head and made a gesture with one arm that implored the universe to witness his frustration.

'It just didn't work out,' Bunting said.

'Oh, is that right? You don't suppose you could go into a little more detail on that, could you?'

Bunting tried to remember why his date had ended. 'My mother didn't make her doctor's appointment.'

Herko stared at him pop-eyed. 'Your mother ... Does that make sense to you? You're out with a girl, you're supposed to be having a good time, you say: Gee, Mom didn't get over to the doctor's, I guess I better *split*?'

'I'm sorry,' Bunting said. 'I'm not in a very good mood right now. I don't like it when you yell at me. That makes me feel very uneasy. I wish you'd leave me alone.'

'Boy, you got it,' Herko said. 'You have got it, Bobby, in spades. But there are a few vital bits of information it has become extremely necessary for you to have in your possession, Bobby, and I am going to give them to you.'

He stepped backwards and saw his down jacket on the floor. He raised his eyes as if the jacket had disobediently conjured itself off a hook and thrown itself on the carpet. He leaned over and picked it up, ostentatiously folded it in half, and draped it over one arm. All this reminded Bunting sharply, even sickeningly, of his father. The affectation of delicacy had been a crucial part of his father's arsenal of scorn. Herko had probably reminded him of his father from the beginning; he had just never noticed it.

'One,' Frank said. 'I assumed you were going to act like a man. Funny, huh? I thought you would know that a man remembers his friends, and a man is grateful to his friends. A man does not act like a goddamn loony and bring down trouble on his friends. Two. A man does not run out on a woman. A man does not leave a woman in the middle of a restaurant – he acts like a *man*, damn it, and conducts himself like he knows what he's doing. Three. She thought you were a drug addict; did that get through to you?'

'I didn't leave her alone, she left me alone,' Bunting said.

'She thought you were a junkie!' Herko was yelling again. 'She thought I fixed her up with a fucking cocaine freak, right after she broke up with a guy who put a restaurant, a house, and a car up his nose! That's . . .' Herko raised his arms and lifted his head, trying to find the right word. 'That's . . . *miserable! Disgusting!*'

Bunting stood up and grabbed his coat. His heart wanted to explode. It was impossible to spend another second in his cubicle. Frank Herko had become ten feet tall, and every one of his breaths drained all the air from Bunting's own lungs. His screams bruised

Bunting's ears. Bunting was buttoning his coat before he realized that he was walking out of the cubicle and going home.

'Where the hell do you think you're going?' Herko yelled. 'You can't leave!'

Unable to speak, nearly unable to see through the red mist that surrounded him, Bunting hurried out of the Data Entry Room and fled down the corridor towards the elevator.

As soon as he got out of the building he felt a little better, but the woman who stood next to him on the uptown bus edged visibly away. He could still hear Frank's huge, punishing voice. The world belonged to people like his father and Frank Herko, and people like himself lived in its potholes and corners.

Bunting got out of the bus and realized that he was talking to himself only when he saw himself in a shop window. He blushed, and would have apologized, but no one around him met his eye.

He walked into the lobby of his apartment building and realized that it was not going to be possible for him to go back to work. He could never face Herko again, nor the other people who had overheard Frank's terrible yelling. That was finished. It was all over, like the fantasy of Veronica.

He got into the elevator, thinking that he seemed to be different from what he had thought he was, though it was hard to tell if this was for the better or the worse. In the old days he would have been figuring out where to go to get another job, and now all he wanted to do was to get back into his room, pour himself a drink, and open a book. Of course all of these had also changed, room, drink, and book.

By the time he pushed his key into the lock he

realized that he was no longer so frightened. In the psychic background, the waves of Frank Herko's voice crashed and rumbled on a distant beach. Bunting decided to give himself something like a week to recover from the events of the past few days, then to go out and look for another job. A week was a comfortable time. Monday to Monday. He hung up his coat and poured a drink into a clean Ama. Then he collapsed onto his bed and let his head fall back on the pillow. He groaned with satisfaction.

For a time he merely sucked at his bottle and let his body sink into his wrinkled sheets. In a week, he told himself, he would get out of bed. He'd shave and dress in clean clothes and go outside and nail down a new job. He'd sit in front of another computer terminal and type in a lifetime's worth of mumbo jumbo. Soon there would be another Veronica or Carol, an Englishwoman or a Texan or a Cuban with an MBA from Wharton who was just finding her sea legs at Citibank. It would be the same thing all over again, and it would be terrible, but it would be okay. Sometimes it would even be sort of nice.

He sucked air, and lifted the bottle in surprise and found that it was empty. It seemed that he had just declared a private holiday. Bunting rolled off the bed and went through the litter to the refrigerator. He dumped more vodka into the little bottle. Vodka could get you through these little blue periods.

Bunting closed the freezer door, screwed the top onto the bottle, and held the nipple clenched between his teeth while he surveyed his room. One week, then back into the world. Bunting remembered his vision of the raging Jesus who had stormed through Battle Creek. Suffer the little children.

He crossed to his bed and picked up the telephone. 'Okay,' he said, sucked from the bottle, and sat down. 'Why not?'

'I ought to,' he said.

He dialled the area code for Battle Creek, then the first three digits of his parents' number.

'Just thought I'd call,' he said. He pulled more vodka into his mouth.

'How are things? I don't want to upset anybody.'

He dialled the last four numbers and listened to the phone ring in that little house so far away. Finally his father answered, not with 'Hello', but with 'Yeah'.

'Hi, Dad, this is Bobby,' he said. 'Just thought I'd call. How are things?'

'Fine, why wouldn't they be?' his father said.

'Well, I didn't want to upset anybody.'

'Why would we get upset? You know how your mother and I feel. We enjoy your calls.'

'You do?'

'Well, sure. Don't get enough of 'em.' There was a small moment of silence. 'Got anything special on your mind, Bobby?'

It was as if the other night had never happened. This was how it went, Bunting remembered. If you forgot about something, it went away.

'I guess I was wondering about Mom,' he said. 'She sounded a little confused, the other night.'

'Guess she was,' his father said in an abrupt, dismissive voice. 'She gets that way, now and then. *I* can't do anything about it, Bobby. How're things at work? Okay?'

'Things could be better,' Bunting said, and immediately regretted it.

'Oh?' Now his father's voice was hard and biting.

'What happened, you get fired? They fired you, didn't they? You screwed up and they fired you.'

He could hear his father breathing hard, stoking himself up like a steam engine.

For a second it seemed that his father was right: he had screwed up, and they had fired him. 'No,' he said. 'They didn't. I'm not fired.'

'But you're not at work, either. It's nine o'clock in the morning here, so it's ten where you are, and Bobby Bunting is still in his apartment. So you lost your job. I knew it was gonna happen.'

'No, it didn't,' Bunting said. 'I just left early.'

'Sure. You left at eight-thirty on Monday morning. What do you call that, premature retirement? I call it getting fired. Just don't try to kid me about it, Bobby, I know what kind of person you are.' He inhaled. 'And don't expect any money from the old folks, okay? Remember all those meals at fancy restaurants and all those trips to Europe, and you'll know where your money went. If you ever had any, and if any of that stuff was true, which is something I have my doubts about.'

'I took the day off,' Bunting said. 'Maybe I'll take off tomorrow, too. I'm taking care of a few details around here.'

'Yeah, those kind of details are likely to take care of you, if you don't watch out.'

'Look,' said Bunting, stung. 'I'm not fired. You hear me? Nobody fired me. I took the day off, because somebody got on my back. I don't know why you never believe me about anything.'

'Do you want me to remind you about your whole life back here? I know who you are, Bobby, let's leave it at that.' His father inhaled again, so loudly it sounded as if he had put the telephone into his mouth. He was calming himself. 'Don't get me wrong, you got your good points, same as everybody else. Maybe you just ought to cut down on the wild social life, and stop trying to make up for never going out when you were a teenager, that's all. There's responsibilities. Responsibilities were never your strong point. But maybe you changed. Fine. Okay?'

Bunting felt as if he had been mugged on a dark street. It was like having Frank Herko yell at him about manhood all over again.

'Let me ask you something,' he said, and pulled another mouthful of Popov out of the Ama. 'Have you ever thought that you saw what reality really was?'

'Jesus wept.'

'Wait. I mean something by that. Didn't you ever have a time when you saw that everything was alive?'

'Stop right there, Bobby, I don't want to hear this shit all over again. Just shut your trap, if you know what's good for you.'

'What do you mean?' Bunting was almost yelling. 'You mean I can't talk about it? Why can't I talk about it?'

'Because it's crazy, you dummy,' his father said. 'I want you to hear this, Bobby. You're nothing special. You got that? You worried your mother enough already, so keep your trap shut. For your own good.'

Bunting felt astonishingly small. His father's voice had pounded him down into childhood, and he was now about three feet tall. 'I can't talk any more.'

'Sleep it off and straighten up,' his father said. 'I mean it.'

Bunting let the phone slide back into the cradle and grabbed for the Ama.

By the time he decided to get out of bed, he was so drunk that he had trouble navigating across the room and into the bathroom. As he peed, a phrase of his father's came back to him, and his urine splattered off the wall. *I don't want to hear this shit all over again.* All over again? If he weren't drunk, he thought, he would understand some fact he did not presently understand. But because he was drunk, he couldn't. Neither could he go outside. Bunting reeled back to his bed and passed out.

He woke up in the darkness with a headache and a vast, encompassing feeling of shame and sorrow. His life was nothing – it had always been nothing, it would always be nothing. There could be no release. The things he had seen, his experiences of ecstasy, the moment he had tried to describe to Marty: all were illusion. In a week he would go back to DataComCorp, and everything would return to normal. Probably they would just take him back – he wasn't important enough to fire. The only difference would be that Frank Herko would ignore him.

His whole problem was that he always forgot he was nothing special.

He promised himself that he would stop making things up. There would be no more imaginary love affairs. Bunting walked over to his window and looked down upon men and women in winter coats and hats who had normal, unglamorous, realistic lives. They looked cold. He got back into bed as if into a coffin.

TWELVE

The next morning, Bunting poured all of his vodka and cognac down the sink. Then he washed the dishes that had accumulated since his last washing. He looked at the sacks of garbage stowed away here and there, put the worst of them into large plastic bags, and took them all downstairs to the street. Back in his apartment, he swept and scrubbed for several hours. He changed his sheets and organized the magazines and newspapers into neat piles. Then he washed the bathroom floor and soaked in the tub for half an hour. He dried himself, brushed his teeth, combed his hair, and went straight back to bed. One of these days, he told himself, he would begin regular exercise.

The next day he fought down the impulse to get another bottle of vodka and went to the supermarket on Broadway and bought a bag of carrots, a bag of celery, cartons of fruit juice and low-fat milk, a loaf of whole-grain bread, and a container of cholesterol-free margarine. Such a diet would keep the raging Jesus at bay.

Bunting spent most of Thursday lying down. He ate two carrots, three celery sticks, and one slice of dry bread. The bread tasted particularly good. He drank all of his fruit juice. In the evening, he tried switching on the television, but what came out was a stream of language so ugly it squeaked with pain. He fell soundly asleep at nine-thirty, was awakened by the sound of gunshots around three in the morning, and went promptly back to sleep.

On Friday he rose, showered, dressed in a conservative grey suit, ate a carrot and drank two or three ounces of papaya juice, put on his coat, and went outside. It was a bright brisk day, and the air, though not as fresh as that of the Montana plains in 1878 or Los Angeles in 1944, seemed startlingly clean and pure. Even on Upper Broadway, Bunting thought he could smell the sea. The outline of a body had been chalked on a roped-off portion of the sidewalk, and as Bunting walked between two parked cars and stepped down onto insanitary, untidy Broadway to walk alongside the traffic in dazzling sunlight, he merely glanced at the white outline of the body and then firmly looked away and continued moving towards the traffic lights and the open sidewalk.

Bunting walked for miles. He looked at the watches in Tourneau's windows, at the shoes in Church Brothers, the pocket calculators and compact disc players in a string of windows on lower Fifth Avenue. He came at length to Battery Park, and sat for a moment, looking out towards the Statue of Liberty. He was in the world, surrounded by people and things; the breeze that touched him touched everyone else, too. To Bunting, this world seemed new and almost undamaged, barren in a fashion only he had once known and now nearly wished to forget.

If a tree fell in the forest, it would not make a sound: no, none.

He began walking back uptown, remembering how he had once sat comfortably astride a horse named Shorty and how a worried perfume executive in a flannel suit had handed him a photograph of his mother. These experiences too could be sealed within a leaden casket and pushed overboard into the great psychic sea. They were aberrations: silent and weight-less exceptions to a general rule. He would get old in his little room, drinking iced tea and papaya juice out of baby bottles. He would outlive his parents. Both of them. Everybody did that.

He took a bus up Broadway, and got off several blocks before his building because he wanted to walk a little more. On the corner a red-faced man in a shabby plaid coat sat on a camp chair behind a display of used paperback books. Bunting paused to look over the titles for a Luke Short or a Max Brand, but saw mainly romance novels with titles like *Love's Savage Bondage* or *Sweet Merciless Kiss*. These titles, and the disturbing covers that came with them, threatened to remind Bunting of Marty seated across from him in a Greenwich Village restaurant, and he stepped back from the array to banish even the trace of this memory. A cover unlike the others met his eye, and he took in the title, *Anna Karenina*, and realized that he had heard of the book somewhere – of course he had never read it, it was nothing like the sort of books he usually read, but he was sure that it was supposed to be very good. He bent down and picked up and opened it at random. He leaned towards the page in the light of the street lamp and read. *Before the early dawn all was hushed. Nothing was to be heard but the night sounds of the frogs that never ceased in the marsh, and the horses snorting in the mist that rose over the meadow before the morning.*

A thrill went through his body, and he turned the page and read another couple of sentences. *A slight wind rose, and the sky looked grey and sullen. The gloomy moment that usually precedes the dawn had come, the full triumph of light over darkness.*

Bunting felt a strange desire to weep: he wanted to stand there for a long time, leafing through this miraculous book.

A voice said, 'World's greatest realistic novel, hands down.'

Bunting looked up to meet the uncommonly intelligent gaze of the pudgy, red-faced man in the camp chair. 'That right?'

'Anybody says different, he's outa his fuckin' mind.' He wiped his nose on his sleeve. 'One dollar.'

Bunting fished a dollar from his pocket and leaned over the rows of bright covers to give it to the man. 'What makes it so great?' he asked.

'Understanding. *Depth* of understanding. Unbelievable responsiveness to detail linked to amazing clarity of vision.'

'Yeah,' Bunting said, 'Yeah, that's it.' He clutched the book to his chest and turned away towards his apartment building.

He placed the book on his chair and sat on the bed and looked at its cover. In a few sentences, *Anna Karenina* had brought shining bits of the world to him – it was as close as you could get to *The Buffalo Hunter* experience and still be sane. Everything was so close that it was almost like being inside it. The two short passages he had read had brought the other world within him – which had once seemed connected to a great secret truth about the world as a whole – once again into being – had awakened it by touching it. Bunting was almost afraid of this power. He had to have the book, but he was not sure that he could read it.

Bunting jumped up off the bed and ate two slices of

wholegrain bread and a couple of carrots. Then he put his coat on and went back to the cash machine at the bank and to the drugstore across the street.

That night he lay in bed, enjoying the slight ache in his legs all the walking had given him, and drinking warm milk from his old Prentiss. Beneath him, odd and uncomfortable but perfect all the same, was the construction he had made from eighty round plastic Evenflos and a tube of epoxy, a lumpy blanket of baby bottles that nestled into and warmed itself against his body. He had thought of making a sheet of baby bottles a long time ago, when he had been thinking about fakirs and beds of nails, and finally making the sheet now was a whimsical reference to that time when he had thought mainly about baby bottles. Bunting thought that sometime he could take off all the nipples and fill every one of the Evenflos beneath him with warm milk. It would be like going to bed with eighty little hot-water bottles.

He held the slightly battered copy of *Anna Karenina* up before him and looked at the cover illustration of a train which had paused at a country station to take on fuel or food for its passengers. A snowstorm swirled around the front of the locomotive. The illustration seemed filled with the same luminous, almost alarming, reality as the sentences he had found at random within the book, and Bunting knew that this sense of promise and immediacy came from the memory of those passages. Opening the book at all seemed to invoke a great risk, but if Bunting could have opened it to those sentences in which the horses snorted in the mist and the wind sprang up under a grey morning sky, he would have done so instantly. His eyes drooped, and the little train in the illustration threw upwards a white flag of steam and jolted forward through the falling snow.

THIRTEEN

On Monday morning the telephone rang with a fussy, importunate clamour that all but announced the presence of Frank Herko on the other end of the line. Bunting, who was in the seventh day of his sobriety, could imagine Herko grimacing and cursing as the phone went unanswered. Bunting continued chewing on a slice of dry bread, and looked at his watch. It was ten o'clock. Herko had finally admitted that he was not coming in again, and was trying to bully him back to DataComCorp. Bunting had no intention of answering the telephone. Frank Herko and the job in the data entry room dwindled as they shrank into the past. He swallowed the last of his papaya juice and reminded himself to pick up more fruit juices that morning. At last, on the thirteenth ring, the telephone fell silent.

Bunting thought of the horses snorting in the cold morning mist when everything else was silent but the frogs, and a shiver went through him.

He stood up from the table and looked around his room. It was pretty radical. He thought it might look a little better if he got rid of all the newspapers and magazines – his room could never look ordinary any more, but what he had done would mean more if the whole room was a little cleaner. The nipples of baby bottles jutted out from two walls, and a blanket of baby bottles, like a sheet of chain mail, covered his bed. If there were very little else mess in the room, Bunting saw, it would be as purposeful as a museum exhibit. He could get rid of the television. All he needed was one table, one chair, two lamps, and his bed. His room would be as stark as a monument. And the monument would be to everything that was missing. Bunting was a little uncertain as to what precisely was missing, but he didn't think it could be summed up easily.

He washed his plate and glass and put them on the drying rack. Then he unplugged his television set, picked it up, unlocked his door, and carried the set out into the hall. He took it down past the elevator and set it on the floor. Then he turned round and hurried back into his apartment.

Bunting spent the morning stuffing the magazines and newspapers into black garbage bags and taking them downstairs to the sidewalk. On his fourth or fifth trip, he noticed that the television had disappeared from the hallway. Bango Skank or Jeepy had a new toy. Gradually, Bunting's room lost its old enclosed look. There were the two walls covered with jutting bottles, the wall with the windows that overlooked the brownstones, and the kitchen alcove. There was his bed and the bedside chair. In front of the kitchen alcove stood his little dining table. He had uncovered another chair which had been concealed under a mound of papers, and this too he took out into the hallway for his neighbours.

When he came up from taking out the last of the garbage bags, he closed and locked the door behind him, pulled the police bar into its slot and inspected his territory. A bare wooden floor, with dusty squares where stacks of newspapers had stood, extended towards him from the exterior wall. Without the newspapers, the distance between himself and the windows seemed immense. For the first time, Bunting noticed the streaks on the glass. The bright daylight turned them silver and cast long rectangles on the floor. Rigid baby bottles stuck out of the wall on both sides, to his right going towards the bathroom door and the kitchen alcove, and to his left, extending towards his bed. The wall above and beyond the bed was also covered with a mat of jutting baby bottles. A wide blanket of baby bottles, half-covering a flat pillow and a white blanket, lay across his bed.

After a lunch of carrots, celery, and bread, Bunting poured hot water and soap into a bucket and washed his floor. Then he poured out the filthy water, started again, and washed the table and the kitchen counters. After that he scrubbed even his bathroom – sink, toilet, floor and tub. Large brown mildew stains blotted the shower curtain, and Bunting carefully unhooked it from the plastic rings, folded it into quarters, and took it downstairs and stuffed it into a garbage can.

He went to bed hungry but not painfully so, his back and shoulders tingling from the work, and his legs still aching from his long walk down the length of Manhattan. He lay atop the blanket of bottles, and pulled the sheet and woollen blanket over his body. He picked up the old paperback copy of *Anna Karenina* and opened it with trembling hands. For a second it seemed that the sentences were going to lift up off the page and claim him, and his heart tightened with both fear and some other, more anticipatory emotion. But his gaze met the page, and he stayed within his body and his room, and read. *And all at once she thought of the man crushed by the train the day she had first met Vronsky, and she knew what she had to do. With a light, rapid step she went down the steps that led from*

the water tank to the rails and stopped close to the
approaching train.

Bunting shuddered and fell into exhausted sleep.

He was walking through a landscape of vacant lots and
cement walls in a city street that might have been
New York or Battle Creek. Broken bottles and pages
from old newspapers lay in the street. Here and there
across the weedy lots, tenements rose into the grey air.
His legs ached, and his feet hurt, and it was difficult
for him to follow the man walking along ahead of him,
whose pale robe filled and billowed in the cold wind.
The man was slightly taller than Bunting, and his dark
hair blew about his head. Untroubled by the winter
wind, the man strode along, increasing the distance
between himself and Bunting with every step. Bunting
did not know why he had to follow this strange man,
but that was what he had to do. To lose him would be
disaster – he would be lost in this dead, ugly world.
Then he would be dead himself. His feet seemed to
adhere to the gritty pavement, and a stiff wind held
him back like a hand. As the man receded another
several yards down the street, it came to Bunting that
what he was following was an angel, not a man, and
he cried out in terror. Instantly the being stopped
moving and stood with his back to Bunting. The pale
robe fluttered about him. A certain word had to be
spoken, or the angel would begin walking again and
leave Bunting in this terrible world. The word was
essential, and Bunting did not know it, but he opened
his mouth and shouted the first word that came to
him. The instant it was spoken, Bunting knew that it
was the correct word. He forgot it as soon as it left his
throat. The angel slowly began to turn around. Bunting

inhaled sharply. The front of the robe was red with blood, and when the angel held out the palms of his hands they were bloody too. The angel's face was tired and dazed, and his eyes looked blind.

FOURTEEN

On Tuesday morning, Bunting awoke with tears in his eyes for the wounded angel, the angel beyond help, and realized with a shock of alarm that he was in someone else's house. For a moment he was completely adrift in time and space, and thought he might actually be a prisoner in an attic – his room held no furniture except a table and chair, and the windows seemed barred. It came to him that he might have died. The afterlife contained a strong, pervasive odour of soap and disinfectant. Then the bars on the windows resolved into streaks and shadows, and he looked up to the bottles sticking straight out on the wall above his head, and remembered what he had done. The wounded angel slipped backwards into the realm of forgotten things where so much of Bunting's life lay hidden, and Bunting moved his legs across the bumpy landscape of baby bottles, his fakir's bed of nails, and pulled himself out of the bed. His legs, shoulders, back and arms all ached.

Out on the street, Bunting realized that he was enjoying his unemployment. For days he had carried with him always a slight burn of hunger, and hunger was such a sharp sensation that there was a small quantity of pleasure in it. Sadness was the same, Bunting realized – if you could stand beside your own sadness, you could appreciate it. Maybe it was the same with the big emotions, love and terror and grief. Terror and grief would be the hardest, he thought, and for a moment uneasily remembered Jesus slapping a bloody palm against the side of his old house in Battle Creek. Holy, holy, holy.

The extremely uncomfortable thought came to him that maybe terror and grief were holy too, and that Jesus had appeared before him in a Battle Creek located somewhere north of Greenwich Village to convey this.

A white cloud of steam vaguely the size and shape of an adult woman rose up from a manhole in the middle of Broadway and by degrees vanished into transparency.

Bunting felt the world begin to shred around him and hurried into Fairway Fruits and Vegetables. He bought apples, bread, carrots, tangerines and milk. At the checkout counter he imagined the little engine on the cover of the Tolstoy novel issuing white flags of steam and launching itself into the snowstorm. He had the strange sense, which he knew to be untrue, that someone was *watching* him, and this sense followed him back out onto the wide, crowded street.

A woman-sized flag of white steam did not linger over Broadway, there was no sudden outcry, no chalked outline to show where a human being had died.

Bunting began walking up the street towards his building. Brittle pale light bounced from the roofs of cars, from thick gold necklaces, from sparkling shop windows displaying compact discs. In all this brightness and activity lurked the mysterious sense that someone was still watching him – as if the entire street held its breath as it attended Bunting's progress up the block. He carried his bag of groceries through the cold bright air. Far down the block, someone called out in a belling tenor voice like a hunting horn, and the world's hovering attention warmed this beautiful sound so that it lingered in Bunting's ears. A taxi slid forward out of shadow into a shower of light and revealed, in a sudden blaze of colour, a pure and molten yellow. The white of a Chinese woman's eyes flashed towards Bunting, and her black hair swung lustrously about her head. A plume of white breath came from his mouth. It was as if someone had spoken secret words, instantly forgotten, and the words spoken had transformed him. The cold sidewalk beneath his feet seemed taut as a lion's hide, resonant as a drum.

Even the lobby of his building was charged with an anticipatory meaning.

He let himself into his bare room and carried the groceries to his bed and carefully took from the bag each apple and tangerine, the carrots, the bread, the milk. He balled up the bag, took it and the carton of milk to the kitchen alcove, flattened out the bag and folded it neatly, and then poured the milk into three separate bottles. These he took back across his sparkling floor and set them beside the bed. Bunting took off his shoes, the suit he was wearing, his shirt and tie, and hung everything neatly in his closet. He returned to the bed in his underwear and socks. He turned back the bed and got in on top of his fakir's blanket of baby bottles, and pulled the sheets and blanket up over his body without shaking off any of the objects on the bed. He doubled his pillow and switched on his lamp, though the cold light still cast large bright rectangles on the floor. He leaned back under the reading light and arranged the fruit, carrots, bread, and bottles around him. He raised one of the bottles to his mouth and clamped the nipple between his teeth. There was a pleasant brisk coolness in the air that seemed to come from the world contained in the illustration on the cover of the book beside him.

Bunting drew in a mouthful of milk and picked up the copy of *Anna Karenina* from the bedside chair. He was trembling. He opened the book to the first page, and when he looked down at the lines of print they rose to meet his eye.

FIFTEEN

The supervisor of the building looked down as he fitted the key into the lock. He turned it, and both men heard the lock click open. The super kept looking at the floor. He was as heavy as Bunting's father, and the two sweaters he wore against the cold made him look pregnant. Bunting's father was wearing an overcoat, and his shoulders were hunched and his hands were thrust into his pockets. The breath of both men came out in clouds white as milk. Finally the super glanced up at Mr Bunting.

'Go on, open it up,' said Mr Bunting.

'Okay, but there are some things you probably don't know,' the super said.

'There's a lot I don't know,' said Mr Bunting. 'Like what the hell happened, basically. And I guess you can't be too helpful on that little issue, or am I wrong?'

'Well, there's other things, too,' the super said, and opened the door at last. He stepped backwards to let Mr Bunting go into the room.

Bunting's father went about a yard and a half into

the room, then stopped moving. The super stepped in behind him and closed the door.

'I fucking hate New York,' said Mr Bunting. 'I hate the crap that goes on down here. Excuse me for getting personal, but you can't even keep the heat on in this dump.' He was looking at the wall above the bed, where many of the bottles had been splashed, instead of directly at the bed itself. The bed had been cracked along a diagonal line, and the sheets, which were brown with dried blood, had hardened so that they would form a giant stiff V if you tried to take them off. Someone, probably the super's wife, had tried to mop up the blood alongside the cracked, folded bed. Chips of wood and bent, flattened bedsprings lay on the smeary floor.

'The tenants are all mad, but it's a good thing we got no heat,' the super said. 'I mean, we'll *get* it, when we get the new boiler, but he was here ten days before I found him. And I'll tell you something.' He came cautiously towards Mr Bunting, who took his eyes off the wall to scowl at him. 'He made it easy for me. See that police bolt?'

The super gestured toward the long iron rod leaning against the wall beside the door frame. 'He left it that way – unlocked. It was like he was doing me a favour. If he'd a pushed that sucker across the door, I'd a had to break down the door to get in. And I probably wouldn't have found him for two more weeks. At least.'

'So maybe he made it easy for whoever did it,' said Bunting's father. 'Some favour.'

'You saw him?'

Mr Bunting turned back to look at the bottles above the bed. He turned slowly to look at the bottles on the front wall. 'Sure I saw him. I saw his face. You want details? You can go fuck yourself, you want details. All they let me see was his face.'

'It didn't look like anybody could have done that,' the super said.

'That's real clever. Nobody did it.' He saw something on the bed, and moved closer to it. 'What's that?' He was looking at a shrivelled red ball that had fallen into the bottom of the fold. A smaller, equally shrivelled black ball had fallen a few feet from it.

'I think it's an apple,' said the super. 'He had some apples and tangerines, some bread. And if you look close, you can see little bits of paper stuck all over the place, like some book exploded. All the fruit dried out, but the book . . . I don't know what happened to the book. Maybe he tore it up.'

'Could you maybe keep your trap shut?' Mr Bunting took in the bottles above the bed for an entire minute. Then he turned and stared at the unstained bottles on the far wall. At last he said, 'This is what I don't get. I don't get this with the baby bottles.'

He glanced at the super, who quickly shook his head to indicate that he did not get it either.

'I mean, you ever get any other tenants down here who did this kind of thing?'

'I never see anyone do this before,' said the super. 'This is a new one. These bottles, I gotta take the walls down to get 'em off.'

Mr Bunting seemed not to have heard him. 'First my wife dies – three weeks ago Tuesday. Then I hear about Bobby, who was always a fuckup, but who happens to be my only kid. When they decide to give it to you, they really give it to you good. They know how to do it. Now on top of everything else, there's this crap. Maybe I should have stayed away.'

'You saw his face?' the super asked.

'Huh?'

'You said you saw his face.'

Mr Bunting gave the super the glance that one heavyweight gives another when they touch gloves.

'Well, I did too, when I found him,' the super said. 'I think you ought to know about this. It's something, anyhow.'

Mr Bunting nodded, but did not alter his expression.

'When I came in . . . I mean, your son was dead, there was no doubt about that. I was in Korea, and I know what dead people look like. It looked like he got hit by a truck. It's crazy, but that's what I thought when I saw him. He was smashed up against the wall, and the bed was all smashed . . . Anyhow, what got me was the expression on his face. Whatever happened happened all right, and, pardon me, but there's no way the police are ever gonna arrest a couple of guys and get 'em on this, because no couple of guys could ever do what I saw in this room with my own eyes, believe me . . .'

He inhaled. Bunting's father was looking at him with flat, impatient, indifferent anger.

'But anyhow, the point is, the way your son looked. He looked happy. He looked like he saw the greatest god-damn thing in the world before *whatever* the hell it was happened to him.'

'Oh yeah,' Mr Bunting said. He was shaking his head. 'Well, he didn't look that way when I saw him, but I'm not too surprised by what you say.' He smiled for the first time since entering his son's room, and started shaking his head again. The smile made the other man's stomach feel small and cold. 'His mother never understood it, but I sure did.'

'What?' asked the super.

'He always thought he was some kind of big deal.' Mr Bunting included the whole apartment in the gesture of his arm. 'I couldn't see it.'

'It's like that sometimes,' the super said.

INTERLUDE:

Bar Talk

It was an ordinary side-street bar, its only oddity being its placement on the second floor over an Indian restaurant. The patrons of the bar never entered the restaurant, and the customers and staff of the restaurant never came upstairs to the bar. The people who went there liked the long, dark, dull wood of the bar, the mirror, the wooden panelling and old beer signs on the walls. Few people bothered to look any more at the photographs of poets and novelists who had been regular patrons once, or at the pictures of boxers and anonymous show business people who had also been regulars, though at another time. Nobody ever looked out of the windows, which were the unremarkable windows of the apartment the bar had once been. It was as if the new regulars did not wish to be reminded they were above the street, once they had climbed the stairs.

These patrons were the people of the neighbourhood, and they used the bar to escape from their apartments. None of them was young or rich, and most of them seemed to have settled into their various lives. They did not talk very much, except to Max, the bartender. Sometimes they seemed to be waiting for the bartender to return to them, so that they could continue their conversation, and to be impatient with the customer who had delayed him. Max was often the youngest person in the room – he wanted to be a stand-up comedian, and he liked to present his own experience in a comic, representative fashion.

In the autumn, on one of the first cold days of the year, a new person started coming upstairs to the bar. He dressed in camouflage fatigues, a leather jacket, and worn black running shoes. The fatigues seemed faded from thousands of washings, and darker patches showed where tags and insignia had been torn off. He had long, thick, black hair, and he wore heavy round glasses. The man always carried a book with him, and he sat down at the far end of the bar, ordered a vodka on the rocks, and opened his book and read for a couple of hours. He had three or four drinks. Then he closed the book, paid up, and left. Pretty soon he was there every day. Some of the regulars started nodding hello to him, and he nodded back or smiled, but he never said anything, not even to Max.

After a couple of weeks, he turned up one day in a black turtleneck and a pair of jeans so faded they were almost white. One of the regulars, a woman in her sixties named Jeannie, couldn't stand it any more and went over to him when he opened his book. 'What happened to the fatigues?' she asked. 'You finally wash them?'

Max laughed.

'I have a lot of fatigues,' the young man said.

'You must like to read,' Jeannie said. 'Every time I see you, you're reading something.'

'I have a lot of books, too,' he said, and laughed, startled by his own words.

Everybody else in the bar, even Max, was staring at them, and Jeannie inexplicably turned red. She stepped away from the young man, but he put his hand on hers, and she moved back beside him. Max drifted up the bar, and everybody else went back to their conversations or their silences. After a while Max began talking to an old merchant seaman named Billy Blue, and Billy began to laugh. Max turned to another of his regulars and told the same story, and both customers started laughing. Everybody forgot about Jeannie after a while. Then Max or someone else looked down at the end of the bar, and she was sitting there by herself. The man had dropped some bills on the bar and left without anybody noticing. Jeannie had a funny look on her face, as if she were remembering something she'd be happier to forget.

'That guy say something to you, Jeannie?' Max asked. 'He get nasty?'

'No, nothing like that,' Jeannie said. 'He was fine. Really.'

She stood up and carried her glass over to the window and looked down onto the street.

'He was *fine*?' Max said. 'What the hell does that mean?'

'You wouldn't understand,' Jeannie said. She turned away from all of them and looked down. Some of the regulars thought she might be crying, but they couldn't really tell. Everybody was sort of embarrassed for a little while, and then Jeannie finally turned away from the window and went back to her old place at the bar. The guy with the book never came back; after a couple of weeks, Jeannie began going to a bar further down the block.

Something About a Death,
Something About a Fire

The origin and even the nature of Bobo's Magic Taxi remain mysterious, and the Taxi is still the enigma it was when it first appeared before us on the sawdust floor. Of course it does not lack for exegetes: I possess several manila folders jammed to bursting with analyses of the Taxi and speculations on its nature and construction. 'The Bobo Industry' threatens to become giant.

For many years, as you may remember, the inspection of the Taxi by expert and impartial mechanics formed an integral portion of the act. This examination, as scrupulous as the best mechanics could make it, never found any way in which the magnificent Taxi differed from other vehicles of its type. There was no special apparatus or mechanism enabling it to astonish, delight, and terrify, as it still does.

When this inspection was still in the performance — the equivalent of the magician's rolling up his twinkling sleeves — Bobo always stood near the mechanics, in a condition of visible anxiety. He scratched his head, grinned foolishly, beeped a tiny horn attached to his belt, turned cartwheels in bewilderment. His concern always sent the children into great bouts of laughter. But I felt that this apparent anxiety was a real anxiety: that Bobo feared that one night the Einstein of mechanics, the Freud of mechanics, would uncover the principle that made the Magic Taxi unique, and thereby spoil its effectiveness forever. For who remains impressed by a trick once the mechanism is exposed? The mechanics grunted and sweated, probed the gas tank, got on their backs underneath the Taxi, bent deep into the motor, covered themselves with grease and carbon so that they too looked like comic tramps, and, at the end of their time, gave up. They could not find a thing, not even registration numbers on the engine block, nor trade names on any of the engine's component parts.

In appearance it was an ordinary taxi, long, black, squat as a stone cottage, of the sort generally seen in London. Bobo sat at the wheel as the Taxi entered the tent, his square behatted head flush against the plexiglass window that opened onto the larger rear compartment. This was empty but for the upholstered back seat and the two facing pull-down seats. It was the very image of the respectable, apart from the sense that Bobo is not driving the Taxi but being driven by it. Yet, though nothing could look so mundane as a black taxi, from the first performance this vehicle conveyed an atmosphere of tension and unease. I have seen it happen again and again, consistently: the lights do not dim, no kettle drums roll, there is no announcement, but a curtain at the side opens, and, unsmiling, Bobo drives (or is driven) into the centre of the great tent. At this moment, the audience falls silent, as if hypnotized. You feel uncertain, slightly on edge, as if you have forgotten something you particularly wished to remember. Then the performance begins again.

Bobo does strikingly little in the course of the performance. It is this modesty that has made us love him. He could be one of *us* – fantastically dressed and pummelling the bulb of his little horn when confused or delighted. When the performance concludes, he bows, bending his head to the torrential applause, and drives off through the curtain. Sometimes, when the Taxi has reached the point where the curtain begins to sweep up over the bonnet, he raises his white-gloved, three-fingered hand in a wave. The wave seems regretful, as if he wishes he could get out of the Taxi and join us up in the uncomfortable stands. So he waves. Then it is over.

There is little to say about the performance. The performance is always the same. Also, it differs slightly from viewer to viewer. Children, to judge from their chatter, see something like a fireworks display. The Taxi shoots off great exploding patterns which do not fade but persist in the air and enact some sort of drama. When pressed by adults, the children utter merely some few vague words about 'The Soldier' and 'The Lady' and 'The Man With a Coat'. When asked if the show is funny, they nod their heads, blinking, as if their questioner is moronic.

Adults rarely discuss the performance, except in the safety of print. We have found it convenient to assume a maximum of coincidence between what we have separately seen, for this allows our scholars to speak of 'our community', 'the community'. Exegetes have divided the performance into three sections (the Great Acts), corresponding to the three great waves of emotion that overwhelm us while the Taxi is before us. We agree that everyone over the age of eighteen passes inexorably through these phases, led by the mysterious capacities of the Magic Taxi.

The first act is The Darkness. During this section, which is quite short, we seem to pass into a kind of cloud or fog, in which everything but the Taxi and its attendant becomes indistinct. The lights overhead do not lessen in intensity, they do not so much as flicker. Yet the sense of gloom is undeniable. We are separate, lost in our separation. At this point we remember our sins, our meagreness, our miseries. Some of us weep. Bobo invariably sobs, the tears crusting on his white make-up, and blasts and blasts his little horn. His painted figure is so akin to ours, and yet so foolish, so theatrical in its grief, that we are distracted from our own memories. We are drawn up out of unhappiness by our love for this tinted waif, Bobo the benighted, and the second act begins.

This section is known as The Falling because of the physical sensations it induces. Each of us, pinned to the rickety wooden benches, seems to fall through space. This is the most literally dreamlike of the three acts. As the sensation of falling continues, we witness a drama that seems to be projected straight from the Taxi into our eyes. This drama, the 'film', is also dreamlike. The drama differs from person to person, but seems always to involve one's parents as they were before one's own birth. There is something about a death, something about a fire. Our own figure appears, radiant, on the edge of a field. Sometimes there is a battle, more often there is walking upwards on a mountain path through deciduous northern trees. It is Ireland, or Germany, or Sweden. We are in the country of our great-great-great grandfathers. We belong here. At last, we are at home. It is the country that has been calling to us all our lives, in messages known only to our cells. In it we are given a brief moment to be heroic, a long lifetime to be moral. This drama elates us and prepares us for the final section of the performance, The Layers.

The beam of light from the Taxi disappears into our

eyes, like a transparent wire. When our eyes have been
filled by the light, the Taxi, Bobo, the sweaty lady
sitting on your right and the man in the blue turtleneck directly in front of you, all of them disappear.
The first sensation is that of being on the fuzzy edge of
sleep; then the layers begin. For some, they are layers
of colour and light through which the viewer ascends;
for some, layers of stone and gravel and red sandstone;
an archaeologist I know once hinted to me that in this
part of the performance he invariably rose through
various strata of civilizations, the cave-dwellers, the
hut-builders, the weapon-makers, the iron-makers,
until he was ascending through towns and villages that
had been packed into the earth. I, for my part, seem to
rise endlessly through scenes of my own life: I see
myself playing in the leaves, making snowballs, doing
homework, buying a book – I cry out with happiness,
seeing the littleness of my own figure and the foolish-
ness of all my joys. For they are all so harmless! Then
the external recurs again before us, Bobo waves driving
through the curtain, and it is finished.

In the first years, when the Taxi was of interest to
only a few, we did not worry much about meanings.
We took it as spectacle, as revelation – a special added
attraction, as the posters said. Then the scholars of
C— University issued their paper asserting that Bobo's
Taxi was the representation of 'common miracle', the
sign that the world is infused with spirit. The scholars
of the universities of B— and Y— agreed, and issued a
volume of essays entitled *The Ordinary Splendour*.

G—, however, and O— disagreed. They pointed to
the sordidness of the surroundings, the seedy costumes
of the other acts, Bobo's little horn, his tears, the
difficult benches and the smell of candyfloss, and their

volume of essays, *The Blank Day*, was much given to analogies to Darwin, Mondrian, and Beckett. Like many others, I skimmed the books, but did not feel that they had touched the real Bobo, the real Taxi: their resonant arguments, phrased with such tact and authority, battled at a great distance, like moths bumping their heavy wings against a screen door. A remark uttered by a friend of mine indicates much more accurately than they the actual quality of the Taxi's performance.

'I like to think,' he told me, 'of Bobo before he became famous. You must know the theory that he used to be an ordinary man with an ordinary job. He was a doctor, or an accountant, or a professor of mathematics. My sister-in-law is certain that he was the vice-president of a tobacco company. "It's in his posture," she says. Anyhow, what I like to picture is the morning that he walked out of his house, going to work in the ordinary way, and found the Taxi waiting for him at the kerb, not knowing that it was his destiny, entirely unforeseen, black and purring softly, pregnant with miracle.'

INTERLUDE:

The Veteran

After two divorces, he lives in a two-bedroom sub-urban home near Columbus, Ohio, with a pit bull terrier called Lurp. Most of his clothing refers to Vietnam – he has a large collection of T-shirts with pictures of elaborate dragons and slogans like *IF YOU WEREN'T THERE, SHUT THE FUCK UP.* The second bedroom is his exercise room, where he works out with weights every morning and afternoon. Although he never read for pleasure during his youth, and in fact still reads very little, he earns his living by writing action-adventure novels about Vietnam.

He writes facing a wall in his living room covered with framed covers of his own books, photographs of Asian women, photographs of himself and his old unit, and a framed poster once issued by his publishers. At eyelevel, just to the left above the monitor of his computer, is a frame containing the medals he was awarded in Vietnam. The living room curtains are always drawn.

He works eleven or twelve hours a day, and goes out as seldom as possible. His wives wanted him to go to psychotherapy or at least join a veterans' group, but he said that his books were his psychotherapy. He con-trols his drinking, as he controls everything else – a man without control, he thinks, isn't a man at all.

Every night he comes thudding out of sleep, covered in sweat and staring into the dark. Something huge and scaly is twisting away into nothingness. There you are again, he thinks, there you are, old friend.

Mrs God

For Lila Kalinich

Take a line. What is it about? What is it referring to? What picture can I think of to replace it?

It is as if it doesn't care about me but just stares. (He, She, – .) (Trees, Rocks, Planets, Stars.) Still, I am inside it as much as under or across. I stare back at myself.

Content's Dream, CHARLES BERNSTEIN

ONE

Standish had not realized how tense he was until the jet finally left the ground and his body, as if by itself, began to relax. Nothing could call him back now, neither Jean's anxiety nor his own reservations. It was settled; he was on his way. The startlingly graphic map of lights that was New York City appeared in the window to his left, then slipped out of view. They were at some alarming, dream-like attitude to the earth that would have meant certain death during Isobel Standish's day — but what might she, in whose name her almost-grandson had ditched both home and seven-months-pregnant wife, not have done with the experience of being revolved about the earth in a metal tube?

The anxiety of the past months continued to ebb from him. Like sweat or semen, anxiety was a physical substance that poured from a self-replenishing well. Of course he was right to go; even Jean had eventually agreed that Esswood was a wonderful opportunity for them both. Three or four weeks at Esswood could lay the groundwork for his tenure, for a book about Isobel — his almost-grandmother — for the whole next stage of his life. When he returned he ought to be carrying in his briefcase the germ of a secured future as surely as Jean once again carried another kind of future life within her womb. And to put it crudely, his would pay for hers.

On the strength of that comfort, he ordered a martini from the stewardess. Of course some of his anxiety had been caused by Esswood itself. Esswood had been know to withdraw its Fellowships, occasionally at times very awkward for the prospective Fellow. The Seneschals, Esswood's owners, appeared to be almost fabulously remote from the details of American academe, but Standish had known two men who, after a period of discreet crowing about being accepted for a term at Esswood, had abruptly ceased to speak about it at all. They had been thrown out before ever getting there.

Ten years ago the first of these, Chester Ridgeley, had been one of the tenured faculty at little Popham College in Popham, Ohio where Standish had begun his academic career. A stiffly eccentric, prematurely aged fixture of the English Department, Ridgeley had been invited to spend a sabbatical semester in Esswood's famous library going over notes and drafts of poems by the obscure Georgian poet Theodore Corn, who thirty years before that had been the subject of his dissertation. Theodore Corn had apparently been a frequent guest at Esswood, and once had actually said that no one who had not seen Esswood House and its grounds – 'the far field and lazy mill beyond the plangency of pond' – could fully understand his poetry.

'There's nothing quite like it,' another faculty member, at the time still thought to be a friend, had said to Standish – the trusting young Standish. 'The place is nearly a secret, in spite of everything they're supposed to have in that library. It's still privately owned, and the Seneschals accept only one or two

researchers every year. Apparently it's changed a good
deal from the glory days when Edith Seneschal ruled
the roost and artists made merry in the West Wing,
not to mention the hayloft. The family still lives there,
but in straitened circumstances – even rather *odd*
circumstances, one gathers.' He was in every sense a
great gatherer, this treacherous so-called friend. Slyly,
fox-like, he gathered and gathered. 'Ridgeley was lucky
– six months to potter around in that great library,
discovering crates of unpublished stuff by that ninny
Theodore Corn. He'll be able to soak up the landscape
around Esswood House, which is supposed to be stun-
ning. And maybe he'll discover the secret. For there is
supposed to be a secret, you know. Very clever of our
Chester.'

Because he had not yet been certain, Standish had
not replied to this sly, supposed friend, his name and
his person both redolent of cough lozenges, that his
own grandmother's sister, his grandfather's first wife,
had been a guest of the Seneschals at Esswood. He
could not even be certain that it was not the allusion
to secrecy and a secret that put the notion in his mind.
But he thought he remembered that his grandmother's
sister had died at an English country house whose
name was similar to that of Ridgeley's benefactor; he
made no more connection than these two dim coincidences. In those days at Popham, coincidence was still
possible.

Just before the end of the fall semester, Standish saw
Ridgeley in the English Department office and had to
suppress an involuntary gasp of dismay. Ridgeley's
scholarly stoop was a positive hunch, his fallen cheeks
looked grey, and his eyelids sagged to reveal hectic
pink linings. Never truly steady on his feet, now he

shuffled like a sick old man. According to Standish's informed hypothetical friend, Ridgeley had sublet his apartment and arranged to store his goods, only to be informed that the Seneschal family had learned of certain indiscretions in his history and were regretfully impelled, as they had put it, to withdraw for the immediate future his invitation to join them as an Esswood Fellow.

Indiscretions? Standish asked. Ridgeley?

Well, said his friend, apparently there was some talk about Ridgeley a long time ago. This man, this false pseudo-friend whose name evoked the humble lozenge, a corrupt and musky forty-six to Standish's dewy twenty-four, had heard in his first years at Popham only the last echoes of an ambiguous, long-dead situation too vague to be called a scandal. Ridgeley might have mishandled an affair with a student; the student might have chucked her studies and returned to a bleak hometown and died, perhaps even in childbirth. Nothing was certain. For his part, Ridgeley had denied everything and then wisely refused to speak about the situation. The question was, said the treacherous pseudo-friend, how had the people at Esswood learned of this musty old affair? Did they hire private detectives? Ridgeley's term at Esswood had not been withdrawn absolutely but only for an unspecified number of terms – maybe they learned no more than Standish. You have to grant, said the foul seducer, that they take themselves very seriously.

Of course Ridgeley had survived, had been able to cancel his sabbatical and keep his apartment and his job; but as far as Standish knew, the summons to Esswood had never been renewed.

The other case came after a fantastic act of betrayal

that resulted in bloodshed, real bloodshed, though the
blood in question was neither Standish's nor the ser-
pent-friend's, also after the loss of a certain *thing*, a
thing never to be regarded as human but lost indeed,
most powerfully and irrevocably lost, wrapped in the
bloodied sheets and discarded, burnt or flushed away
into psychic oblivion. The other consequence of the
act of betrayal had been Standish's eventual removal
and appointment to a far, far superior college: Zenith
College, in Zenith, Illinois. Standish never understood
how Jeremy had managed to get invited to Esswood in
the first place – Jeremy Starger, a naïve, untrustworthy
twenty-five-year-old instructor in English, fresh from
Ann Arbor with a Ph.D., often literally reeling from
drink in the early afternoon. Jeremy's bright little eyes
popped and jiggled above his rufous beard as he dis-
coursed inordinately, unstoppably about D. H. Lawrence, the subject of his 'research' and the object of his
passion. Lawrence had spent several weeks at Esswood,
his visits timed so as not to coincide with those of
Theodore Corn, whom he detested. (Lawrence had
called Corn a 'beetle' and a 'maggot' in letters to
Bertrand Russell.) Standish was surprised that Jeremy
knew of Esswood's continuing existence, even more
surprised to be buttonholed in a corridor of Zenith's
Humanities Building and told that he, Jeremy, had
been 'taken on' as an Esswood Fellow. Three months,
beginning in mid-June. Standish, who was under considerable pressure to complete his own Ph.D., had
become acutely aware of Esswood by this time.

After this news Jeremy became increasingly erratic.
He often cancelled or failed to meet his classes. One
day Standish had seen a slim grey envelope in Jeremy's
departmental mail slot, its printed return address – at

which Standish peeked – only Esswood Foundation, Esswood, Beaswick, Lincolnshire. He had taught a class and returned to the office just as Jeremy, flushed and jubilant, opened the envelope and pulled out the letter. Standish lounged nearer and noticed that it was handwritten. Jeremy glanced at the letter, then sat down heavily in another man's chair. When he saw Standish's enquiring look, he flushed even more darkly and said, 'They've reconsidered.'

'Oh, no,' Standish said. 'I'm very sorry, of course.'

'Sure, I just bet you are,' Jeremy said. 'The only emotions you feel, Standish, are – ' He stopped talking and shook his head. 'I'm sorry. I'm upset. I can't *believe* this. Maybe it's a mistake.' He reread the letter. 'How could they do this?'

'I gather they can be unpredictable,' Standish said. Jeremy's attack made him feel stiff and formal. 'Do they give any reason for withdrawing your Fellowship?'

'*It has become necessary for us to reconsider your appointment,*' Jeremy read. '*We apologize for the undoubted inconvenience this must cause you, and offer our sincerest regrets that we shall not be seeing you in England this summer.*' Jeremy crumpled the letter into a ball and tossed it into his waste-paper basket.

'I don't really suppose you know anything about this, do you, Standish?'

'What could I know?' Standish asked. 'If someone wrote to the Seneschals that their D. H. Lawrence scholar might spend more time in the local public house than the famous library? I don't know anyone who would do that.'

Jeremy bared his teeth at him and stormed out,

undoubtedly on his way to the Stein, the bar most favoured by Zenith's faculty.

A year later the effusive Jeremy had exiled himself to an assistant professorship in central Oklahoma, and William Standish had begun to realize what Esswood could do for him. His investigations into the poetry written by his grandfather Martin's first wife had led him to believe that this restless, impatient woman, completely unknown, had been an important precursor of Modernism – a lost talent, minor but significant. If she had spent weekends at Garsington, if she had *died* at Garsington, where half of Bloomsbury plus T. S. Eliot would have celebrated her, taken her under its angelic, malicious wings, above all promoted her, she would now be a famous poet. But Isobel Standish had spent weekends with Edith Seneschal instead of Ottoline Morrell, and had died and remained obscure. (Theodore Corn spent entire months at Garsington but, compared to Isobel, Corn was a mellifluous blockhead.)

Isobel Standish had published only one book, the slender *Crack, Whack, and Wheel*, Brunton Press, 1912. Half of its five hundred copies had been donated to libraries or distributed to friends. The remainder, unnoticed, unreviewed, was left cased in the basement on Brunton Street in Duxbury, Massachusetts of Martin Standish, who had paid for the publication of his wife's odd little book. It must have looked very odd indeed to unliterary Martin. To William Standish's more educated eye, the poems were astonishingly original, using speech rhythms, nonsense passages, irregular lines, gnomic diction. This poetry implicitly rebuked sentimentality and celebrated its own off-centre gravity. Isobel Standish deserved to take her

place among Stevens, Moore, Williams, Pound, and
Eliot. She was in some ways the Emily Dickinson of
the twentieth century, and she was William Standish's
private property.

By this time he had come to realize that his dissertation on Henry James had quietly expired. He was
still married, and though he and Jean were again now
able, after all their trials, to think about trying to
become parents, his career at Zenith was growing more
imperilled year by year. Two books about Isobel Standish, an edition of her complete work edited by himself
and a consideration of her place in contemporary
poetry, would satisfy the tenure committee and enable
him to keep his job. He could make an end run round
the ghastly corpse of his dissertation and then fly free
of Zenith altogether – to come to rest in some far more
suitable, even ivied, world.

Nine months before the committee had informed
him that publication of some kind would be an absolute requirement of his staying on at Zenith, he had
written to Esswood enquiring if in fact Isobel had en-
joyed the hospitality of the Seneschals, if she had
worked at Esswood – above all, if she had left papers
in the celebrated library. If so, might this letter be
considered an application for a Fellowship of whatever
duration Esswood might deem most appropriate for a
thorough study of her work? He had not neglected to
describe his enthusiasm for Isobel's work and his sense
of its importance, nor to allude to his odd relationship
to the poet.

Esswood had returned a prompt acknowledgement
signed with the initials R. W. His application would be
decided upon 'in due course'. Standish informed the
members of the committee that he expected to have

news for them soon and allowed them to conclude
from that what they might.

Three months went by without word from England.
In the fifth month of his ordeal, Jean Standish learned
that she was pregnant again and that the child was due
in late September. In the third month of her pregnancy
Jean developed alarming symptoms – high blood pressure, one unaccountable instance of vaginal bleeding –
and was ordered into bed for four weeks. She dutifully
took to her bed. At the end of this time, eight months
after his application, Standish finally received another
letter from Beaswick, Lincolnshire. He had been
accepted. For a period of three weeks he was to be
given free access to the Isobel Standish papers and
whatever else he might find helpful. ('We do not
believe in unnecessary circumscriptions on scholarly
work,' wrote R. W., now revealed as one Robert Wall.)
Robert Wall had added a bland sentence of apology for
the delay, which went unexplained. Standish thought
that they had offered the Fellowship during August to
someone else, and the other person had eventually
turned them down. Or they had withdrawn their
appointment, as with Jeremy Starger and Chester Ridgeley. This seemed more likely. Someone else's failure
had been his salvation.

For salvation it was. Standish's chairman agreed to
postpone for a year any decision about his future at
Zenith College. Within that time Standish was to
prepare his edition of Isobel's work, write a lengthy
introduction, and arrange for publication of the
volume.

Jean had been the last obstacle. How do you know
they won't withdraw it at the last minute? Maybe they
do this all the time. (Unfortunately, Jean knew all

about Chester Ridgeley and Jeremy Starger.) Have you ever known anyone who actually went there? Maybe the whole place is a fantastic practical joke, maybe it's just another one of your crazy fantasies, maybe they'll find out about *you*. Don't you think about that, Bill? Why do you need them, anyhow? Flushed, fearful, Jean woke him at night and drilled questions at him until she, not he, broke down into tears of doubt. The next day she adopted an uncharacteristic meekness, barely speaking when he returned to the apartment after school – she was a walking apology.

When he said that he was taking the appointment for the sake of their shared future, she said, 'Don't pretend that you want to go for my sake.' During the final months of the semester, Jean wavered between a meek deceptive acceptance of his plans and an increasingly violent opposition to them. By June, she wept whenever either of them mentioned the trip. It was impossible for him to leave – especially now. There were other colleges besides Zenith. And even if no other colleges would hire him, weren't there always high schools? Would that be such a disgrace?

And what if I lose this baby? Don't you realize it could happen?

But she never said: And what if I lose this baby too? And she never blamed him, except perhaps once, for the loss of the *thing* wrapped in the bloody sheets and flushed away into null-world, oblivion.

Sometimes during these weeks Standish looked at his obese wife, her hair hanging in loose, damp disarray around her red face and wondered who she was, who it was that he had married. He reminded her that she was healthy, that he would be back three weeks before the birth.

You won't, she said. *I know it. I'll be all alone in the hospital, and I'll die.*

If it's that bad, he finally told her, I'll write to Esswood and tell them I can't go because of problems at home.

You think I'm bullying you, you're so weak, you don't understand, you don't even remember.

What don't I understand?

This baby is real. Real! I am going to have this baby! Do you know for certain there is an Esswood? How can you be so sure you'll write a book there?

Especially, she meant, since you've never been able to write one here at home.

Do you remember, do you, do you, do you, do you even remember what you made me do?

It doesn't matter, Standish thought; in a week or two I'll get the flat grey envelope with its single, handwritten paragraph.

He sat with Jean in the evenings. He talked about his classes, they watched television. Jean spoke of very little but food, soap operas, and the movements of the baby in her womb. She seemed two-dimensional, like someone who had died and been imperfectly resurrected. One night he took his *Crack, Whack, and Wheel* from the shelf and began making notes. Jean did not protest. Oddly, the poems seemed lifeless to him, untalented and childish. They too seemed dead.

The grey envelope would come any day, he thought, and put an end to this charade. Mail came to the department office between three and three-thirty, and each day after his Freshman class Standish approached the office with a familiar heartsickness. He looked at the slot bearing his name as soon as he came through the door.

After six working days he found a grey envelope in the slot. It bore the return address of the Esswood Foundation. Standish glanced reflexively towards the littered desk that had been Jeremy Starger's, and the bearded young Eighteenth Century specialist who used it now looked up at him and frowned. 'Keep away from me, Standish,' he said. Not bothering to reply, Standish took the envelope from his slot, along with the bundle of publishers' announcements that was his usual mail. He was surprised to find how disappointed, almost frightened, he was. Standish dropped the textbook announcements into the overflowing departmental waste-paper basket and carried the grey envelope to his desk. He felt hot. He knew he was blushing. Robert Wall had found him out. Sighing, he ripped open the envelope and pulled out a sheet of hieroglyphic non-sense that after a few seconds resolved itself into a mimeographed map illustrating how to drive from Heathrow Airport to Beaswick, where Esswood was located. His heartbeat and his flush faded. A lightly pencilled X marked Esswood's location. Standish felt the profound relief of one who after being sentenced to death receives a full pardon.

That night he gave the map to Jean as she sat before the television set. 'Nice,' she said, and held it out towards him. In the glare from the set her cheeks were as puffy as bolsters. As Jean's belly had expanded, so had the rest of her body, encasing her in an unhappy overcoat made of ice cream and doughnuts. He took the map from her bloated fingers. He imagined that Isobel Standish had remained slim all her life.

'. . . good it's going to do,' she muttered to the screen.
'What?'

'I wonder how much good that map is going to do you.' She did not bother to look at him.

'Why would you wonder about that?' he asked, unable to keep a sudden quickening from his voice.

'Because it shows you how to get to that place from Heathrow.' Then she did turn her head to face him.

'Heathrow is the name of the London Airport.'

'But you're not going to London. You're going to some place called Gatwick.'

The name Gatwick did sound familiar. Standish went upstairs to the bedroom, pulled his airline ticket out of his dresser drawer, and read what was printed on its face.

'You're right,' he said when he came back downstairs. Jean grunted. Standish wondered if she had prowled through his dresser drawers. The television seemed very loud. He turned to the bookshelf and pulled out an atlas and turned to the index for England. Gatwick was unlisted.

Standish sat down in the chair beside Jean's and unfolded Robert Wall's little map, with its complications of roads and motorways and interchanges. None of the towns in black boldface type were Gatwick. He could see Gatwick nowhere between London and Lincolnshire. Gatwick was literally off the map. Well, he would find the place once he got there. Gas stations all had maps. England had to have gas stations, didn't it?

Though Standish checked his mail every day, Robert Wall never wrote that Esswood had found it necessary to withdraw his appointment; and now here he was, thirty thousand feet above the Atlantic Ocean. Standish had two more drinks on the long flight, and nearly ordered a fourth until he remembered Jeremy Starger.

You couldn't turn a ridiculous red-bearded little drunk loose in the Esswood library, could you? You couldn't let that happen.

Standish took *Crack, Whack, and Wheel* from his carry-on bag. Feeling pleasantly honourable and muzzy from gin, he opened Isobel's book. His underlinings, notes, and annotations jumped reassuringly out at him, testimony to the merits of Isobel's poetry and the depth of his own thought. Here were the physical traces of an alert, scholarly mind at work on a worthy object. *Cf. Psalm 69*, read one of his notes, *world does not answer the cry for pity, ironic intent, ref. Husband?* In ink of another colour he had added *eloquent offer of charity, attribute of the poetic self.* And in pencil above this was added *anti-narrative strategy.* Isobel Standish's work was full of anti-narrative strategy. At some point Standish had scrawled *Odysseus, Dante* in the crowded margins. The title of the poem he had annotated so industriously was 'Rebuke'.

> Neither found he any, the vagrant said
> Under the mouldering eaves of the house
> Full of heaviness and no one to comfort,
> No one wavering up to say
>
> 'Put on your indiscretions, little fool,
> But first take your glasses off. Why, Miss
>   Standish . . .'
> This glowing moon. The crowd
> Has already gathered on the terraces.
>
> The history of one who came too late
> To the rooms of broken babies and their toys
> Is all they talk about around here —
> And rebuke, did you think you'd be left out?

Blurry with hangover, he ate the terrible airline meal, drank one glass of red wine that tasted of solvent, and

nursed another through the movie. He was not accustomed to drinking so much. Jean did not approve of
wine with meals, and Standish did not usually appreciate the sluggishness and confusion with which more
than a single drink afflicted him. Yet this was not at
all the life to which he was accustomed – the safety of
home was thousands of miles behind him, and he was
suspended in midair with a copy of *Crack, Whack, and
Wheel*, on his way somewhere utterly unknown. Every
aspect of this circumstance felt ripe with anxiety.
Three weeks seemed a very long time to be immured
in a remote country house looking at manuscripts of
poems he still was not sure he understood.

Standish fell asleep during the movie, and woke up
in dim morning greasy with sweat, as if covered with
a fine film of oil. The stewardess had put a blanket
over him, and he thrashed and kicked, imagining that
some loathsome thing, some fragment of a nightmare,
lay atop him . . . Fully awake, he wiped his greasy face
with his hands and looked around. Only a few goggling
idiots had observed his moment of panic. Standish
pulled the blanket off the floor and only then noticed
that he had an erection. Like some huge beast diving
into concealment, his dream shifted massively just
beneath the surface of his memory.

The aeroplane began to descend shortly after he had
eaten. Standish pushed up his window cover, and cold
grey light streamed into the cabin. They seemed to
descend through layer after layer of this silvery under-
sea light. At last the plane came through a final layer
of clouds filled with a pure, unliving whiteness, and an
utterly foreign landscape opened beneath them. Tiny
fields as distinct as cobblestones surrounded an equally
tiny airport. In the distance, two great motorways met

and mingled on the outskirts of a little city surrounded by rows of terraced houses. A long way past the toy city lay a forest, a great flash of vibrant green that seemed the only true colour in the landscape. *England*, Standish thought. A thrill of strangeness passed through him.

The plane landed at some distance from the terminal, and the passengers had to carry their hand baggage across the tarmac. Standish's arms ached from the weight of the various small bags he had filled at the last minute with books and cassettes. His Walkman bumped his chest as it swung on its strap. He felt a queer, fatalistic exhilaration. The silvery light, a light never seen in America, lay over the tarmac. Two dwarfish men in filthy boiler suits stood in the shadows beneath the aeroplane watching the passengers trudge towards the terminal. Standish knew that if he could overhear the words the men passed as they squinted through their cigarette smoke, he would not understand a one.

But he had no trouble understanding or being understood as he passed through the airport. The customs official treated him courteously, and the Immigration Officer seemed genuinely interested in Standish's response to the question about the purpose of his visit. And when Standish asked him for directions to a village in Lincolnshire, he said, 'Don't worry, sir. This is a small country, compared to yours. You can't get too lost.' Every word, in fact every syllable of this charming little speech was not only clear but musical: the Immigration Officer's voice rose and fell as did no American's, and so did that of the girl behind the rental desk, who had never heard of Esswood or Beaswick but pressed several maps on him before she

walked him to the terminal's glass doors and pointed
to the decade-old turquoise Ford Escort, humble and
patient as a mule, he had rented. 'The boot should hold
all your bags,' she said, 'but there's lashings of room in
the back seat, if not. You'll want to begin on the
motorway directly ahead and go straight through the
interchange. That'll see you on your way.'

Standish wondered if all over England people played
tunes at you with their voices.

TWO

Driving on the left, so counter to his instincts, elated
him. Like all driving it was largely a matter of fitting
in with the stream. Standish found that it took only a
small adjustment to switch on the radio with the left
hand instead of the right, to pass slower cars on the
wrong side – but he was not sure how long this control
would last in an emergency. If the car ahead of him
blew a tyre or began to skid . . . Standish saw himself
creating a monumental crack-up, a line of wrecked,
smoking cars extending back a mile. His heart was
beating fast, and he smiled at himself in the rear-view
mirror. He was tired and jet-lagged, but he felt foolishly, shamelessly alive.

Only the roundabouts gave him trouble. The stream
of traffic swept him into a great whirling circle from
which drivers were to choose alternate exits marked
by a great spoke-like diagram. At first Standish could
not tell which of the spokes was his, and drove sweating around the great circle twice. When at last he had
seen that he wanted the third of the exits, he found
himself trapped in the roundabout's inner lane, unable

to break through the circling traffic. He went around once more, straining to look over his shoulder, and set the windscreen wipers slapping back and forth before he located the turn indicator. As soon as he began to move out of his lane several horns blared at once. Standish swore and twisted the wheel back. Around once more he went, and this time managed to enter the stream of cars on the outer edge of the roundabout. When he squirted into the exit his entire body was damp with sweat.

Fifteen miles further north, the whole thing happened all over again. His map slipped on the seat, and he panicked – he was supposed to stay on this north-bound dual carriageway, but at some point he did have to turn off onto a trunk road, and from that onto a series of roads that were only thin black lines on the map. He drove round and round and doubt over-whelmed him. His turn indicator ticked like a bomb. Sweat loosened his grip on the wheel. At last he managed to penetrate the honking wall of cars and escape the roundabout. He pulled off to the side of the road and scrabbled amongst the maps strewn on the floor. When he had the proper map in his hands, he could not locate the roundabout he had just fled. It did not exist on the map, only in life. His earlier feelings of relaxation and purposefulness mocked him now. They were illusions; he was lost. At length the desire to weep left him and he calmed down. He found a roundabout on the map, an innocuous grey circle, which almost had to be the one he had just escaped. He was not supposed to get off the dual carriageway for another thirty-seven miles, where a sign should indicate the way to Huckstall, the village where he picked up the next road. He would not have to brave any more roundabouts. Standish pulled out into the traffic.

After a time, the landscape became astonishingly empty. Dung-coloured bushes lay scattered across flat colourless land. Far away in the distance was a gathering of red-brick cottages. Standish wondered if this might be Huckstall.

He looked at the tiny village through the passenger window and saw a pale face pressed against a second-floor window, a white blur surrounded by black just as if – really for all the world, Standish thought, just as if a child had been imprisoned in that ugly two-storey building, walled up within the red brick to stare eternally towards the cars rushing past on the dual carriageway. Smaller white blotches that might have been hands pressed against the glass, and a hole opened up in the bottom of the child's face, as if the child were screaming at Standish, screaming for help!

He quickly looked away and saw that a low black hill had appeared before him on the right side of the dual carriageway. Bare of vegetation, the hill seemed to fasten onto the empty landscape rather than grow from it. Other hills like it cancelled half the horizon. They looked dead, like garbage piles – then he thought they looked like black, blood-soaked sheets, bloody towels and pads thrown onto the abortionist's floor.

The air carried a sour, metallic tang, as if it were filled with tiny metal shavings. Standish came up beside the first low hill and saw that it was a mound of some material like charcoal briquets – stony chips of coal. Now and then rockslides of the chips ran down the flanks of the hill. Between the black hills of coal dusty men rode toy-like bulldozers. Completely ringed by the black hills was a world of men rushing around in blackened, murky air beneath strings of lights. Obscure machines rose and fell. Yellow flares burned beside the black mounds. *Slag heaps*, Standish thought, not knowing if he was right. What were slag heaps, anyhow?

Even the sky seemed dirty. Rhythmic clanks and thuds as from underground machines filled the air. It was like driving through a hellish factory without walls or roof. Standish had not seen a road sign or marker for what must have been miles. There was nothing around him now but the shifting black hills and the dusty men moving between the flares. Suddenly the road seemed too narrow to be the dual carriageway.

He decided to keep driving until he saw a road sign. The thought of getting out of his car in this brutal and desolate place made his throat tighten.

Then the entire world changed in an eye-blink. The black hills, strings of lights, men on toy bulldozers, and tiny flares fell back behind him, and Standish found himself driving through dense, vibrant green. On either side of the car fat, vine-encrusted trees and wide bushes pushed right to the edge of the road. For ten or fifteen minutes Standish drove through what appeared to be a great forest. The interior of the car grew as hot as a greenhouse. Standish pulled up to the side of the road and wiped his forehead. Leaves and vines flattened against the side window. He looked at his map again.

North-east from the second roundabout extended the road to Huckstall. The map indicated woodlands in green, but none of the green covered the roadway. Sickeningly, Standish thought that all this right–left business had so confused him that he had travelled south from Gatwick instead of north – by now he would be hundreds of miles out of his way. He groaned and closed his eyes. Something soft thumped against his windscreen. Standish moaned in dismay and surprise, and reflexively covered his face with his arms.

He lowered his arms and looked out. On the upper right-hand side of the windscreen was a broad, smeary stripe which he did not think had been there earlier. Standish did not at all want to think about what sort of creature had made the smear. An insect the size of a baby had turned to froth and spread itself like butter across the glass. Death again, messy and uncontainable. He wiped his face and started forward again.

The woodland ended as abruptly as it had begun, and without any transition Standish found himself back in the empty, burnt-looking landscape. Twice he passed through other, smaller outdoor factories with their slagheaps and dusty men wandering through flares. He felt as if he had been driving in circles. There were no signs to Huckstall or anywhere else. Unmarked roads intersected his, leading deeper into the undulating russet landscape. *Full of heaviness and no one to comfort*, Standish remembered from 'Rebuke'. He longed for signs to Boston or Sleaford or Lincoln, names prominent on the map Robert Wall had sent him.

In minutes a low marker, a small stone post like a tooth set upright beside the road, came into view before him. Standish pulled up across from it. He got out of the car and walked around to see the worn words carved on the marker: 7m. Seven miles? Seven miles from what?

'Lost?'

Standish snapped his head up to see a tall thin man

standing directly behind the little stone tooth. He might just now have jumped up out of the earth. His loose baggy brown trousers, spattered boots, and rumpled mackintosh were nearly the colour of the landscape. He wore a dark cap pulled low on his forehead. The man slouched and grinned at Standish. He was missing most of his teeth.

'I don't really know,' Standish said.

'Is that right?' said the grinning man. His tongue licked the spaces between his teeth.

'I mean, I'm trying to figure it out,' Standish said. 'I thought this marker might help me.'

'And does it?' The man's voice was a sly, quiet burr, remarkably insinuating. 'There's precise matter to be read here. A man might do a great deal with information as accurate as that.'

Standish hated the man's dry, insulting mockery. 'Well, it doesn't do *me* any good. I thought I was on the dual carriageway, going towards Huckstall.'

'Huckstall.' The man pondered it. 'Never heard of Americans making their way to Huckstall.'

'I'm not really going *to* Huckstall,' Standish said, infuriated at having to explain himself. 'I just thought I might have lunch there. I was going to pick up the road to Lincolnshire.'

'Lincolnshire, is it? You'll want to do a good bit of driving. And you thought you were on the dual carriageway. Is this how dual carriageways look in America, then?'

'Where *is* the dual carriageway?' Standish cried.

'Kill a bird? Little baby?'

'What?'

'With your car?' He pointed his chin towards the smear on the windscreen.

'You're crazy,' Standish said, though he had feared exactly this.

The man blinked and stepped backwards. His tongue slid into one of the spaces between his teeth. Now he seemed uncertain and defensive instead of insolent. He was crazy, after all – Standish had been too startled to see it.

'Where are you from?' he asked, hoping that the man would answer: Huckstall.

The man tilted his head back over his shoulder, indicating wide, empty blankness. Then he took another backward step, as if he feared that Standish might try to capture him. The stranger came into focus for Standish: he was not at all the ironic, almost menacing figure he had seemed. The fellow was deficient, probably retarded. He lived in that empty wilderness and he slept in his clothes. Now that he was no longer afraid of the man, Standish could pity him.

'Killed something, that'll *do* you,' the man said. His eyes gleamed like a dog's, and he edged a bit further away. 'That'll be bad luck, that will.'

Standish thought the bad luck was in meeting an oaf straight out of Thomas Hardy. 'Where is Huckstall, would you know?'

'I would. That I would. Yes.'

'And?'

'And?'

'And where is it?' Standish shouted.

'Up there, up there, right up that road, which is the very road you're on.'

Standish sighed.

'*They flee from me,*' the man said.

Standish put his hands in his pockets and began to

move around the front of the car without quite turning his back on the vagrant.

'*That sometime did me seek,*' the man said. '*With naked foot stalking in my chamber.*'

Standish stopped moving, aware that he was, after all, in England. No addled American tramp would quote Thomas Wyatt at you. The English teacher in him was piqued and delighted. 'Go on,' he said.

> '*Once have I seen them gentle, tame, and meek,*
> *That now are wild, and do not once remember,*
> *That sometime . . .*'

He paused, then intoned, '*Timor mortis conturbat me,*' quoting from another poem. Evidently he was a ragbag of disconnected phrases.

'Hah! Very good,' Standish said, smiling. 'Excellent. You've been very helpful to me. Thank you.'

The man closed his eyes and began to chant.

> '*In going to my naked bed as one that would have slept,*
> *I heard a wife saying to her child, that long before had wept,*
> *She sighed sad and sang full sweet, to bring the babe to rest,*
> *That would not calm but cried still, in sucking at her breast.*'

'Um, yes,' Standish said, and quickly got into the car. He turned the key in the ignition and glanced sideways at the man, who had come out of his trance and was shuffling towards the car, reaching for the handle of the passenger door. Standish cursed himself for not locking the doors as soon as he had got in. The engine caught, and Standish pulled away before the

man reached the handle. He looked in the mirror and
saw the creature staggering up the middle of the road,
gesturing with both hands. Standish looked ahead
quickly.

He drove through the emptiness for perhaps five
minutes before coming to a small green sign which
read HUCKSTALL 10m.

It was, when he came to it, a village of narrow lanes
lined with brick cottages, so ugly and uninviting that
he nearly decided to pass through it and continue on.
But the next village appeared to be at least twenty
miles away, and it would take thirty minutes to drive
that distance over the country roads. And when he
came up to the market square in the centre of town,
Huckstall did not seem so grim.

Triangular plastic pennants on strings marked off
separate areas of the cobbled square – on market days,
each area would belong to a separate stallholder.
Beyond the strings of pennants lay reassuring signs of
civilization, a bow-fronted shop called Boots the
Chemist, the imperial stone facade of a Lloyds Bank,
and the plate-glass window, filled with brightly coloured paperbacks, of a W. H. Smith bookshop. On the
corner opposite Standish and his Escort crammed with
luggage stood a large double-fronted, half-timbered
building with bay windows, a small blue sign with the
words TAKE COURAGE below a golden rooster, and a
much larger sign depicting crossed duelling pistols
which bore the legend THE DUELLISTS. The windows
sparkled, the blue paint and white trim gleamed.
Standish had a sudden vision of a roasted pig on a
serving platter, thick wedges of crumbly yellow
cheese, overflowing tankards of ale, a fat, smiling man

in a toque carving slices of rare roast beef and pouring thick brown gravy onto Yorkshire pudding.

He could make it to Beaswick and Esswood in another three or four hours. *Stopped off for a pub lunch*, he would say. *Beautiful little place in Huckstall called The Duellists. Do you know it? Ought to be in the guidebooks, if you ask me.*

Standish left his car parked on the side of the square and walked through the chill grey air towards the glistening pub. His stomach rumbled. It came to him that he had driven a strange car hundreds of unfamiliar miles, he was the recipient of a distinguished English literary fellowship, he was about to enter an English interior for the first time. He fairly bounded up the steps and opened the door.

His first impression was of the pub's size, his second that it must have closed for the afternoon. The interior of The Duellists was divided into a series of enormous rooms furnished with round tables and padded booths. A red tartan carpet covered the floors, and the walls were artificially half-timbered. In the hazy light from the windows, Standish saw a stocky black-haired man washing glasses behind the bar on the far side of the rows of empty tables. The air stank of cigarette smoke. The bartender glanced up at Standish hovering inside the door, then resumed pulling large, vaguely pineapple-shaped glasses out of hot water and setting them up on the bar.

Standish wondered if he still had time to get a sandwich. He walked to the bar. The tops of the tables were slick with beer, and most of the ashtrays were filled. Crumpled packs of Silk Cut and Rothmans lay beside the ashtrays.

'Yes,' the barman said, looking up sharply before plunging his hands into the water again.

'Are you open?'

'Door's not locked, is it?'

'No, I thought maybe the licensing laws – '

'Been a change then, has there? And about bloody time, too.'

'Well, I wondered – '

The man fixed Standish with an impatient stare, wiped his hands on a towel, and leaned against the bar.

'You're not closed,' Standish said.

The man held out both hands palm-up and moved them outward in a gesture that said: see for yourself. 'So if you'll place your order, sir . . .'

'Well, I was hoping to get a beer and something to eat, I guess.'

'Menu's behind the bar.' He tilted his head towards a blackboard advertising steak and kidney pie, shepherd's pie, ploughman's lunch, ham sandwich, cheese sandwich, scotch egg, pork pie, batter-fried prawns, batter-fried scallops.

Standish was charmed all over again. In this list he saw how far he had come from Zenith. He suspected the food might be humble by English standards, but he wanted to taste it all. Here was the simple nutritious food of the people, shepherds and ploughmen.

'It all looks so *good*,' he said.

'Oh, aye?' the barman frowned and turned around to look at the blackboard himself. 'You'd better order some of it, then, hadn't you.'

'Ploughman's lunch, please.' Standish envisioned a big steaming bowl with potatoes and leeks and sausages all mixed up in a rich broth. 'It's good, is it?'

'Good enough for some,' the barman said. 'Chutney or pickle?'

'Why, a little of both.'

The man turned and disappeared through a door at the far end of the bar. After a moment Standish realized that he had gone into the kitchen to place the order. The bartender returned as abruptly as he had left – his face had an odd, flinty, concentrated look that made him seem always to be performing some unwelcome task. '*And*, sir?'

'And?'

'And what did you want from the bar? Pint of bitter? Half pint?'

'What a wonderful idea!' Standish exclaimed, knowing that he sounded like an idiot but unable to restrain himself. *A pint of bitter*. Standish was suddenly aware of the smallness of England, of its *cosiness*, the snugness and security and warmth of this island nation.

The bartender was still staring at him with that tense, flinty expression.

'Oh, a pint, I guess,' Standish said.

'A pint of what, sir?' He swept his hand towards old-fashioned pump taps with ceramic handles. 'The ordin'ry?'

'No, what's the best one? I just got off the plane from the States a couple of hours ago.'

The man nodded, picked up one of the pint mugs he had set out to dry, set it beneath a tap marked Director's Bitter, and hauled back on the tap. Cloudy brown liquid spurted out into the glass. The man pushed and pulled the pump until the glass had filled. His face still seemed stretched taut, immobilized, as if a layer of cells deep within had died.

'You folks still drink warm beer over here, is that right?'

'We don't boil it,' the bartender said. He thumped the pint on the bar before Standish. 'You'll let that settle, sir.'

What was still swirling around in the glass looked like something drawn up from a swamp. Little brown silty fecal things spun around and around.

'We don't see many Yanks up this way,' he said.

'Oh, I've still got a long way to go,' Standish said, watching his beer spin. 'I'm on my way to a village called Beaswick. Lincolnshire. I'm invited to a, I guess you'd say, manor house called Esswood.'

'The fellow was murdered there,' the barman said. 'That'll be three pounds forty altogether.'

Standish counted out four pounds from his stash of English money. 'You must be mistaken,' he said. 'It's a kind of foundation. Every year they invite someone – you'd have to say it's a kind of honour.'

'Funny kind of honour.' The barman gave Standish his change. 'American, he was. Like yourself, sir.' He turned away. 'Take a seat, sir. The food will be out directly.'

Standish carried the heavy glass to a table and sat down. He examined the beer. It was calmer now. A thin layer of foam lay on its top like scum. The spinning brown things had dissolved into the murk. He sipped cautiously. Over a strong clear bite of alcohol rode a sharp deep tang more that of whisky than of beer. It was like drinking some primitive tribal medicine. Standish felt a healthy, cheering distance between himself and the standards of Zenith. He took a longer swallow and told himself he was getting to like this stuff.

'That's strong, that is, the Director's,' said a female voice behind him, and Standish jerked his hand in surprise and soaked his cuff with beer.

'Beggin' your pardon,' the girl said, smiling at Standish's sudden consternation. She was a pretty blonde in her late teens or early twenties with wide, rather blank eyes of an almost transparent pale blue. She wore a red woollen sweater covered by a stained, bulging white apron that for some reason reminded Standish of a nurse's uniform. He noticed that she was very pregnant before he saw that she was carrying a plate with a large wedge of cheese and the heel of a loaf of French bread. 'Your food.'

'I'm sorry, but that isn't what I ordered,' Standish said.

'Of course you ordered it,' she said, all her amusement gone in an instant. 'You're the only bloody customer in the place. D'you think I could make a mistake like that with but the one order?'

'Wait. This is cheese and — '

'Ploughman's lunch, that is. With pickles *and* chutney.' She thrust it before him so that he could see the two puddles of sauce, brown and yellow, beside the wedge of cheese.

She set the plate roughly on the table and rapped a knife and a fork down beside it. 'Wouldn't you call that right?' A glance at him. 'He came into the kitchen and said, "Ploughman's lunch, pickle and chutney," and I said, "Wants both, does he?" because I'd looked out of the window and seen you making for the pub and I knew you were a Yank by your clothes and the way you walked. Just like a Yank it was. You needn't think I'm ignorant just because I live in Huckstall and work in a pub. I'm educated better by far than your

great ignorant American girls – I've got five O levels –
and my husband *owns* this pub. You should see the
envy on their faces when we go home, you should
see – '

About midway through this astonishing speech
Standish became aware of the meaning of the rigid
expression on the barman's face: *not this, not again.*
The girl was breathing hard, and she placed one hand
on her chest.

'Enough,' the barman said from behind Standish.

The girl glared down at Standish and turned away to
move quickly through the empty tables, tugging at the
tie of the apron as she went. She dropped the apron at
the door and pushed through to the outside.

Standish looked up in amazement at the barman. He
was wiping his hands on a white towel, and he looked
back down at Standish with a stony rigidity.

'Closing time, sir,' he said.

'What?'

'You'll be leaving now. Time.'

'But I haven't even – '

'Your money will be refunded, sir.' He took a
crumpled wad of bills from his pocket, found four
single pound notes, and set them down on Standish's
table, where they immediately wilted in a puddle of
spilled beer.

'Oh, come on,' Standish said. 'I could wait here if
you want to go out and bring her back. Honest, I
understand – my wife's pregnant too. She said a lot of
crazy things just before I left – '

'Time,' the man said, and put a hand as heavy as a
bag of cement on Standish's shoulder. 'Take the
cheese. I am closing now, sir.'

Standish gulped down a mouthful of the awful beer.

He stood. The barman slid his hand down Standish's arm to his elbow. 'Now, sir, please.'

'You don't have to push me out!' Standish grabbed the wedge of cheese as the barman began to move him towards the door. The man's face was concentrated and expressionless, as if he were moving a heavy piece of furniture.

He permitted Standish to open the door of the pub.

Outside in the bright grey air, Standish looked down at the empty market square with its fluttering flags. The pregnant girl had disappeared. Standish heard the clanking of heavy bolts behind him.

'Jesus,' he said. He looked down at the wedge-shaped piece of cheese. From somewhere came a pervasive distant thunder like the noise of a hidden turbine. It seemed to him that people were peering at him from behind curtains.

He looked across the square. A shiny, half-flattened bag flipped across the cobbles in a moist breeze, dribbling out crumbled potato crisps. The cheese in his hand had begun to adhere to his fingers.

Of course, he thought. In a place this size everybody knows everything – that crazy woman chased them all out of the pub before I showed up. They were waiting to see how long I'd last.

The homely little turquoise mule across the square sat in a dazzle and sparkle of water or of quartz embedded into the cobbles. Standish walked towards it along the perimeter of the square. Other people's lives were like novels, he thought. You saw so little, you had only a peek through a window, and then you had to guess about what you had seen.

For a moment, he quite clearly saw before him the

pretty quadrangle, crisscrossed by intersecting paths, that was the centre of the Popham campus.

At a scuffle of movement behind him he turned round and nearly stumbled. The crowd he had imagined was not there. In an arch between The Duellists and a tobacconist's shop he glimpsed two people watching – a blonde woman in a red jersey and a tall man in a cap and a long muddy coat. It took Standish a moment to realize why this man looked familiar: he was the tramp who had startled him on the road to Huckstall. They vanished beneath an arch. Standish heard the footsteps of the tramp and the publican's wife clattering down the hidden street.

But the tramp had been about ten miles out of town. He could not have walked so far in the short time since Standish had seen him.

They flee from me that sometime did me seek.

He jumped at a sudden noise, and saw only the shiny bag flipping over the stones. The odd rumbling of unseen engines persisted.

Standish looked at the darkened pub and saw the source of the mysterious sound. Beyond the top of the pub, the distance of a field away, a steady stream of trucks and cars rolled north on an elevated road. It was the dual carriageway he had managed to lose at one of the roundabouts.

The rest of the drive to Lincolnshire passed with what seemed to him surprising ease. The dual carriageways swept him uneventfully towards his destination; the tangle of lines on Robert Wall's map resolved itself, after frequent inspection, into actual roads with actual identities that led to actual places; he lost his way only once, by overshooting a badly marked intersection. By all his earlier standards, it was a difficult and confusing journey, but by the standards of the morning it was nearly painless.

The light faded. In the growing darkness Standish began to see dykes and canals in the fields, which even in the diminishing light were of a glowing, almost electrical green. The map led him past tiny Lincolnshire villages and through broad marshes. A pale phosphorescence, as of something dead come back to uneasy life, now and then glowed far off in the marshes.

He came to Beaswick in the dark, at ten o'clock at night. The village was a mean affair of ugly terraced houses interspersed with pubs and chip shops. In ten minutes he had passed through it, still following his map.

A few minutes later he came to an unmarked road that led into a darkness of massive oaks. He drove through an iron gate and up a drive which went looping through the monumental trees. He rounded a final curve and saw before him an immense white house at the top of a wide flight of steps. Behind the house his headlights shone upon a descending series of terraces before they flashed across the windows of the house. Standish pulled up before the steps and got out of his car. When he took his first long look at Esswood House, an entirely unforeseen thing happened to him. He fell in love with it.

THREE

Standish had never been to France or Italy, he had never seen Longleat, Hardwick Hall, Wilton House, or any of the twenty country estates that were Esswood's

equal; it would have made no difference if he had.
Esswood struck him as perfect. The clear symmetrical
line of the house, broken regularly by great windows,
delighted him. He tried to remember the name for a
façade like this, but the word would not come. It did
not matter. The whole great white structure seemed
balanced, in harmony with itself and the countryside
around it. What might have been forbidding – the
whiteness and severity of its façade, the flight of steps
that might have reminded him of a government building – had been humanized by constant use. A single
family, the Seneschals, had lived here for hundreds of
years. People had moved familiarly up and down these
steps and through every one of the rooms. Generations
of children had grown up here. Even in the darkness
the stairs showed worn patches, eroded by generations
of Seneschals and hundreds of poets and painters and
novelists. Here and there the paint was flaking, and
water damage had left dark linear stains at the corners
of some of the noble windows. These small blemishes
did not disturb Esswood's perfection.

Standish opened the boot of the car and lifted out
two of his large suitcases. They seemed much heavier
than they had in Zenith, and Standish dropped them
one after the other onto the gravel before he closed the
boot. Then he picked them up and trudged towards the
staircase.

Someone in the house heard the sounds he made as
he struggled towards the door. A light passed down the
row of dark windows at the front of the house and
moved towards the door. Standish wondered if a servant girl were rushing towards Esswood's main
entrance with a lighted candle, as would have happened centuries earlier. Would they still have servant

girls, he wondered, and then began to wonder if he should be using the main entrance. There had to be an entrance at ground level, probably beside the staircase or off to the side of the house, where he had seen a trellised arbour. He grunted and hauled the two big suitcases up onto the terrace atop the steps. The massive, heavily ornamented door opened onto a blaze of light and colour, and a woman in a well-cut, grey pinstriped suit with a tight-fitting skirt stepped back, smiling, to welcome him in. She appeared to be about his own age or slightly older, with long, loosely bound hair and an intelligent, hawklike face with bright, animated eyes.

Anxiety and surprise undid him. He said, 'Is this the right door? Did I come to the right place?'

'Mr Standish,' the woman said. Her voice was warm and soothing. 'We've been wondering where you might be. Please come in.'

He fell another notch deeper into infatuation with Esswood.

'I've been wondering where I might be, too,' he said, and thought he saw a flash of approval in her lively eyes. Then he ruined it. 'This where they all come in? This is the right door?' She nodded, smiling now at his fatuity instead of his wit, and he carried his heavy bags over the threshold. They seemed fatuous too. Everything inside the entrance seemed very bright – the woman's smile, the gleam of mirrors and polished floorboards and brass and lustrous fabrics. 'You're not carrying a candle,' he said.

'Britain isn't that old-fashioned, Mr Standish. You needn't have carried your bags by yourself, you know. The staff is here to make things easier for you. I'll get

someone to take your things to your rooms straight-
away, and you may go up to relax a bit after your
journey. Then we shall see you in the dining room. Mr
Wall has been waiting for this moment.' Now the
beautiful smile was pure warmth again. 'You must be
famished, poor man.'

Standish wondered if there was even the slightest
chance that this woman might marry him.

'I take it there's nothing else in the car?'

She clearly expected him to say no. The light in her
eyes informed him that he had brought too many
clothes, and that she held out these two great straining
bags to him as a joke she trusted him to share. He
wished that the car and everything inside it would
sink down into the drive and disappear.

'I guess I did bring a lot of stuff,' he said. 'I had to
leave some things in the car.'

'We'll fetch them up for you. We don't want you
straining your back before you set to work.'

She smiled as if in forgiveness of his inexperienced
packing and turned away to lead him towards his
rooms. Standish paused after a few steps. She hesitated
and looked back at him. He gestured towards his
ridiculously heavy suitcases, which sat like intruders
in the polished entryway. 'They'll be seen to,' she said.
'Everything will be seen to. You'll learn our ways, Mr
Standish.'

He set off after her down the entry hall, which he
now saw to be a screened passage lined with vast
tapestries. Between the long tapestries he looked into
a hall the size of a ballroom in which brightly
upholstered furniture had been arranged before a tall
stone fireplace with Ionic columns. Big gloomy paintings of huntsmen, children, and horses hung on the

panelled walls. The next time Standish came to one of
the openings between the screens, he saw a gallery
running above the far side of the room. Curved wooden
beams and arches overhung the gallery.

'That's the East Hall, the oldest part of the house,'
the woman said, looking back at him. 'Elizabethan, of
course.'

'Oh, sure,' Standish said.

They reached the end of the screen passage and
turned left towards a staircase that seemed nearly as
wide as the stairs in front of the house. Portraits of
eighteenth-century noblemen glowed dully on either
side of the staircase, which divided into two smaller,
curving staircases at its top. Standish's guide began
ascending the stairs, and he followed.

'I'm afraid there are more stairs, but you will be
staying right above the library, in the Fountain Rooms.
It's where we always put our scholarly guests, and
they've always seemed quite comfortable there.'

'Is there really a fountain?'

'In the courtyard, not in the room, Mr Standish.'
Turning into the left branch of the staircase, she
smiled again at him over her shoulder. 'You have an
excellent view of the courtyard from your rooms.'

A question that had occurred to him in Zenith came
to him now.

'Am I the only one? I mean, aren't there other people
working in the library now?'

'No, of course not,' she said, giving him a rather
severe, questioning look and at last pausing to allow
him to catch up with her. 'I assumed you would have
known. Do forgive me. I seem to have forgotten that
you've never been here before. We never invite more
than one guest to make use of the library at any time.

Scholarship seems a very individual activity, I suppose, and I think we always wanted our guests to be able to make full use of Esswood. Didn't want to have two people trying to use the same set of papers – your sort of work is actually very intimate, isn't it? Sharing it would be like sharing, oh, I don't know, a toothbrush or a bathtowel or – '

A bed, Standish thought.

'Well,' she said. Her eyes glowed. 'At any rate, yes, you are the only one. You have three weeks in which all of Esswood, especially the papers in the library, is yours. In a manner of speaking.'

'Do you think I might be able to get an extension for another week if it turns out I need it?'

'I should think it possible. We are nearly there now.'

They were climbing the narrower side-stairs together, and she smiled up at him.

'The Fountain Rooms are just ahead through the Inner Gallery. And the Inner Gallery is just beyond this . . .'

She opened a door at the top of the staircase and led him into a room or passageway that seemed as dark as a movie theatre after the dazzle of his introduction to the house. About the size of the bedroom he shared with Jean back in Zenith, the dark room seemed crowded with furniture, uncomfortable and cramped. 'Lighting's wonky here. Must get it seen to. Study, this is, not used much now.' In the gloom Standish picked out heavy chairs with ottomans, books in dim, dull ranks on the walls. Shadowy and indistinct, the woman moved like a blur before his eyes, almost melting into the room, and threw open another door at its far end. She slipped through into a rectangle of yellow light.

Standish felt as though he were pursuing her.

He burst out into the next, brighter room half-expecting to see her moving ahead of him down a corridor. But she stood facing him from a point about six feet into a long, high-ceilinged space too wide to be a corridor and too long and narrow to be a room. One side of this museum-like space was decorated with large paintings of horses and dogs and boats at sea, beneath which were arranged low, uncomfortable-looking benches. The other side, Standish's left, was lined with a series of enormous windows that looked out onto the lighted windows of another vast house. Then Standish realized that the other house was another section of Esswood, and that he was looking out over the courtyard.

'Nearly there, Mr Standish. This is the Inner Gallery, so called because there is another gallery, the West Gallery, on the second floor at the front of the house. The West Gallery was added in the seventeen-thirties when Sir Walton Seneschal redid Esswood's façade in the Palladian style.'

Palladian, Standish thought. That was the word he had not been able to remember. Then he remembered seeing the light, as of a flashlight or candle, passing behind the windows as he approached the house.

'The Gallery is on the second floor?' he asked.

'Both of them, yes.'

'And the second floor is where I entered, at the top of the stairs?'

She stopped. 'Oh no – you entered on the first floor. The one below is the ground floor. Americans always take a little time to learn our system.' She began to move forward past the large dark windows.

Maybe he had been mistaken. 'And you didn't carry

a candle, or something like a candle, past the front windows when you heard me coming?'

She stopped again and looked up at him in a way that seemed almost tense with worry. Then her face softened. 'Are you teasing me?'

And there it was again, the note of a subdued flirtatiousness just beneath the surface of her manner.

'I don't think I'd know how to tease you,' Standish said. The flirtatiousness disappeared so quickly that Standish wondered if he had imagined it. 'I mean, I thought I saw someone carrying a lamp past the first-floor windows.'

Her face smoothed out into a deliberate absence of expression. 'I'm afraid that's not possible, Mr Standish.' She continued down the gallery a step ahead of him.

'And now we have arrived,' she said, opening the door at the gallery's end. 'Everything's been prepared for you. Your bags should be here in a moment. As soon as you're ready, Mr Wall will be waiting in the dining room, which you can reach by returning to the ground floor, turning to the right of the main staircase, and going straight through the West Hall. Or you might take the back staircase from your room to the library; go past the library, and keep turning left in the corridor until you come to the double doors – that'll be the dining room.'

'Fine.'

She stepped back instead of leading him into the room, as he had hoped. To keep her from leaving, he said, 'Are the Seneschals here now?'

She nodded. 'They're seldom elsewhere. Miss Seneschal is an invalid and rarely leaves the family wing. Of course, they're both quite old.'

'They have no children?'

Her extraordinary face flickered, as if this time he really had gone too far, and she gestured towards the half-opened door to the Fountain Rooms. 'Remember not to keep poor Mr Wall waiting long – he'll be quite overcome with relief when he sees you. As overcome as you will be to see your dinner, I imagine.'

'I look forward to seeing both of them. And to seeing you again, too.'

She shot what he took as a glance of humorous appreciation at him with her wide intelligent eyes, and she turned away.

Standish stepped through the door into the Fountain Rooms and turned to watch her walk away. He realized that she had never told him her name. He could not call out to her – he could not shout in Esswood. She opened the door at the far end of the gallery, and then she was gone.

His rooms were not what he had expected. The splendour of the rest of the house and the name 'Fountain Rooms' had led Standish to anticipate extravagance: gold and velvet, decorative antiques, a canopied bed. The reality of the Fountain Rooms was as mundane as a room in a slightly rundown old hotel.

It was a suite of two small rooms. The living room was furnished with stiff, high-backed chairs and a couch covered in a floral chintz. A small table with ancient copies of *Country Life* and *The Tatler* stood before the couch. Standard lamps with big yellow shades shed mild light. A stuffed fox and a terrarium with dark green ferns stood on the mantel of the fireplace. Against a wall with rose-patterned paper there was a writing desk with a leather top and a green

library lamp. A bookshelf beside the desk was
crammed with novels by Warwick Deeping, Compton
Mackenzie, John Buchan, and Agatha Christie. The
books looked welded into place. On the pale walls
with roses had been hung pictures of men in wigs and
embroidered waistcoats playing cards in what looked
like the East Hall downstairs, people in slightly more
modern dress playing croquet on a terrace beneath the
rear elevation of Esswood House, of a carriage drawn
by prancing horses coming up the drive where Standish
had left his car. A small spotted spaniel trotted alongside the carriage, his head raised. Through the windows on the left side of the room Standish saw the
Seneschals' windows glowing back at him from across
the courtyard. The room contained no television,
radio, or telephone.

Slightly smaller than the living room, the bedroom
was fitted with a narrow single bed with a bedside
table and carved wooden headboard, a comfortable-
looking wing-backed chair, a sofa covered with the
same dark blue floral material as the bedspread, a
second small desk, and a large wooden press for hanging clothes. Beside the press was a tall wooden door
which must have led to the back staircase. There was
another chest-high bookshelf, this one filled with what
appeared to be a complete set of the writings of
Winston Churchill. On the mantel of the bedroom
fireplace was a pair of heavy, ornate silver candlesticks,
and above it hung a geometrical steel engraving which
proved to be a plan of Esswood's terraces, showing a
long pond, what appeared to be a little forest with a
circular clearing like a druidical site, and fields. The
shutters of the bedroom windows had been closed, and

the entire room looked hazy in the low golden light of the lamps.

Standish pulled at the handles of a pair of mirrored doors, expecting to find a closet, and looked into a tiled bathroom. He stepped inside, closed the door behind him, and used the toilet. Afterwards, he washed his hands and inspected his face in the mirror.

The rims of his eyelids showed a faint pink like the eyes of a rabbit. Grey smears of dust lay across his cheeks. His receding hair, flat as seaweed, stuck to his head. Standish groaned. This was the face that the wonderful quick-witted woman had seen. What he had taken for flirtation had only been civilized pity. He had turned up hours late with an absurd amount of luggage; he had gaped like a tourist; he had undoubtedly leered. Yes, he had leered. Oh, God. Standish took off his jacket and unbuttoned his shirt. He filled the basin with hot water and washed his hands and face. Then he emptied and refilled the basin and quickly washed his hair.

He came out of the bathroom and saw his shirts, socks, and underwear laid out on the bed beside his bathroom kit. His four bags stood beside the bed. On the little desk was *Crack, Whack, and Wheel*. His suits and jackets and trousers had been hung in the press, his shoes arranged beneath them, his ties on a tie rack.

Standish put on a clean shirt, a new tie, and a blazer from the press. He changed his shoes for a pair of shiny loafers. The mirrored doors told him that he once again looked like a respectable young scholar. He felt light-headed with hunger, and decided that the back way to the dining room sounded faster than working his way through the gallery, the dark little study, and down the staircase. He marched up to the door beside the press and pulled it open.

FOUR

On the other side was a bare, unpolished wooden landing. A narrow flight of stairs dropped past a window and then curved out of sight. Low-wattage bulbs set in old gas fixtures gave the stairs a dim but even illumination. Standish moved across the landing and began to descend the stairs.

After the third or fourth turning of the staircase he looked back up the way he had come and saw only the smooth skin of the walls and the steep dark risers of the steps. He wondered if he had somehow missed the exit onto the first floor and was descending into the scullery, or the dungeon, or whatever they had in the basement here. Then he remembered the height of the hall with the enormous stone fireplace, and kept going downwards. After another series of turns he came to a place where the light bulbs had burned out, and he continued down slowly, touching the walls on both sides. When the stairs turned again Standish expected to emerge into the light, but the darkness continued. He felt his way down another nine or ten steps in the dark. At another turn of the staircase, light from below began to wash the outer wall, and after another few steps he saw that his hands and the sleeves of his blazer were grey with spider webs.

A little while later he saw the bottom of the staircase beneath him. A flagged corridor illuminated by the same altered gas fittings led to a tall, narrow door identical to the one in his bedroom. This must have been the door to the library. Standish came down the final few steps and went down the corridor to stand in front of the door. Almost guiltily he placed his hand on the brass doorknob. He looked sideways down the empty corridor. After all he had been through this day, no one would begrudge him a private treat. He had been invited to use the library: and Isobel had written a good deal of her verse on the other side of this door.

Standish turned the knob, so intent on seeing the library that when the door resisted him he turned it again and rattled it back and forth, as if he could force it open. Why was it locked? To keep the servants out? To keep *him* out? Standish remembered the dead lamps in the staircase, and wondered how long it had been since the last scholar had been invited to Esswood. Then he remembered what the publican in Huckstall had said about an American being murdered at Esswood, and quickly turned away from the door.

After about fifteen yards he came to a sharp left-hand turn in the corridor, marked by an Italianate marble statue of a small boy rising up on his toes, arms outstretched, as if for a kiss. Standish went past the statue into the new wing of the corridor and moved on in silence for another thirty or forty feet. Again there was an abrupt left-hand turn, this time into a wider, but still flagged and dimly lighted corridor. At the turn another marble statue, of a woman cowering back with her hands over her face, stood on a round, marble-topped table. Now Standish could hear low voices and soft noises coming from somewhere within the house. At last he stood before a wide set of double doors. He knocked softly and saw dingy wisps of spider webs adhering to his cuff. He hastily wiped them off. No one answered his knock. Standish turned the knob,

and heard a satisfying *thunk* as the lock withdrew into
its stile. He pushed, and the thick door opened before
him.

A man with a square, sturdy face and thick grey hair
that fell over his forehead blinked at him, then smiled
and stood up on the far side of a long table that took
up the middle of the room. A single place setting had
been laid opposite them on the smooth white cloth.
The man was several inches taller than Standish. 'Ah,
at last,' he said. 'Mr Standish. How good it is to see
you. I am Robert Wall.'

As soon as Standish stepped forward he saw that the
table was too wide for them to shake hands across it.

'Lost a bet with myself,' Wall said. 'You stick there,
and I'll make the trek round.'

Wall smiled at him with a touch of ruefulness and
began to walk round the bottom of the table to greet
him. He wore a beautifully cut, grey tweed suit, a dark
blue shirt, and a pink tie of raw silk. Wall was not
quite what Standish had expected – he looked like a
college president, not the administrator of an obscure
literary foundation. His handsomeness struck Standish
as an irrelevance, almost a hindrance. Wall marched
up to him with his hand outstretched, and Standish
realized how Jean would respond to the sight of this
man.

'Allow me to welcome you properly,' Wall said. He
gave Standish a dry, brisk handshake. 'You *have* had a
day of it, haven't you? Care for a drink before we have
the opportunity of feeding you? Splash of whisky?
Single malt? Something special, I promise you.'

Standish never drank whisky, but heard himself
agreeing. Up close, Robert Wall's face looked dusty
with fatigue. Tiny wrinkles like razor cuts nicked

the corners of his eyes and mouth. Wall grinned at Standish and turned away towards a pantry located behind a door at the bottom end of the table. Standish trailed after him. The size and splendour of the dining room both stimulated and oppressed him. Portraits of dead Seneschals frowned down from the walls, and wherever Standish looked he saw some unexpected ornamental detail: dental moulding around the ceiling, the pattern of the parquet floor around the edges of the Oriental carpet, plaster rosettes around the light fixtures on the wall. The flatware set around his plate, and the plate itself as well as the rim of the wine glass beside it, were of gold. A golden plate! A golden fork, a golden spoon, a golden knife! The casualness of this opulence unsettled him, as if he had inadvertently stepped outside ordinary reality into the world of fairy tales.

Behind the glass-fronted cupboard doors in the pantry stood ranks of the golden plates, and in the cupboard at the far end was an array of bottles. A narrow staircase like the one Standish had taken from his room led downstairs, presumably to the kitchen. Robert Wall took a bottle from the shelf and two glasses from another cabinet.

'You said you lost a bet with yourself?'

'Yes, I did,' Wall said, smiling at him as he passed back into the dining room. His obvious exhaustion and the tiny cuts around his eyes and mouth utterly negated his good looks when you were this close to him – he looked as though he were still recovering from a skin graft.

Then for an instant Standish thought that Robert Wall did not look exhausted or ill but simply hungry, like a man who has never ceased to long for the great prizes that he has seen hovering, all his life, just out of reach, like a man who has never given up wanting more than he has decided to settle for.

Wall eased past him in the narrow space of the pantry and, as both men emerged back into the dining room, Standish realized that it was he, not Wall, who was hungry – he was famished, ravenous as a starving wolf.

Carrying the bottle and the short glasses, Wall went up one side of the table, Standish the other. Wall gestured towards the place that had been set, and Standish sat.

'The bet was that you'd have taken the main staircase back downstairs, and come in here from the West Hall. You're very intrepid, finding your way by the backstairs.'

Wall poured whisky as he spoke. He leaned far over to pass Standish his glass, and then sank gracefully down into his own chair. For a moment filled with dismay, Standish found himself wondering if Wall was married to the woman who had shown him to his rooms.

Are you teasing me? For a moment he saw the woman's hawklike face looking up at him.

'A woman showed me to my room,' he said.

Wall nodded and raised his glass, giving Standish a look of vague disinterest. Standish took an experimental sip. The whisky tasted like a rich, smooth food. It was ambrosial. Wall was waiting for whatever he would say next. 'The woman knew about the back staircase – that's how I knew about it. Who is she, by the way? She didn't tell me her name.'

'Couldn't say. You're settled in all right?'

'Dark hair, very long and sort of *loose*? Extremely good-looking? About my age?'

'Mystery woman,' Wall said. 'You really are intrepid.' He looked at his watch. 'Your dinner should be ready in a moment. Just a question of warming it up. Do you like the malt?'

'Wonderful.'

'Excellent – intrepid and blessed with good taste as well. It *is* rather special – seventy years old.'

'You mean you don't know who she is?'

'I tend not to have much to do with that sort of thing. You had a peaceful journey?'

Standish described getting lost on the roundabout and miraculously finding his way to Huckstall, and the scene in the pub there. 'I was thinking afterwards that the whole thing was like an Isobel Standish poem – an Isobel Standish kind of *experience*, if you see what I mean.'

'A pity you should have chosen Huckstall for your first excursion into English life, but it can't be helped, can it?'

'Are they famous for waylaying visitors?'

'Not exactly. During dinner I'll spin you a tale.' He glanced at his watch. 'Where *is* your dinner? They should have brought it up by now. I expect they're waiting for us to finish our whisky even as we wait for them to bring your meal.' He stood up and went down the table and slipped through the pantry door. Standish heard him speaking to someone on the other side of the pantry door, then a low female laugh. Wall backed through the door with a tray in his hands. 'Good job I didn't startle her into dropping this. They've given you a meal with a bit of a history. Loin of veal with morel sauce, some green beans too, I see. I'll open a nice Bordeaux to go with that, shall I?'

Standish nodded. The smell of the food on the tray made him salivate. Wall set the plate down before him, and it fitted perfectly into the larger golden plate. Wall carried the tray to the pantry, and reappeared instantly with a bottle of red wine and a corkscrew.

'I'll join you, if I may. We could continue our conversation until you want to go to bed. I must be off tomorrow afternoon, so I won't be here for a little time. Though I could have breakfast with you, if you like?'

'Please,' Standish said, happy not to be abandoned to the dining room. He tried a small section of the veal, and a variety of tastes so subtle and powerful spilled into his mouth that he groaned out loud. He had never tasted anything even faintly like it. The cork came out of the bottle with a solid pop, and Wall poured deep red wine into his gold-rimmed glass. Standish swallowed, and the food continued to ring and chime in his mouth.

'You know why you're given veal with morels, of course?' Wall sat down on the other side of the table.

Standish shook his head. He continued to eat as Wall spoke, now and then pausing to sip the wine, which was as extraordinary as the food.

'Isobel Standish's favourite meal.' Wall smiled at him. 'When they heard that in the kitchen, there was no restraining them. We use fresh mushrooms, of course, and good veal can be had in the village. I'm happy you approve.' He paused, and the benign expression on his face altered. 'So you knew nothing of Huckstall before you stopped there? Its fame had not crossed the Atlantic?'

Standish shook his head. A circle of warmth in the centre of his being was spreading outwards millimetre by millimetre, bringing peace and contentment to every cell it touched.

'Little bit of trouble there, earlier this summer,' Wall said. 'Man killed his wife and her lover, then was killed himself. A publican.'

Standish saw the stony, immobile face of The Duellists' proprietor vividly before him, and the wonderful food congealed on his tongue.

'Not much of a scandal by American standards, of course,' Wall went on, 'but it made quite a splash here. The woman was pregnant. The husband chained them up in the cellar of the pub and tortured them for several days. Finished up by decapitating both of them. The boyfriend was a prominent fellow locally – local poet, something of the sort. I didn't mean to spoil your meal, Mr Standish.'

'No, it's fascinating,' Standish said. 'It reminds me so much of the people I saw there.'

Wall looked pleasantly bemused.

'In that pub, The Duellists.'

'Ah.' Wall smiled indulgently. 'See what you mean. Can't remember the name of this fellow's pub at the moment. Lord Somebody-Or-Other's, I think. Couldn't have been your place anyhow.'

'Why not?'

'Chap burned it down after he committed the murders, didn't he? Completely off his head, of course. Excuse the pun, if that's what that was. Anyhow, he put the heads in bags of some sort and tossed them onto a slag heap. Probably thought that no one would ever find them. Or didn't care. His own life was useless to him anyway, wasn't it? He jumped in front of a

speeding car just outside the village. Have some more
of that wine, won't you?'

Standish saw with astonishment that his glass was
empty. He lifted the bottle and poured. Wall pushed
his own glass forward and Standish stood up to pour
for him too.

'The impact killed him, but nobody discovered the
body until the next morning – all busy fighting the
fire, do you see? The pub went up like tinder. Danger
the entire street might go up with it. And then, of
course, after they'd put out the blaze they found the
bodies, which had escaped most of the effects of the
fire. Being in the cellar, you know. Oh!' His eyes
flashed at Standish. 'I'd forgotten – the chap, the
boyfriend fellow, wasn't the local poet. All part of the
scandal. He *had* been important – not any more.
Fellow had been the librarian, something like that,
headmaster perhaps, but had gone seriously downhill
years before. Became a drunk. No job. Lived rough.
Pub fellow couldn't take the humiliation of being
cuckolded by a virtual tramp.'

Standish ate steadily while Wall spoke, in reality
now only half-tasting the wonderful food.

'This *is* a terrible tale for dinnertime, isn't it?'

'Not really,' Standish said. 'When I was in The
Duellists – '

'I must tell you the rest. The next day, as I say, the
body of the publican was found on the road. Man had
been crushed by the car that struck him. Car was still
there, you see – driver's door open, engine still running. No driver in sight. He had panicked and scarpered
across the moor. Never knew he was innocent – never
knew the whole tale.'

'Didn't they track him through his car?'

'Rented. Fellow may have used a false name, as far as I know. He's still running, I suppose.'

'The man in The Duellists told me that someone had been murdered here.'

'At Esswood?'

'Yeah! An American, he said.'

'That's very odd.' Wall seemed entirely unperturbed. 'I'm sure I should have heard of it. After all, I'm generally somewhere about the place.' He was frowning-smiling, the frown being a disguise for a smile. It was perhaps the most ironic expression Standish had ever seen.

'I thought it sounded funny,' Standish said.

'Can't really think when we last had a murder.' Wall was nearly smiling outright. 'And I've been around here most of my life. Your fellow had the name confused with Exmoor, or something of the sort. You weren't worried about it, I hope?'

'Of course not. Not at all. Nope.'

'You were clearly a good selection for an Esswood Fellowship, Mr Standish.'

'Thanks.' Unsettled by the flattery, Standish wondered if he should ask Wall to call him William. Would Wall ask to be called Robert?

'Did you happen to peek into the library on your way through the back hallway? If I were in your shoes, don't think I could have resisted.'

'Well, not really,' Standish said, and Wall raised his eyebrows. 'That is, to tell you the truth, I did try the door, but it was locked.'

'I'm afraid that isn't possible. The library doors are never locked. Could it have been another door?'

'Near the bottom of the stairs?'

'Hmm. No matter. Sounds as if it didn't want to let

you in. We may have to reconsider your application, Mr Standish.'

Now he knew he was being teased. He sipped his wine, and then met Wall's continuing silence with a question. 'You said you've been at Esswood most of your life. Were you born here?'

'I was, in fact. My father was the gamekeeper before the first war, and we lived in a cottage beyond the far field.' Wall poured for himself and Standish. 'In those days, what drew guests here to Esswood was Edith Seneschal's hospitality and the fame of her kitchen, which as you see continues to be pretty good, but the pleasure they had in one another's company and whatever they found to enjoy in Esswood itself kept them coming back. Their gratitude for that pleasure led them to contribute to our library – which is, of course, why it is unique. Every literary guest we had donated manuscripts, papers, diaries, notebooks, drafts, material they knew to be significant as well as things they must have considered nearly worthless. Of course, some of the latter have turned out to be among our most important possessions.'

'Manuscripts and diaries? T. S. Eliot and Lawrence and everybody else? Even Theodore Corn – even Isobel?'

'Oh, even Isobel, I assure you,' Wall said, smiling. 'Especially Isobel, I might say. I don't quite know how it began, but before long it had become a custom to give something of that sort to the house, as a token repayment for Edith's hospitality, as an indication of one's gratitude for Esswood's beauty and seclusion . . . it was part of coming here at all, to leave something like that behind when you left.'

'That's extraordinary,' Standish said. 'You mean that

all these famous people donated original manuscripts and diaries every time they came?'

'Every time. Year after year. Isobel Standish came to Esswood twice, and I believe she left some very significant items for the library.'

'And were these, um, donations copies of more widely known works? It doesn't sound – '

'Nor should it. I *think* I'm right in saying that everything of that sort we have is unique to us. None of it can be published or reproduced elsewhere, except by arrangement. Those were the conditions that evolved, you see.'

Standish felt as though he had licked his finger and pushed it into a socket. The place was a treasure-house. Manuscripts of unknown works by some of the century's greatest writers, early handwritten drafts of famous poems and novels! It was like coming on a warehouse full of unknown paintings by Matisse, Cézanne, and Picasso.

Robert Wall must have seen some of his excitement in his face, for he said, 'I know. Rather takes the breath away, doesn't it. If you're the sort of person who can appreciate it properly. Of course, you can see why we are very careful each year in selecting the Esswood Fellows – they have a great deal to live up to.'

'Wow,' Standish said. 'Absolutely.'

'And that was its attraction for me too, I imagine. Apart from its being the only home I've ever really known. I went to school and then university – the Seneschals were always very generous when they felt generosity was called for – but I'm afraid I always felt a deep connection to Esswood. So after university I did my best to make myself indispensable, and I've been here ever since. Called up in the second war, of course, but I couldn't wait to get back here. Still the gamekee-per's boy at heart, I fear. And I do like to think I've helped Esswood move into the modern world without losing anything of its past.'

Wall smiled at Standish. 'That's the thing, you see. The past of Esswood is really still quite alive. I can remember walking out past the long pond with my father one morning and seeing Edith Seneschal, who seemed to me the loveliest woman in the world, wander towards me with a tall woman, also beautiful, and a stout, distinguished, elderly gentleman, and introducing me to Virginia Woolf and Henry James. James was very old then, of course, and it was his last visit to Esswood. He bent down to shake my hand, and he admired my coat. "What a lot of buttons you have, young man," he said to me. "Is your name Buttons?" I was tongue-tied, hadn't a clue what to say to him, just gawped up like a gormless fool, which he took awfully well. Later on in life I read everything I could about them, James and Woolf, as well as all their work – I tried to learn everything possible about all our guests. Scholars included, of course. I see that as one of the essential tasks of running Esswood properly. We screen everybody pretty thoroughly beforehand, and try to get to know them even better while they're with us. We want to be well-matched with our guests. It won't *work* as well as it should if it isn't a proper mating. The people who come here must love Esswood.'

Standish nodded.

'But you see, I'm an advanced case. I love it so much I've never left.'

'You're a lucky man.'

'I agree. It's better never to leave Esswood.'

Never to leave Esswood. Standish heard some unspoken message, a kind of silent resonance, in Wall's last
words. Even Wall's posture, his head tipped back and
his fingers wrapped around his glass, seemed to com-
municate the aura of an unspoken meaning. Then
Standish realized at least one of the things Wall must
have meant: he had been something like ten in 1914,
and therefore must now be over eighty years old. The
man looked to be somewhere in his fifties.

'Esswood has been good to you,' he said.

Wall smiled slowly, and nodded in agreement. 'Esswood and I try to be good to each other. I think it will
be good to you too, Mr Standish. We were all very
happy when we received your application. Until then
it looked as though there might not be an Esswood
Fellow this year.'

'I couldn't have been the only applicant!'

'No, we had about the usual number of applicants.'

Standish raised his eyebrows in curiosity, and Wall
indulged him. 'Something over six hundred. Six
hundred and thirty-nine, to be exact.'

'And mine was the only one you considered?'

'Oh, you had some competition,' Wall said. 'There is
always a period of several months while things sort
themselves out. We do take what we consider to be
more than usual care.' He smiled with the same slow
ease, and looked nothing like the son of a gamekeeper.
'If you're finished, we could peek in at the library.
Then I'll let you get the rest I'm sure you need. Unless
you have some questions?'

Standish looked down at his plate. Most of the
wonderful meal seemed to have consumed itself. 'I
guess I can't help wondering when I'll have the chance
to meet the Seneschals.'

Wall stood up. 'They're not in the best of health.'

'The woman who greeted me said that Mrs Seneschal – '

Again Wall stopped him with a look that told him not to trespass. 'Let us try that troublesome door, shall we?'

Standish stood up. For a moment his head swam and he had to steady himself on the back of his chair. Some words that Robert Wall said to him vanished like everything else into grey fuzz, and then his head cleared and his vision returned. 'Sorry.'

'Do you feel all right?'

'Just a little spell. I missed what you said, I'm sorry.'

Wall opened the door through which Standish had entered the dining room. 'All I said was, you must have heard this mysterious person incorrectly. There is no Mrs Seneschal.'

Standish passed by Wall, and the deep grooves like scars in his face came into focus.

'It's Miss Seneschal. She and Mr Seneschal are brother and sister. Edith's two surviving children.'

'Oh, I was sure – '

'Simple mistake for a weary man.' Wall gestured down the length of the flagged corridor. 'Unlike most of our guests on the first night, you already know this way quite well, don't you?' He set off in the direction from which Standish had come. 'Yet another sign of our good judgement in selecting you.'

They walked on a few paces, Wall striding like a youthful and well-exercised man.

'You're married, aren't you, Mr Standish?'

They turned right at the statue of the woman shrinking back.

'Yes, I am.'

'Children?'

'Not yet,' Standish said, the skin at the back of his neck prickling. He thrust away from him the vision of a lighted window in a Popham apartment house, a drawn shade behind which two people, one of them a faithless wife and the other a faithless friend, clawed at one another in bed. Wall was looking at him inquisitively, and he added, 'Jean is pregnant – expecting in two months.'

'So we'd better get you home safe and sound before that, hadn't we?'

Standish nodded vaguely.

They turned right again, past the reaching boy.

'In any case, this is what you've come all this way to see. Let us try this puzzling door.'

They stood before the tall, narrow, wooden door. Wall's face was a shadow beneath his handsome grey hair. Entirely unwillingly, Standish saw Jean folding herself into Wall's arms, rubbing her face fiercely against his chest. Jean often made a fool of herself with handsome men.

'Seems to work normally.' Wall turned his shadowy face towards Standish. 'Perhaps you turned the knob the wrong way.'

He had not turned the knob the wrong way. For an instant it was as if Jean, or her shade, had witnessed his humiliation, and Standish felt a ferocious blush leap across his face like a rash.

Wall stepped inside and flicked a switch. Warm bright light filled the door. 'Come in, Mr Standish.'

Standish followed him into an enormous room which seemed at first to contain a disappointingly small number of books. Most of the room consisted of vast empty space. Bright white Corinthian columns

shining with gold leaf at top and bottom stood before
curved recesses ranked with books. Books spanned the
library beneath classical murals. Almost immediately
he realized that there were thousands and thousands
of books, books on shelves all around the massive
room, books reaching nearly to the barrel-vaulted ceiling as ornate as a Wedgwood china pattern, books and
manuscript boxes everywhere, in every moulded, flow-
ing section of the huge room. Chairs and chaises of red
plush with gilded arms stood at intervals along the
walls, and a massive chair sat before a wooden writing
desk in the middle of the room, on the centre rosette
of a vast, peach-coloured Oriental carpet. Over the
mantel of the marble fireplace on the left side of the
library hung a large portrait of a gentleman in eighteenth-century clothes and white wig looking up from
a folio propped on the library's writing desk. The
library's walls, and the section of the high-vaulted
ceiling not covered with ornate plaster palmettes,
husks, arabesques, and scrolls, were painted a cool,
almost edible colour hovering between green and grey
that seemed lit from within. The entire space of the
library was filled with radiant light that came from no
visible source. Standish had spent much of his life in
libraries without seeing one like this. He wondered if
he really could walk through it – it seemed too good to
use, like some delicate clockwork toy or Fabergé egg.

'Rather good, isn't it?' Robert Wall was leaning back
against one of the pillars, his arms crossed over his
chest. 'It's a Robert Adam room, of course. One of his
most successful, we think.'

'What are those columns made of? I thought they
were painted, but – '

'Alabaster. Striking, isn't it? As good as anything at

Saltram House. They look freshly painted until you see those delicate veins in the stone.' In his ambiguous face was a full understanding of just what Standish was feeling.

Wall pushed himself forward and stood up. 'Now I must take you through the main entrance and point you up the staircase. It's a little late to creep through the servants' corridor. Though I daresay in the old days the servants' corridor saw a great deal of surreptitious movement.'

Standish smiled before he understood what Wall meant. Wall led him out through an archway set between two of the alabaster columns, then through a pair of ornately carved wooden doors and into another high, vast room that seemed cold and museum-like after the library.

Before them, across an expanse of dark carpet and through the middle of a double row of stiff chairs like soldiers, was another set of carved doors.

'Dining room can be reached through there,' Wall said, indicating the far doors, 'and the main staircase which takes you up to the Inner Gallery and the Fountain Rooms is directly ahead of you. Until we meet again, then. We will see to your car tomorrow. Don't give it a thought.'

The two men began to move down past the soldierly chairs.

'I can't help but wonder what happens to the place once Edith's children die. Who inherits the place?'

'I'm afraid there's no proper answer to that.'

'What does that mean? That you can't tell me?'

Instead of answering, Wall opened the door at the far end of the uncomfortable room, and stood waiting for

Standish to go through. For a moment he reminded Standish of the landlord of The Duellists.

'I'm sorry if that was an awkward question.'

'I'm sorry if you didn't like my answer. But if you want to know anything else, ask away. You may have three questions.'

'Well, I guess I'm curious about Isobel. I mean, I know she died here, and I guess I always assumed that she had some illness. Do you remember anything about it?'

Wall continued to hold the door and look down at Standish. His expression had not changed in any way.

'Did she have influenza?'

'Is that your second question?'

'Well, I know there were influenza epidemics around then ... Do you remember Isobel at all? I've never even seen a picture of her.'

'That is your third question. Of course I remember Isobel. It was a great loss for all of us when she died. Everyone here cared for her deeply.' He motioned Standish through the door, and followed him out into the great hall. 'She died in childbirth, to answer your real question. I'm rather surprised that you should not have known.'

'I didn't even know that she'd had a child,' Standish said.

'The child died too.' Wall smiled and stepped away. 'You do remember how to get back to the Fountain Rooms?'

When Standish reached the top of the wide staircase he turned to look back down at Robert Wall, but the entire first floor of Esswood was dark. He heard a burst of female laughter from beneath him, as if it had risen up the stairs like smoke.

In the bedroom he undressed and discovered that the sheets were delightfully cool and the bed just as firm as he liked a bed to be. He heard the lights in the Inner Gallery click off. Far away a door closed softly.

FIVE

Standish and a number of other men were being held captive in a large bare cabin with a plank floor and rough wooden walls. Armed guards in brown uniforms lounged against the walls, idly watching the prisoners and speaking to one another in low, unintelligible voices. At one end of the huge wooden room was a low raised platform where a man whose grey hair had been shaved close to his bullet head sat behind a desk. Stacks of pages lay on the surface of the desk, and the man examined papers one by one before transferring them from one stack to another. He was dressed in a baggy grey suit and a wide florid necktie, and the points of his shirt collar turned up. Like the uniformed guards, he looked bored. The faces of all the men, the guards and the official behind the desk, were broad, fleshy, masculine, roughened by alcohol and comfortable with brutality and death. Through windows cut into the sides of the building Standish saw snow falling steadily onto a white landscape. At irregular intervals a man holding a rifle and bundled into a fur cap and a heavy dark coat struggled past the windows, gripping the leashes of two straining dogs. All of these men were at ease with the cold and the perpetual snow. They were at ease with everything they did. The atmosphere was of unhurried bureaucratic peace.

Fearful, Standish stood in the middle of the room

with the other captives. All but he wore colourless
woollen garments that resembled pyjamas. Standish
knew that in time he too would be stripped of his
jacket, shirt, tie, trousers, and shoes, and be dressed in
the woollen pyjamas. There was no possibility of
escape. If he managed to get outside and evade the
guards and the dogs he would die of exposure.

The shoulders of his fellow prisoners were bent,
their heads cropped, their faces shadowy. They had
reconciled themselves to death; in a sense they were
already dead, for nothing could move or touch them,
nothing could jar them out of their apathy.

Standish experienced the purest dread of his life.

The man at the desk was selecting the order in
which Standish and his fellow prisoners were to be
executed. There was no possibility of pardon. Sooner
or later this bored extermination machine was going
to snuff out each one of them. There was nothing
personal about it. It was business: a matter of moving
papers from one stack to another.

The man at the desk looked up and uttered a mono-
syllable. One of the guards straightened up, walked
towards the group of prisoners, and seized one man by
the elbow. The prisoner got to his feet and allowed
himself to be pulled towards the door. Nobody but
Standish watched this. The guard opened the door and
handed the prisoner almost gently to a man in a dark
coat and fur hat. This second guard pulled the prisoner
away into the snow, and the door closed.

Standish knew that the prisoner was going to be
beheaded. Somewhere out of his range of vision was a
wooden chopping block and a basket that caught the
severed heads.

He glanced towards the door, and knew that one of

the guards would shoot him if he even touched the
knob.

Standish paced around the middle of the room under
the eye of the guards. Some of the other prisoners were
also walking aimlessly around the room, and Standish
avoided looking at them closely. Some of the men sat
on the floor, their backs bowed, and some curled up on
the planks as if asleep, hiding their faces in their hands.
Standish did not want to see their faces. If you saw one
of the faces . . . then you saw it tumbling off the block,
its eyes and mouth open, the brain still conscious, still
recording and reacting to the shock, the terrible
knowledge . . .

Standish realized that he was not dreaming. Somehow he had ventured into this wretched country, been
captured, condemned to death, and transported to this
penal outpost with these degraded men. He looked
wildly around, and the two nearest guards watched
him closely. Standish forced himself to walk slowly up
to one of the cabin's walls. He placed his hand on the
cold wall. A swift, continuous draught flowed into the
room from the gaps between the boards.

The official called out another name, and in the blur
of sound Standish heard *st* and *sh*. His blood thinned.
A languid guard pushed himself off a wall and walked
towards him. Standish could not move. The guard
advanced, looking at him expressionlessly. Standish
opened his mouth and found that he could not form
words. He saw large black pores on the guard's stony
face and a long white scar, puckered like a vertical
kiss, running from his right eye to the middle of his
cheek.

The guard brushed past Standish and grasped the
upper arm of a man in grey pyjamas just behind him.

The guard began to jerk the man towards the door. As they passed Standish, the prisoner lifted his head and looked directly into Standish's face. His eyes were black and flat as stones. Standish stepped backwards, and the guard pulled his prisoner away.

Standish turned round and saw a baby lying on a blanket that had been folded on a small table against the opposite wall. The baby jerked its hands towards its face, then froze. The baby's hands drifted down to its sides as slowly as if the baby were under water. It was a new baby, red-faced, only a few days old. It wore coarse woollen baby clothes of the same material as the prisoner's pyjamas. The baby seemed to gasp for air. Standish took a step forward, and the baby's arms jerked spasmodically towards its head. Puffy, swollen-looking pads of flesh covered the baby's eyes.

One of the guards shouted at Standish, who stopped moving and pointed at the baby. 'I want to pick it up. What can be wrong with that?'

The man behind the desk carefully placed the paper in his hand on a neutral space on his desk and uttered a short series of monosyllables that caused the soldier to lower his rifle and retreat to the wall. Standish swallowed.

The official turned his head to look at Standish. His eyes were the colour of rainwater in a barrel. 'This not your baby,' the official said in a low, heavily accented voice. 'Possible you understand? This baby not your baby.'

And then Standish understood that he had lost everything. He was to be beheaded in this ugly country, and the baby gasping on the table was not his baby. Black steam filled his veins. He groaned, at the end of his life, and woke up in a sunny bedroom at Esswood.

SIX

'Got it wrong again,' said Robert Wall. It was half an hour later. Carrying two pencils, a legal pad, and his copy of *Crack, Whack, and Wheel*, Standish closed the door from the servants' corridor and came near the table. Two places had been set. Golden domes with handles covered the plates. 'You are indeed a fellow who prefers the less-travelled road, Mr Standish.'

'I guess I am,' Standish said.

'As your tastes in literature would indicate. Let us see what is beneath these covers, shall we?'

They raised the golden domes. On Standish's plate lay an entire dried-out fish with bulging eyes.

'Ah, kippers,' Wall said. 'You're a lucky fellow, Mr Standish. We're a bit short-handed here just now – in fact I'm off to Sleaford in an hour or so to interview some prospective help – and you can never be sure what they'll serve up at breakfast. Last week I had porridge four days running.'

Standish waited until Wall had separated a section of brown flesh from the kipper's side, exposing a row of neat, tiny bones like the bars of a marimba, and inserted it in his mouth. When he tried to do the same, bristling bones stabbed his tongue and the inside of his cheeks. The fish tasted like burned mud. He chewed, glumly tried to swallow, and could not. His throat refused to accept the horrible wad of stuff in his mouth. Standish raised his napkin to his mouth and spat out the bony mess.

'And now,' Wall was saying, lifting the cover from a dish that stood between them. Standish prayed for real food – scrambled eggs, toast, bacon.

'This *is* good luck,' Wall said, exposing a pasty yellow-white, partially liquefied substance. 'Kedgeree.' He began loading it enthusiastically onto his plate. 'An aquatic morning, this. Do help yourself.'

'Do you suppose there's any toast around here?' Standish said.

'Beside your plate.' Wall gave him a surprised look. 'Under the toast cover.'

He had not even seen the second, more elongated golden lid next to his plate. He lifted it off and uncovered a double row of brown toast in a metal rack. Between the rows of toast stood a pot of orange marmalade and another of what looked like strawberry jam, each with a golden spoon. Standish ladled marmalade onto a wedge of toast.

'Something amiss with your kipper?'

'Wonderful, great,' Standish said.

'I hope you had a comfortable night?'

'Fine.'

'No trouble sleeping? No discomfort of any kind?'

'Nothing.'

'Very good.' Wall paused, and Standish looked up from smearing jam on another triangular wedge of toast. 'There is one matter I must discuss with you. It's of minor importance, I'm sure, but I didn't want to bring it up last night.'

'Oh?' Standish held the jam-spoon in one hand, the triangle of toast in the other.

'There seems to be some confusion about the circumstances under which you left your first teaching position. Popham College, was it?'

Standish looked at him in an excellent imitation of genuine wonderment. 'Confusion?' After a bit he looked down at the objects in his hands. Thoughtfully he applied jam to the toast.

'Certainly nothing that should cause you concern, Mr Standish, for if it were you would not be here today. But – well, I don't think I am betraying confidences if I say that we had intimations of a conflict of some kind, though nothing ever seemed positively worrisome to us.'

'Popham was a very small college,' Standish said. His underarms had become damp. 'A small college is like a small town. Especially the English Department of a small college. There's an unbelievable amount of gossip. In fact, when I arrived, people were still talking about something that had happened thirty years earlier between a student and an English professor named Chester – '

'I see,' Wall said, smiling at him.

'What happened was really very simple.' He closed his eyes and remembered how Jean had struggled on the steps to the ordinary little house in Iola, Popham's larger neighbour, how she had given up on the doorstep when the nurse who was not a nurse had opened the door, how the purity of his hatred had moved him through days when sorrow or love would have killed him. 'I saw things clearly,' he said, and cleared his throat. 'A little more clearly than most of the other people on the faculty. It was obvious that most people in my department resented me. One man in particular, a false friend, behaved unspeakably. You could use the word betrayal. There was no unpleasantness, of course – '

'No,' said Wall.

' – but it just sort of became clearer and clearer that Popham and William Standish were not made for each other.'

'They were jealous of you?'

'Right. After a while we all understood that I'd be happier elsewhere. I think I'm still trying to find the right place for me. Zenith is all right, but I can't spend the rest of my life there.'

Wall now looked embarrassed to have brought the matter up. 'Yes, I see,' he said, helping himself to another spoonful of kedgeree. For a time the two men ate their separate meals in silence. When Standish glanced up and caught Wall staring at him, he instantly dropped his eyes.

'Yes,' Wall said. 'Well, it's of no real importance.'

'I don't see how it could be.' Standish felt a flash of hot impatience, another flash of memory too – of standing on a summery street swaddled in a Burberry and hat, looking up at a shaded window on the worst day of his life. 'I could say a lot more, you know, but I don't think – '

'Nor do I,' Wall said, and the two men finished their breakfasts in a silence Standish attributed to the other man's tact.

'So today you begin,' Wall said as they pushed themselves away from the table.

They walked side by side through the great rooms.

Wall opened the library doors and for a moment both men stood mutely in the entrance. Like Standish's bedroom, the library was filled with morning light. The brightness and splendour of the gold trim on the pillars and the furniture seemed utterly fresh in the sunlight, and the long carpet glowed. Standish heard himself sigh.

'I know,' Wall said. 'I feel that way every time I see it.'

Through a window set between bookcases at the library's far end, Standish could see Esswood's terraces falling away into a hazy green distance. Stands of trees that might have been painted by Constable bent towards the pond at the bottom of the terraces. Everything, grass, trees, and pond, looked as if it had just been born. A windmill revolved in slow motion atop a distant hill.

'Isobel's never really been taken seriously before,' Wall said. 'You're convinced, are you, that she was a poet of the first rank? She was something other than a normal guest, you know.'

Standish turned to face him, and the taller man edged sideways.

'Perhaps it's the wrong time for this discussion,' Wall said. 'Let me show you where the Isobel Standish material is kept.'

Standish was surprised by the extent of his desire to be left alone. Wall had insulted him twice, obscurely, and with ironic English good manners.

'It's in the first recess, straight through and on the right.' He hesitated, as if puzzled by Standish's sudden diffidence. The 'hungry' look was very clear on his face. 'Well. I suppose there's nothing left to do but wish you luck in your research.'

Standish thanked him.

'I'll leave you to it, then.'

'Fine, good, okay.'

Wall seemed to decide not to say something that came into his mind. He nodded and walked away with what seemed a deliberate lack of hurry.

* * *

Standish walked around the great room, trying to familiarize himself with the library as a whole. He peeked into the recesses but did not leave the central room until he thought he understood its basic organization.

The Seneschals had laid down their library in almost geological layers. The first serious accumulation of books seemed to begin in the seventeenth century, with a strong preponderance towards religion. Shelf after shelf had been filled with theology, the patristic writings in huge leather folios, Greek and Latin commentaries, and church histories. Bound volumes of sermons filled two shelves. In the eighteenth century, the focus of the collection shifted towards politics, geography, and natural history. The only items of literary interest amongst the volumes concerning antipodean flora and parliamentary papers were complete collections of *The Spectator*, Johnson and Boswell, as well as various editions of Shakespeare, Marlowe, and other Elizabethan dramatists. In the nineteenth century Esswood's library had nearly doubled in size, and for the first time became primarily concentrated on literature. Standish idled past books by Dickens, from *Sketches by Boz* to *The Mystery of Edwin Drood* in the part-numbers in which some of them had first appeared, in individual volumes, and in bound sets; past complete collections of Trollope, Thackeray, Wilkie Collins, Cardinal Newman, Tennyson, Keats, Shelley, Matthew Arnold, Browning, Mrs Gaskell, and the Brontë sisters; past ranks of *The Cornhill* in brown leather bindings; and Swinburne and Dowson and Oscar Wilde; and Henry James – an astonishing amount of Henry James, which took Standish up to the twentieth-century collection.

Edith Seneschal took over around the time of *The Ambassadors*, Standish reckoned, and continued as the main force behind the library until a few years after the publication of *The Waste Land* and *Ulysses*. Everything in between, Georgians, Edwardians, Vorticists, Imagists, Futurists, War poets and Modernists, in little magazines, broadsides, pamphlets, chap-books, every sort of publication possible, was represented as only a passionate collector could manage it. The approximately thirty-five years of Edith's reign occupied' as much shelf space as the whole of the nineteenth century. Afterwards, the collection dwindled away to a few almost randomly selected novels: on the library's last shelves, looking far too contemporary and almost out of place, were books by Auden, Spender, MacNeice, Isherwood, E. F. Benson, P. G. Wodehouse, Waugh, Kingsley Amis. The last few books, thrust in almost carelessly, were *Lunch Poems*, *The Tennis Court Oath*, and *Anglo-Saxon Attitudes*. The Seneschal children had never seriously tried to augment the Esswood library in the way their ancestors had.

Standish felt a pure and uncomplicated longing to be like Robert Wall. He yearned to live in this place, unencumbered by any other attachments, for ever.

Maybe he could become Robert Wall. Someone had to care for the library after Wall's death. Why not a dedicated young American scholar?

Robert Wall was aptly named: he *was* a wall.

Standish walked to the window and looked down over the pond to the fields. The sun had grown higher. Everything before Standish was drenched in warmth and suffused with a relaxed, quiet, accumulating energy. A woman in a long dress of a pale green stood down at the bottom of the terraces on the far side of the long pond. She must have just emerged from the trees. Her face was a white smudge. Standish saw tension in her posture and the set of her legs and realized that she was angry or distressed. She turned from the house and began to pace down the length of the pond. In a moment she had vanished beneath the final terrace.

Standish leaned forward and touched his forehead against the glass. The woman did not reappear. He supposed that she must have been old Miss Seneschal.

He left the window and walked between two columns to the first recess.

It was a wide alcove stacked with bookshelves on both sides. The vaulted ceiling in the recess was patterned with plaster pineapples, candlesticks, and scrolls. Soft, even light filled the recess, illuminating the curved backs of brown, green, and yellow boxes made from leather and thick board. Each of these boxes was stamped in gold with a single name.

For a moment Standish felt almost reverent.

The names stood like golden statuettes before the material hidden in the boxes. Everything in the boxes was alive because it had not been brought out to dry and harden in the air: what was contained in the boxes stayed alive because it was secret.

For a second he saw Wall's shadowy figure poised over an open file box, his face dripping red.

Then at the end of the third shelf on the right-hand side of the recess he saw his own last name stamped on three of the fat file boxes. He went up to the boxes stamped *Standish* and touched the first of them. It was of sturdy dark green ridged board.

Standish slid the box, heavy as a carton of bricks, off the shelf.

He set the box down on top of the desk in the centre of the library. Standish lowered himself into the chair and tilted his head and looked up. In the central panel of the vault, surrounded by an oval of ornate white plaster, a stern, bearded god leaned out of a whirling storm and levelled his index finger at Standish. Standish swallowed.

He bent forward and sprung the catch to open the box. Loose sheets of paper immediately spilled out onto the desk. Tiny, impenetrable black handwriting, Isobel's, covered the pages. Standish's heart began to thump. His trembling hands caused another waterfall of papers from the box.

Standish peered at a dense page. Many words and lines had been crossed out, and every inch of the margins had been covered with additions and second thoughts. To Standish it looked very like a page from the manuscript of a novel. In the top right-hand margin, encircled by scribbled words, was the number 142. Standish deciphered the words *I, project, imposs-ible*. Another set of squiggles resolved themselves into *immortality*.

Just for a moment Standish felt as if an invisible hand had seized his heart and given it a light but palpable squeeze.

It is cruel, he read at the bottom of the page. The words that followed leaped into legibility. *It is cruel, this bargain we make with the Land. Too cruel, but is not eternity cruel, and immortality, and art? Once chosen, you cannot refuse.* Then the writing again dissolved into hieroglyphs and squiggles.

He grunted and heaved the eighty-pound box from the desk and deposited it on the floor. He reached in and removed a thick handful of papers.

The box contained as many as eight hundred loose pages and one manila folder. Standish removed the folder and opened it. The top page bore the initials B. P. Beneath them Isobel had written her own initials. The next page was numbered 65, and was no clearer than the other densely scrawled pages in the box.

Standish sorted through the papers until his stomach growled. Afternoon light filled the library. He looked at his watch and found that it was nearly two. He was hungry again. Samples of Isobel's tiny crowded writing lay across the desk like fragments of one great sentence fallen from the sky, dropped perhaps by the irritated god – with his frown and his pointing finger he was telling Standish to put all that stuff back together again.

In the dining room, a golden cover kept a golden plate warm. Golden utensils were placed beside it. A bottle of wine stood in a golden ice bucket filled with cold water and floating chips of ice. Esswood's invisible servants had declared him a wine drinker. Standish pulled the dripping bottle halfway out of the bucket. Puligny-Montrachet, 1972. Presumably that was okay stuff. He raised the cover from the plate and found beneath it, as fragrant as the night before, slices of loin of veal with morel sauce.

Standish sat down and saw a note beneath the wine glass.

Mr Standish, I may be away from Esswood longer than anticipated. If you find that you require anything in my absence, simply leave a note listing your requirements outside the library door. Other guests have found that this arrangement permits them to work undisturbed.

Luncheon will be served at approximately one o'clock and dinner is generally around eight.

Until my return, RW

After lunch Standish took 'his' corridor back to the library and returned to his desk. He felt heavy and slow, but pleasantly numb. Impulsively, he wrote *box of paperclips, 3 ballpoint pens, 3 manila folders, 3 notebooks* on a sheet of legal paper, tore off the sheet, and carried it through the alabaster pillars to the entrance. He opened the door and set the long yellow sheet on the carpet.

Back at his desk, he opened the folder and riffled through forty or fifty pages of *B. P.* The numbers were out of sequence; some pages had no numbers at all. Standish yawned, then amazed himself by farting hugely. The eighteenth-century Seneschal frowned down at him, the dyspeptic god threw a thunderbolt as Standish fell into sleep as a stone falls down a well.

Some time later he came to with a pounding in his head and an ache in his bladder. His mouth tasted like a sewer. He stood up shakily, and the stack of papers in the file spilled out of his lap onto the floor. He groaned and bent down to stuff them back into the file. He stood up and moved away from the desk. Now he had a clear view of the window. The shadows of the gnarled trees slanted towards the fields. His watch said that it was four-thirty. Then there was a movement near the trees, and Standish ignored his bladder long enough to move closer to the window. A woman in a soft, close-fitting hat and a long, pale dress had come out of the trees near the long pond. Around her the hedges and fields sizzled with that same irrational bursting energy he had sensed earlier. The woman took a step forward, then hesitated and turned round. She looked as if she were arguing with someone who stood hidden in the trees. She looked up at Standish's window, and he moved back even before he realized that he was frightened. Still holding the folder, he let himself out into the servants' corridor.

A huge spider web he had broken on his first night fluttered and rippled as he passed through it, sending out loose grey tendrils like fingers. At last Standish burst into his room, grimacing with effort and already unbuckling his belt. He got to the toilet just in time. Panting, he leaned backwards and saw the folder on the shelf behind the tub, where he had dropped it. He picked it up and opened it.

B. P., he thought. He ripped toilet paper from the roll.

The Birth of the Poet.

That was it — Standish felt as if he had heard it spoken in Isobel's own voice. She had written an account of her experiences at Esswood and donated it with the rest of her papers.

As he washed his hands he decided to read the memoir at night. It would be an invaluable backdrop to the poems. Then it seemed to him that the memoir too ought to be publishable. He foresaw another lengthy introduction, another crucial book. *Isobel Standish at Esswood: A Poet at the Crossroads.*

Standish trotted down the curving staircase.

This discovery meant that he would need much more than three weeks at Esswood. It would take another month to work his way through the hundreds of pages of Isobel's handwriting. At the same time, he had to conduct a thorough investigation of her poetry. He wondered if Wall would give him another month. If he presented a well-argued case which alluded to the advantages to Esswood itself in publicizing Isobel's account of her productive time here ... And Jean would forgive him taking the extra time as long as he got back before she gave birth. A small, almost invisible flare of anger and humiliation went off in his chest at the thought of his wife. He imagined fat Jean squatting to give birth: blood and gore flopping out of her along with the child. Standish shook his hand at the flapping tendrils of the spider web, dismissing these feelings as well as whatever lay behind them – he had no time now for destructive emotions. The stairs wound round and round, going farther and farther down, far past the point where he thought they ended. At length he reached the bottom of the stairs and rushed the short distance down the corridor and let himself in.

He nearly sighed with pleasure. The desk was heaped with papers, the columns stood guard, the beautiful rows of books lined the walls. The portrait commanded him to sit and work. Then he remembered Wall's note and his response to it, and turned to the main entrance.

In a straight line on the carpet outside the doors, arranged like the corpses of mice brought in by a loving cat, were a box of number one paperclips, three yellow Bic pens, three stenographic notebooks, and three manila folders.

SEVEN

The low sun was still visible when Standish had finished separating what appeared to be drafts of poems from the far more numerous pages of prose. The next day he could sort out the second box and, if he had time, begin to divide the pages of poetry into published and unpublished; after dinner tonight he could begin paginating and reading the memoir.

There was an hour before dinner. He decided to walk down the terraces and enjoy the hazy light and long shadows.

At the end of the screen passage he let himself out onto the wide terrace at the top of the marble stairs and inhaled air so sweet and heavy with fragrance that it was like a drug. No wonder literary Londoners had so readily trekked to Beaswick: after the smoky London of the early twentieth century, Esswood would have seemed a paradise. Standish went down the steps, his knees stiff from the day behind his desk. Four steps from the bottom he looked back up at the house. *Americans always take a little time to learn our system.*

And: *Are you teasing me?*

Ah, a joke within a joke.

It struck him that the house looked empty. The servants were somewhere inside, old Miss Seneschal and old Mr Seneschal must have been pottering around inside the East Wing, but that side too looked abandoned. A reflected cloud scudded past a row of third-floor windows.

At the bottom of the steps he walked across the crunchy gravel to the right side of the house.

Large smooth flagstones ran beneath the arch of the trellis, which was densely grown with thick green vines and broad dark leaves. Halfway down the side of the house, the trellis parted around a low wooden door. At its far end he emerged again into bright sunlight and saw the land falling away before him in three broad terraces to the long dark pond. This was bordered at either end by the stands of gnarled, leaning trees

from which the woman in green had emerged. A steep
metal staircase, painted black, ran down the slope of
the terraces.

He moved towards the staircase. Far away, on the
other side of the long pond and a little forest, a wide
field striped by a mower sloped upwards to a row of
straight, feathery trees which served as the border of
another, higher field. White sheep like dots of wool
stood so motionless they looked painted. At the top of
the far field the blades of a windmill shaped like a
beehive turned slowly in a drifting breeze.

An unchanging paradise would have such fields,
such ponds and trees, even the unmoving sheep and
the drowsy windmill. It came to him that he was
wholly happy for the first time since boyhood.

The black paint on the iron railing was flaky and
pitted with rust. The entire structure clanged when
Standish moved onto the first step. He grasped the
gritty railing and looked back at the house.

From the rear the building had the massivity of a
prison. The rough stone facing of the ground floor gave
way to undistinguished brick. The windows at the
back of the house were uniformly smaller than those
at the front. Here and there blackened timbers, relics
of some earlier Esswood, were visible within the brick-
work. Only the library windows were not curtained.

Standish began to move down the iron staircase.

White iron lawn chairs and a sturdy iron table had
been set out on the first terrace. The second was a
smooth green swatch of lawn, oddly blank, like an
empty stage.

When he reached the bottom of the stairs his palm
was stained orange from the rust. Behind him the
staircase chimed and vibrated against the bolts.

Over the tops of the trees Standish could see the feathery trees and the field topped by the windmill. A thick, buttery odour hung in the air – an almost sexual smell of grass, water, and sunlight. It occurred to Standish that this was a perfect moment: he had been inhabiting a perfect moment since he had come out from under the trellis. He walked across a track of crushed red gravel and bent to immerse his hand in the pond. The water met his flesh with a cool live shock that refreshed his entire body. Had they swum here, Isobel and Theodore Corn and the others? He swirled his hand gently in the water, watching the rust deposit drift away like a cloud of orange blood.

Shaking his right hand, he stood up and turned towards the house. From the pond it looked less ugly, more like the prosperous merchant-landowner's house it had been before Edith had turned it into a sort of art colony.

An enormous butterfly with deep, almost translucent, purple wings like fragments of a stained-glass window bobbled in the heavy air over the pond, and Standish's breath caught in his chest as he watched it zigzag upwards with aimless grace. Its angle to the light altered, and the thick wings became a dusty non-colour. Then Standish half-saw, half-sensed a movement in the house, and he looked up the terraces and saw a figure standing in the library window. A smudge of face above a blur of green hovered behind the glass. His viscera went cold. The woman was shouting at him: a black hole that must have been her mouth opened and closed like a valve. He had a sense of anger leaping like a flame. The pale blobs of her fists flattened against the glass. With a rush of panic, he remembered driving north on the motorway and seeing the child shut up in the red-brick house: it was as if she had pursued him here, still demanding release.

Standish put his hand on his chest and breathed hard for a moment, then began to move round the pond towards the house. The woman stepped back from the window and disappeared. Red dust lifted from the stones each time he took a step.

EIGHT

At five minutes to eight he backed awkwardly into the dining room through the door from the secret corridor. Cradled in his arms were two bulky folders, one filled with drafts of poems, the other with partially ordered pages of *The Birth of the Poet*. He planned to go through the poetry while he ate, and to make a sustained effort at reading the memoir in the Fountain Rooms after dinner.

When he turned round he saw his place laid in the now-familiar manner: the golden tableware, the domed covers, and the gold-rimmed wineglass. An opened bottle of red Burgundy stood beside the glass. Two candles burned in golden candlesticks.

He put the files on the table and sat down. He placed his hand over the cover. He hesitated for a second, then lifted the cover and looked down at slices of veal loin covered with a brownish sauce and morel mushrooms. 'Now wait a second,' Standish said to himself. He replaced the cover.

He saw the face of the marvellous woman who had let him into Esswood looking back up at him over her shoulder. There were two women in the house – one, old Miss Seneschal, who distrusted him and peered at him through windows; and the other, who teased. He stood up and went into the butler's pantry.

'What are you trying to do, fatten me up for the kill?' he called out.

A burst of giggles floated towards him from the kitchen.

An even, diffuse light, like the soft light in the library, filled the narrow stairwell. Standish trotted down to a bend in the staircase, around a half-landing, and down again. He felt a bubble of elation rising to his throat from the centre of his life, deep, deep within.

'You have to eat this stuff with me, at least,' he called, and came down into the kitchen.

A row of old iron sinks stood against one bright white wall, an electric dishwasher and a long, dark green marble counter beside them. White cabinets hung on the wall. On the opposite side of the room was a huge grey gas range with two ovens, a griddle, and eight burners. In the middle of the room was a large work surface covered with the same green marble. A golden corkscrew with handles like wings lay on the marble.

'Hey!' Standish shouted. 'Where are you? Where'd you go?'

Laughing, he threw out his arms and turned around. 'Come on!'

She did not answer.

His laughter drained away. 'Aw, come on,' he said. He peeked around the side of the big counter. 'Come on out!'

Standish walked all the way round the divider and touched the front of the range, which was still hot.

'Please.'

He leaned against the marble counter, thinking that

at any moment she would pop, giggling, out of a closet. On the far side of the iron sinks was an arched wooden door, painted white. A long brass bolt had been thrown across the frame. Standish pulled back the bolt and opened the door. He stepped outside into the middle of the arched trellis.

'Hello!' he shouted. Then he realized that the door had been bolted from the inside.

He went back into the kitchen. Once more he walked all around the kitchen, hearing nothing but the sound of his own footsteps on the stone floor. His emotions swung wildly within him, vacillating between frustration, rage, disappointment, amusement, and fear without settling on any one of them. He put his hands on his hips. 'Okay,' he said. 'We'll play it your way.' At length he went back up the narrow staircase. On the table in the suffocatingly formal dining room were his folders, the cover over his food, the bottle of wine.

Dinner could wait another few minutes. He went back into the pantry, opened the liquor cabinet and removed the bottle of malt whisky and two glasses. The bottle said COMMEMORATIVE HERITAGE 70 YEARS OLD. He set the glasses down beside the sink and poured an inch and a half of whisky into each glass, then replaced the bottle and carried the glasses into the dining room.

He sat down and drank while staring at the pantry door. The whisky tasted like some smooth dark meat.

He finished the whisky in his glass, picked up the other glass, and tilted all the liquid in it into his mouth and swallowed.

As he ate, he flipped through drafts of unfamiliar poems. They seemed to make even less sense than was

usually the case in Isobel's poetry. Most of them
seemed to consist entirely of randomly selected words:
Grub bed picture dog, Hump humph laze sod. He
wondered if Isobel had evolved towards or away from
outright meaninglessness. He drank some red wine,
which he noticed tasted as good as the Esswood
whisky, though in an entirely different way. Perhaps
Isobel had written drunk. He revolved the bottle and
looked at the label. It was a Pomerol, Château Petrus,
1972. And the veal was so good that it was almost
worth eating at every meal.

In fact . . . Standish stopped chewing for a moment.

In fact, it was like being with Isobel, eating this
particular meal at this particular table. It was as if time
did not exist in the conventional linear sense at all and
she were somewhere just out of sight.

The P of the title meant *Past*, Standish realized.

He closed the folder of poems, pushed it aside, the
drew the thick folder of the memoir nearer to his plate.
He drank wine, he chewed at his food and drank again.
He read.

An unmarried young woman from Duxbury, Massachusetts came to a great estate in England. A beautiful
woman named E. greeted her. E. led her up the staircase to a long gallery and a suite of rooms that
overlooked a playing fountain. The young woman from
Massachusetts bathed and rested before going downstairs to meet the other guests, knowing that she was
in this place to find her truest self. She experimentally
opened a door in her bedroom and discovered a staircase that seemed like a secret known only to her . . .

Standish tried to pour wine into his glass and found
that the bottle was empty. A few mushrooms lay in
congealed grey sauce on his plate. The brightness of

the dining room hurt his eyes. Back in time again, he yawned and stretched. Somehow it had got to be nearly midnight. Standish stood up and went back to the pantry to pour himself another inch of seventy-year-old whisky. If his body was tired, his mind was not – he would have trouble sleeping.

Carrying his folders and glass, he moved through the room to the main entrance, not feeling like struggling up his and Isobel's 'secret' corridor this late at night.

He mounted the great staircase and took the right wing towards the little anteroom before the Inner Gallery. He knew that the door to the gallery was opposite the door to the staircase. Therefore he felt as if his body had betrayed his mind when he bumped into a large piece of furniture, somehow got turned around in the dark, and could not find the other door.

He told himself to stay calm. He ceased blundering from one piece of furniture to another. The room seemed even darker than it had when his beloved had led him through it. He forced himself to breathe steadily and slowly. In the darkness he could see the large, clumsy shapes of high-backed leather chairs. All four walls seemed covered with a uniformly mottled grey-brown skin that refused to resolve into rows of books. He stepped forward and banged his right leg painfully against a hard surface. He swore under his breath, stepped sideways, and inched forward.

A space opened up before him, and he moved more confidently towards the hovering plane of the wall. After a single step he tripped over some low piece of furniture, screamed, and fell. The glass flew out of his hand and shattered far off to his left. He landed on his left arm, still clutching Isobel's papers. Sharp, definite pain shot from his elbow to his shoulder, then settled into a constant throb. Standish began to push himself along the floor like a grub. He realized that he was very drunk.

From somewhere above him, he heard a woman laugh.

His entire body grew cold, and his testicles shrank back up into his body. He tried to speak but his throat would not work. The laughter expired in a short, happy sigh. The severed tendons of Standish's throat reattached themselves. 'Where are you?' he whispered.

Silence.

'Why are you doing this to me?'

He heard a soft flurry of movement behind him, then thought he heard rapid footsteps moving down the staircase.

Standish groped his way across the room until his outstretched fingers found a wooden door.

He came out into the blaze of light that was the Inner Gallery, rubbing his eyes with his left hand. Reality wavered around him, golden plates and golden forks and a deserted mansion and severed heads and a woman who vanished into laughter and a baby not his baby in a past that . . .

The Birth of the Past.

He shook his head. He needed sleep. Cool draughts moved around Standish's ankles. He looked through the dark windows and saw the windows of the Seneschals' suite shining back at him.

While he watched, a small dark shadow scuttled across the shade of the window on the left, and the lights went off as abruptly as the slamming of a door. It had not seemed the shadow of an ordinary human being. All the contradictory feelings within Standish

melted into a single act of acceptance: he was in the
Land, and he would follow where he was led.

Standish let himself into the Fountain Rooms,
moved unseeing through the living room, and threw
himself onto the bed.

NINE

... *born in Huckstall, the fleeing blue-eyed boy it
was?*

Standish's bed stood beside the long pond in cool
moonlight, and a disembodied voice had just spoken
lines about Huckstall and a blue-eyed boy which,
though nonsense, had caused a turmoil in his breast.
The dark pond stretched out before him. He held a
sleeping baby in his arms, and the baby slept so rosily
because it had just nursed at his breasts, which were
womanly, large and smooth-skinned, with prominent
brown nipples. A drop of sweet milk hung from his left
nipple, and with his free hand Standish brushed it
away. The peace of holding the baby in the bed beneath
the moon was a kind of ecstasy. Then he remembered
the speaking voice and the creature in the window,
and looked down the side of the pond to the group of
leaning trees. Their twisting branches concealed a
being, male or female, who wished to remain hidden.
Standish felt a simple, profound apprehension that this
being wanted to harm his baby. It – he or she – would
kill him too, but the threat to himself was a weightless
scrap, a nothing, against his determination to protect
his baby. As if in response to the threat, his breasts
tingled and ached and began to express tear-shaped

drops of white milk that leaked, rhythmically as drips
from a tap, from his nipples.

From somewhere either in the depths of the silvery
trees or beyond them a woman began to laugh . . .

. . . and in the darkness of the Fountain Rooms, without breasts or baby, Standish flew into sudden wake-
fulness. His heart banged, and his body felt as if it had
been torn from an embrace. Someone else was in the
room: the dream-danger had been supplanted by this
real danger. Whoever was in the room had just ceased
to move, and now stood frozen in the darkness, looking
down at him.

The publican of The Duellists had told the truth and
Robert Wall had lied: an American had been lured here
and lulled to sleep with rich food and strong wine, and
the murderer had crept into his room and killed him.

Standish felt with a horrible certainty that the murdered American had been decapitated.

He tried to see into the darkness. His baby had been
taken from him, and a being who meant him nothing
but ill stood wrapped in darkness ten feet away.

'I know you're there,' Standish said, and instantly
knew she was not.

There were no giggles now. Standish lifted his head,
and nothing else in the room moved. He was now as
alone as when he followed the woman's laughter down
the kitchen stairs. Yet it seemed to him a second later
that someone *had* been in the room with him, someone who circled all about him, someone who was a
part of Esswood, Miss Seneschal or his beloved (it
occurred to Standish that his beloved might actually
be Miss Seneschal), someone who needed only the

right time to appear before him. She could not show
herself to him now, for he did not know enough now.

She would show herself when he had earned the
right to see her.

He remembered dreaming of having large breasts so
engorged with milk that they leaked, and absently
rubbed his hands over his actual chest, slightly flabby
and covered with a crust of coarse black hair. Something about Huckstall pushed at his consciousness
urgently enough to make him sit up in bed – he felt
pricked by a pin. But what could Huckstall have to do
with his work, which of course was the meaning of the
baby in his dream?

Standish got out of bed to pee. A haze of light
touched the bedroom window, and he turned just in
time to look through the slats of the shutter and see
the Seneschals' light snap off again.

TEN

An impossible thing happened the next morning. On
the way to the dining room by way of 'his' staircase
and corridor, Standish lost his way inside Esswood and
found himself wandering around strange corners, down
unfamiliar steps, past locked and unlocked doors.

Standish had suffered very few hangovers, but each
of them had made him unreasonably hungry. He
wanted only to get downstairs and devour whatever
was on the table, even if it had a funny name and
looked like earwax. He almost ran down the stairs. His
head pounded, and his eyes were oddly blurry – no
more alcohol, not ever, he promised himself. He passed
through the remnant of the huge spider web and pawed

at it in revulsion. After a time, it seemed to him that
he had circled round and round so many times that he
must have gone past the first floor. He slowed down.
The walls of the staircase were of whitewashed stone
that was cold to the touch. When had the walls
changed to stone? He looked over his shoulder. The
curve of the wall, the iron sconce, even the dim grey
light seemed strange.

Soon he reached the bottom of the staircase. The
corridor seemed both like and unlike the one he knew.
Just ahead was a tall door and a dim hallway. Everything seemed a little darker and dirtier than he remembered. He could not be certain that he was in a new
part of the house until he had hurried down to the end
of the corridor and found a blank wall where a statue
of a boy should have been. He turned the corner and
saw another, smaller flight of steps leading down to a
concrete floor.

He stopped moving. Now it seemed to him that he
had turned both right and left, blindly, several times
without paying attention – his stomach had led him.
He had a vague impression, like an image from a
dream, of corridors branching off in an endless series
of stone floors and dingy concrete walls. He felt a
flutter of nausea. He turned round. A dark hallway
extended past thick wooden doors and ended at a T-
junction. He groaned. For a moment the sense of being
lost overwhelmed his hunger. He backtracked down
the hallway and tried the nearest door. It was locked.

The next door opened into a room filled with irregular, thin white things, bits of kindling. Dusty frames
containing dead moths and butterflies hung on the
wall. High in the opposite wall was a little window
like the window in a prison cell. The air smelled dead.

Standish peered into the room and recognized that the objects piled on the floor were bones. Dozens, perhaps hundreds, of skeletons had been dismembered here. He suddenly remembered the story of Bluebeard's wife, and the ache in his head instantly became a red-hot wire of pain. Standish looked up and down the corridor and took a step into the awful room.

Skulls with long antlers lay in a corner. Standish walked nearer to the piles of bones. Many of them looked like the bones of animals. The faded colours of butterflies in a frame caught his eye, and he noticed a handwritten label taped beneath the glass. Nile Expedition, 1886. He began breathing again. Some cracked old Seneschal who fancied himself a naturalist had brought back these bones and butterflies from Africa in a crate.

He left the roomful of bones and hovered in the corridor. He could not retrace his steps through the series of rights and lefts he had unthinkingly taken. Opposite the bone room were two more doors, and Standish stepped up to one of them and opened it.

Things he could not see moved out of sight – he had an impression of fat little bodies diving behind the stacks of newspapers and magazines that filled the room. He imagined that malevolent eyes peeked at him, and thought he could smell fear and hatred. His eye snagged on the headline of a *Yorkshire Post* that lay on the floor, as if one of the little creatures had dropped it. PREGNANT WIFE, LOVER, TORTURED THEN BEHEADED. *Grisly Discovery on Huckstall Slagheap.* From somewhere quite near came a sly, breathless *tick, tick, tick* of sound that might have been laughter.

Standish stepped back. The entire room seemed

poised to strike at him. He backed across the threshold
and slammed the door. Standish felt light-headed,
scared, unexpectedly brave – his discovery of this part
of Esswood could not be accidental. He had been
intended to find his way here. There were no accidents,
no coincidences. He was *supposed* to be here. He had
been *chosen*.

He tried the other door on that side of the corridor,
and found it locked. Standish moved to the end of the
corridor and went slowly down the steps.

A lower, narrower hallway led to an open door to a
tiny cement room in which a greasy armchair two feet
high sat beneath a hanging light bulb. On the far side
of the chair was another door. Standish stepped inside.
To one of the cell's concrete walls had been taped a
reproduction of a painting in the Fountain Rooms – a
small dog scampered before a carriage drawing up to
Esswood. Standish crossed the room and opened the
other door. Beyond it was a dark chamber that contained a huge, squat body with a Shiva-like forest of
arms that snaked to every part of the low ceiling.
Gauges and dials decorated the furnace, and beyond it
other machines leaned against the far wall: penny-
farthing bicycles, a row of axes in descending sizes like
a hanged family, a sewing machine with a treadle, a
vacuum cleaner with a long, limp neck and a distended
bladder.

This was the library's rhyme, Standish saw. Up
there, subtle spiritual things breathed and slept in file
boxes; here, dirty things pumped out heat.

He went deeper into the basement. Standish peered
into rooms filled with dolls and broken toys, with five
cribs and five baby beds and five black perambulators
as high off the ground as a princess's carriage, with

musty, folded sheets and blankets, with faded children's books, wooden blocks and stuffed animals. He came to an ascending staircase and looked back to see the flaring nostril of a rocking horse through an open door. He had found 'Rebuke's' *rooms of broken babies and their toys.*

The unfamiliar stairs took him up past row after row of wine bottles in tall cases like bookshelves, then transformed themselves into a wide, handsome set of stairs with an onyx balustrade that led him into the splendour of East Hall.

Breakfast had been laid on a fresh white tablecloth. Standish sat down and lifted the golden cover. The smoked corpse of a fish regarded him with dead eyes. Standish slid onto his fork a pasty mess that looked as hairy as a caterpillar. He put the paste in his mouth and bit down on a pincushion. Small sharp bones stung every square millimetre of his palate. Other slender bones slid between his teeth. He spat onto the golden plate.

ELEVEN

Soon after, under the eyes of the great-great-great-great grandfather and the pointing god, he nudged the bones lodged between his teeth with his tongue and made notes to himself on a legal pad. *If truly no accident or coincidence in universe, then narrative is superseded for everything is simultaneous. To be here is to be within Isobel's poetry, literally and metaphorically, for world without coincidence is world which is all metaphor. It is childhood once again. Key to the nonsense poems. Syntax the only source of meaning.*

*Question: toys, dolls, beds, etc. seen by Isobel, as in
'Rebuke'. What happened to the children that used
them? Why 'broken'? How many children did Edith
Seneschal have?*

Must ask Seneschals about siblings.

Could the secret be some horrible family disease?

Standish thought a moment, then wrote another
line.

Research in churchyard?

He looked down at the pad for a moment, then
ripped off the sheet and wrote a few words on the next.
This too he tore off, and took it outside the library
door and laid it on the carpet. When he returned to the
desk he looked at his guardian spirits and decided that
he had spent enough time on the poems for the
morning. *B. P.* was what he wanted to read.

With a happy sigh he pushed the poems aside and
pulled the bulkier prose manuscript towards him. He
began reading on page 26, where he had broken off the
previous night. For some twenty minutes Isobel's
handwriting squirmed before him on the page. Then
time ceased to be a linear sequence of events, and
Standish entered the Land with Isobel.

The young woman from Massachusetts found herself
growing fonder of the house each day. A happy accident had led to her meeting her hostess, E., the well-
known patroness of the arts, in Boston; and when E.
had asked to see the young woman's work – and been
impressed by what she described as its 'bravery' – she
had invited her new friend to join her at her estate. So
the young woman felt an initial gratitude to E., but the
speed with which she worked, once introduced to the
Land, warmed this emotion to love. She found herself

writing both prose and poetry more easily than ever
before in her life, coming into her own voice a little
more surely every day. And after readings in the West
Gallery during the evenings, she was praised and
applauded by writers whom she had earlier known
only as revered names. Encouraged, she began to jetti-
son from her work nearly everything that made it
resemble the poetry of her own time.

That's my girl, Standish thought.

The young woman from Massachusetts spent her
mornings writing in the Fountain Rooms, took lunch
with E. and the other guests, and in the afternoon
wandered through the Land – her name for Esswood.
The physical world excited her nearly to euphoria. She
felt that Esswood's beauty called to her, spoke to her,
welcomed her. In the afternoon guests not busy writing
played croquet, bathed in the pond, read by themselves
in the library or the East Hall, or read to one another
beneath sun umbrellas on the great terrace overlooking
the pond and the far fields. Dinners were lavish:
gourmet meals and great wines. The young woman
declared a preference for loin of veal with morel sauce,
and did not object when the Land teasingly offered it
to her every night for a week. The wines too were
ambrosial. On her first night the guests were given a
1900 Château Lafite-Rothschild, and on the second
night, an 1872 Château Lafite-Rothschild. On the third
night the guests were given an 1862 Lafite-Rothschild,
reputedly the greatest vintage of the past hundred
years, and considered likely to surpass all other wines
for the next hundred as well.

The young woman's euphoria was more substantial

than that given by wine, more permanent than could
be provided by good company, and more profound even
that that found in artistic progress. The feelings the
young woman began to associate with the Land were
not overtly religious, but were intensely spiritual – a
force like music or disembodied spirit seemed to
inhabit every aspect of the estate. What was most
remarkable about the web of feelings linked to the
Land was its release of gaiety. Not naturally high-
spirited, the young woman joined the other guests in
play – charades and *tableaux* and laughing
conversations.

The young woman found herself indulging a previously unsuspected taste for practical jokes: she used
her 'secret' corridor to move unseen about the house,
and delighted in disarranging a fellow poet's papers or
effects, and in appearing like a spectre in their rooms
at night, then vanishing.

Riveted to the pages before him, Standish felt his heart
slam against his ribs.

Although she had never taken any great interest in
children, the young woman felt that much of the
Land's strange and tender appeal to her was due to her
hostess's two surviving children.

Again, Standish's heart nearly stopped.

E.'s calm was all the more remarkable in the light of
her children's fates. She had married a second cousin
with the same surname, a man uninterested in either
the arts or country life and far more devoted to French
brandy, Italian women, and the House of Commons

than to his family: yet he had given her five children, three of whom had died in their earliest years. The two living children, R. and M., endeared themselves to the Land's young guest by their quiet, sweet, rather stricken charm: they had little energy, for they too were supposed to have contracted the disease that had killed their siblings. This awful disease, it was rumoured, had been transmitted to the children by their father, and was something of a family curse; a family secret, too, for the exact nature of the disease was not known.

Both children tired easily and were often inordinately hungry – it was a symptom of the disease that to sustain even low levels of energy, the sufferer had to take in large quantities of food, though what sort of food remained a mystery. The children were always fed in private. Despite their special diet, little R. and little M. seemed to be wasting away before the young guest's eyes. The sister more so than her brother: while *he* could still appear to be something like a normal child, *she* was weaker by the day. *He* was pale; *she* was pallid, even waxen. At times the poor child's skin seemed damp and oddly ridged, or pocked, or swollen, or all three at once, and so white as to be almost translucent – as if she were in the process of changing into another kind of creature altogether.

Standish looked up and saw that the light in the library had grown rich and golden. His watch said that it was one-thirty. He was half an hour late for lunch. Numbly, he got to his feet.

He knew that he had not even begun to assimilate what he had read. He would have to understand what

Isobel had written even more than Isobel had understood it. This seemed crucial: Standish had heard the
music too, and he had experienced Isobel's euphoria
the first time he had stepped out into the Land in
daylight. But Isobel had taken everything at face value.
The words *timeless, eternity, gaiety, children, disease,
transformation* swirled through Standish's head.
Spectre, laughter, disembodied spirit.

An idea of the morning presented itself to him with
even greater force, and he walked on complaining legs
to the great door. When he opened it he saw an ignition
key on the carpet.

After lunch, groggy from veal and wine, he opened
Esswood's great front door and inhaled fragrant
summer air. For an instant he pictured the two living
children, little R. and little M., seated on the marble
steps. Then he saw the car on the drive and gasped. It
was a Ford Escort, painted turquoise.

Standish flew down the steps, noticing that the car
was far cleaner than the one he had driven from
Gatwick to Lincolnshire. He was sure that it was a
different car. When he reached the drive he walked up
to it and touched its warm, smooth, well-waxed hood.
It *was* a different car. Like everything else that had
been taken into the Land, it shone and sparkled.

Standish got in behind the wheel and fitted the key
into the ignition.

It took nearly an hour to find the local church. When
Standish finally forced himself to stop and ask for
directions, he found that he could scarcely penetrate
the harsh, slow-moving local accent. Trying to make
sense of the garble of lefts and rights given him by two
grudging men outside a pub, Standish wound up on

Beaswick's High Street, where teenagers stared at his car and mumbled remarks he did not have to understand to know were obscene. The town was grey and dirty. Overweight women with piled-up hair and flaming faces peered into the car. Then, as suddenly as slag heaps and flares had turned into thick forest, the ugly little sweetshops and tobacconists became open fields and desolate marshes.

Eventually he saw a six-foot heap of grass and earth bristling with thick roots at an intersection and remembered that one of the hostile men before the pub had told him to turn one way or the other at a 'hummock'. Perhaps this was a hummock. Far away stood a farmhouse. Two sway-backed horses stared gloomily at him from the middle distance. On the other side of the hummock a hill led up to a small grey church and a graveyard of tilting headstones. On the crest of the hill above the church stood a beehive-shaped windmill he had seen before. He was three minutes from Esswood: he could have walked across the field to get to the church.

Standish drove up onto the wet grass before the stone church and left the car to walk round to the graveyard.

On the other side of the church was a smaller, even uglier stone building like a cell with curtained windows. Standish walked between the two buildings to the cemetery gate.

Enclosed by a waist-high iron fence, the cemetery covered an acre of sloping ground and contained several hundred graves. The oldest headstones, those directly before Standish, resembled wrinkled old faces, sunken and blurred beneath a pattern of shadows and scratches. Standish began to move down the middle of the graveyard. None of the stones bore the name Seneschal. Other names recurred again and again – Totsworth, Beckley, Sedge, Cooper, Titterington. He kept moving slowly through the cemetery.

A door slammed behind him, and someone began working towards him through the graves. Standish turned round to see a black-haired man in a long buttoned cassock approaching with one hand upraised, as if to stop traffic. The vicar's heavy red face sagged as if against a strong wind, and he leaned forward, ducking his head, as he hurried towards Standish.

'I say, I say.'

Standish waited for the man to reach him.

Close up, the vicar presented a hearty, smiling manner that seemed a disguise for some other, more bullying quality. He was in his late fifties. The odours of beer and tobacco enveloped Standish as the man came nearer. He spoke in the harsh accent of the village. 'Saw you from the vicarage, you know. Don't get many strangers here, don't get accustomed to strangers' faces.' A big yellow smile in the red face, as if to balance what might otherwise have been simple rudeness. 'American, are you? Your clothes.'

Standish nodded.

'Interested in our Norman church? You'd be welcome to walk round inside, but it makes me a bit uncomfortable to see a man I don't know walking about our little, um, our little garden of souls here. Seems irregular.'

'Why?'

The vicar blinked, then showed Standish his false smile. 'You might think our ways are odd, but we are just a tiny little bit of a community, you know. Just paused on your way through, did you?'

'No.' The vicar irritated Standish so profoundly that he could scarcely bring himself to talk to the man.

'Came all this way to do grave rubbings? We've nothing to interest you in that line, sir.'

Standish frowned at the vicar. 'I wanted to see if I could locate any family graves. My name is Sedge, and my people came from this village.'

'Ah. Well, now. You're a Sedge, then, are you?' The vicar was squinting at him, half-smiling, as if trying to make out a family resemblance. 'Where did you say you were from in America?'

'Massachusetts,' Standish said. 'Duxbury, Massachusetts.'

'You should find Sedges right the way through this little cemetery. When did your people arrive in America, then?'

'Around 1850, maybe a bit earlier,' Standish said. 'I traced us back right here to Beaswick, and a local family invited me to stay with them; so I wanted to see if I could find any of their people here too. I'm curious about them.'

He turned away from the vicar and began inspecting headstones again. Capt Thomas Hopewell, 1870–1898. An angel leaned weeping back from an open book. A marble woman shrank back from grief or death, her face over her hands – he recognized the statue as the twin of one at Esswood. Behind him he felt, with senses suddenly magnified, the exasperation of the vicar. He waited for the man to come thundering after him, and then realized that the vicar's manner was that of a man with a secret.

The soft heavy tread came up behind him. 'Local family, is it? Might I ask which local family?'

'Of course.' Standish stopped moving and turned

round to the sagging red face. Behind the vicar he
caught a glimpse of a marble monument atop a child's
grave – a small boy reaching up with outstretched
arms. This too was a copy of a statue in Esswood's
'secret' corridor. 'The Seneschals.'

The vicar actually licked his lips. His entire manner
had changed in a moment, along with the atmosphere
between himself and Standish. 'That's really very
interesting, that is.'

'Good.' Standish turned away to inspect the name
on the base of the monument of the grieving woman.
SODDEN. He fought the impulse to giggle. 'Where are
they buried, then?'

'Prominent family, of course.' The vicar scuttled up
beside him. 'You'd say, *the* prominent family in our
little corner of the world. You're putting up with them,
are you, Mr Sedge? In Esswood House?'

'That's right.'

'Quiet over there, is it, Mr Sedge?'

'Yes, it's very peaceful,' Standish said.

'I daresay.' The man licked his lips again. Standish
was startled by the sudden realization that the vicar
looked frightened.

'I think it's strange that I don't see any of their
graves. Edith's children, I mean – the three who died
so young.'

'Strange? I should think it is strange. And what
about Edith herself? Miss Edith Seneschal, who
became Mrs Edith Seneschal: now surely you would
think she would be buried here as well. Wouldn't you,
Mr Sedge?'

The man was peering at him with his head cocked
and his lips pursed. Rusty brown stains like stripes
covered his cassock.

'And her husband too, don't you think? The Honourable Arthur Seneschal, a dim figure granted, a willing partner one might say, very willing I'd wager, in all his wife's ambitions. You'll be wanting to see his headstone as well, won't you?' There was a venomous lilt in his voice, and Standish had the feeling of some unspoken complicity between them.

'What's wrong with you?' he said.

'He wonders what's wrong with me,' the vicar said to the air. 'Mr Sedge is curious, isn't he? The odd fact is, there hasn't been a Sedge in Beaswick since 17 – what was it now?' He darted over the low grass to a tilting headstone. '1789. I thought it was that. Charles Sedge. A bachelor, by the way. An only son. He'd be amused by your story. He'd be especially amused that you claim to be staying with the Seneschals.' The vicar astonished Standish by leaning over the tombstone and braying: 'This fellow claims to be a Sedge – long-lost American cousin, Charles! Wants to pay his respects. Says he's putting up at Esswood House. Wants to find the graves of Edith's children. Can you give him any assistance, Charles?'

He straightened up. An unhealthy mirth had turned his face an ever darker shade of red. 'Or perhaps I heard the name wrong. Did you want to say that your name is Titterington? Or Cooper? You couldn't be a Beaswick Sedge, in any case, could you? They were all dead by the time you claim your family arrived in America. And no descendant of a Beaswick Sedge would walk through the doors of Esswood House.'

Standish said, 'I don't know what you're talking about. Are you accusing me of lying?'

'I'm accusing you of ignorance,' the vicar said. 'I wonder where you really are staying. I wonder where

you really are from. If you don't know that we would
refuse to give burial to any Seneschal, you have no
connection to Beaswick. Which makes me wonder
what it is that you are doing in my churchyard, telling
me tales about staying at Esswood House.'

'Why shouldn't I be staying at Esswood House? I *am*
staying there – I'm a guest, I was invited – '

'Nobody is staying at Esswood House. I very much
doubt whether anyone is still living in Esswood House.
There are a couple of students hired to discourage
intruders and keep the place clean, but they're not
local people – not even Lincolnshire folk.' He looked
down at a flat, grassy grave and rustled the folds of his
cassock. To Standish it looked as though the vicar
were dancing inside his body, whirling about in furious
glee. 'You needn't think I'm so stupid I can't see, that
I'm such a blockhead I didn't know what you were
immediately I saw the cut of your jacket.' A joyful
defiance filled his eyes. 'I knew someone like you
would appear – someone from a tawdry American
magazine, some bit of trash you'd call a newspaper –
but it never in my most ambitious dreams came to me
that when a jackal like you appeared you would claim
to be looking for the graves of Edith's children.'

'But that's what I *am* looking for!' Standish shouted.

Now the vicar was virtually twitching. 'Then you'll
need directions to Esswood House, won't you? I saw
how you came up – I saw your car. You didn't come
from the house. You drove from the village.'

Standish thought of protesting that he had lost his
way. Instead he said, 'What's the quickest way to get
to the manor?'

'Aha! Truth! The unfamiliar guest, truth, has
entered our conversation. To reach Esswood House

you proceed straight back the way you came until you reach the hummock, then turn right, not left, and proceed directly on past the Robert Wall – '

'The what?'

'The Robert Wall – it's only a local name, needn't be alarmed. I thought the gutter press would be less easily startled. Won't fall down on you: the old wall's been standing on the boundary of the Seneschal estate for four centuries.'

'Why is it called the Robert Wall?'

'Because, I suppose, a man named Robert built it. He wanted to keep the Seneschals in, didn't he?'

Standish began walking away. He brushed past the vicar without looking at him. The vicar stepped back on a grave and laughed. 'You're going to discover their secret, is that what you're going to do, Mr Sedge?' Standish heard him laughing as he walked past the ugly church.

TWELVE

Two days later, at the end of the afternoon, a sentence at the top of the page jarred him back into the waking world.

I have found my vagrant, my scholar-gypsy with cornflower eyes.

It was a surprise to see Isobel stoop to the conventional period mush of 'cornflower eyes', but the young woman from Massachusetts had found a soulmate, someone with whom she could take long walks and discuss literature. *I have found my vagrant* – Standish remembered the mad creature who had materialized on the outskirts of Huckstall, shuddered, and continued reading. Isobel found the vagrant an untutored genius, a lone figure in the world, without wife or child. At the bottom of the page Isobel had written *Matter for another tale*. The 'vagrant' promptly disappeared from the manuscript.

Standish read for the rest of the day. The library faded away around him and he wandered through the Land with Isobel. The details of her days did not vary much, but Standish found the similarities to his own routine very pleasing. In Isobel's descriptions of writing, eating, strolling round the house and its grounds, an unstated purpose, some transformation, hovered just out of sight. Whatever the young woman looked at burned in her vision. The long pond *simmered*, the far field was *a green hide nailed to the sun*. The library was an *oven*, *a volcano*, and poetry was *lava*. Every surface *shimmered* and *gleamed*, everything *trembled* with the pressure of the force beneath it.

Until nearly eight o'clock Standish remained immersed in Isobel's memoir, not so much reading as *being read*. His boyhood and the other, more real world that existed within or beside this one took shape around him, and with it came the memory of Popham, the feelings and atmosphere of the wonderful and terrible time that had really begun when in his Burberry on a blazing day he had tracked Jean to another's apartment and really ended with the nurse who was not a nurse and the bloodied sheets around a discarded utterance, a non-noun, an aborted word in a deleted sentence. There was a truer self within him, and he had felt it struggling to be born.

A superstitious vicar in a stained cassock could not hope to understand it.

When he looked up and noticed that it was nearly dinner-time, Standish was aware of a tremendous glory, like the beating of a great pair of wings, in the air around him. For a moment, the library seemed charged with an absence, not an abrupt withdrawal, but the anticipatory, trembling absence just before the appearance of a radiant and necessary being.

This time Standish took the longer route to the dining room. He moved almost ceremoniously to his chair and lifted the cover from the veal in its sauce. Beside the gold-rimmed glass on the tablecloth was a bottle, streaky with dust, of Château Lafite-Rothschild, 1862.

After dinner he took the main staircase to the upper floor. The sound of absent laughter filled the air of the little study; so did the odour of malt whisky, from both the glass he had spilled two nights before and the one he carried before him, aiming it like a key at the study's opposite door. He emerged into the Inner Gallery. He thought he heard a small agile body skittering out of sight behind him, dodging back into the shadows. No, the vicar of Beaswick would not, would never, understand. A folder of papers nestled between his elbow and his ribs.

He was not drunk. He was not. He was moving in a straight line down the gallery between the big panes of glass and the looming paintings, and he could have touched his nose with his finger. On his right side English horses grazed in a painted field; on his left, the Seneschals' windows glowed pale yellow, and in their bedrooms two Seneschals, male and female created He them, lay separate or entwined in their beds or bed. Standish heard sounds from the courtyard, and stepped nearer the windows and looked down. A glittering shower of diamonds, lava, golden blood, shot upwards and flew apart before falling back to earth. This eruption resolved itself into a fountain illuminated by lights sunk into the gravel around its base.

Esswood was taking him in, accepting him, *using* him, as it had used and accepted Isobel.

He placed the folder on the bed, undressed, and went into the bathroom. A flushed, radiant demon filled with blood gazed at him from the mirror. Standish brushed his teeth, his eyes held by the gleaming eyes of the demon in the mirror. Froth bubbled comically from his lips. He rinsed his mouth with cold water, spat into the sink, looked once again at his demon's eyes, then splashed his face with cold water.

His cock stuck out before him in the mirror, rigid as a ruler and curved slightly upwards. A translucent drop appeared at its tip.

Standish masturbated over the pretty blue-patterned sink, as he did so fantasizing that he stood in the grove of twisted, gestural trees in cool night air. A certain woman stood by the edge of the long pond, outlined by the silver moonlight so that her naked body was a curved pane of pure black. He could feel crushed leaves, small twisted roots, and rounded stones beneath his feet. Cool air prickled the skin on his arms. The hieratic figure by the pond stepped forward. Her eyes shone white in the blackness. Standish gasped, for he actually *was* out in the cool night beside the pond, not in the bathroom of the Fountain Rooms. What he felt – the chill, the leaves beneath his feet – was what he felt, not a fantasy, and the beloved woman, who with her shining eyes and outlined body seemed half a tiger, moved forward again. His body

His body uttered a massive affirmation, a million nerves slammed one door shut and threw another open, and gouts of semen shot out of him like the water from the fountain and flew into the darkness. Standish instantly felt drained, as if he had lost a quart of blood. The terrifying figure before him seemed to be smiling in acceptance of his offering. He closed his eyes in terror and fell down in a faint ... but opened them in the bathroom, where he had propped himself against the sink with locked arms. A final cloud of white semen oozed across the pattern of blue flowers. The gooseflesh was fading from his arms. He shook his head and looked at himself in the mirror. His face was tired and ordinary, white with shock. He splashed his face and swished water around in the sink. He felt as if he had just stepped out of a rollercoaster.

In the bedroom, he buttoned himself into clean, pressed pyjamas which had been laid out on the bed. His cock felt hollowed out. When he got into bed he first smelled, then saw, the glass of malt whisky he had placed on the bedside table. Unhesitatingly he picked up the glass and swallowed half the contents. A ball of warmth began to grow like a seed in his stomach. Now he felt light, nearly boneless. The folder fell from his hands onto his chest. Just before he fell asleep he realized that he had not looked to see if the Seneschals had turned off their lights.

But they had turned them off when he awakened several hours later. Once again he had the feeling that someone was in his room, but this time the alien presence was not frightening. His bedroom was utterly dark, without even the faint haze of yellow on the louvres of the shutters. From the presence in the room

flowed a sense of unhappiness, even of rage, too powerful not to be felt.

That she had returned at all spoke of how much she
needed him.

'I know you're here,' he said softly.

And then William Standish nearly fainted, for a
slight form paler than the rest of the room separated
itself from the darkness and advanced a minute distance towards his bed. Until that moment Standish
had inhabited a world of suppositions, hypotheses,
imaginings, and fancies – but the figure shyly advancing towards the bed was a proof, a confirmation. His
mouth went dry.

The pale figure drew nearer. Now he saw that she
was holding something before her with both arms. It
was a baby. His heart moved with sorrow. He could
see the top of the figure's head, and her hair falling in
long, smooth wings. Her paleness gave her an insub-
stantiality like transparency. She looked faded, worn
away, like cloth that had been rubbed against a stone.
Above its wrapping he could see only a portion of the
child's face, a waxen nose and lifeless eyes. The
woman slowly began to lift her head as she continued
coming towards him. He saw her wide forehead, her
thick eyebrows, the bridge of her nose. His emotions
jammed together like a traffic accident. Taller, thinner,
plainer, more intense than his beloved, this was the
woman whom he had seen looking up at him from
beside the long pond. Later she had appeared in the
library window, looking down at him. She was Isobel
Standish. Isobel was awkward and wilful, sensitive in
all the wrong ways. He realized that he more or less
disliked her on sight.

She needed his help.

As if this were all that she had come to tell him, Isobel Standish turned away and began to melt back into the darkness with her baby. 'Don't go,' he said, and groped for the switch on the bedside light. Sudden, stabbing light froze everything in the room into place, as if the candlesticks and the heavy press and the blue sofa had come to life in the dark and now had to pretend to be inanimate again. The woman with the dead baby had vanished. Standish heard water splashing in the courtyard and a loud rasping sound that was his own breathing. He began to shake.

There was no point in trying to get back to sleep. Standish threw back his covers and got out of bed. He rushed to the window and peered through the slats of the shutters. The Seneschals' windows flashed like a signal and went dark again.

He could still feel the cool air on his bare skin, the prickly roughness of the leaves beneath his feet, and how the being had called him, how it had smiled and hungered . . . White dots appeared before his eyes. He sat down. Then he lifted his left foot and saw that the sole was black with dirt. Small, dark particles clung to his skin. His blood actually seemed to stop moving. He lowered his foot. Here and there on the carpet were dusty footprints the size of his feet.

For a moment Standish knew beyond doubt that flabby white creatures moved all around him in the dark house, searching for his traces, needing him: he could hear the grown sick babies crawling in the secret corridors and the Inner Gallery.

Once chosen . . .

Standish jumped up and turned on another light. He picked up the folder. *Birth of the Past*, he thought –

that was an Esswood title. He sprawled on the blue
sofa to read until morning.

THIRTEEN

Isobel's handwriting had degenerated into a nearly
illegible scribble. Entire paragraphs tied themselves up
into a private code that insisted on staying private.
Lying on the blue couch, almost too frightened to read,
too frightened not to read, Standish recognized the
signs of great emotional pressure.

The young woman from Massachusetts, now no
longer quite so young, had returned to the Land. In the
three years of what she thought of as her 'exile', her
work and her marriage had deteriorated. She had written nothing worthwile since leaving Esswood, and had
ceased to tolerate the attentions of her husband. She
felt that her appearance had deteriorated, leaving her
with limp hair, dull eyes, and a sunken face. It was as
if she had been cut off from some necessary nourish-
ment. In great pain she had written to her 'saviour',
'the gardener of her soul', and begged to be invited
back. *Of course*, E. had written, *we have been waiting
for you.* The husband had apparently decided not to
oppose her going, and indeed must have known by his
wife's raptures that to try to keep her from going
would be to end his marriage. Martin Standish, as
astonishingly complaisant as ever: perhaps he had
thought to save his wife's sanity by giving her Esswood
once again. After seven weeks' travel, the young
woman collapsed into E.'s arms at the train station
and soon was driven up the gravel drive between the
trees. A small brown-and-white King Charles spaniel

yapped at the wheels of her carriage. She wept the
instant she saw the Palladian façade. She was home
again. *We have needed you*, E. said to her. That night,
she ate loin of veal with morel sauce and felt health
and strength returning to her body. In honour of her
homecoming, E. said, they drank an 1860 Château
Lafite-Rothschild. The life she had needed, the one
that gave life back to her, had again taken her into its
arms.

Standish looked up and saw moonless night through
the chinks in the shutters. A faint murmurous sound
that had faded in and out of his awareness revealed
itself to be the splashing of the fountain. He guessed
that it was something like four o'clock.

For a time the young woman was conscious of nothing
but her joy in being reunited with territory so sacred
to her. She took her chair in the library in a daze of
happiness. She wandered down the terraces and
crossed the fields, letting them soak into her. She often
found herself weeping, as if her life had been rescued
from a barely perceived danger. The pitch of perception
she had reached three years ago now returned effortlessly, and everything about her carried the charge of
its own energy. The earth *burned*. The bindings in the
library *gleamed*, the fat white sheep *blazed* in the
fields. Poetry came in a vivid, almost frightening rush
that left her exhausted and trembling. Every day there
were two, three, four new poems – and dozens of pages
of her journal. She was like an adept of a religion that
worshipped creation itself, for what infused the Land
with energy and made her writing leap sizzling onto
the page was an original sacred force without a god,

without Jesus, without priests or ceremonies – a trans-
figuring force that was its own god, saviour, priest,
ceremony. She had been *chosen* more decisively than
before. She would never leave by choice, and if someone dragged her away – if she were expelled like waste
into the inert world of Brunton Road, Duxbury, Massachusetts – she would inhale grey death and die.

For among the other guests was the 'vagrant', the
'scholar-gypsy' who had helped awaken her. The
famous cornflower eyes seemed dimmed and faded, his
clothing even shabbier; he was not perhaps even nota-
bly clean. To Standish he seemed a distressingly seedy
character. Yet they worked side by side in the library,
they dined together, they walked together in the summery fields. They spent many hours in the Seneschals'
suite with E., who had fallen ill, and her son. The girl's
illness had progressed, and she was kept secluded in
another room. *My daughter cannot be seen*, E. said,
waving away their request with a limp hand. *She is on
a journey she must make alone – though she has
needed you, my dear. We all have needed you.* The
boy, as beautiful as ever, like his sister with the same
hawklike beauty of their mother, had become
abstracted and wan. He slept most of the day, but
when awake he seized the young woman's hand and
begged her for stories. *We have all needed you.* The
young woman caught on both their drawn, grave,
'hawk' features a look of hunger that was more a cast
of features than a passing mood, as if it underlay all
their charm and accomplishment.

Stung out of his trance, Standish looked up. A faint
light had begun to seep through the shutters. Outside
the house, hundreds, maybe thousands, of birds

seemed to be spinning in circles, raising an amazing joyous clamour as they flew round and round.

Need and hunger, thought the appalled Standish. Hawk features.

Did he know of the secret staircase and the secret corridor? the young woman asked her scholar-gypsy. She saw in the raised eyebrow that he thought she was teasing him – adding a literary mystery to their tale. I'm not joking, she said, there really is a secret staircase. Oh, is there now, asked the scholar-gypsy. And what have you been reading, you Duxbury romancer, *The Castle of Otranto? The Monk?* No, nor *Varney the Vampire*, she answered, but how do you imagine I travel about the house without being seen? Do I transport myself by magick? Show me, my girl, I am in your thrall, uttered the scholar-gypsy, and the young woman led him up the grand staircase and through the disused chamber that in the days, now gone, when E.'s husband had deigned to spend the Parliamentary recess in Lincolnshire had been his study, which was a misnomer for any activity ever carried on in *that* little room – and when were the servants ever going to do anything about that wonky light (as E. called it)? – and then down the Inner Gallery past the view of the fountain, not neglecting to wave to the dear grave boy watching who knew what from his mother's window, and into the young woman's cherished Fountain Rooms. Her soulmate admired the stuffed fox and the terrarium while she slipped into the other room and through the door to the staircase and called out *can you find me?* He homed towards the sound of her laughter. And opened the door and came through to join her behind the walls, saying: cowslip, bluet, lily,

hyacinth, rose. Now you know my secret, she said.
And took him down the long staircase to the library. *I
hear strange creatures moving here at night. But I
have an advantage, strange night creatures or no.* No
– you have *the* advantage, said the vagrant scholar-
gypsy; you have a special place in this house, you have
been taken in, you heard E., they need you. Because I
need them more, she said, and he smiled and shook his
head. Yet sometimes I feel quite terrified, a great
change is coming upon us all and I do not know if I
have courage for it. Then, because he looked puzzled
and downcast, she said *Behold I have mysterious
treasures*, and took his hand in her private realm
behind the walls and led him down and down the
staircase until they were in darkness beneath the earth.
You will see what I have seen, she said, and led him
through a rat's run of stone passages.

You can find your way back?

Oh, there is no way back but to go forward.

At length she gripped his hand and said: *Here*. It was
a passage like any other, stone and dark and lined with
doors. She threw open the nearest and said, here is the
chamber of the bones, where previous guests have
gathered. Who is laughing? he said, following into a
vault heaped with dry nibbled bones, not you nor I, but
some laughter follows us. The treasure is laughing,
said she, and took him out and down and through
another door where three great doll's houses stood side
by side beneath a reproduction of the painting in which
a gay King Charles spaniel scampers by the right
offside wheel of a carriage coming up to Esswood
House. The doll's houses reproduced Esswood House
in miniature, and in one front window of each little
house a low light as of a candle burned.

Inch-Me and Pinch-Me and Beckon-Me-Hither are landlords here, she said. Within each house are rooms with little golden plates and little golden goblets and the room where little wine bottles fill rack upon rack and the dark little library where Inch-Me and Pinch-Me and Beckon-Me-Hither pretend to read like the great grand folks upstairs. And I must still show you the enormous furnace room where the live furnace they tend burns and burns, and the last room, the final room, the, as you might say, ultimate room – and they both heard a stir of sound behind them and turned, the young woman with an almost fearful ecstasy, to see not whatever it was that she expected but E.'s young son, the inheritor of the Land and all its treasures should the miniature live furnace continue to burn in his narrow live chest, Robert.

Of course, said William Standish to himself, and heard that the birds had ceased their racket. I knew it all along. I knew who he was. And I knew who *she* was, too.

Looking for poems? the boy asked. I often wondered where poems come from, and now I see two poets and I know. Have you seen enough of our cellars? I can show you other aspects, if you please? His smile played, and the young woman and her scholar-gypsy pleased that he show them wonders, new wonders. And the boy took them past the furnace room and the tiny chair empty of the tiny furnace-tender and up into the house again and through the screen passage and outside into the blazing warmth. The boy's face, so like his mother's, was full of an odd, translucent light thrown up by the marble steps. He led them through the trellis to the top of the terraces.

E. and several other guests sat upon a Turkey carpet unrolled in the shade, and their hostess waved to the party of three. The other guests were G., a poet newly arrived in London from Yorkshire; N., a painter of portraits, and his mistress, O., so pale and weary of attitude that the young woman suspected her of indulging in opium; Y., D., and T., young novelists who had come down from Oxford to vanquish the literary world, lived together in a house in Chalk Farm, and reviewed books for the *TLS*; and J., a literary banker and book collector from New York. These were not a particularly brilliant bunch, the young woman felt. Even E. had lost interest in Y., D., and T., whose laboured epigrams, languid mannerisms, and excessive enthusiasm for the wine cellar had assured that they would never receive a second invitation.

All of these people waved to the threesome that crossed their vision, and E. called out to the young woman as she might to a servant a request that she speak to the cook about the quality of the lamb to be found in the local market – the young woman had come to be involved in some of the day-to-day matters of the house.

They clattered down the iron staircase to the long pond and the gnarled trees. The boy Robert led them to the trees, saying, Oh, in all your wanderings did you ever wander *here*? I hear the laughter again, the vagrant said, who is laughing? He thought to balk, but the young woman took his hand and pulled him after the dancing boy into the trees. Inch-Me and Pinch-Me and Beckon-Me-Hither, said she. The gamekeeper's boy, said the vagrant, looking out for foxes. And does old

William have a boy now? called out Robert. I thought he lived without woman or get. Our young lady must be right, though I doubt I ever heard the names ere now.

From the terraces it looked as though only a small number of trees separated the pond from the fields, but in fact a considerable growth of trees lay beyond the pond, the illusion created by a valley or fold in the land into which the boy led them now. Sunlight fell in patches and spangles on the soft ground. My brothers and sisters are here, you know, he said, and the ground became level again and the trees separated before him like ladies drawing back from an unpleasantness. A round clearing lay open to the sun but out of sight of the house, visible only to the kites and blackbirds overhead.

Three low mounds occupied the centre of the clearing, which was overgrown with long, silky grass. The young woman's first thought raised gooseflesh on her arms – the long, extremely comfortable-looking grass appeared well fertilized, well *fed*, that is – and she tightened her grip on her friend's arm. They have no headstones, he said, and answered the boy, they need none, we know their names. His young face filled with sly shadows. A magickal place, the young woman thought, thinking magick by no means as comfortable as the long-haired grass. A bird, some bird, cackled in the midst of the trees. You see our heart, I suppose you might make poems of it, the boy said, and his face became so complex that the young woman cried aloud – from pain or fear she did not know.

The boy was gone when she looked up from the protection of the scholar-gypsy's arms, and a dizzying male scent seemed to raise her from the ground. She was weeping in the pouring sunlight, and the gypsy kissed her and she moaned and the gypsy lifted her and laid her on the grass and made her clothing and his clothing disappear as he kissed her neck and shoulders; and she screamed with joy as he thrust his torch within her and they made love not for the first time and not for the second or third, nor even the tenth or the twentieth.

Standish put down the pages. His outside, his shell, seemed to have detached itself from his interior and become capable of movement while the interior Standish, the real Standish, sat numb and frozen. He was visited by the acute memory of standing sweating in his hat and raincoat on the Popham street and looking up at the window behind which his loathsome, treacherous friend was screwing his equally loathsome and treacherous wife. He should have expected exactly this, he realized: Isobel's return to England was too passionate not to be at least partly romantic; of course she had been having an affair all along. Martin Standish and Duxbury, Massachusetts had stifled her talent, and the 'gypsy' who had set it free had killed her by fathering her child.

'*They flee from me,*' Standish said to himself – and saw again, as from beneath the brim of a hat on a hot airless night as traffic hummed and roared like bees at his back, a lighted window in an apartment building. The bee-noise shook the world. A week before Jean had told him that she was pregnant, and expected him to believe that the child was his.

Standish shuddered, and for a moment feared that he was going to vomit upon the manuscript. *B. of P. Birth of the Past* or *Birth of the Poet! Betrayal of the Professor. Bastard of the Pretender.*

Childish giggling laughter came to him from the next room. He pushed the manuscript aside and watched his body get out of bed and cross to the door and open it. His body must have wanted to do this, because the inner Standish could not command the body to stop. All was well, however, all was well. The scampering little people from the basement had not overturned any tables or broken any lamps. He began to relax. Then both inner and outer Standish froze again. On the rug before the door the Inner Gallery lay a long white envelope.

He *had* heard them. Inch-Me and Pinch-Me and Beckon-Me-Hither had come and left a message. Welcome to reality, it would say, you don't need your hat and raincoat now; no more standing about on street corners with a dry mouth and a pounding heart. No, sir! He stepped up and looked fearfully down at the envelope. It bore an English stamp, his name, the Esswood address. His name and the address had been written in a sloping, pushed-together handwriting he gradually recognized as his wife's. Standish bent down and picked up the envelope. It had been postmarked in London.

He experienced a wave of instantaneous and pure revulsion. Jean and the magpie in her belly had tracked him down: they could not give him even a week's seclusion. They would crowd through the door and waddle in, dripping cookie crumbs and shreds of doughnuts.

Braced for everything, braced multi-dimensionally, Standish sat down, ripped open the envelope, and removed his wife's letter.

FOURTEEN

Dear William,

I bet you didn't expect to hear from me so soon. It's the funniest thing, yesterday I ran into Saul Dickman, who said that he was spending the rest of the summer in England. He only wished he was going to be in a cushy spot like you, with an exciting project like yours. Anyhow, I asked him if he could take a letter with him and mail it when he got to London, and if you get this, that's what he did. Three-day delivery, not bad, right?

I wanted to write for a lot of reasons — William, you seemed so tense before you left. When I took you to the airport, you were frothing at the mouth whenever anyone passed us, and when they called your flight you were so worked up you wouldn't have said goodbye if I hadn't reminded you. You had that awful look in your eye. This makes me so worried. But I don't know how much I should say, because I don't know how mad you'll get. Anyhow, I sure hope you got some sleep on the plane because some of this was just plain old lack of sleep. And William, you were never really a relaxed kind of guy anyhow, were you? I mean, a lot of stuff is just kind of normal for you, and I guess I'm not perfect either, you know what I mean.

But you know why I'm worried, too. You should know. I don't want to make you mad at me, and things have been pretty good between us for the past couple of years. But neither one of us will ever forget what happened at Popham. Of course everything was hushed up and you landed on your feet. I got over it. We managed to forgive each other, didn't we? You even got another job. But it still happened. William, I don't want any of that to ever happen again. I'm not going to lose this baby, you can bank on that, but it's just as important that you take care of yourself.

If you start feeling that old way again, just come home. COME HOME. Don't lose yourself. Don't forget me. Everything is all right.

*Zenith is nice, but couldn't we live anywhere? As long as
you stay* William.

*I need reassurance too. A lot of it, like you. I don't know
if I'm trying to give it to you or to me by writing to you like
this – I know I'd find it really hard to say things like this to
you in person. I hope you'll write to me or even call me,
maybe just to cheer me up. I'm so heavy I can hardly walk
to the bathroom, and I pee every time I burp. I have
heartburn that won't go away. I'm afraid that something is
going to go wrong – I know there's no reason for this, but
I'm afraid that it'll be like that other time, our terrible time,
and that I'll have to talk to lawyers and policemen, and
when I get so worried I wish you were here so I could see
you were okay.*

Please write, do good work, and come home soon.
Love,
Jean

*P.S. I looked up your place in a reference book – Oxford
Companion to English Literature? Something like that.
What a place! Have you found out* ANYTHING?? *Is there
really a big dark secret? Or shouldn't I ask?*

FIFTEEN

Saul Dickman, Standish thought. That figured. Yesterday I ran into Saul Dickman. Yesterday I just happened
to find myself talking to good old Saul, who's been
married twice and can be counted on to see the sex
object in even an abject blob of hysteria like Jean
Standish. Standish crumpled the letter and threw it
into the wastebasket.

Showered and dressed, he emerged into the Inner
Gallery twenty minutes later. A small razor nick
beside his Adam's apple printed a constellation of red-
brown spots onto his collar as he walked past the

windows. He twisted his neck to look at the Seneschals' windows and imagined seeing a boy with a
shadowy angelic face, the younger duplicate of Robert
Wall's, staring back at him. He could not see the boy
unless he looked with Isobel's eyes – and then he could
see, with dreamlike clarity, the dark-haired boy who
would grow up to call himself Robert Wall, leaning
against the glass across the way. The boy followed him
in a manner that looked casual at first but was actually
charged with an electric attention. It was what *they*
had seen as they walked through the Inner Gallery.
The seeming languor, the actual hunger. *It's better
never to leave Esswood* – that was how they did things,
by tossing these gauzy little spider webs over you and
seeing if you figured out the pattern before they melted
away. Oh, you were ten years old in 1914, were you,
Mr Robert Wall? and are you implying that your
general appearance at the age of eighty-six, not to
mention your sister's at the relatively even more
astonishing age of eighty-three or four, is part of the
reason why it's better never to leave Esswood?

Standish passed into the dark study and saw in his
mind the eyes of the woman who had come into his
room with her dead baby: he imagined Isobel locking
him in her arms, clamping him into her stony embrace,
all that desperation pouring itself into a romantic
mould and overflowing it.

He ran down the staircase, seeing everything as it
had been seventy-odd years earlier. These old men
were two generations nearer, and what went on
beneath their gaze was a deliberate mockery. Earlier
Seneschals had lived quietly, buried their dead,
improved the library, and hidden their afflicted. Unfortunates like the late Mr Sedge had fed their awful

appetites. Through Isobel's eyes Standish saw the riot
with which Edith had replaced the secretive old order.
Imaginary throngs sprawled over the furniture, talked
ceaselessly, raided the wine cellar, stripped the kitchen
of its food. They dirtied the sheets and stained the
carpets and filled every room with a blur of sound and
smoke and colour. Chattering, impudent ghosts – full
of spurious, accidental 'life', some of them diseased,
some of them coughing into their fists, some of them
as drunk as Jeremy Starger, some as prissy as Chester
Ridgeley, some men always pawing at women's
breasts, touching, touching, some women glancing
always at men's fly buttons, in secret touching, like
Jean Standish on the other side of an upstairs window
in Popham. In the East Hall he saw them standing in
pairs, twisting their hands together, their lips moving
in their endless clever talk-talk, never dreaming what
dreamed about *them* from behind the walls and waited.

You have been chosen, said 'Robert Wall'.

He gasped in the sudden heat as he trotted down the
stairs. His clothing felt hot and confining, and he
yanked the blazer off his shoulders and tossed it aside
as he reached the bottom step. Standish ran over the
gravel to the side of the house and ducked into the
trellis.

A hot, swarming smell, sharply sexual, surrounded
him. From behind the interwoven green walls and
ceiling came a steady, intense, live buzz of sound, as
from a hive. Standish burst out of the trellis, expecting
to see a swarm of bees or wasps dancing over the
terrace, but the air was clear and hot and empty. The
intense, sizzling noise continued, coming from everywhere at once. Popham. The sweat dripping down his
forehead. Standish paused and wiped his face on his

sleeve. Imaginary guests looked up from their lawn
chairs and tilted beards and sharp eyes at him and
pretended to flick dust from the sleeves of their perhaps too carefully selected garments. He turned from
their whispers as Isobel had done and trotted towards
the iron staircase. Large dark splotches rose up out of
his body and printed themselves on his shirt. Beneath
the thin, distracted heat-sounds emanating from real
insects and the faint susurrus of leaves from the grove
beyond the pond, there endured the buzzing of a hive,
as of busy, indifferent traffic at the back of a man in a
Burberry raincoat in Popham, Ohio on a night as hot
as this. A week before she said she was pregnant. And
expected him to believe the magpie was his. He
reached the staircase and ran down the terraces in the
sun.

At the bottom he could see with Isobel's eyes the
slight figure of a beautiful boy, in a cream shirt
perhaps, open at the neck perhaps, watching with
tilted head from the top of the rusting staircase. No
gamekeeper's boy, for old William lived without
woman or get. Standish pretended to be indifferent to
the traffic on the Popham street outside the apartment
of a man whose name he would never permit even
now to enter his mind, except in disguise as when the
eye fell upon the wrapper of a certain cough-drop or in
suchlike contact, as if you loathed a gentleman named
Park and on a business trip to Gotham found yourself
in Central.

Try not to think of a white bear. Standish had grown
very good at not thinking of white bears.

The buzzing, humming, hive-like noise of the
Popham street became louder at the bottom of the
terraces.

Standish began moving more slowly towards the grove of gestural trees at the right of the long pond. It was from here that the hive-like sound came, and as he passed between the first of the trees Standish imagined that this sound underlay the earth everywhere, that it was an impersonal world sound, not to be noticed any more, like the word Park unless you were in Central.

The twisting trees were oaks, hundreds of years old. Long ago they had been deformed by some process equivalent to foot-binding. The limbs rolled out and splayed into labyrinths around their thick, dwarfish bodies. His ferocious beloved had stood here, watching him.

Standish gazed through the branches to the green rise of the fields dotted with fat unmoving sheep.

Nothing is known once only, nothing is known the first time. A thing must be told over and over to be really told.

Before him, invisible except as a fold in the landscape from even the topmost terrace, the trees continued down a slope and gathered so thickly that he could not see the bottom of the slope. He began to move downhill. Eighty years ago, when these trees were young, there would have been paths through them; now the branches had grown together. Standish had come down ten or twelve feet, but the locked trees would not allow him to go farther. He circled sideways, searching for an entrance to the web, and finally he moved back a bit towards the pond and got to his knees and crawled beneath the locked branches.

SIXTEEN

Beneath his hands was a smooth brown carpet of crumbling leaves and loose, pebbly earth that felt as if it had passed through the digestive system of an enormous insect. The dwarf oaks formed a kind of low-arched entrance, though Standish saw none of the patches of light through which Isobel had moved on her way to the clearing. The darkness increased as he worked his way forward, and he found himself moving wearily through an intermittent night. After a time Standish knew he was lost. He had inadvertently crawled away from the path to the clearing. His knees were wet, and his hands were gritty. Standish collapsed onto the damp earth. Sweat steamed from his body. He lay his head on the backs of his hands. The earth hummed and moved in almost impalpable tremors like the shifting of an animal's hide. He forced himself back to his knees.

Perhaps five minutes later the darkness modulated into mild grey, and soon after that sunlight began to pierce the locked arms of the trees. Blotches of light struck the ground. His back heated. The hive noise had grown louder, more dense, many voices working together to form one great voice. Then Standish was where Isobel and the gypsy had followed the boy Robert, for the interlaced fingers had separated above him and he was looking down at his squat, square, headless shadow.

The sizzling noise had ceased – he was at its centre. Standish grunted himself up onto his feet. His knees were filthy and soaked, and his shirt was dark with

sweat. He stood on the far edge of a circle of trees
surrounding a round clearing perhaps fifteen feet in
diameter, like something stamped out of the woods by
a giant machine. Long, soft grass blanketed the clearing. At its centre stood the three mounds Isobel had
seen. They were barely distinguishable from one
another and the ground beside them. *They have no
headstones, they need none, we know their names.*

Standish exhaled, understanding everything at last,
and heard the sound instantly disappear into the louder
but still inaudible sound of the soul-traffic that was
the noise of the hive. *Magick*, Isobel had written, using
the old spelling, and for once she had been right. It was
magick. It had always been a sacred place, probably,
for that was one way to put it, but now it was more so
because of the people they had used and buried here.
Edith was not buried here, and neither were any of her
children, for none of them was dead. Others were.

Standish went through the grass and stood before
the mounds. With a groan he threw himself down onto
the mass grave. Against his cheek the grass felt like
the long, cool hair of his beloved. He spread his arms
and embraced the grave. The sun poured down on his
back. He groaned again, and gripped the silken grass
with his fingers. Down in the soil with Isobel lay a lost
child who screamed for release with all the others,
screaming like a pale creature pressed against a
window.

What power a lost child has, what a lever it is, what
a battery of what voltage.

Standish pushed himself off the grave. He made a
feeble effort to brush the dirt and broken leaves from
his trousers. Then he wiped his dirty hands on the
sides of his trousers and gazed up at the birds wheeling

overhead. They had the proud wing-spread of preda-
tors, raptors. Esswood's centre kept shifting, widening
out as one thing rhymed with another in the poem it
was. Standish turned from the grave towards the circling wall of trees. Directly before him was the path
on which Isobel and her lover had followed young
Robert Seneschal to the clearing. In the earth beneath
the twined branches he could see the marks of his own
passing. He lowered himself to his knees, which cried
out in pain, and began to crawl back into the woods.

In what seemed half the time of the trip to the
clearing, light began to reach him and the trees separated and he was looking at the slope leading back to
the pond and the first terrace. He stood and walked up
the slope, now and then grasping a branch to pull
himself forward.

SEVENTEEN

At the top of the iron staircase he walked across the
burning grass towards the trellis. A crowd of languid
ghosts raised their teacups and from the corners of
their eyes watched him pass. Standish slipped into the
trellis. Fat green leaves, dark as spinach, cupped the
trembling liquid of the sunlight. He entered the house
through the unbolted kitchen door and moved towards
the stairs to the pantry and dining room. Beside these
enclosed stairs was a door he had not tried earlier. It
opened onto the basement stairs.

Downstairs, he turned towards the furnace room,
retracing backwards his earlier route through the basement. Doors stood open in the stone passageway, and
he passed the room filled with stuffed tigers and dusty

plush dogs. All the doors he had opened remained open. Standish hurried along.

He turned through the open door of the concrete cell with its small worn chair. In the picture on the wall the playful dog scampered at the carriage wheel. Standish went through the second open door and proceeded past the black furnace to the far wall, to the family of axes.

He took the largest axe from its bracket, hefted it, replaced it in the bracket, and took the next largest. This one felt less likely to tip him over. He carried the axe back into the corridor.

From the furnace room he trotted up the short flight of steps towards the two locked doors he had tried on his earlier trip to Esswood's basement.

At the top of the steps he came out into another dark corridor. Here were four closed doors. Standish walked towards the first, swinging the axe beside him as he went. This was the second locked door he had tried, beside the room stacked with old newspapers. He twisted the knob. The door was still locked. Standish stepped backwards, lifted the axe over his head, and swung it at the middle of the door.

The head of the axe sank into the wood. Standish yanked it out and swung again. Sweat blinded him. He rubbed his eyes with a dirty hand and smashed the axe into the door again. Finally the door began to splinter, and after several more swings Standish was able to put his arm through a hole in the wood and turn the knob from the inside. A knife of raw wood cut into his arm, and blood bubbled happily from the wound and ran down his arm.

Standish opened the door.

He had expected big dolls' houses, cut away on one

side to allow a child access to every room, but these
were actually miniature Esswoods, larger than he had
expected and identical to their model down to the
water stains dripping from the corners of the windows.
They were actual houses, lined up like houses on a
suburban street. High on the wall above, like the sun
in a suburban sky, hung another reproduction of the
painting in his sitting-room – the capering dog, the
rolling carriage. A low light burned in each third
window from the right. Standish's breath caught in his
chest. It was as if three little people were due home
from work any minute now. The floor was a mess of
small white bones – chicken bones – so dry they
snapped when Standish stepped on them.

The stairs before the miniature houses were of
marble, cut by craftsmen who had been extravagantly
paid for their silence. He looked into one of the
windows and saw tapestries two feet long and carpets
three feet square, and ornate red and gold chairs a foot
high. There would be golden plates three inches across,
and golden forks half the size of his little finger, and
little wine glasses that would snap in his hands. And
did they sleep on beds, or had Edith ordered them
pallets woven from soft wool? And had they screamed
at night in pain and terror, and had Edith come down
to comfort them?

That was not very likely, Standish thought. Their
mother had been like God in the heaven of the picture
above their houses, loved or hated but invisible –
vanished into the sky.

Before Edith's generation had there been other Seneschals who occupied the little houses, afflicted Seneschals who lived concealed from everyone who came to
the great house around them? That was likely, for in

the twentieth century the only man Edith had found
to marry had been her unsatisfactory second cousin,
who likewise had found no one but Edith to marry
him.

And had any of Edith's illustrious guests ever known
or suspected her secret? That was even more likely,
Standish thought, for after a time all who came were
scribblers like Y., D., and T., and eventually no one at
all came: no cars, no carriages for little dogs to follow.
And think of what they had written! Henry James and
his mad governess who arrived at a remote house to
care for two afflicted children, E. M. Forster and his
tales of people living in a great hive, Eliot's waste land
and hollow men . . . Many of Esswood's guests had
walked part of the way into knowledge. Isobel had
gone farther than any of them, and Isobel had never
left.

It's better never to leave Esswood, Standish
remembered.

He stepped back, raised the axe, and brought it down
on the first little house. The thin plaster wall crumbled
like stale bread, and little paintings in little frames and
little chairs and a little bed fell from a guest bedroom
into the West Hall. Another blow smashed the main
staircase into splinters and toothpicks. Another shot
miniature books from miniature shelves, and cleaved
the portrait above the mantel. The floors broke apart
like kindling, and the foot-high furnace fell into clanking sections of pipe. The library's vaulted ceiling shattered into a rain of candy. Standish swung his axe
again, and the contents of a kitchen cabinet exploded
upwards into the ruins of the dining room. A table
three feet long slid down a tilting floor and crashed
into a miniature sink. Matchstick bones and tissue

butterflies flew up like tinder. The East Hall disinte-
grated, and the bedrooms of the East Wing splattered
against the wall. It took Standish nearly an hour to
smash the first little house into a heap of broken
shreds and shards from which protruded a length of
bookcase, a porcelain sink, a little book bound in
Moroccan calf, and the curved wooden corner of a
window frame. Then he moved on to the second house
and, a little more than forty-five minutes later, to the
third.

When that one was destroyed too he threw his shirt
behind him. His arms felt as if he had been rowing
through heavy seas, and his back was one vast ache.
Standish dropped the axe, and it smashed a patterned
china teacup to powder. He picked up the axe again
and discovered from a sharp stab of toothache in his
right palm that he had developed a blister the size of
an orange. He settled the axe handle into the blister
and felt the sharp awakening presence of pain.

The other locked door stood across the cement
corridor. Standish spared both the axe and his hand
and kicked at the stile beside the lock. The door rattled
in its jamb. He kicked again with the flat of his foot,
then drove the whole strength of his leg against the
lock. It broke with a loud snap like the breaking of a
bone, and the door flew open on its hinges. Standish
dragged the axe into Isobel's ultimate room.

There was no window: the light came in with him.
He wiped sweat from his forehead and waited for his
eyes to adjust. A dry *tock*, *tock*, *tock* that sounded
faintly like frightened laughter came to him from the
corridor.

At last Standish could see that he had broken into
an empty room. He was not sure what he had expected

– nothing as overt as skeletons or a chopping block, but something that would *shake* him. The floor sloped towards a central drain. Before the back wall the cement floor was scuffed, as if a heavy piece of equipment had stood there a long time. There were long, faint scratches in the floor. Finally Standish saw what appeared to be a series of oblong frames on the wall to his left. They reminded him of the framed butterflies in the bone room, and as he stepped nearer he saw that the frames contained photographs.

There were six of them, ordinary snapshots of unremarkable couples. From what Standish could see of the clothing worn by the two people in the first photograph, it had been taken in the late twenties or early thirties. In the third photograph, the man wore the uniform of an American army officer. Thereafter the men reverted to suits. The women next to the first two men wore veils; all the other women wore large-brimmed hats, or had turned their faces from the camera, or were in shadow. Two of the photographs had been taken on the first terrace of Esswood House, and two had been taken on the path that circled the long pond – shadows of the twisted oaks turned the woman's face to darkness. Then Standish recognized the face of one of the men beside the pond.

The face was sunken and unhealthy, with prominent knobs of bone above the eye sockets, and the man's shoulders had a decided stoop. He was smiling – smiling in ecstasy. It was Chester Ridgeley, some ten or eleven years older than when Mr and Mrs Standish, William and Jean, had left the serpent-infested Eden of Popham College in the town of Popham.

But there was no Mrs Chester Ridgeley.

The woman beside the old scholar had turned away

from the camera into the shade of a deformed oak. She appeared to be in her mid-thirties, strong of body, square-shouldered, with the sort of inherent, self-sustaining physical confidence with which even otherwise ordinary women are sometimes blessed, and which makes them anything but ordinary. Ridgeley held her hand trapped between his two old hands.

It was her because it had to be her. It was her because it could be no one else.

Standish went down the row of photographs and peered at each couple. The men, he guessed, were all academics – Esswood Fellows. The woman was always the same woman, always with the same air of physical confidence in the set of her shoulders, the carriage of her arms, the balance of her hips. In the fifty or sixty years represented by the photographs, she had not aged ten. When she had opened the door of Esswood House to him, she had appeared a strikingly youthful forty.

Standish stepped away from the photographs, aware for a moment that he was half-naked, dirty, out of breath, bleeding from many small cuts and abrasions, that he stank . . .

He turned from the photographs and stared down at the drain in the centre of the floor. He wondered if Ridgeley had ever returned to Popham. Had they received a telegram announcing his retirement? A letter declaring his intention to devote the remainder of his life to research on the life of that absolutely inessential literary figure Theodore Corn?

I feel certain that you will understand my excitement at having made many discoveries here, also my unwillingness to sacrifice my remaining years to classroom lecturing when so much (and so much, also, in the personal sense) remains to be done . . .

Standish left Isobel's ultimate room. Little bodies
scurried here and there in the room stacked with old
newspapers. He leaned in, and all motion ceased.
Standish looked down at the copy of the *Yorkshire
Post* and its glaring headline, then lowered himself
onto his sore knees and flipped the newspaper over and
stared at the photographs he knew would be there.

But these photographs, of a burly publican with a
face like a thrown rock, a hard-faced woman with high,
bleached hair, and a weak-chinned lover, were of
strangers. *Tock*, *tock*, *tock* went the mechanical,
mirthless laughter. He forced himself up on his feet
and looked down again at the meaningless faces.

A puzzling gap in experience, a piece of experience
missing from the universe – a loss for which the
universe yearned, ached, grieved without awareness of
its suffering – went with Standish as he wandered with
his axe beneath Esswood. He came to a modest set of
stairs going upwards to an open arch, and carried his
axe up into the known world.

He passed through the arch and found himself at the
back of 'his' staircase, in 'his' secret corridor that had
been Isobel's. He walked down the hall to the dining
room and opened the door. The smell of his cooling
lunch was faintly nauseating. He went to the table and
pulled the open bottle of white wine from the bucket.
Then he carried the dripping bottle down the corridor.

The library seemed larger, lighter, even more beautiful than on the night 'Robert Wall' had first shown it
to him. The long peach carpet glowed, and the alabaster pillars stood like sentinels before the ranks of
books.

Standish swigged from the bottle, then looked at the
label. Another 1935 Haut-Brion, ho hum. He swigged

again, and winked at great-great-great-great grandfather. He set the bottle on the desk and carried the
axe across the shimmering room into the first recess.
Here were the broad file boxes stamped STANDISH and
WOOLF and LAWRENCE, all the names which had been
the lures for the men whose photographs hung in the
ultimate room. He had been right, his first day in the
library, when he had imagined 'Robert Wall' drinking
blood from these fat containers.

Standish raised his axe and smashed open the second
of Isobel's file boxes. A tide of yellowing paper spilled
from the ruptured box and splashed on the floor.
Standish swung his axe again, and the blister on his
hand screamed like a child. Papers fluttered around
him like birds. He drove the axe into the third STAN-
DISH box and, instead of disintegrating into a shower
of handwritten pages, the box slid along the shelf until
it slammed into a wooden upright. Standish wriggled
the axe out of the cardboard, and the box spilled off the
shelf, dumping small square photographs to the ground
like confetti.

Grunting with surprise, Standish bent down and
picked up a handful of the photographs. And here, in
the first photograph, was the image of a tall, intense-
looking woman in a pale dress and close-fitting hat
standing on the path beside the long pond. Standish
knew that the dress was green, though the seventy-
year-old photograph was black and white; and he knew
the woman's face, in the photograph no more than a
blur, had the long chin and narrow nose he had already
seen. Here was Isobel at the chair in the library; here
she was reading a fat book in the West Hall; here
Isobel stood beside a rotund, open-mouthed man
whom Standish eventually recognized as Ford Maddox

Ford. Standish tossed the photographs aside and
grabbed another handful from the smashed file box.
Isobel posed uncomfortably beside an equally
uncomfortable T. S. Eliot. Isobel with a sleek dark-
haired man who might have been Eddie Marsh; Isobel
in the far field, trying to look pastoral; Isobel holding a
drinks tray – serving cocktails – and smiling ruefully.
The poor mutt.

Standish struck the box with his axe one more, and
photographs flew all around him. Then he took aim at
JAMES, and cracked the first one like a nut with one
blow of the axe. Wads of loose paper cascaded out, and
he kicked them apart.

He drove the axe into the second box of James's
papers, and into the third, and then drove it down into
the papers themselves and cut a great wad of them in
half. Monuments of unageing intellect, Standish
thought, and drove the axe into WOOLF. Then into the
next file box, and the next, and the next, until every
one had been smashed open and its contents spilled on
the floor. After that he dragged the axe across the
library to the second recess and started with FORSTER
and BROOKE – ugh, how did he get invited? – and came
to CORN.

Standish grinned at the thought of Theodore Corn.
He smashed open the box. A few sheafs of paper flew
out – Theodore Corn would of course have sheafs of
paper, preferably slender sheafs – along with another
gout of small square photographs.

The photographs hit the already impressive drift of
papers on the floor with the clatter of falling insects.
Standish bent down to pick up a random handful,
assuming he would see more photographs of lumpy
literary people.

They were strikingly like the photographs of Isobel. *I should have left this idiot's box alone,* Standish said to himself, feeling a premonitory tingle. He turned over various small squares of paper which had been printed with the same scant margins, the same dingy range of tones from sepia to light grey, and the same landscapes and furniture of Isobel's pictures. Many of the faces too were also in Isobel's photographs – Ford breathing through his mouth, Eliot hunching and making a face like a cat. The principal figure in this set of images was in some ways Isobel's male counterpart. A tall skinny figure in wrinkled suits, wearing unbuttoned shirts with flyaway collars, sometimes in a sleeveless Fair Isle pullover too small for him, he looked at the camera with a long, lopsided rural face seamed and pocked by childhood diseases, adolescent acne, and a long attachment to alcohol. His left front tooth and incisor were missing, and his hands, twice the size of Standish's own, had joints like bolts.

What had reminded Standish of Isobel was none of this, but the man's air of aggrieved disappointment – the sense of having been cheated lifted from the photograph like an odour. Coarser than Isobel, he was just as embittered. His sly, drunken face proclaimed *I deserve more, I need more.* Standish detested him even before he realized who he had to be, and then recognized that he detested him because he recognized himself in the man. If this person were an American of the 1980s instead of an Englishman of seventy years before, he might be married to someone like Jean Standish and be teaching in some dead Midwestern Zenith. He would dress better and a crown would fill the gap in his mouth. He would profess the Nineteenth

Century Novel, not very well but at least as well as William Standish.

Standish flipped over another of the dark little photographs and saw the man leaning against the back of Esswood House with a leer spread across his gappy mouth and a scarf tied around his neck like a rope.

He was, of course, Chester Ridgeley's darling, Theodore Corn.

Then Standish realized that he knew one more piece of the puzzle: Isobel had taken these photographs, just as Corn had taken all the photographs of Isobel.

And this led to the final fact — as Isobel might have said, the ultimate fact — which had prompted Standish's sense of foreboding when he had seen photographs spilling from Corn's box. The ninny Corn was the man Isobel had met at Esswood. Theodore Corn was her vagrant, her scholar-gypsy. He had been the father of her lost child.

Standish held the loose wad of photographs in his hands for a moment entirely empty of thought or feeling. He let them drop, and they clattered onto the strewn papers. Standish kicked at the mess on the floor. Everything about him seemed meaningless and dead. The meaninglessness was worse than death, because the meaninglessness existed at the centre of a mystery, like the whorls of a beautiful pink and ivory shell that wound deeper and deeper into the glowing interior until they came to – nothing.

Theodore Corn looked up at him from a hundred photographs, sly and hayseed and unknowable.

Standish waded through the ruck of papers and smashed the axe into POUND. Another mass of papers flew up from a shattered box and fell, thick as leaves, to the ground. He saw Isobel seated beside Theodore

Corn at the dinner table, gazing at him over the golden rim of her wineglass. He swung his axe and demolished another box.

Eventually Standish waded out of the second recess and went to the desk. The original file still sat beside the red gilt chair. Atop the desk stood the bottle of Haut-Brion. Standish looked down at Isobel's poor papers and considered carrying them over to the recess and tossing them on the pile. He nudged the papers with his foot and watched them spill sideways, exposing lines and sentences of Isobel's busy handwriting. That was good: that was better. Now the sentences could lift off the page and escape into the sky.

Standish put the bottle to his mouth and drank. He examined the library impartially and found it beautiful. He looked up, and the god glared down at him, pointed his ineffectual finger. The god was made entirely of paint a fraction of an inch thick, and that the finger came forward to point was an illusion created by a man named Robert Adam, who had loved great houses and fine libraries. Standish hefted the axe in his hands. He raised it and let it fall on the desk. The axe cracked its top open. Objects Standish had not noticed, Bic pens and legal pads, fell into the desk. Other insignificant things went sailing into the library.

Late afternoon sun came streaming through the windows.

Standish dropped the axe and saw blood spatter onto the carpet. The carpet instantly drank the blood, shrinking the red spots and hollowing them into pale pink rings almost invisible against the peach.

As hungry as the house, his stomach growled.

Standish thought for a moment, then smiled and sat at the ruined desk. He found a pen nestled beside long,

polished splinters. He wrote *matches* on a legal pad.
Then he tore the sheet off the pad and wobbled towards
the door.

In the dining room the table was set for dinner. An
open bottle of red wine stood on the tablecloth. Standish's mouth felt as if he had been eating ashes, and he
filled the gold-rimmed glass to the top and gulped
several mouthfuls before he bothered to look at the
label. 1916 La Tâche. It could have been the year Isobel
returned to the Land, in search of immortality and the
greedy embraces of Theodore Corn. What else had
Isobel been looking for in 1916, in the midst of a world-
engulfing war? The final curve inside the pink shell,
the story inside the story, the new sentence, the source
of the sound. Standish's hand slowly dripped blood on
the tablecoth, and the tablecloth sucked the drops to
pale circles. He smiled, and set down the glass to wrap
his right hand in one of Esswood's broad linen napkins.
Then he sat and lifted the golden cover. Isobel's meal
steamed on the golden plate.
    Standish ate. The room tilted to his left, then to his
right. His whole body ached. Eventually his eyelids
insisted on coming down over his eyes, and he lowered
his head to the table and slept. In the midst of a grove
of trees a shining baby lifted its arms and tilted up its
head for a kiss. Standish stretched out his torn arms,
but his feet were caught in thick silken grass like
ropes. Blood dripped from the palms of his hands, and
the shining baby turned its face away and cried.
    Standish too wept, and woke up with his wet face
cradled in the bloody napkin wound around his hand.
'Oh, God,' he said, imagining that he had to go back to
the library and write a book about Isobel. A tide of

relief radiated out from the memory of what he had done in the library.

He wiped his face and stood up. The axe lay beside his chair like a sleeping pet, and he carefully knelt and reached for the handle. It glided into his hand and fitted itself into the folds of the napkin.

Standish dragged himself down Isobel's secret corridor to the library. He toiled through the great empty space and opened the main door. On the carpet of the West Hall lay a large yellow box of Swan kitchen matches.

Standish carried the matches back into the library, leaned the axe against a column, and went to the second recess. He pushed open the box, and an astonishing number of matches fell out into the heap of papers and photographs. He stared stupidly at the box for a moment before realizing that it was upside down. He turned it over and saw that the other, covered end of the box still contained hundreds of matches. Standish removed one and scratched the head against the cross-hatched strip. The match exploded into bright flame.

He bent down the touched the flame to the corner of a piece of paper. As soon as the paper ignited, he moved the match to another sheet. Then he tossed the burning match far back into the recess. A thin wire of smoke ascended, and a curl of fire followed it.

Standish backed out of the recess and watched the flames eat at the papers. The paint on the bookshelves blackened and burst into circular blisters just before the fire jumped to take the wood beneath the paint. Then he crossed the library to set the papers in the other recess alight.

He dropped the rest of the matches on the floor and

left by the main doors. He had more than enough time to do what had to be done next.

Standish went out into the entrance hall. An ornate clock on a marble table told him that it was five minutes to ten. He wandered down the screen passage and tugged at the front door. Velvet darkness began at the edge of the light that spilled from the house. The trees beyond the drive were a solid wall reaching from the dark ground to the vivid purple of the sky. Overhead were more stars than Standish could ever remember seeing, millions it seemed, some bright and constant and others dim and flickering, in one vast unreadable pattern that extended far back into the vault of the sky, like a sentence in a foreign language, the new sentence that went on and on until first the letters and then whole words became too small to read.

Standish walked out to stand beneath the great sentence. All of that writing in the library, the pages stuffed with words like bodies stuffed with food, would float upwards to join the ultimate Esswood that was the sentence in the sky. Beyond it, invisibly, did an angered god point a finger from a whirling cloud?

Standish carried his axe back into the house.

EIGHTEEN

As he went up the stairs he caught the faint odour of burning, but when he turned off to the left into unfamiliar territory the faraway smell of smoke faded into the odours of old leather and furniture polish and the fresh evening air that entered the house through open windows. He passed under an arch at the top of the left-hand wing of the staircase and went into a room that was the larger counterpart of the study at the other end of the house.

A light fixture hung from the central rosette. Empty bookshelves covered two of the walls. A single rocking chair had been pushed up against a bare wall with pale rectangles where pictures had hung.

At the far end of the empty room was another arch through which Standish could see a bleak corridor. A bare light bulb dangled from a cord. Dust gathered on the floorboards, and cracks ran across the plaster walls. Two large windows with brown shades stood on one side of the hallway, two dusty brown doors on the other.

These were the windows he had seen from the Inner Gallery and the Fountain Rooms. He tugged on the ring of a window shade and gently released it upwards. Across the dark courtyard his old windows glowed yellow around the outline of a misshapen child-sized figure peering out. Standish froze. Inch-Me or Pinch-Me or Beckon-Me-Hither stared at him, and Standish stared back. Then the small, featureless shape disappeared. A grey whorl of smoke moved into the frame of the window. Standish imagined the secret stairs filling with smoke dense enough to push back at you if you tried to move through it. Another, deeper rift of smoke appeared in his window.

He still had all the time he needed.

Standish turned from the window and placed his hand on the first doorknob. He quietly opened the door.

Light from the corridor spilled into the first few feet of a room in which Standish made out the shape of an iron bed, a cheap wooden chair, an open suitcase on the floor. Paperback books lay scattered around the

chair. He moved through the opening and closed the
door. In the darkness he became aware of the pain in
his hands and his back. Oily grime covered his body.
He could smell fear, sweat, blood – he stank like an
animal in a cave.

Inside his head he heard the sound, more an echo
than sound itself, of a baby crying. Standish began to
move on tiptoe across the room towards the untidy
bed. When he was a foot or two from it he was able to
make out the pattern on the thrown-back coverlet.
The sheets were white and rumpled, and the dented
pillow lay across them like a fat slug. From the
wrinkled sheets floated up an odour of perfume and
powder. A spattering of his own blood fell on the
sheets.

Standish turned around and left the room as quietly
as he had come in. The door let yellow, meaningless
light flood over and around him.

In the window on the other side of the hallway he
saw the reflection of a crouching half-human animal,
its body smeared with dirt and blood, come creeping
around a door. It carried an axe in one hand. With
something like glee, Standish saw that this stooped,
monstrous creature was himself – the inner Standish.
Twenty-four hours ago he had glimpsed him in the
bathroom mirror, but now he was really out in the
open. It seemed that he had been waiting for this
moment all of his adult life. '*Why, Miss Standish,*' he
whispered, and pressed a hand to his mouth to keep
from giggling.

Through the creature's body he saw the square of
fire that was the window of his old room.

He turned towards the next door. The bent creature
with the axe turned too. Bloody, matted hair covered

its shoulders. Its dark hand was still pressed to its
mouth. He watched the creature float down the corridor until it moved out of the window.

A few mincing steps brought him to the second door.
His slippery fingers touched the knob. He ground his
teeth and soundlessly turned the doorknob. The door
moved inwards a few inches, and Standish tiptoed with
it. A few inches more, and he slid into the room.

A pair of shoes stood on the bare floor. A white shirt
draped over the back of a chair glided towards him like
a spirit out of the breathing dark. He closed the door
behind him. The shirt looked like a spirit waiting to
be born, maybe through the pair that occupied the bed
across the room. Slow sweet exhalations and inhala-
tions came from them. Over his own stink Standish
caught the delicate scent of perfume and the other,
coarser odours of sweat and sex.

He sighed.

As his eyes grew used to the dark, he saw the bare,
dim walls that would be white in daylight, the masculine clutter of socks and sweatshirts and jeans on the
floor. A tennis racquet leaned against the wall. The
bed was an untidy tangle of long white limbs and wild
hair.

Now Standish felt as if he had awakened from a long
trance. He was simply himself, what all the days,
weeks, hours had brought him to. He was a stunted
monster carrying an axe. For perhaps the first time
since his childhood, Standish entirely accepted
himself.

'Mnnn,' came a voice from the bed.

Standish stood inside the door breathing slow shallow breaths. He could imagine himself in bed with the

couple, lying in a loose tangle of arms and legs, absorbed into them.

But soon they would begin to hear the fire and smell the smoke. He waited until they had settled down into one another's arms and begun to snore light, funny, almost charming snores. He stepped forward. There was no response from the bed. He took another gliding step forward. The beautiful double animal on the bed lay still. Standish moved directly beside it and raised his axe.

He swung it down with all his strength, being both the executioner out in the tundra with his chopping block and the bureaucrat at his desk. The axe landed at the base of one of the animal's two heads and almost instantly cleaved through the vapour of the flesh and the fishbones of the spinal column. The animal's other head lifted itself from the pillow just as Standish raised his axe again. It presented a perfect target, extended in disbelief and confusion that ended with the axe's downstroke.

Now the bed was a bloody sea. Standish dropped the axe and plucked both heads off the soaking sheets by the hair and lowered them to the floor. He picked up two pillows, yanked them from their cases and tossed them back on the bed. Without looking at either of the faces, he stuffed the heads into the empty pillowcases and carried them out into the hallway. They were surprisingly heavy, like bowling balls. Standish trotted down the hallway in misty smoke, went through the arch, and into the barren room at the top of the stairs. The heavy pillowcases swung at his sides.

Black smoke had accumulated against the ceiling in cloudy layers. From what seemed a great distance came the sound of rushing wind. Standish passed through the opposite arch and looked down the left wing of the staircase.

Several distinct layers of smoke hung from the ceiling and moved towards him with a massive gravity. A wall of heat met him at the top of the stairs and pushed him back like a giant hand. As yet there were no flames before him. He began to run down the stairs, and felt as if he had stepped into an oven. The hairs in his nose crisped painfully, and his eyebrows turned to smoke. He saw the thick hair on his chest, arms and belly curl inwards and turn to ash.

When he reached the main body of the staircase a combination of smoke and heat blinded him. He kept running with his right hand on the hot banister. The heads in their pillowcases rhythmically banged against the balusters. His skin felt scalded. His right hand struck the newel cap at the bottom of the stairs, and the things in the pillowcases slammed into the post.

Standish plunged through scalding black soup. A flat, red glare exploded off to his left. When he reached the screen passage he sensed the thick tapestries writhing as their fibres shrank and dried. He ran straight into the door, bounced back, then grabbed the scalding knob with a hand wrapped in hot cotton cloth.

Frigid air rushed over him. Blind and coughing, Standish stumbled out onto the terrace. He tottered down three or four steps, then collapsed backwards and wheezed, trying to fight the smoke out of his lungs. He landed hard on his bottom and lost his grip on the pillowcases. They slid out of his hand and bumped down the steps. Standish felt as if he had been blowtorched. Smoke poured from the fabric of his trousers and clung to his shoes. Down at the bottom of the steps, the pillowcases smoked like smudge-pots.

His legs took him down the steps, and he limped to one pillowcase, picked it up, then limped across the gravel and picked the other up too.

The heads tried to pull the ends of the pillowcases from his hands as he trudged over the gravel. After a few seconds he stopped to look back. Flames showed in the first-and second-floor windows, and smoke poured through the roof.

Standish carried his heavy trophies round the left side of the house. Something inside Esswood let go, and a thunderous crash sent a flurry of sparks and flames into the air. Standish trudged forward through a rain of fire and stepped over a burning chunk of Esswood. He was too tired to look back and see what happened.

Around the left side of the house and across the drive stood a long, low structure with four sets of wide double doors inset with windows. Standish pulled himself towards the building and looked through the first window into an empty darkness.

Through the second window he saw an old saddle and harness hanging on the back wall.

In the third window reflected fire burst through Esswood's roof.

Standish looked through the fourth window and saw the back end of a turquoise Ford Escort. He pulled open the doors and carried the heavy pillowcases inside. As soon as he touched the car he remembered that he did not have the keys, which were probably inside the pocket of a pair of incinerating jeans on the second floor of the East Wing. He opened the door and collapsed into the driver's seat. The two sacks leaked onto the ground between his legs. He reached down and swung both the sacks and his legs into the car.

He put his hands on the wheel and stared at the dashboard, remembering movies in which people jump-started cars. Something heavy fell on the roof of the building. He smelled smoke, and his eyes filmed and his stomach churned. When he had finished coughing and wheezing, he reached over and opened the glove compartment. Two keys linked by a metal ring lay on top of the owner's manual. Standish slid them out.

He inserted a key into the ignition, turned it, and stepped on the accelerator. All these actions seemed to be remembered from some other, very different, past life. He heard the engine catch, and dropped his forehead to the wheel and rested. Another great chunk of Esswood fell onto the roof. Standish forced himself to straighten up. He put the car in reverse and stepped on the accelerator. The Escort smashed into the half-opened doors and rolled out. Standish cut the wheel and turned the car forward. Shreds and dots of fire rained down from the house. Standish jammed the car into Drive and floored the accelerator. The car mushed up a spray of gravel and shot forward. Red light wavered on the drive and the tall, straight oaks. Steam hissed from the trunks of the trees closest to the house. Standish turned on his lights, and streams of yellow floated into the wavering red night. He saw the long drive curling away between the steaming trees, and he aimed for it.

Then he was rolling down the drive, trying to figure out which side he was supposed to be on. Everything was *backward*.

A pair of headlights appeared before him down through the tunnel of trees at the bottom of the drive. Standish let the accelerator drift upwards while he tried to solve the interesting problem of which side of the road was his. He swerved all the way left, then right. The oncoming car flicked its lights off and on. In the rear-view mirror, Esswood blazed merrily. The other car moved into his headlights. It was a Jaguar, and Robert Wall – 'Robert Wall' – was driving it; Standish's beloved, Robert's sister, sat beside him. Both of Edith's children looked startled, perhaps even transfixed. Robert honked his horn and waved at Standish. His beloved spoke words he could not hear. Standish drove on. When he went past the Jaguar, Robert yelled at him and his beloved leaned forward and questioned him with her eyes. Standish picked up speed. Neither one had recognized him.

After a couple of seconds Standish looked in the rear-view mirror and saw Robert Seneschal running down the drive after him. He moved his head to see himself in the mirror. He did not recognize himself either. He was a totally new being, bald, covered with grease and blood, pink and blue-eyed: he was his own baby. The car shot out into the road at the end of the drive, and grinning giggling Standish turned the Escort towards the village.

NINETEEN

After a time the red blur faded from the sky. Standish drove without maps, without memory, guided by a sense of direction that seemed coded into his body. He drove through a landscape of tiny villages filled with cheery lights and flashing signs, of dark fields and dense woods. He saw marsh lights flicker and understood that they too were part of the great sentence that

went on forever until it passed from visibility. Every
human life fitted into that grand and endless sentence.
Occasionally he glanced with admiring satisfaction at
the newborn baby in the rear-view mirror.

He moved swiftly through the villages and fields.
Churches, pubs, and thatched cottages went by in the
dark. Once he saw a house even greater than Esswood
on the crest of a long hill, and Rolls-Royces and
Bentleys and Daimlers were drawn up before it, and
light spilled from every window. Somnolent cows
and horses in the fields swung their heads to watch
him pass by.

Once in a deep wood he struck an animal and heard
it cry out with a terrible cry.

His hands stiffened and froze to the wheel. Still
Standish drove easily through the night. He was a great
fat chuckling baby, and he shat and peed in his filthy
trousers and kept driving.

At last he came to the open-air factories. The strings
of light had been turned off; the torches were put away.
The machines rested in the dark passages, and the
swirling dust had settled for the night. Yet the great
slag heaps rose up into the starry sky, and when
Standish saw them he slowed down.

He peeled his left hand from the steering wheel and
leaned sideways to crank down the passenger window.
When the car drifted alongside the first slag heap,
Standish lifted one of the pillowcases and swung it
through the window. It struck the road and rolled
towards the slag heap. He supposed that was good
enough. He tossed the second pillowcase after the first.
This one made it nearly across the road before it
thumped down and tumbled into a drainage ditch.

Standish groaned and sat up straight again.

Eventually the HUCKSTALL sign flashed in his window and disappeared behind him. Chuckles emanated from the two dripping bags no longer beside him on the passenger seat. An empty world without end or beginning spread out on both sides of the road. Then headlights appeared far ahead down the road. As he drove towards them the figure of a man with outstretched arms stepped forward into the beams of his own lights. Standish was near enough to see in his own headlights that the man was smiling as he waved his arms. The man moved nearer to the centre line. He was not what Standish had expected – a tall smiling man in a sports jacket. His fair hair flopped appealingly over his forehead.

Standish accelerated when he drew near to the man, and when the man began criss-crossing his arms over his head – for this one was used to getting what he wanted, you could see it in his wide-set eyes and smooth cheeks – Standish turned the wheel sharply towards the man and ran straight into him.

The man bounced against the car with enough force to jolt Standish painfully against the wheel. He spun off like a marionette and disappeared beneath the car. There came another, milder jolt. Standish braked to a halt and threw open the door. He put the gear lever at Park but did not turn off the car. He slid off the seat. With slow determined steps, not bothering to inspect the crushed body beneath the car, the poor baby set off into a wide desolation.

Then One Day She Saw Him Again

Then one day she saw him again. It must have been a
year since the first time, because another summer had
passed and the weather was now misty grey and the
air had turned slightly chilly. She had just realized
that, alone of all the people she knew, she was glad to
be out of summer. She preferred these days, for
summer was a pleasure machine like a strong drink
that stroked you and stroked you and never got you
any further than a slow, stunned warmth, but on days
like this – a slight haze hanging in the air, and the tops
of the buildings invisible in the fog – she felt a close,
lifting sense of anticipation, as if some unforeseen
transformation were literally in the air, hovering. Then
she saw him walking towards her again and remembered him perfectly, though she had not seen or
thought of him in the year that had passed.

He might have been wearing the same clothes – a
black sweater and jeans so faded they were almost
white. No, the jeans were different, and the long red
scarf was new. But it was the same young man. The
sense of illumination still clung to him. Neither smiling nor crying now, he was walking along with a
comfortable stride. There was nothing special about
his face, nor was he as young as she had thought, but a
teenage girl turned to look at him curiously as he
passed, and a tall man in a tan raincoat with a heavy,
buttoned lining swung his head to watch him go by. It
was as if a pale light shone upon him, or within him, a

light of which he was absolutely unaware. That was the grace note she had noticed a year ago. He walked past her without pausing. She turned around, hesitated, then began walking after him. She felt faintly silly, even foolish, even a bit ashamed, but her curiosity was too strong for her to let him walk away again. She had a second chance, she saw, and the moment she began to follow him she forgot her plans for the rest of the afternoon in the oddity and interest of her present occupation.

She walked down the avenue half a block behind the man. Her life had changed, it came to her, it would never again be what it had been, and with every step she took the change deepened. She had been set free; this was what had been promised, it was this she had anticipated. An entire year had been wasted in the realm of the ordinary, and now she was slipping away from the ordinary altogether. The air darkened about her, and she followed the man out of everything she had ever known.

AUTHOR'S NOTE

Most of these pieces had their origins or inspirations in other books. The central action of 'Blue Rose' occurred to me while I was reading a neurologist's contentious book about Freud called *The Freudian Fallacy*. 'The Juniper Tree' came to me, very forcefully, while I was reading Marguerite Duras's short novel *The Lover*. 'A Short Guide to the City' was the product of reading a long essay about St Petersburg in Joseph Brodsky's *Less Than One*. And I wrote 'Mrs God' immediately after I had read a great many stories by Robert Aickman so that I could write an introduction to a collection called *The Wine-Dark Sea*, and Aickman's enigmatic and assured example was very much in my mind all the way through William Standish's adventures at Esswood House.

'Blue Rose' and 'The Juniper Tree' have deep connections to another book besides those already mentioned. They are the stories written by Tim Underhill, the secret hero of my novel *Koko*, and represent the first part of Underhill's efforts to comprehend violence and evil by wrapping them in his own imagination. It follows that the Harry Beevers of 'Blue Rose' is not quite the character in *Koko* who bears his name.

'The Buffalo Hunter' was inspired by Rona Pondick's exhibition of sculpture *BED MILK SHOE* at the Fiction/Nonfiction Gallery in New York.

'Something About a Death, Something About a Fire' is one of the first stories I wrote, and I include it here because it is the only early story of mine that I still like and because it fits. Like Bobby Bunting, William Standish, good old Harry Beevers, and the unnamed narrator of 'The Juniper Tree', Bobo lives in a house without a door, and finds there a terror and a splendour he can share with the rest of us.

PETER STRAUB